SPIDER-MAN
SPIDER-VERSE

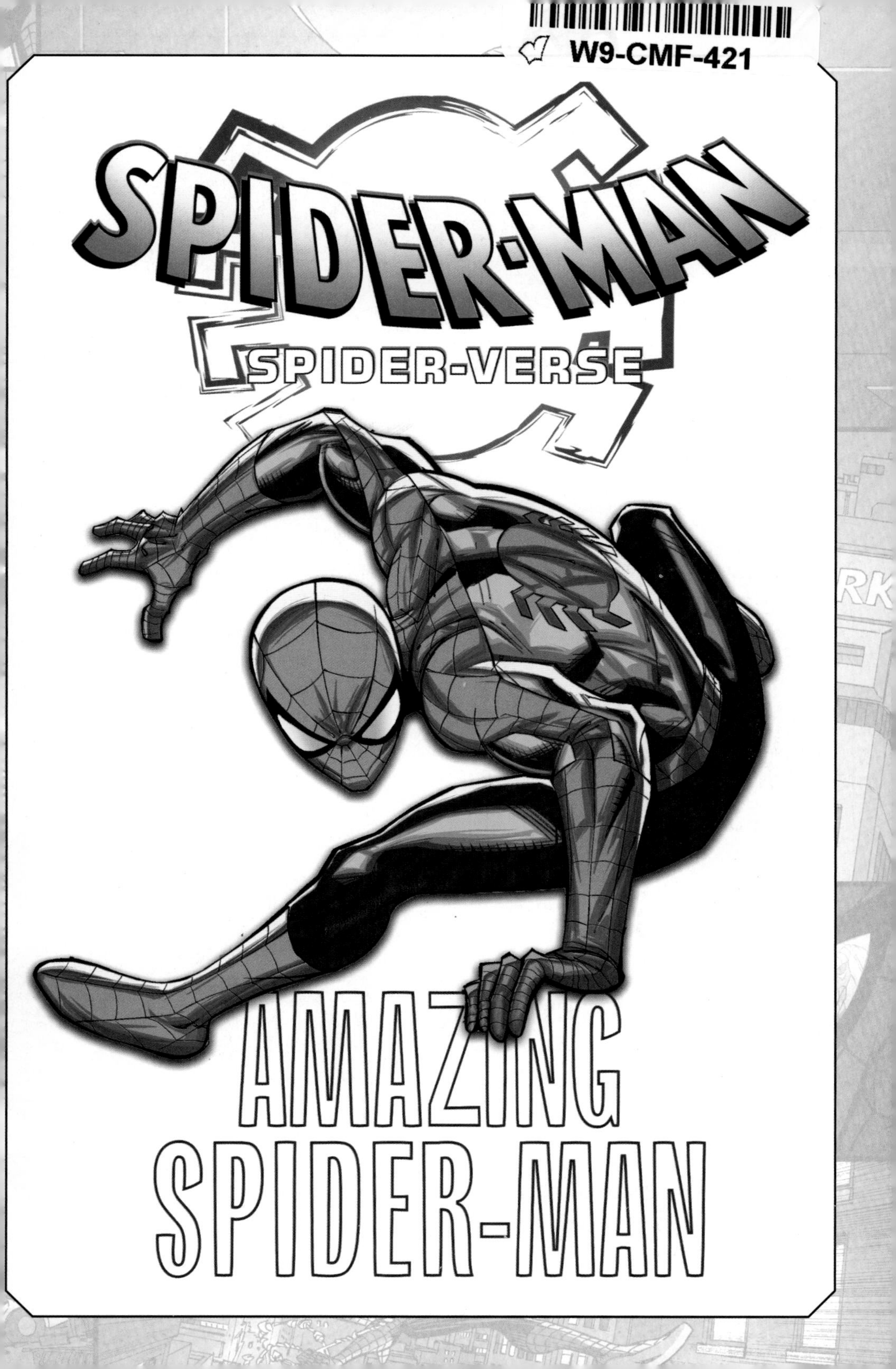

AMAZING SPIDER-MAN

SPIDER-MAN SPIDER-VERSE

AMAZING SPIDER-MAN

MARVEL ACTION ORIGINS #1

WRITER: CHRIS ELIOPOULOS
ARTIST & COLOR ARTIST: LANNA SOUVANNY
LETTERER: SHAWN LEE
COVER ART: LANNA SOUVANNY
EDITOR: ELIZABETH BREI
EDITOR, JUVENILE PUBLISHING: LAUREN BISOM
ASSOCIATE EDITOR, SPECIAL PROJECTS: CAITLIN O'CONNELL

SPECIAL THANKS TO NICK LOWE & BRIAN OVERTON

AMAZING SPIDER-MAN #51-52

WRITER & EDITOR: STAN LEE
PENCILER: JOHN ROMITA SR.
INKER: MIKE ESPOSITO
LETTERER: SAM ROSEN
COVER ART: JOHN ROMITA SR.

SPIDER-MAN: MASTER PLAN

WRITER: **ROBBIE THOMPSON**
ARTIST: **NATHAN STOCKMAN**
COLOR ARTIST: **JIM CAMPBELL**
LETTERER: **VC's TRAVIS LANHAM**
COVER ART: **NATHAN STOCKMAN & JIM CAMPBELL**
EDITOR: **MARK BASSO**

SPIDER-MAN: REPTILIAN RAGE

WRITER: **RALPH MACCHIO**
ARTIST: **CHRISTOPHER ALLEN**
COLOR ARTIST: **RACHELLE ROSENBERG**
LETTERER: **VC's TRAVIS LANHAM**
COVER ART: **TODD NAUCK & RACHELLE ROSENBERG**
ASSISTANT EDITOR: **MARTIN BIRO**
EDITOR: **MARK BASSO**

SPIDER-MAN CREATED BY **STAN LEE** & **STEVE DITKO**

COLLECTION EDITOR: **JENNIFER GRÜNWALD** ASSISTANT EDITOR: **DANIEL KIRCHHOFFER**
ASSISTANT MANAGING EDITOR: **MAIA LOY** ASSOCIATE MANAGER, TALENT RELATIONS: **LISA MONTALBANO**
ASSOCIATE MANAGER, DIGITAL ASSETS: **JOE HOCHSTEIN** MASTERWORKS EDITOR: **CORY SEDLMEIER**
VP PRODUCTION & SPECIAL PROJECTS: **JEFF YOUNGQUIST** RESEARCH: **JESS HARROLD**
BOOK DESIGNER: **SARAH SPADACCINI** SENIOR DESIGNER: **JAY BOWEN**
SVP PRINT, SALES & MARKETING: **DAVID GABRIEL** EDITOR IN CHIEF: **C.B. CEBULSKI**

SPIDER-MAN: SPIDER-VERSE — AMAZING SPIDER-MAN GN-TPB. Contains material originally published in magazine form as AMAZING SPIDER-MAN (1963) #51-52, SPIDER-MAN: MASTER PLAN (2017) #1, SPIDER-MAN: REPTILIAN RAGE (2019) #1 and MARVEL ACTION ORIGINS (2021) #1. First printing 2022. ISBN 978-1-302-94776-7. Published by MARVEL WORLDWIDE, INC., a subsidiary of MARVEL ENTERTAINMENT, LLC. OFFICE OF PUBLICATION: 1290 Avenue of the Americas, New York, NY 10104. © 2022 MARVEL No similarity between any of the names, characters, persons, and/or institutions in this book with those of any living or dead person or institution is intended, and any such similarity which may exist is purely coincidental. **Printed in Canada.** KEVIN FEIGE, Chief Creative Officer; DAN BUCKLEY, President, Marvel Entertainment; DAVID BOGART, Associate Publisher & SVP of Talent Affairs; TOM BREVOORT, VP, Executive Editor; NICK LOWE, Executive Editor, VP of Content, Digital Publishing; DAVID GABRIEL, VP of Print & Digital Publishing; SVEN LARSEN, VP of Licensed Publishing; MARK ANNUNZIATO, VP of Planning & Forecasting; JEFF YOUNGQUIST, VP of Production & Special Projects; ALEX MORALES, Director of Publishing Operations; DAN EDINGTON, Director of Editorial Operations; RICKEY PURDIN, Director of Talent Relations; JENNIFER GRÜNWALD, Director of Production & Special Projects; SUSAN CRESPI, Production Manager; STAN LEE, Chairman Emeritus. For information regarding advertising in Marvel Comics or on Marvel.com, please contact Vit DeBellis, Custom Solutions & Integrated Advertising Manager, at vdebellis@marvel.com. For Marvel subscription inquiries, please call 888-511-5480. Manufactured between 7/1/2022 and 8/2/2022 by SOLISCO PRINTERS, SCOTT, QC, CANADA.

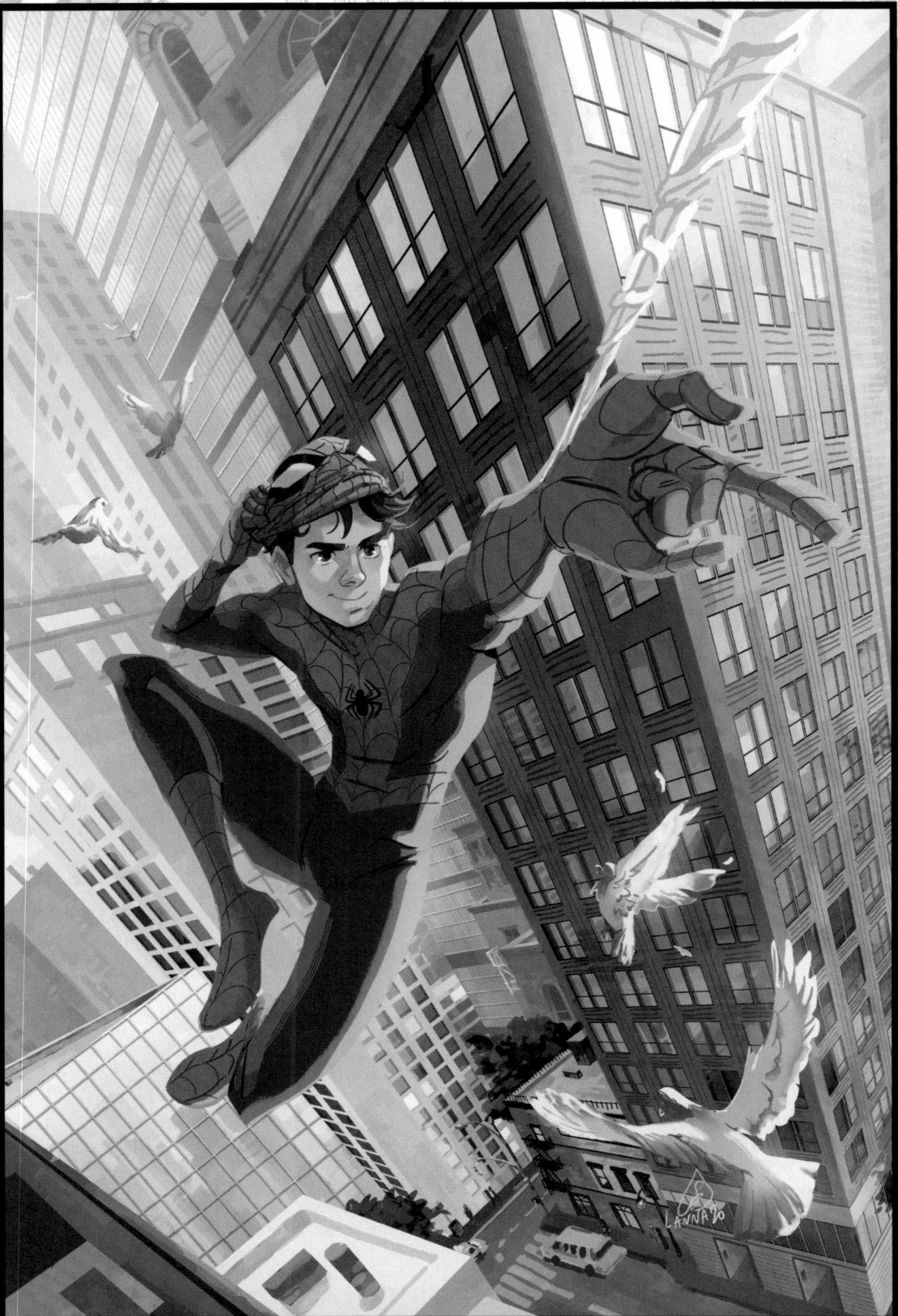

MARVEL ACTION ORIGINS #1

IT'S AN ACTION-PACKED RETELLING OF HOW PETER PARKER'S LIFE CHANGED FOREVER FROM A SPIDER'S BITE!

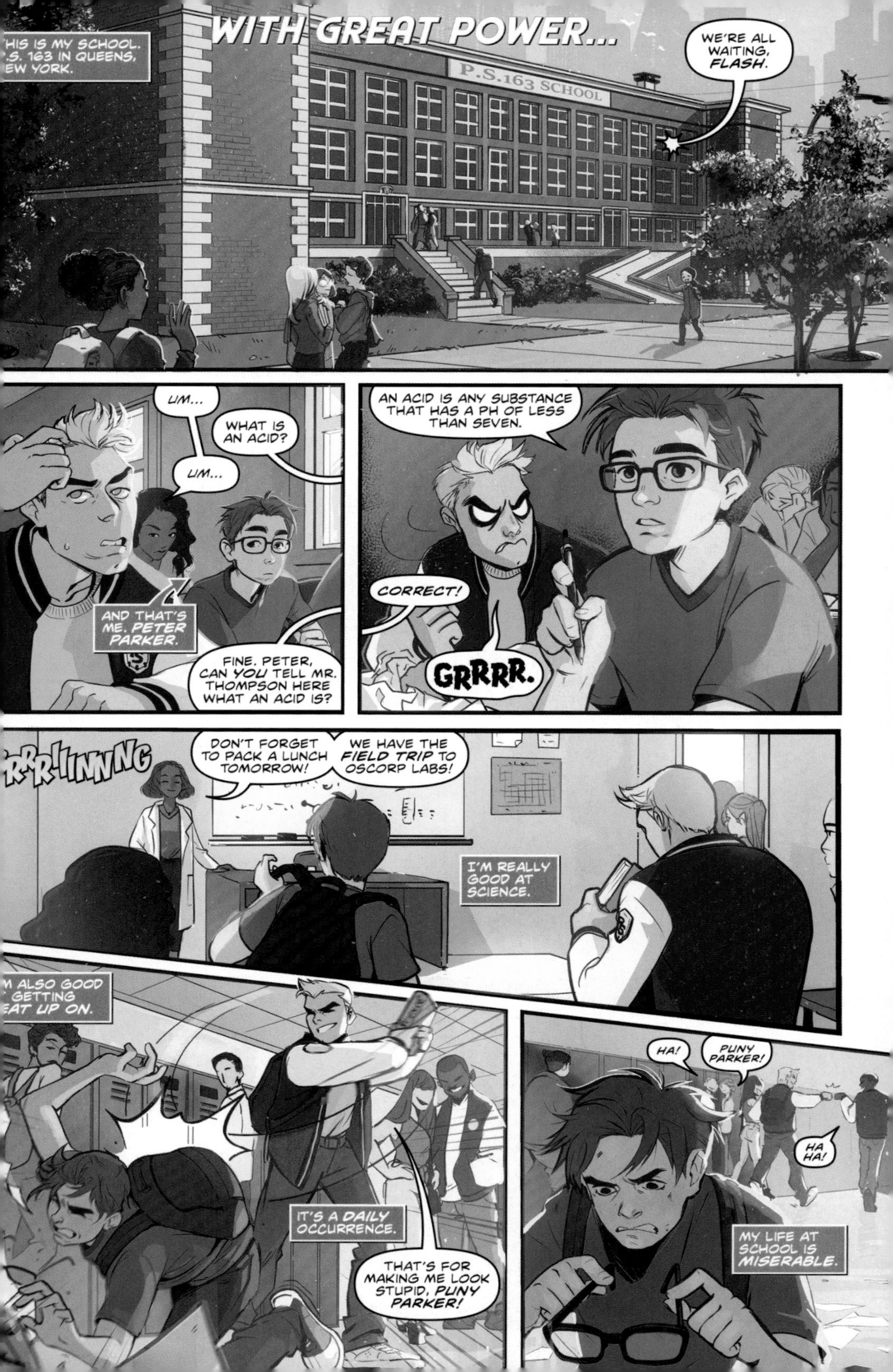
WITH GREAT POWER...
THIS IS MY SCHOOL. P.S. 163 IN QUEENS, NEW YORK.
WE'RE ALL WAITING, FLASH.
P.S.163 SCHOOL
UM...
WHAT IS AN ACID?
UM...
AND THAT'S ME. PETER PARKER.
FINE. PETER, CAN YOU TELL MR. THOMPSON HERE WHAT AN ACID IS?
AN ACID IS ANY SUBSTANCE THAT HAS A PH OF LESS THAN SEVEN.
CORRECT!
GRRRR.
RRRIIINNNG
DON'T FORGET TO PACK A LUNCH TOMORROW!
WE HAVE THE FIELD TRIP TO OSCORP LABS!
I'M REALLY GOOD AT SCIENCE.
I'M ALSO GOOD AT GETTING BEAT UP ON.
IT'S A DAILY OCCURRENCE.
THAT'S FOR MAKING ME LOOK STUPID, PUNY PARKER!
HA!
PUNY PARKER!
HA HA!
MY LIFE AT SCHOOL IS MISERABLE.

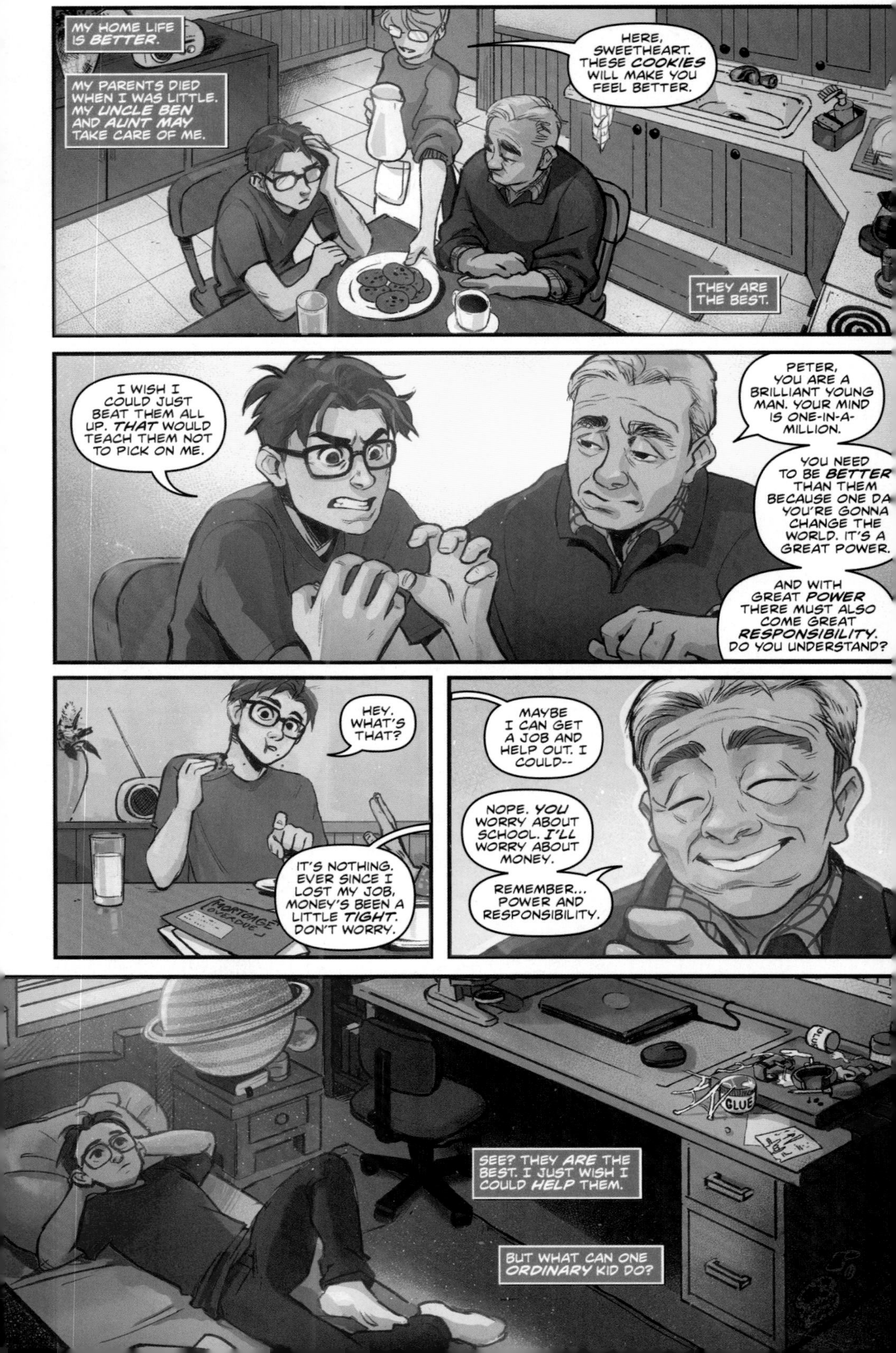
MY HOME LIFE IS BETTER.
MY PARENTS DIED WHEN I WAS LITTLE. MY UNCLE BEN AND AUNT MAY TAKE CARE OF ME.
HERE, SWEETHEART. THESE COOKIES WILL MAKE YOU FEEL BETTER.
THEY ARE THE BEST.
I WISH I COULD JUST BEAT THEM ALL UP. THAT WOULD TEACH THEM NOT TO PICK ON ME.
PETER, YOU ARE A BRILLIANT YOUNG MAN. YOUR MIND IS ONE-IN-A-MILLION.
YOU NEED TO BE BETTER THAN THEM BECAUSE ONE DA YOU'RE GONNA CHANGE THE WORLD. IT'S A GREAT POWER.
AND WITH GREAT POWER THERE MUST ALSO COME GREAT RESPONSIBILITY. DO YOU UNDERSTAND?
HEY. WHAT'S THAT?
IT'S NOTHING. EVER SINCE I LOST MY JOB, MONEY'S BEEN A LITTLE TIGHT. DON'T WORRY.
MORTGAGE OVERDUE
MAYBE I CAN GET A JOB AND HELP OUT. I COULD--
NOPE. YOU WORRY ABOUT SCHOOL. I'LL WORRY ABOUT MONEY.
REMEMBER... POWER AND RESPONSIBILITY.
GLUE
SEE? THEY ARE THE BEST. I JUST WISH I COULD HELP THEM.
BUT WHAT CAN ONE ORDINARY KID DO?

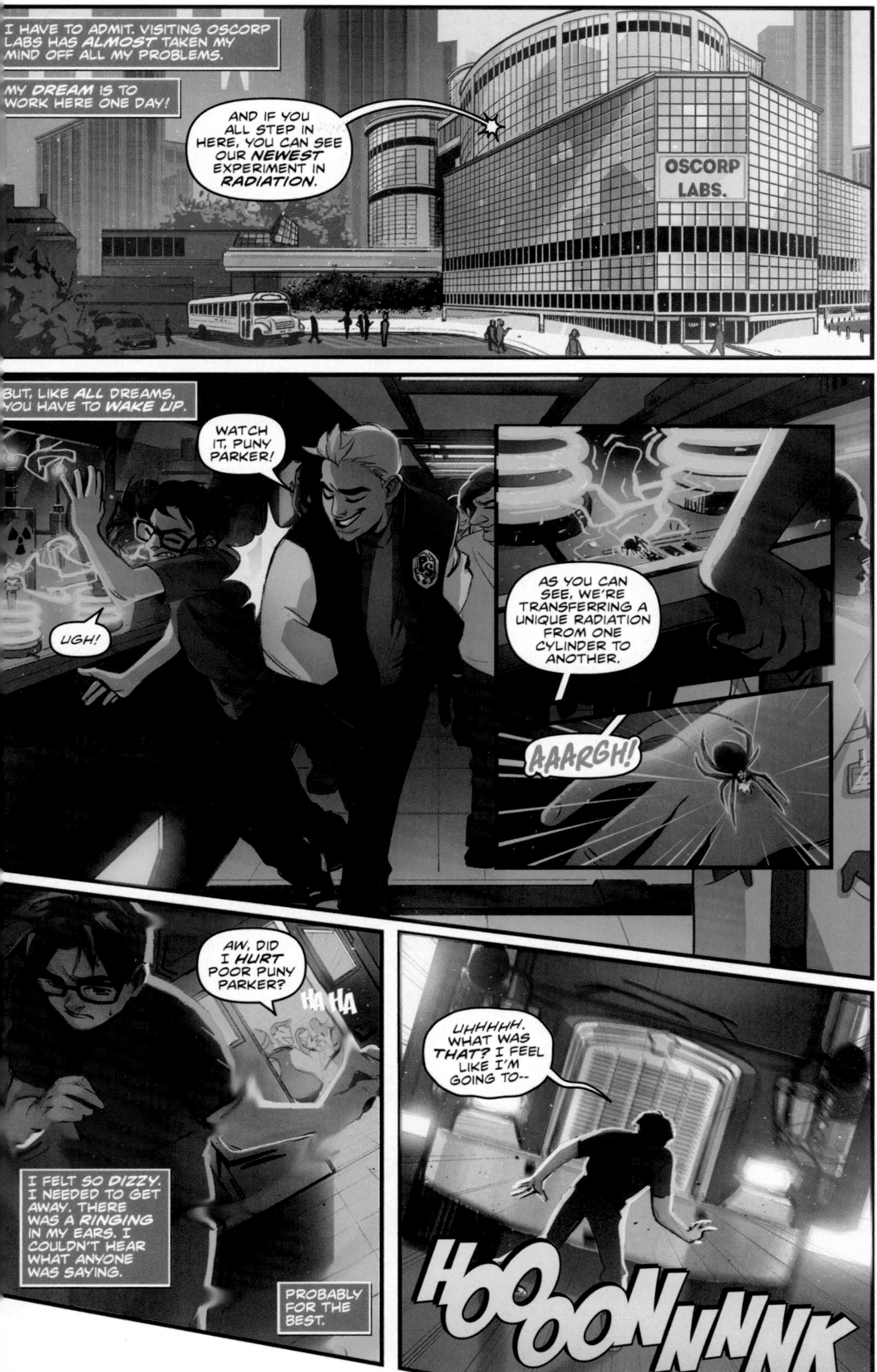
I HAVE TO ADMIT. VISITING OSCORP LABS HAS *ALMOST* TAKEN MY MIND OFF ALL MY PROBLEMS.
MY *DREAM* IS TO WORK HERE ONE DAY!
AND IF YOU ALL STEP IN HERE, YOU CAN SEE OUR *NEWEST* EXPERIMENT IN *RADIATION*.
OSCORP LABS.
BUT, LIKE *ALL* DREAMS, YOU HAVE TO *WAKE UP*.
WATCH IT, PUNY PARKER!
UGH!
AS YOU CAN SEE, WE'RE TRANSFERRING A UNIQUE RADIATION FROM ONE CYLINDER TO ANOTHER.
AAARGH!
AW, DID I *HURT* POOR PUNY PARKER?
HA HA
I FELT SO *DIZZY*. I NEEDED TO GET AWAY. THERE WAS A *RINGING* IN MY EARS. I COULDN'T HEAR WHAT ANYONE WAS SAYING.
PROBABLY FOR THE BEST.
UHHHHH. WHAT WAS *THAT?* I FEEL LIKE I'M GOING TO--
HOOOONNNNK

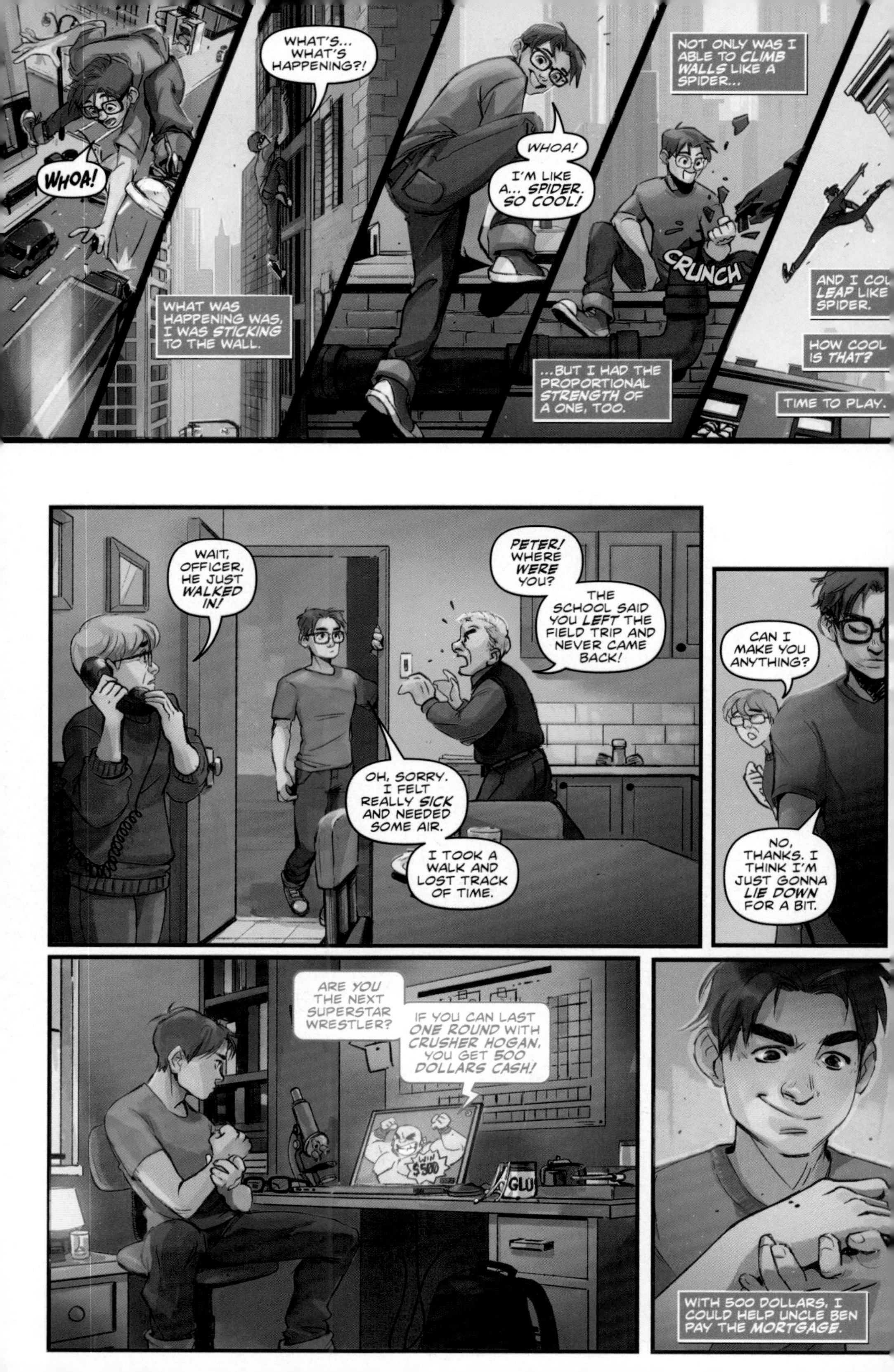
WHOA!
WHAT'S... WHAT'S HAPPENING?!
WHAT WAS HAPPENING WAS, I WAS STICKING TO THE WALL.
WHOA!
I'M LIKE A... SPIDER. SO COOL!
NOT ONLY WAS I ABLE TO CLIMB WALLS LIKE A SPIDER...
CRUNCH
...BUT I HAD THE PROPORTIONAL STRENGTH OF A ONE, TOO.
AND I COU LEAP LIKE SPIDER.
HOW COOL IS THAT?
TIME TO PLAY.
WAIT, OFFICER, HE JUST WALKED IN!
PETER! WHERE WERE YOU?
THE SCHOOL SAID YOU LEFT THE FIELD TRIP AND NEVER CAME BACK!
OH, SORRY. I FELT REALLY SICK AND NEEDED SOME AIR.
I TOOK A WALK AND LOST TRACK OF TIME.
CAN I MAKE YOU ANYTHING?
NO, THANKS. I THINK I'M JUST GONNA LIE DOWN FOR A BIT.
ARE YOU THE NEXT SUPERSTAR WRESTLER?
IF YOU CAN LAST ONE ROUND WITH CRUSHER HOGAN, YOU GET 500 DOLLARS CASH!
WIN $500
GLU
WITH 500 DOLLARS, I COULD HELP UNCLE BEN PAY THE MORTGAGE.

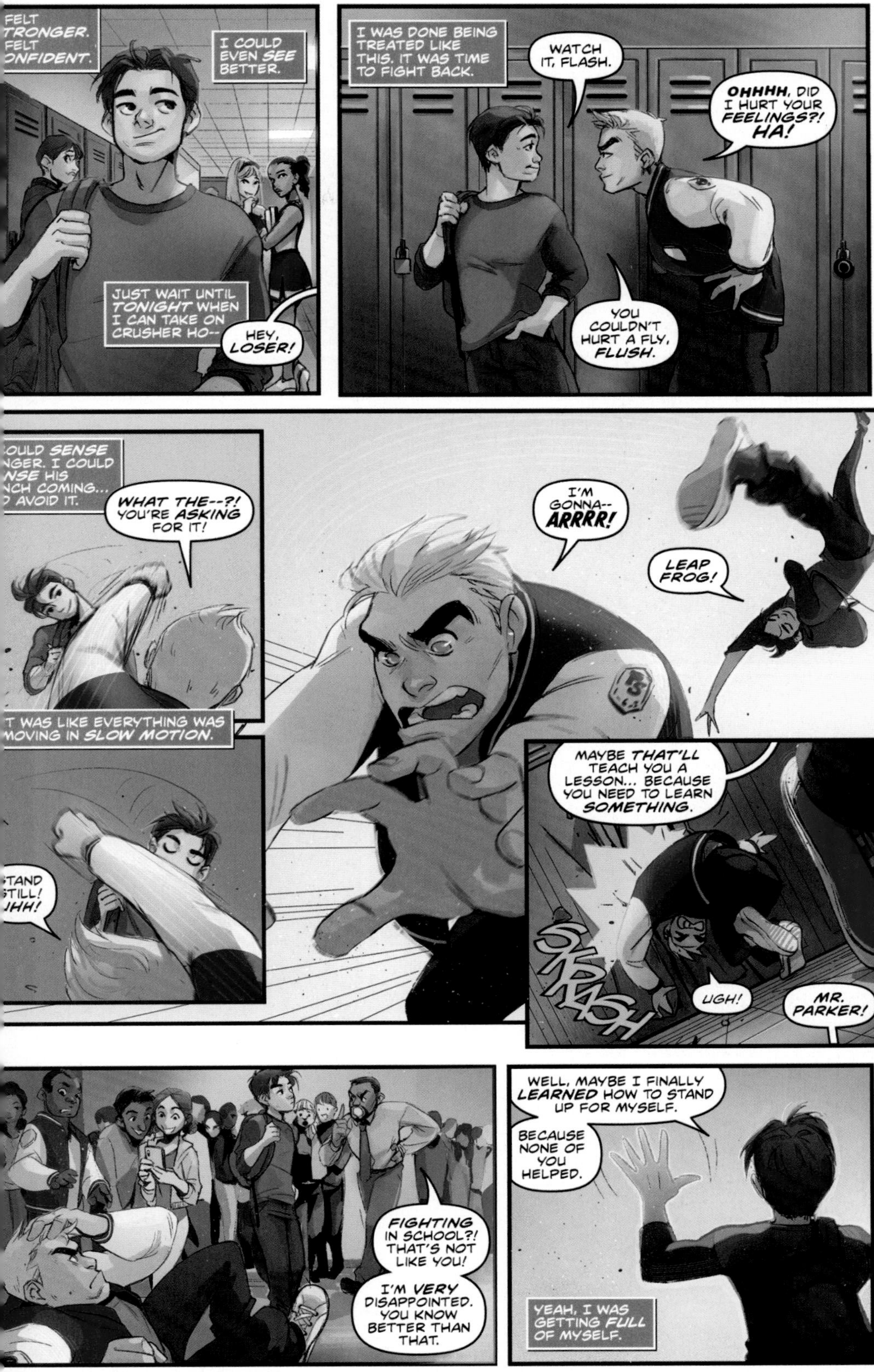
FELT
TRONGER.
FELT
ONFIDENT.
I COULD EVEN SEE BETTER.
JUST WAIT UNTIL TONIGHT WHEN I CAN TAKE ON CRUSHER HO--
HEY, LOSER!
I WAS DONE BEING TREATED LIKE THIS. IT WAS TIME TO FIGHT BACK.
WATCH IT, FLASH.
OHHHH, DID I HURT YOUR FEELINGS?! HA!
YOU COULDN'T HURT A FLY, FLUSH.
OULD SENSE
NGER. I COULD
NSE HIS
NCH COMING...
D AVOID IT.
WHAT THE--?! YOU'RE ASKING FOR IT!
T WAS LIKE EVERYTHING WAS MOVING IN SLOW MOTION.
TAND
TILL!
HH!
I'M GONNA-- ARRRR!
LEAP FROG!
MAYBE THAT'LL TEACH YOU A LESSON... BECAUSE YOU NEED TO LEARN SOMETHING.
SKRASH
UGH!
MR. PARKER!
FIGHTING IN SCHOOL?! THAT'S NOT LIKE YOU!
I'M VERY DISAPPOINTED. YOU KNOW BETTER THAN THAT.
WELL, MAYBE I FINALLY LEARNED HOW TO STAND UP FOR MYSELF.
BECAUSE NONE OF YOU HELPED.
YEAH, I WAS GETTING FULL OF MYSELF.

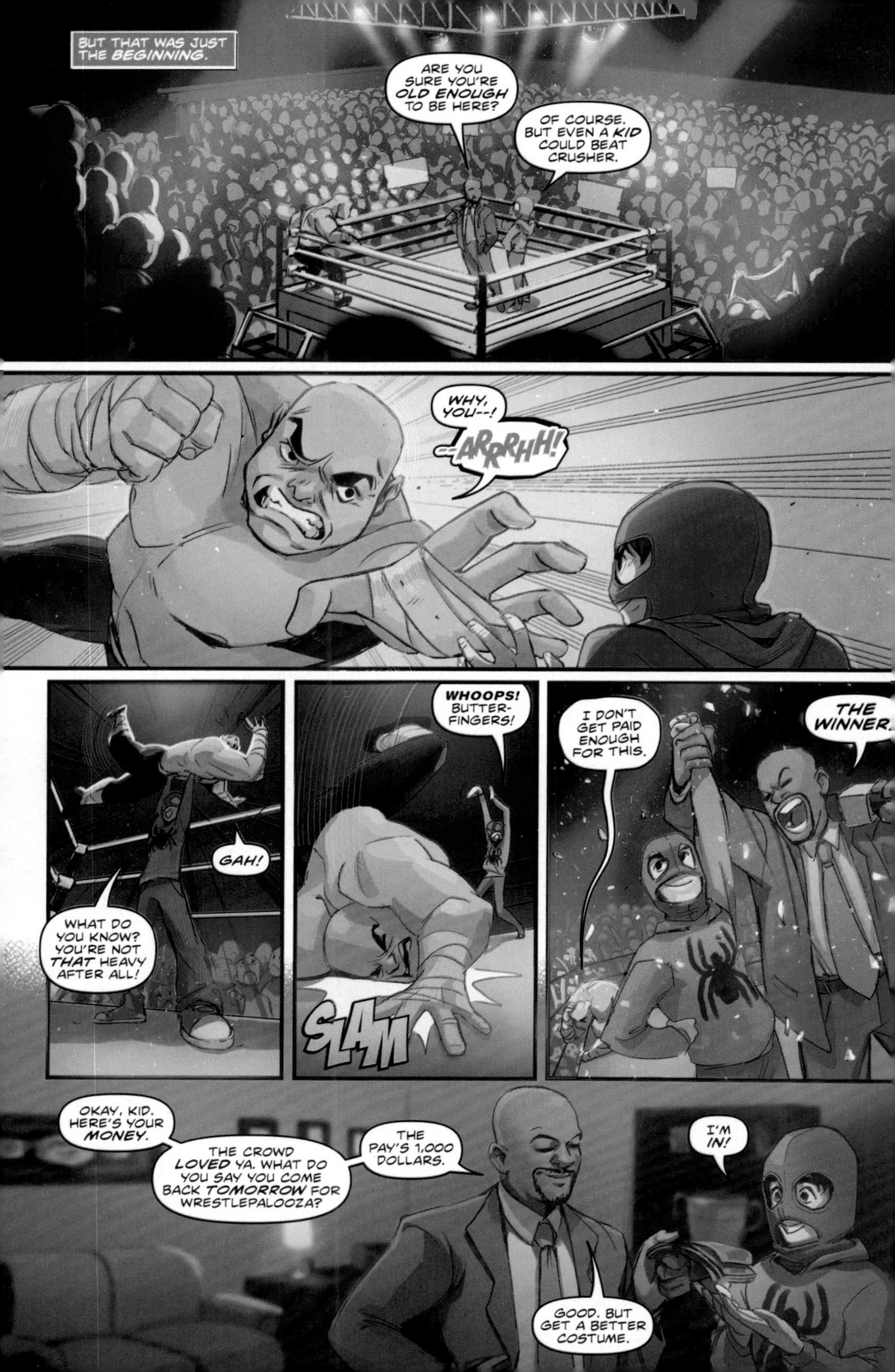
BUT THAT WAS JUST THE *BEGINNING*.
ARE YOU SURE YOU'RE *OLD ENOUGH* TO BE HERE?
OF COURSE. BUT EVEN A *KID* COULD BEAT CRUSHER.
WHY, YOU--!
--ARRRHH!
GAH!
WHAT DO YOU KNOW? YOU'RE NOT *THAT* HEAVY AFTER ALL!
WHOOPS! BUTTER-FINGERS!
SLAM
I DON'T GET PAID ENOUGH FOR THIS.
THE WINNER
OKAY, KID. HERE'S YOUR *MONEY*.
THE CROWD *LOVED* YA. WHAT DO YOU SAY YOU COME BACK *TOMORROW* FOR WRESTLEPALOOZA?
THE PAY'S 1,000 DOLLARS.
I'M *IN!*
GOOD. BUT GET A BETTER COSTUME.

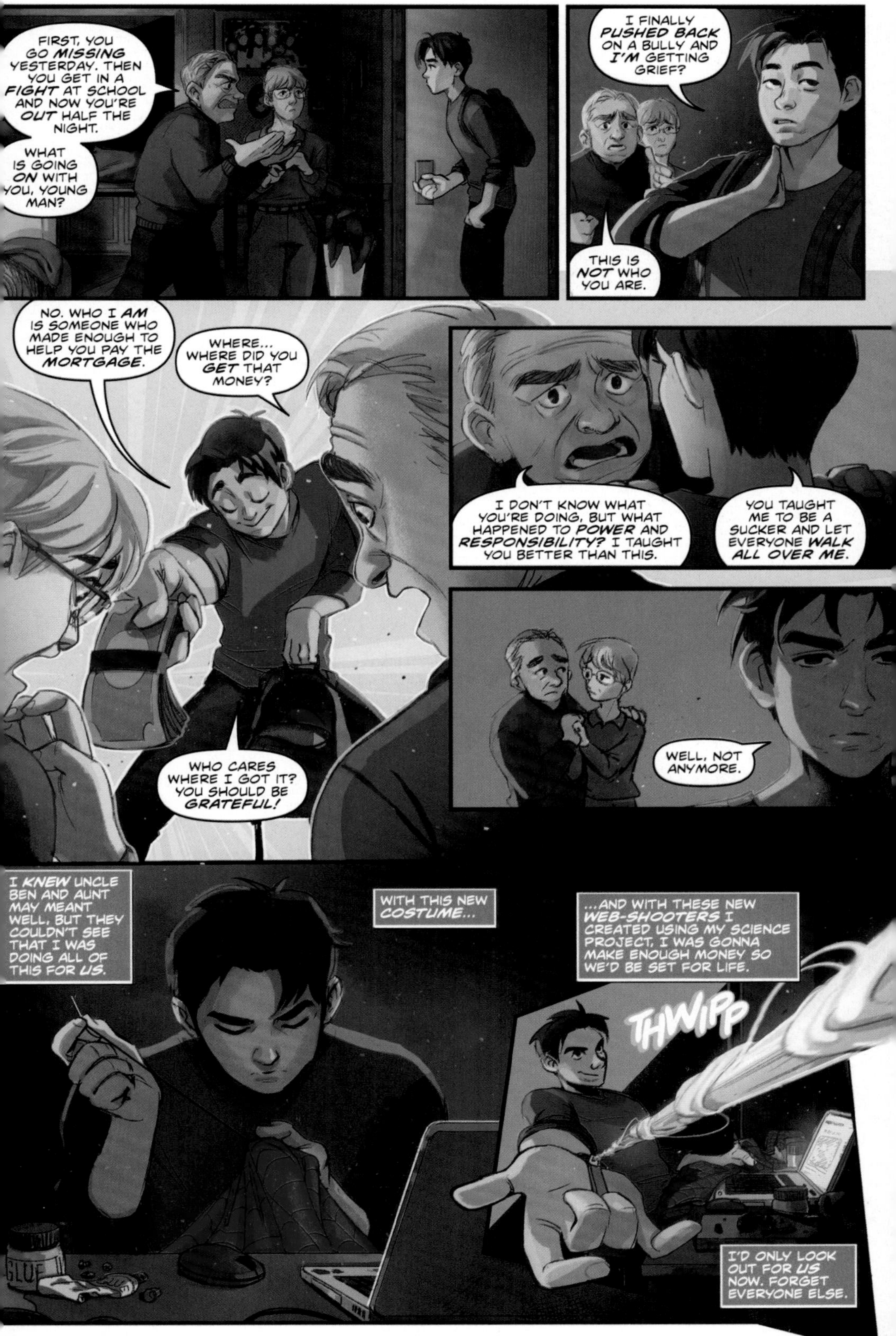
FIRST, YOU GO MISSING YESTERDAY. THEN YOU GET IN A FIGHT AT SCHOOL AND NOW YOU'RE OUT HALF THE NIGHT.
WHAT IS GOING ON WITH YOU, YOUNG MAN?
I FINALLY PUSHED BACK ON A BULLY AND I'M GETTING GRIEF?
THIS IS NOT WHO YOU ARE.
NO. WHO I AM IS SOMEONE WHO MADE ENOUGH TO HELP YOU PAY THE MORTGAGE.
WHERE... WHERE DID YOU GET THAT MONEY?
WHO CARES WHERE I GOT IT? YOU SHOULD BE GRATEFUL!
I DON'T KNOW WHAT YOU'RE DOING, BUT WHAT HAPPENED TO POWER AND RESPONSIBILITY? I TAUGHT YOU BETTER THAN THIS.
YOU TAUGHT ME TO BE A SUCKER AND LET EVERYONE WALK ALL OVER ME.
WELL, NOT ANYMORE.
I KNEW UNCLE BEN AND AUNT MAY MEANT WELL, BUT THEY COULDN'T SEE THAT I WAS DOING ALL OF THIS FOR US.
WITH THIS NEW COSTUME...
...AND WITH THESE NEW WEB-SHOOTERS I CREATED USING MY SCIENCE PROJECT, I WAS GONNA MAKE ENOUGH MONEY SO WE'D BE SET FOR LIFE.
THWIPP
GLUE
I'D ONLY LOOK OUT FOR US NOW. FORGET EVERYONE ELSE.

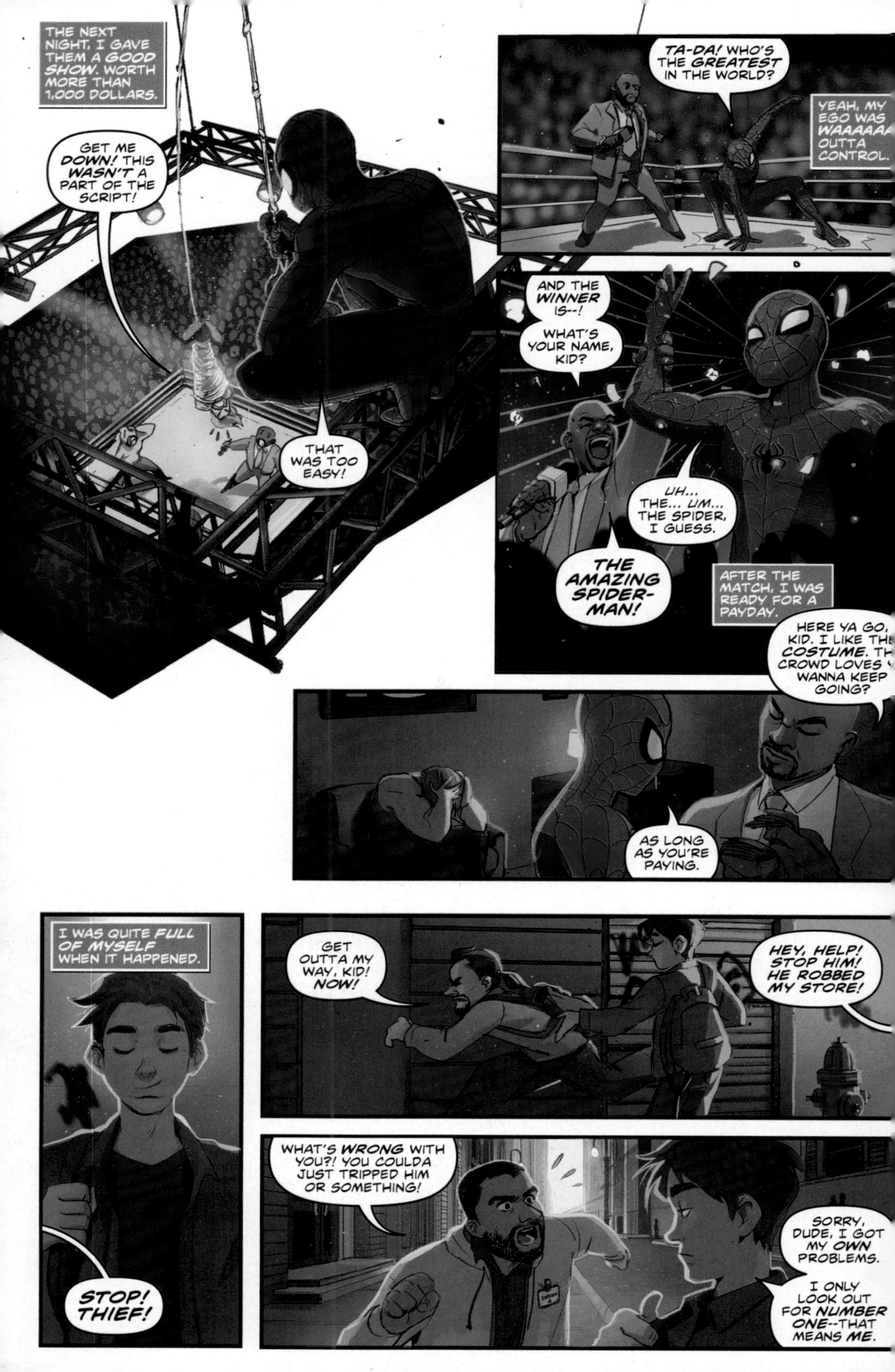
THE NEXT NIGHT, I GAVE THEM A GOOD SHOW. WORTH MORE THAN 1,000 DOLLARS.
GET ME DOWN! THIS WASN'T A PART OF THE SCRIPT!
THAT WAS TOO EASY!
TA-DA! WHO'S THE GREATEST IN THE WORLD?
YEAH, MY EGO WAS WAAAAAA OUTTA CONTROL.
AND THE WINNER IS--!
WHAT'S YOUR NAME, KID?
UH... THE... UM... THE SPIDER, I GUESS.
THE AMAZING SPIDER-MAN!
AFTER THE MATCH, I WAS READY FOR A PAYDAY.
HERE YA GO, KID. I LIKE THE COSTUME. TH CROWD LOVES WANNA KEEP GOING?
AS LONG AS YOU'RE PAYING.
I WAS QUITE FULL OF MYSELF WHEN IT HAPPENED.
STOP! THIEF!
GET OUTTA MY WAY, KID! NOW!
HEY, HELP! STOP HIM! HE ROBBED MY STORE!
WHAT'S WRONG WITH YOU?! YOU COULDA JUST TRIPPED HIM OR SOMETHING!
SORRY, DUDE, I GOT MY OWN PROBLEMS.
I ONLY LOOK OUT FOR NUMBER ONE--THAT MEANS ME.

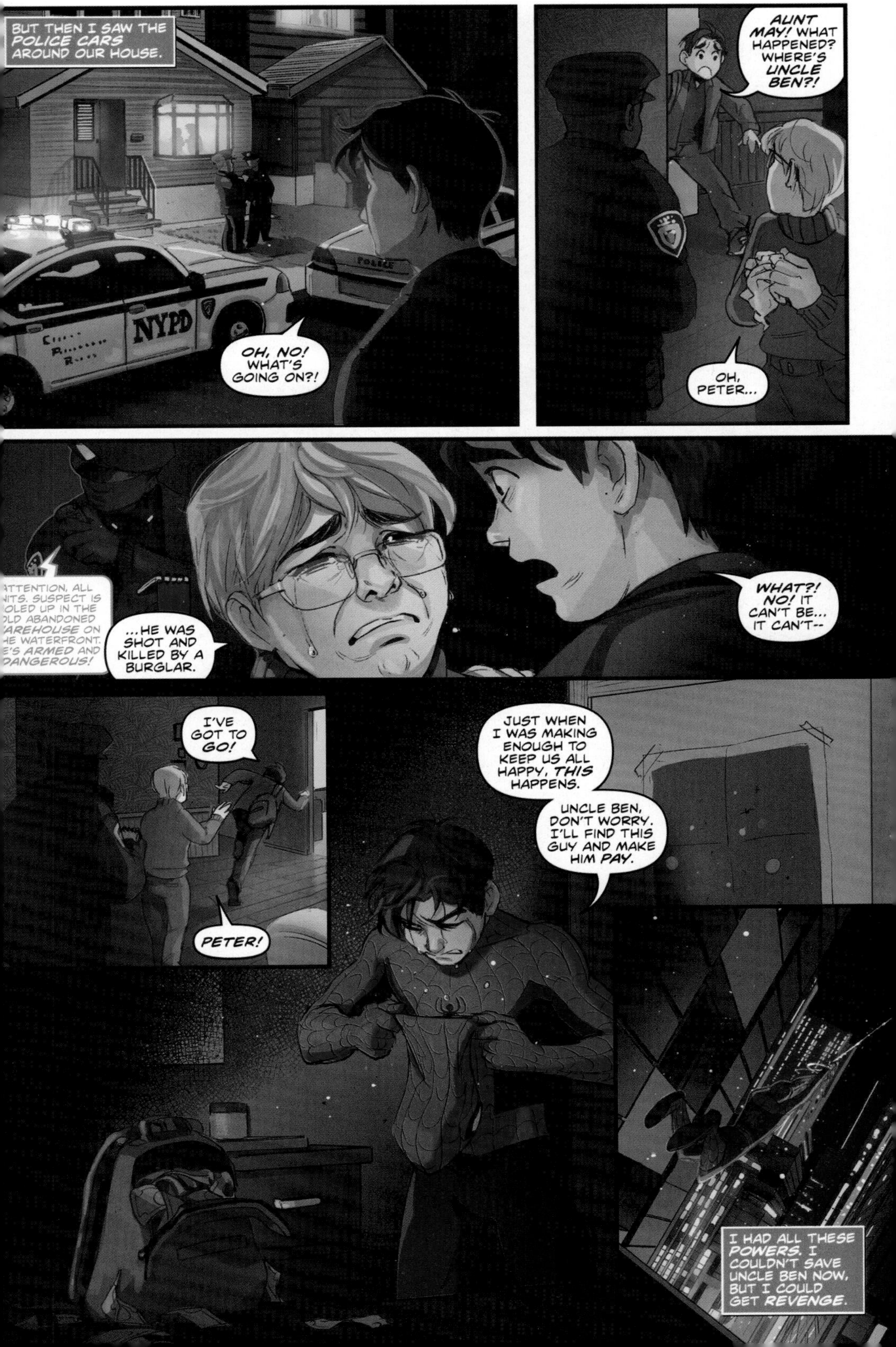
BUT THEN I SAW THE POLICE CARS AROUND OUR HOUSE.
NYPD
OH, NO! WHAT'S GOING ON?!
AUNT MAY! WHAT HAPPENED? WHERE'S UNCLE BEN?!
OH, PETER...
ATTENTION, ALL NITS. SUSPECT IS OLED UP IN THE LD ABANDONED AREHOUSE ON THE WATERFRONT. E'S ARMED AND DANGEROUS!
...HE WAS SHOT AND KILLED BY A BURGLAR.
WHAT?! NO! IT CAN'T BE... IT CAN'T--
I'VE GOT TO GO!
PETER!
JUST WHEN I WAS MAKING ENOUGH TO KEEP US ALL HAPPY, THIS HAPPENS.
UNCLE BEN, DON'T WORRY. I'LL FIND THIS GUY AND MAKE HIM PAY.
I HAD ALL THESE POWERS. I COULDN'T SAVE UNCLE BEN NOW, BUT I COULD GET REVENGE.

EVERYONE STAND YOUR GROUND. HE COULD *PICK US OFF* IF WE GET ANY CLOSER.

THOSE COPS AIN'T GETTIN' *ME.* I ALREADY KILLED *ONE* GUY TONIGHT.

WHAT'S A *FEW* MORE?

NOT IF I HAVE ANYTHING TO SAY ABOUT IT...

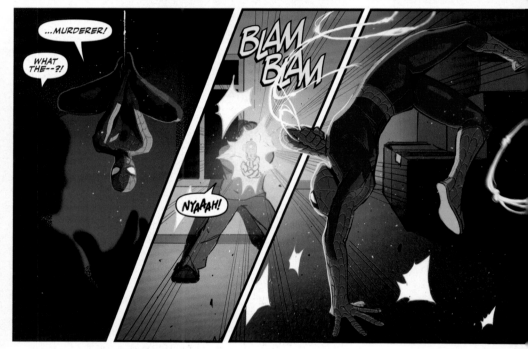

...MURDERER!

WHAT THE--?!

BLAM BLAM

NYAAAH!

SHOTS FIRED! REPEAT, SHOTS FIRED!

KRAK

NOW YOU *PAY* FOR WHAT YOU'VE DONE!

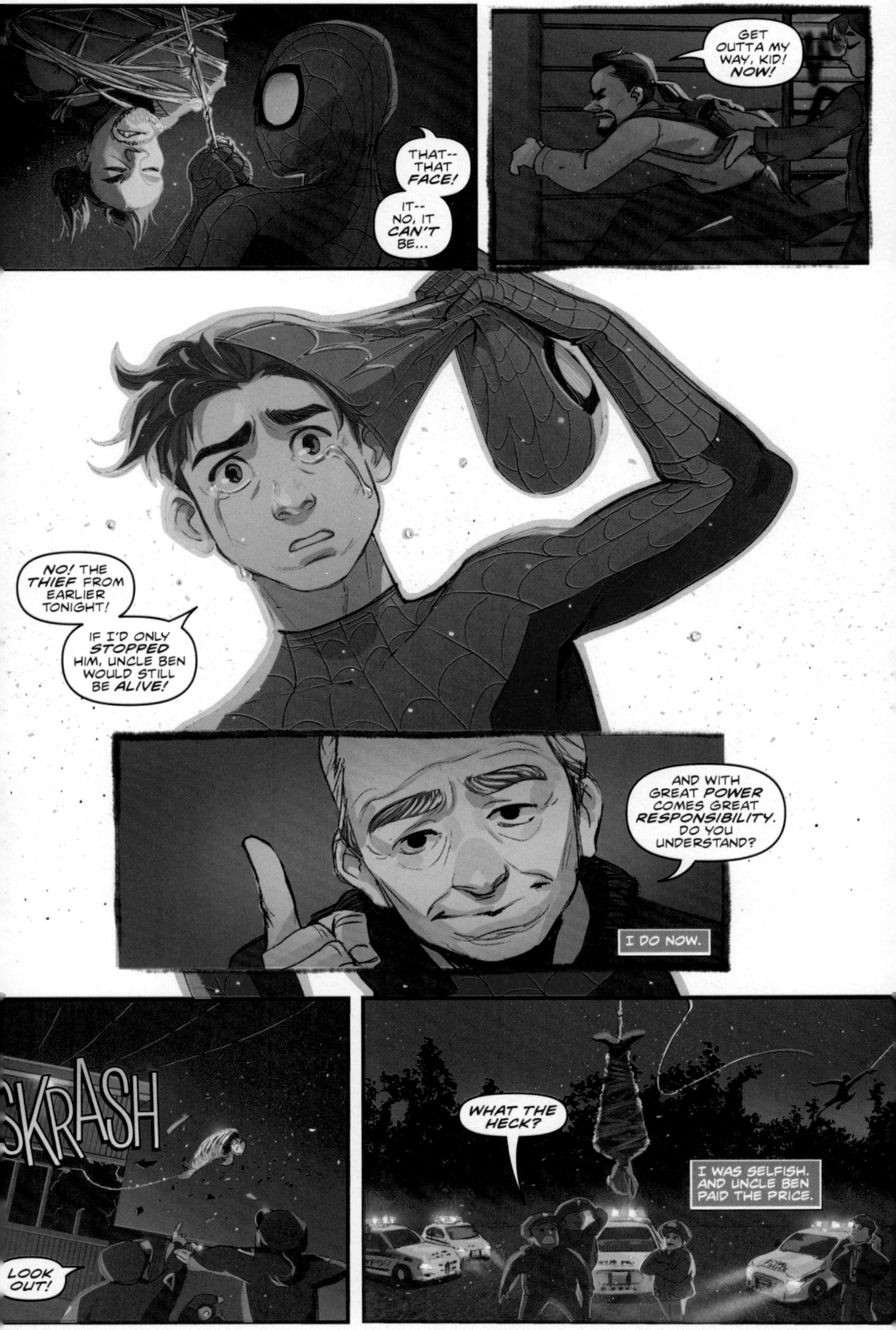
THAT-- THAT FACE!
IT-- NO, IT CAN'T BE...
GET OUTTA MY WAY, KID! NOW!
NO! THE THIEF FROM EARLIER TONIGHT!
IF I'D ONLY STOPPED HIM, UNCLE BEN WOULD STILL BE ALIVE!
AND WITH GREAT POWER COMES GREAT RESPONSIBILITY. DO YOU UNDERSTAND?
I DO NOW.
SKRASH
LOOK OUT!
WHAT THE HECK?
I WAS SELFISH. AND UNCLE BEN PAID THE PRICE.

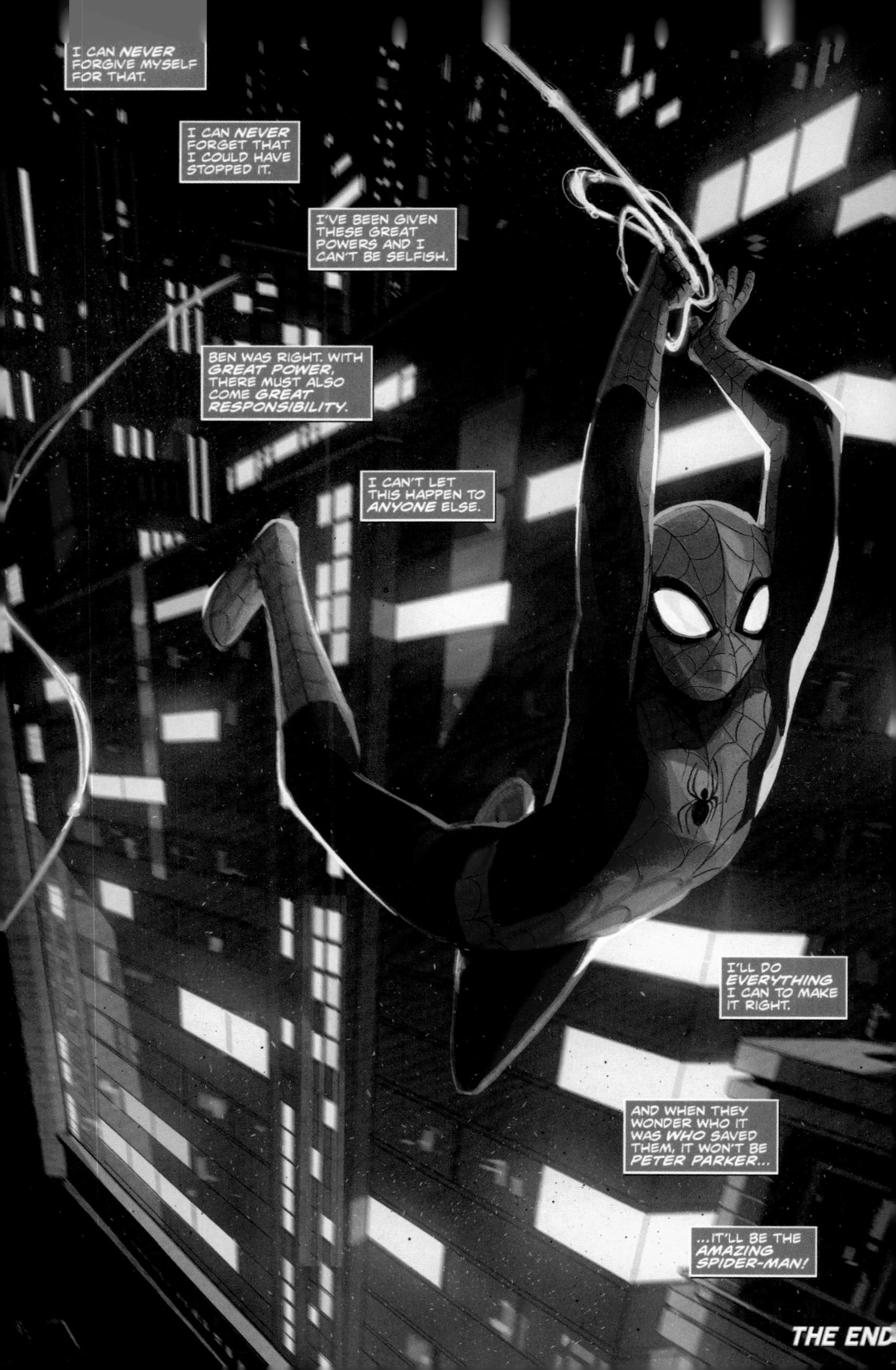
I CAN NEVER FORGIVE MYSELF FOR THAT.
I CAN NEVER FORGET THAT I COULD HAVE STOPPED IT.
I'VE BEEN GIVEN THESE GREAT POWERS AND I CAN'T BE SELFISH.
BEN WAS RIGHT. WITH GREAT POWER, THERE MUST ALSO COME GREAT RESPONSIBILITY.
I CAN'T LET THIS HAPPEN TO ANYONE ELSE.
I'LL DO EVERYTHING I CAN TO MAKE IT RIGHT.
AND WHEN THEY WONDER WHO IT WAS WHO SAVED THEM, IT WON'T BE PETER PARKER...
...IT'LL BE THE AMAZING SPIDER-MAN!
THE END

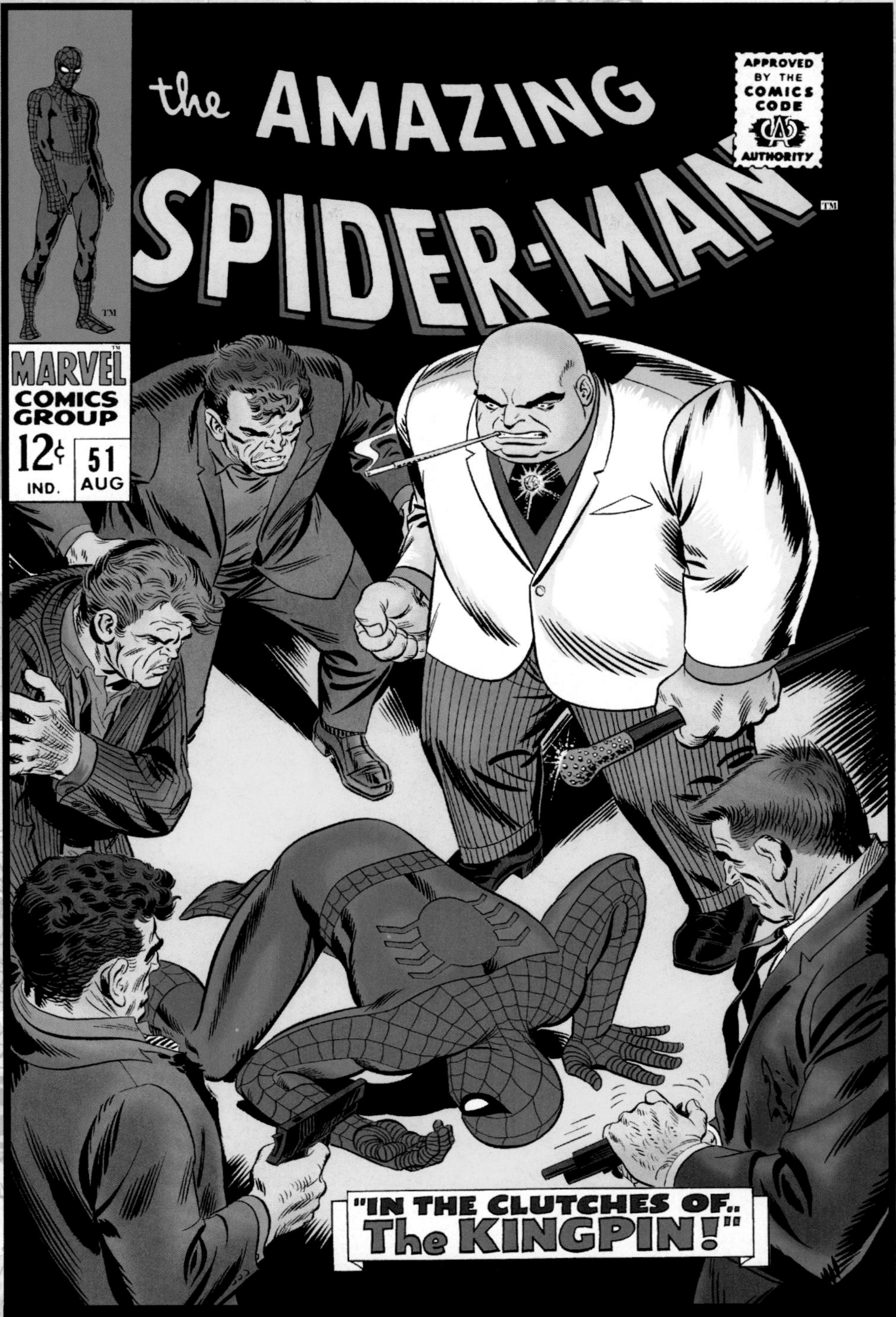
the AMAZING
SPIDER-MAN
APPROVED BY THE COMICS CODE AUTHORITY
MARVEL COMICS GROUP
12¢ IND.
51 AUG
"IN THE CLUTCHES OF.. The KINGPIN!"

AMAZING SPIDER-MAN #51

WILSON FISK IS AFTER J. JONAH JAMESON FOR HIS NEGATIVE PRESS ON FISK'S ILLEGAL ACTIVITIES. CAN SPIDER-MAN TAKE ON THE KINGPIN OF CRIME IN A ONE-ON-ONE BRAWL TO SAVE JJJ?!

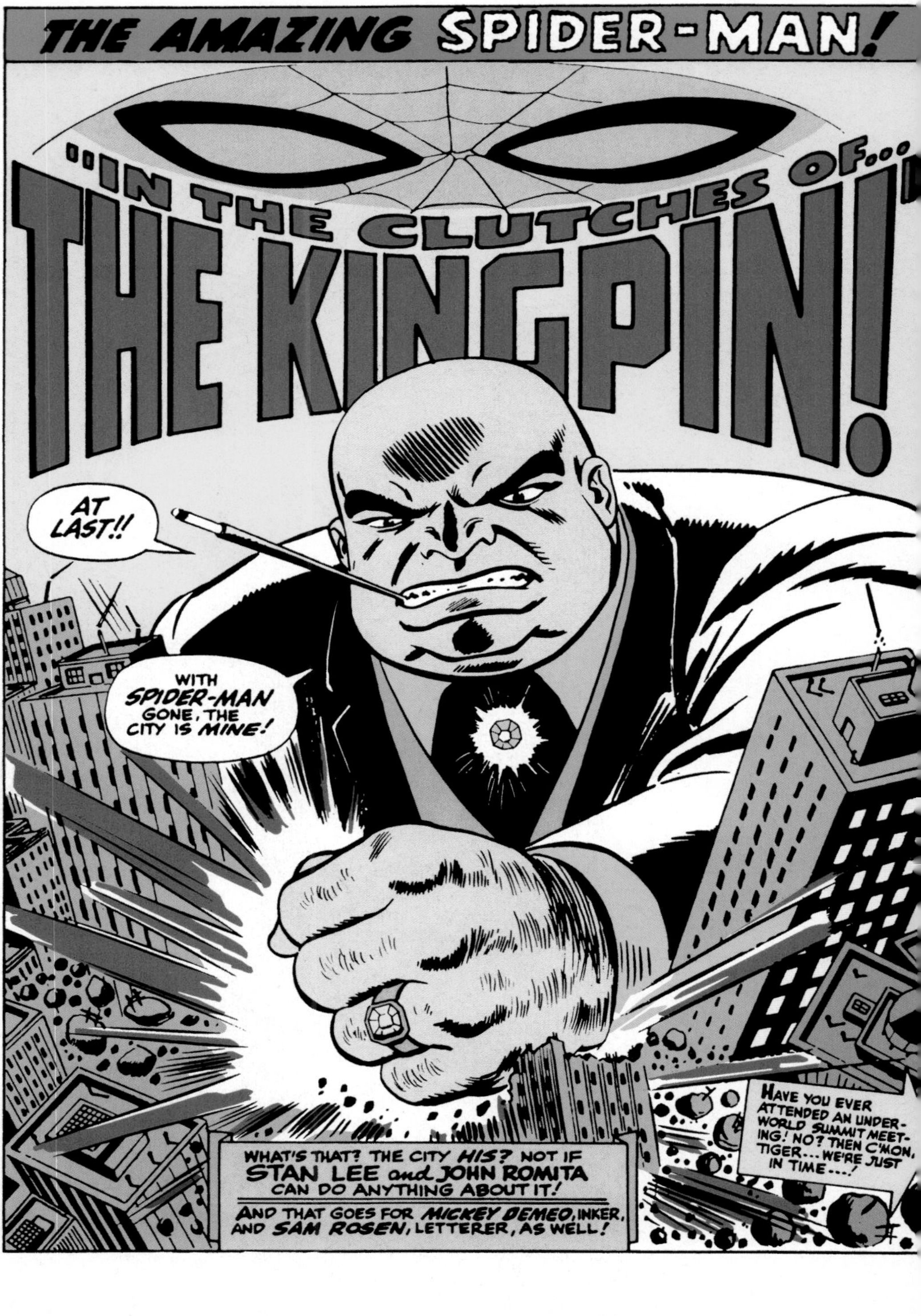
THE AMAZING SPIDER-MAN!
"IN THE CLUTCHES OF..."
THE KINGPIN!
AT LAST!!
WITH SPIDER-MAN GONE, THE CITY IS MINE!
WHAT'S THAT? THE CITY HIS? NOT IF STAN LEE and JOHN ROMITA CAN DO ANYTHING ABOUT IT!
AND THAT GOES FOR MICKEY DEMEO, INKER, AND SAM ROSEN, LETTERER, AS WELL!
HAVE YOU EVER ATTENDED AN UNDERWORLD SUMMIT MEETING! NO? THEN C'MON, TIGER... WE'RE JUST IN TIME...!

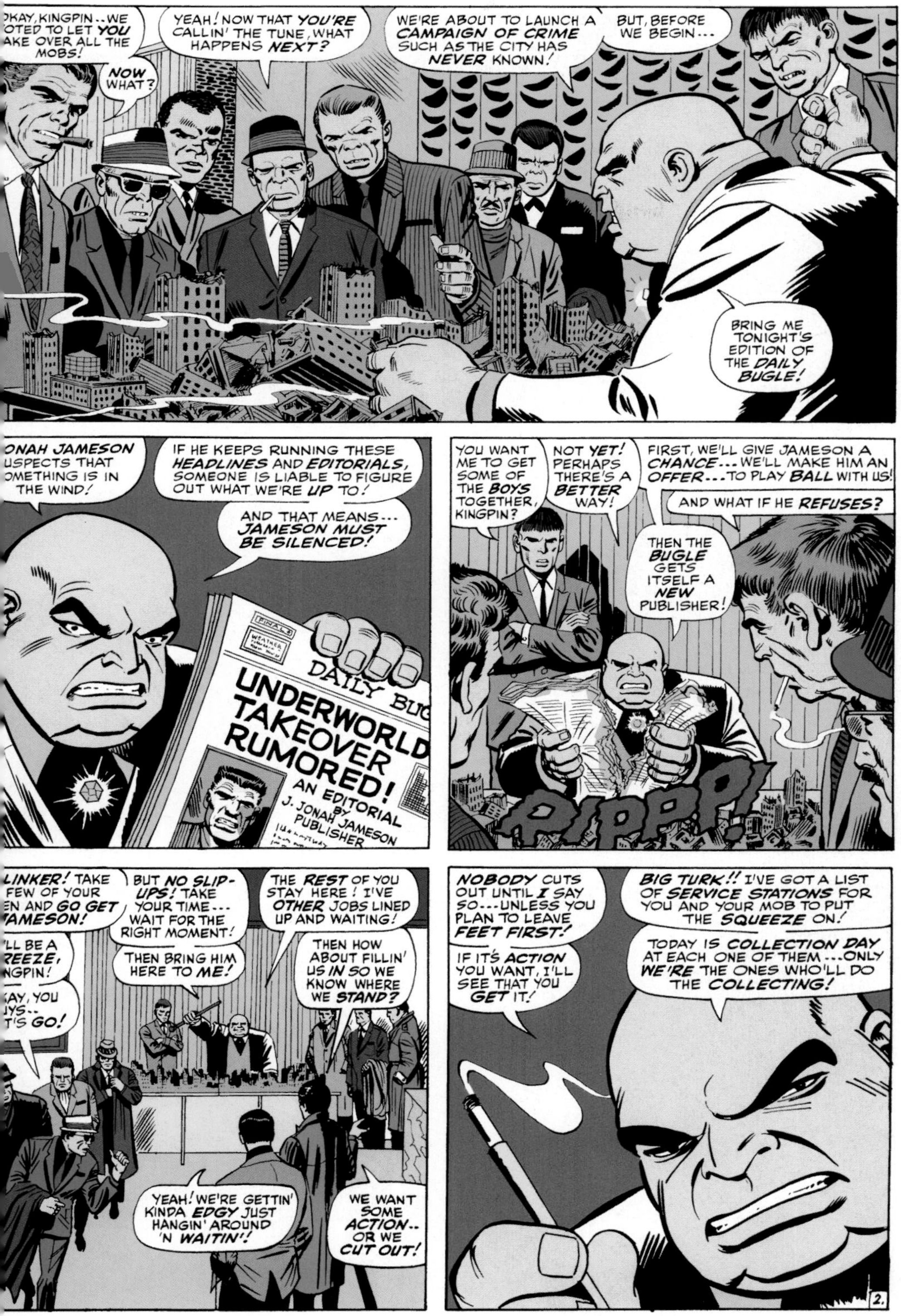

OKAY, KINGPIN.. WE OTED TO LET YOU AKE OVER ALL THE MOBS!
NOW WHAT?
YEAH! NOW THAT YOU'RE CALLIN' THE TUNE, WHAT HAPPENS NEXT?
WE'RE ABOUT TO LAUNCH A CAMPAIGN OF CRIME SUCH AS THE CITY HAS NEVER KNOWN!
BUT, BEFORE WE BEGIN...
BRING ME TONIGHT'S EDITION OF THE DAILY BUGLE!
ONAH JAMESON USPECTS THAT OMETHING IS IN THE WIND!
IF HE KEEPS RUNNING THESE HEADLINES AND EDITORIALS, SOMEONE IS LIABLE TO FIGURE OUT WHAT WE'RE UP TO!
AND THAT MEANS... JAMESON MUST BE SILENCED!
FINAL
DAILY BUG
UNDERWORLD TAKEOVER RUMORED!
AN EDITORIAL BY J. JONAH JAMESON PUBLISHER
YOU WANT ME TO GET SOME OF THE BOYS TOGETHER, KINGPIN?
NOT YET! PERHAPS THERE'S A BETTER WAY!
FIRST, WE'LL GIVE JAMESON A CHANCE... WE'LL MAKE HIM AN OFFER... TO PLAY BALL WITH US!
AND WHAT IF HE REFUSES?
THEN THE BUGLE GETS ITSELF A NEW PUBLISHER!
RIPPP!
LINKER! TAKE FEW OF YOUR EN AND GO GET AMESON!
BUT NO SLIP-UPS! TAKE YOUR TIME... WAIT FOR THE RIGHT MOMENT!
THEN BRING HIM HERE TO ME!
'LL BE A REEZE, NGPIN!
AY, YOU YS.. T'S GO!
THE REST OF YOU STAY HERE! I'VE OTHER JOBS LINED UP AND WAITING!
THEN HOW ABOUT FILLIN' US IN SO WE KNOW WHERE WE STAND?
YEAH! WE'RE GETTIN' KINDA EDGY JUST HANGIN' AROUND 'N WAITIN'!
WE WANT SOME ACTION.. OR WE CUT OUT!
NOBODY CUTS OUT UNTIL I SAY SO... UNLESS YOU PLAN TO LEAVE FEET FIRST!
IF IT'S ACTION YOU WANT, I'LL SEE THAT YOU GET IT!
BIG TURK!! I'VE GOT A LIST OF SERVICE STATIONS FOR YOU AND YOUR MOB TO PUT THE SQUEEZE ON!
TODAY IS COLLECTION DAY AT EACH ONE OF THEM... ONLY WE'RE THE ONES WHO'LL DO THE COLLECTING!

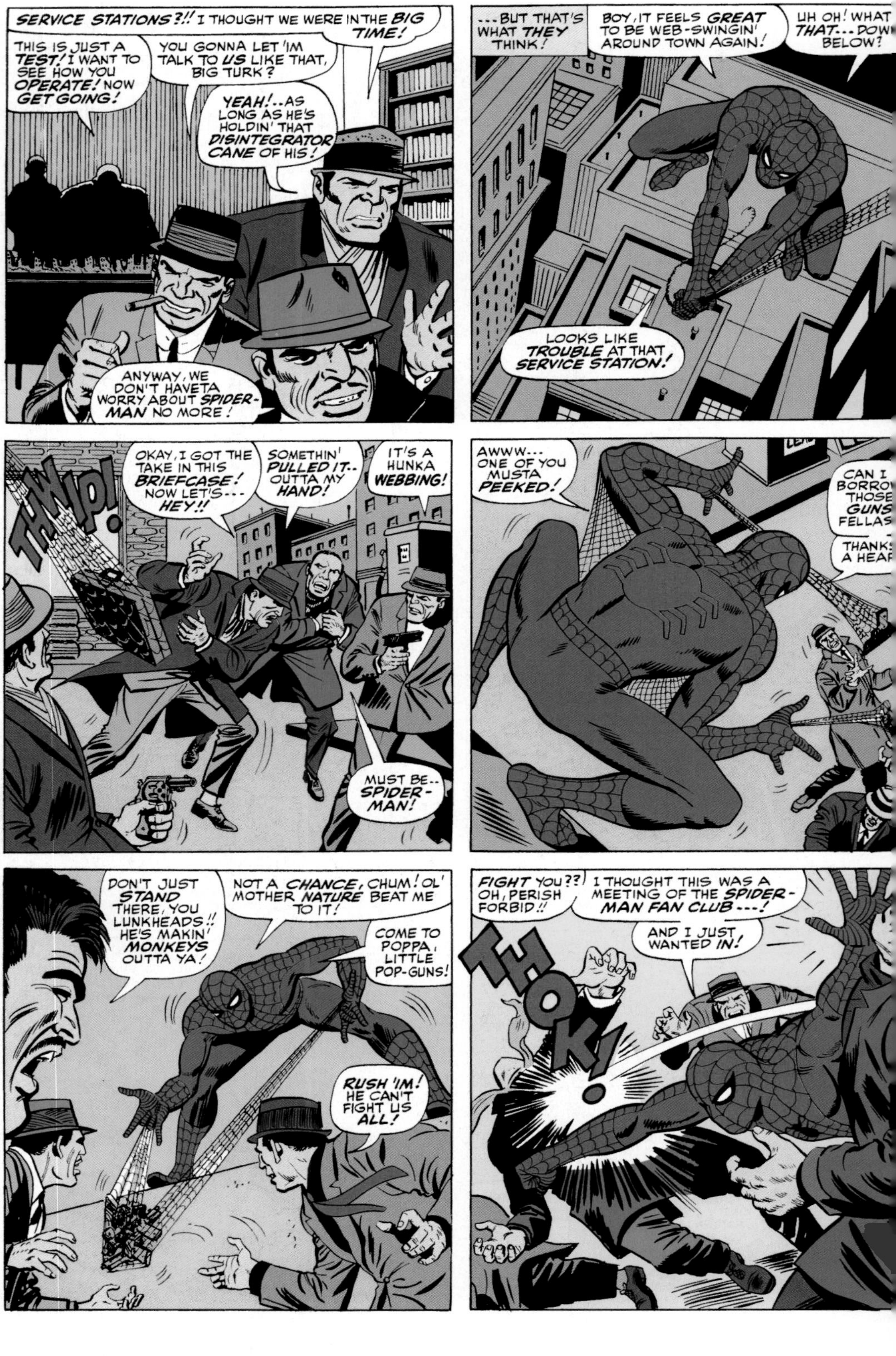
SERVICE STATIONS?!! I THOUGHT WE WERE IN THE BIG TIME!
THIS IS JUST A TEST! I WANT TO SEE HOW YOU OPERATE! NOW GET GOING!
YOU GONNA LET 'IM TALK TO US LIKE THAT, BIG TURK?
YEAH!..AS LONG AS HE'S HOLDIN' THAT DISINTEGRATOR CANE OF HIS!
ANYWAY, WE DON'T HAVETA WORRY ABOUT SPIDER-MAN NO MORE!
...BUT THAT'S WHAT THEY THINK!
BOY, IT FEELS GREAT TO BE WEB-SWINGIN' AROUND TOWN AGAIN!
UH OH! WHAT THAT... DOW BELOW?
LOOKS LIKE TROUBLE AT THAT SERVICE STATION!
THWIP!
OKAY, I GOT THE TAKE IN THIS BRIEFCASE! NOW LET'S--- HEY!!
SOMETHIN' PULLED IT.. OUTTA MY HAND!
IT'S A HUNKA WEBBING!
MUST BE.. SPIDER-MAN!
AWWW... ONE OF YOU MUSTA PEEKED!
CAN I BORROW THOSE GUNS FELLAS
THANKS A HEAP
DON'T JUST STAND THERE, YOU LUNKHEADS!! HE'S MAKIN' MONKEYS OUTTA YA!
NOT A CHANCE, CHUM! OL' MOTHER NATURE BEAT ME TO IT!
COME TO POPPA, LITTLE POP-GUNS!
RUSH 'IM! HE CAN'T FIGHT US ALL!
FIGHT YOU?? OH, PERISH FORBID!!
I THOUGHT THIS WAS A MEETING OF THE SPIDER-MAN FAN CLUB ---!
AND I JUST WANTED IN!
THOK!

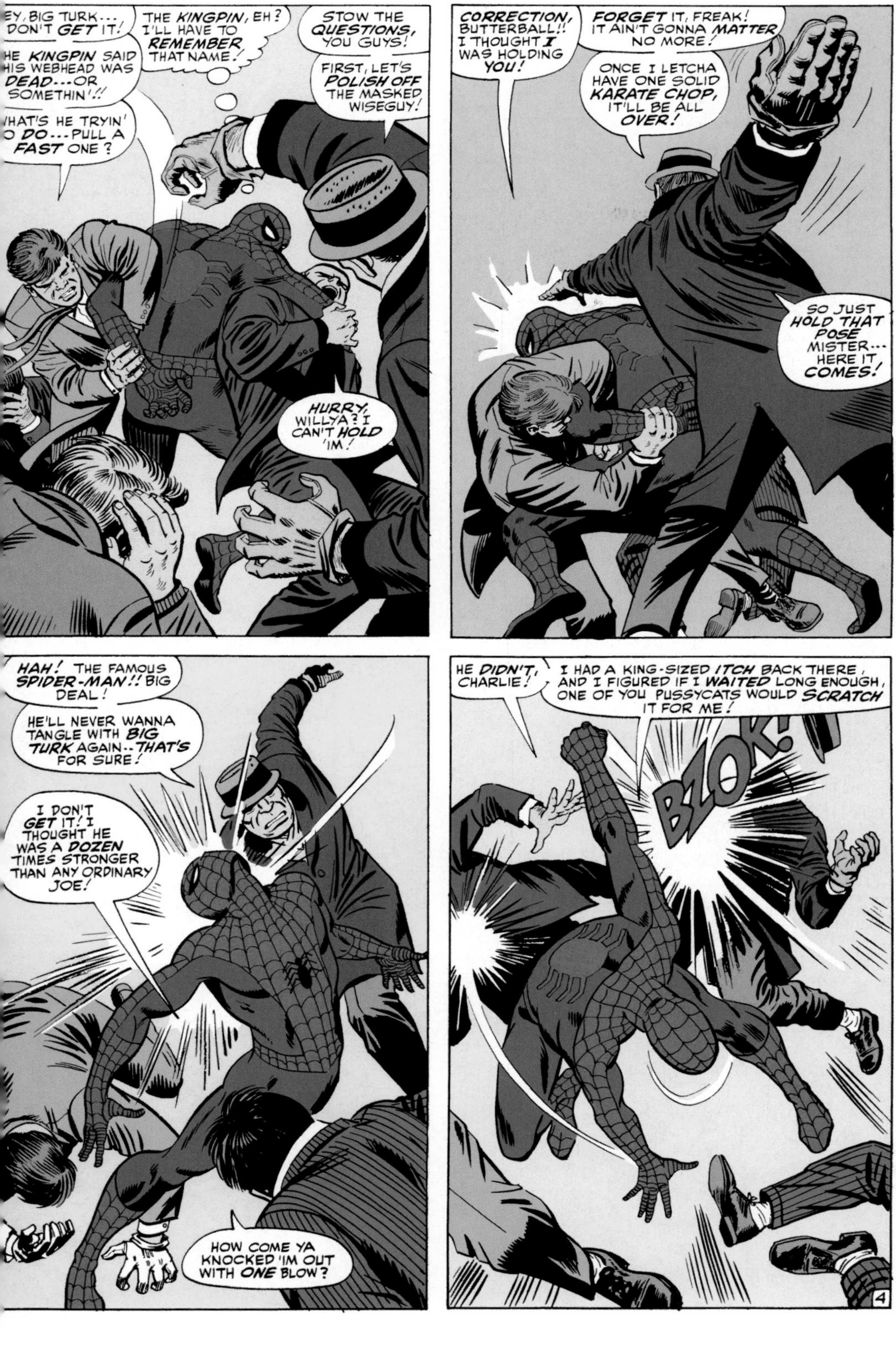

EY, BIG TURK... DON'T GET IT! HE KINGPIN SAID HIS WEBHEAD WAS DEAD...OR SOMETHIN'!!
THE KINGPIN, EH? I'LL HAVE TO REMEMBER THAT NAME!
STOW THE QUESTIONS, YOU GUYS!
FIRST, LET'S POLISH OFF THE MASKED WISEGUY!
WHAT'S HE TRYIN' O DO...PULL A FAST ONE?
HURRY, WILLYA? I CAN'T HOLD 'IM!
CORRECTION, BUTTERBALL!! I THOUGHT I WAS HOLDING YOU!
FORGET IT, FREAK! IT AIN'T GONNA MATTER NO MORE!
ONCE I LETCHA HAVE ONE SOLID KARATE CHOP, IT'LL BE ALL OVER!
SO JUST HOLD THAT POSE MISTER... HERE IT COMES!
HAH! THE FAMOUS SPIDER-MAN!! BIG DEAL!
HE'LL NEVER WANNA TANGLE WITH BIG TURK AGAIN..THAT'S FOR SURE!
I DON'T GET IT! I THOUGHT HE WAS A DOZEN TIMES STRONGER THAN ANY ORDINARY JOE!
HOW COME YA KNOCKED 'IM OUT WITH ONE BLOW?
HE DIDN'T, CHARLIE!
I HAD A KING-SIZED ITCH BACK THERE, AND I FIGURED IF I WAITED LONG ENOUGH, ONE OF YOU PUSSYCATS WOULD SCRATCH IT FOR ME!
BZOK!
4

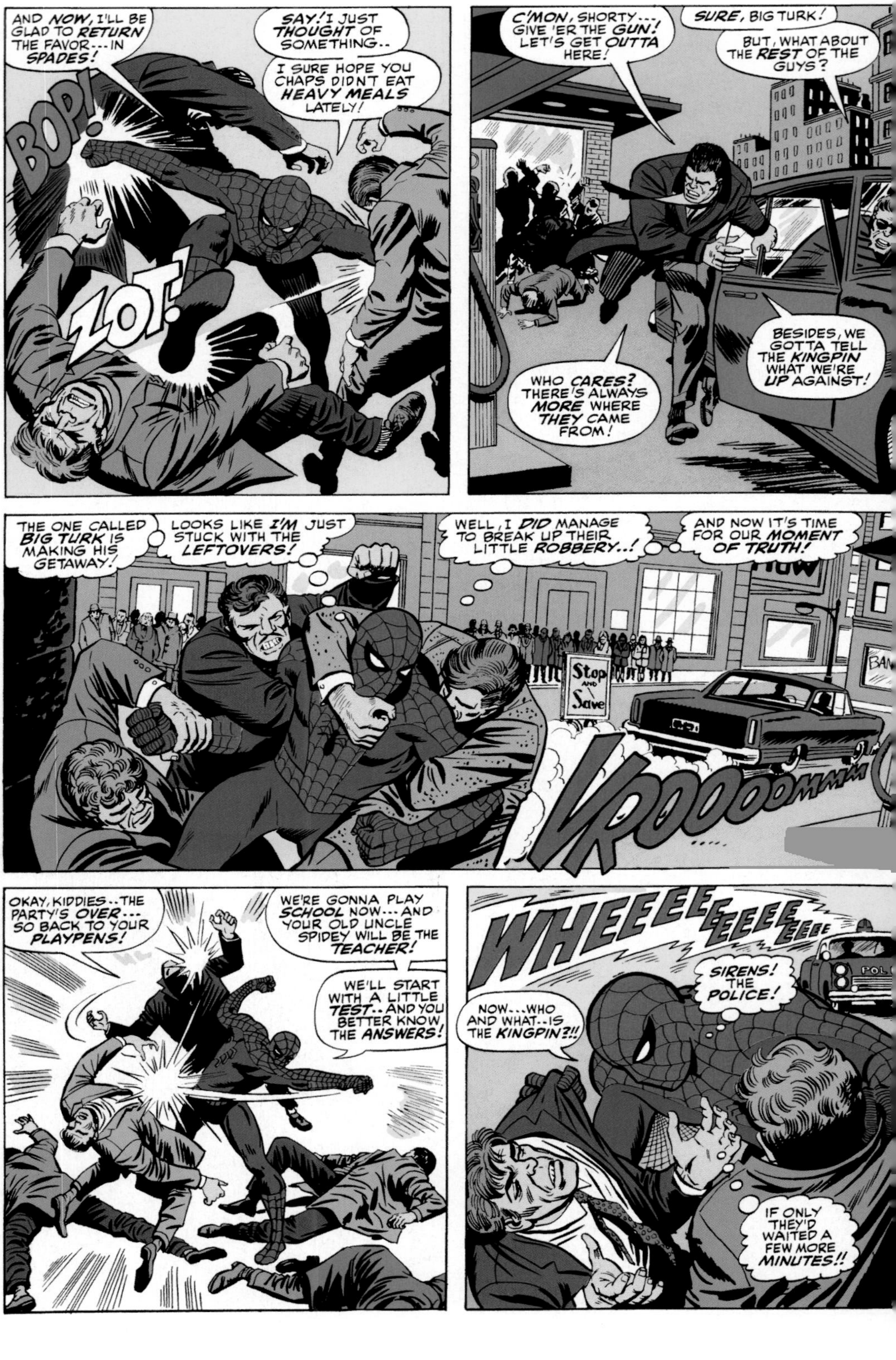
AND NOW, I'LL BE GLAD TO RETURN THE FAVOR---IN SPADES!
SAY! I JUST THOUGHT OF SOMETHING..
I SURE HOPE YOU CHAPS DIDN'T EAT HEAVY MEALS LATELY!
BOP!
ZOT!
C'MON, SHORTY... GIVE 'ER THE GUN! LET'S GET OUTTA HERE!
SURE, BIG TURK!
BUT, WHAT ABOUT THE REST OF THE GUYS?
WHO CARES? THERE'S ALWAYS MORE WHERE THEY CAME FROM!
BESIDES, WE GOTTA TELL THE KINGPIN WHAT WE'RE UP AGAINST!
THE ONE CALLED BIG TURK IS MAKING HIS GETAWAY!
LOOKS LIKE I'M JUST STUCK WITH THE LEFTOVERS!
WELL, I DID MANAGE TO BREAK UP THEIR LITTLE ROBBERY..!
AND NOW IT'S TIME FOR OUR MOMENT OF TRUTH!
Stop AND Save
VROOOOOMMM
OKAY, KIDDIES.. THE PARTY'S OVER--- SO BACK TO YOUR PLAYPENS!
WE'RE GONNA PLAY SCHOOL NOW--- AND YOUR OLD UNCLE SPIDEY WILL BE THE TEACHER!
WE'LL START WITH A LITTLE TEST.. AND YOU BETTER KNOW THE ANSWERS!
WHEEEEEEEEEEEE
SIRENS! THE POLICE!
NOW... WHO AND WHAT.. IS THE KINGPIN?!!
IF ONLY THEY'D WAITED A FEW MORE MINUTES!!

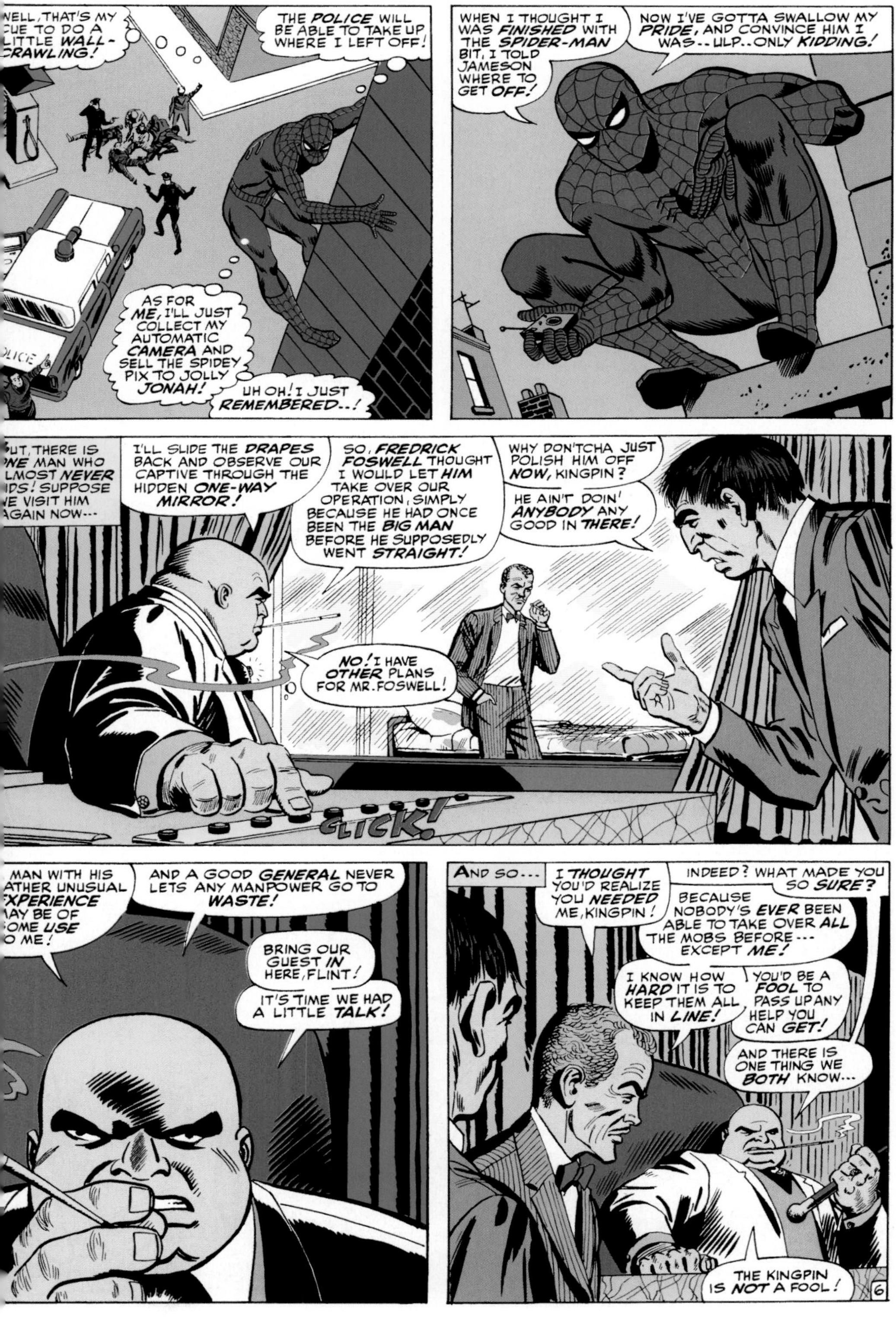

NELL, THAT'S MY CUE TO DO A LITTLE WALL-CRAWLING!
THE POLICE WILL BE ABLE TO TAKE UP WHERE I LEFT OFF!
AS FOR ME, I'LL JUST COLLECT MY AUTOMATIC CAMERA AND SELL THE SPIDEY PIX TO JOLLY JONAH!
UH OH! I JUST REMEMBERED--!
WHEN I THOUGHT I WAS FINISHED WITH THE SPIDER-MAN BIT, I TOLD JAMESON WHERE TO GET OFF!
NOW I'VE GOTTA SWALLOW MY PRIDE, AND CONVINCE HIM I WAS--ULP--ONLY KIDDING!
UT, THERE IS NE MAN WHO LMOST NEVER IDS! SUPPOSE E VISIT HIM AGAIN NOW---
I'LL SLIDE THE DRAPES BACK AND OBSERVE OUR CAPTIVE THROUGH THE HIDDEN ONE-WAY MIRROR!
SO, FREDRICK FOSWELL THOUGHT I WOULD LET HIM TAKE OVER OUR OPERATION, SIMPLY BECAUSE HE HAD ONCE BEEN THE BIG MAN BEFORE HE SUPPOSEDLY WENT STRAIGHT!
WHY DON'TCHA JUST POLISH HIM OFF NOW, KINGPIN?
HE AIN'T DOIN' ANYBODY ANY GOOD IN THERE!
NO! I HAVE OTHER PLANS FOR MR. FOSWELL!
CLICK!
MAN WITH HIS ATHER UNUSUAL XPERIENCE AY BE OF OME USE O ME!
AND A GOOD GENERAL NEVER LETS ANY MANPOWER GO TO WASTE!
BRING OUR GUEST IN HERE, FLINT!
IT'S TIME WE HAD A LITTLE TALK!
AND SO...
I THOUGHT YOU'D REALIZE YOU NEEDED ME, KINGPIN!
INDEED? WHAT MADE YOU SO SURE?
BECAUSE NOBODY'S EVER BEEN ABLE TO TAKE OVER ALL THE MOBS BEFORE--- EXCEPT ME!
I KNOW HOW HARD IT IS TO KEEP THEM ALL IN LINE!
YOU'D BE A FOOL TO PASS UP ANY HELP YOU CAN GET!
AND THERE IS ONE THING WE BOTH KNOW...
THE KINGPIN IS NOT A FOOL!
6

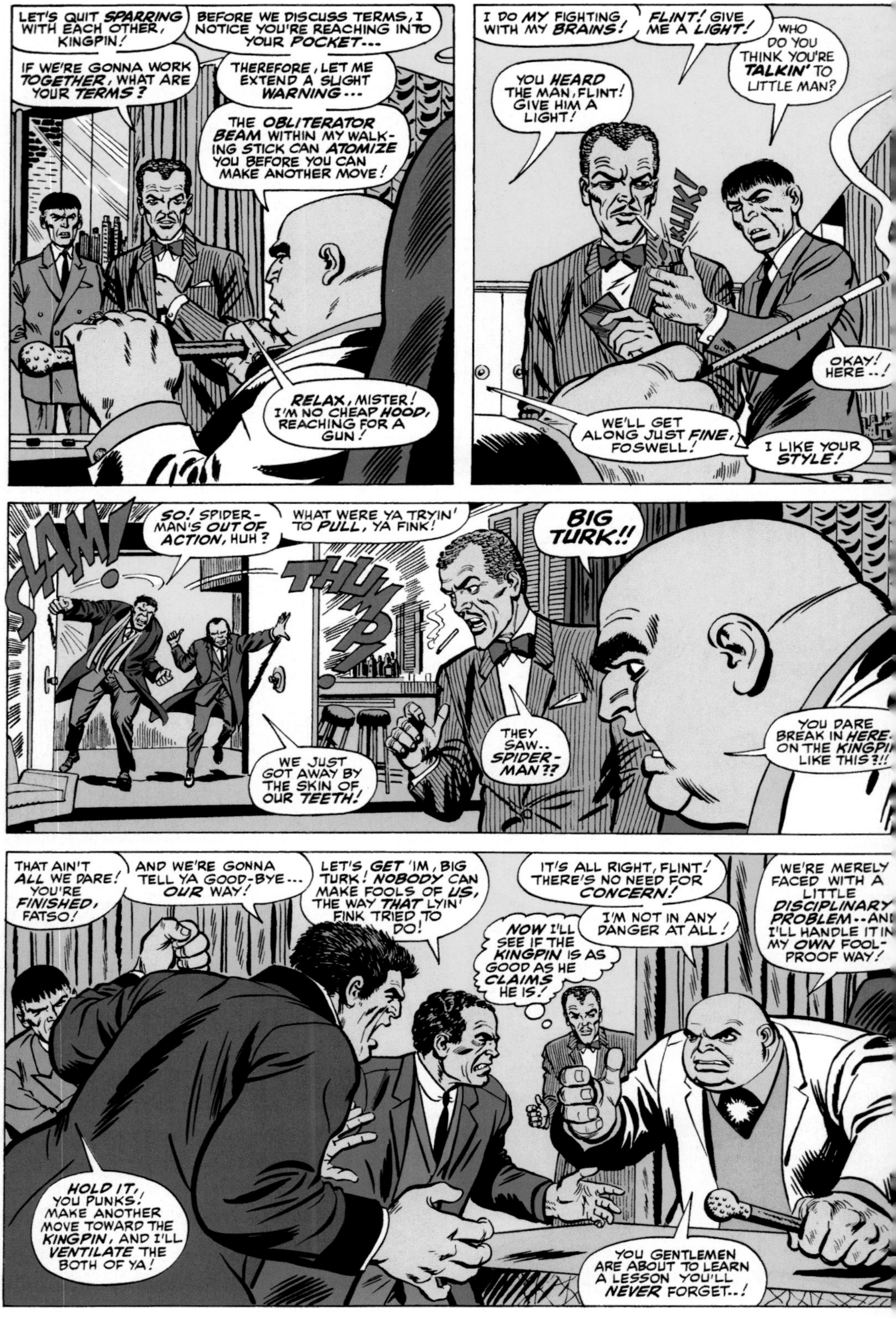

LET'S QUIT SPARRING WITH EACH OTHER, KINGPIN!
BEFORE WE DISCUSS TERMS, I NOTICE YOU'RE REACHING INTO YOUR POCKET...
IF WE'RE GONNA WORK TOGETHER, WHAT ARE YOUR TERMS?
THEREFORE, LET ME EXTEND A SLIGHT WARNING...
THE OBLITERATOR BEAM WITHIN MY WALKING STICK CAN ATOMIZE YOU BEFORE YOU CAN MAKE ANOTHER MOVE!
RELAX, MISTER! I'M NO CHEAP HOOD, REACHING FOR A GUN!
I DO MY FIGHTING WITH MY BRAINS!
FLINT! GIVE ME A LIGHT!
WHO DO YOU THINK YOU'RE TALKIN' TO LITTLE MAN?
YOU HEARD THE MAN, FLINT! GIVE HIM A LIGHT!
KLIK!
OKAY! HERE..!
WE'LL GET ALONG JUST FINE, FOSWELL!
I LIKE YOUR STYLE!
SLAM!
SO! SPIDER-MAN'S OUT OF ACTION, HUH?
WHAT WERE YA TRYIN' TO PULL, YA FINK!
THUMP!
BIG TURK!!
THEY SAW.. SPIDER-MAN??
WE JUST GOT AWAY BY THE SKIN OF OUR TEETH!
YOU DARE BREAK IN HERE ON THE KINGPI LIKE THIS?!!
THAT AIN'T ALL WE DARE! YOU'RE FINISHED, FATSO!
AND WE'RE GONNA TELL YA GOOD-BYE... OUR WAY!
LET'S GET 'IM, BIG TURK! NOBODY CAN MAKE FOOLS OF US, THE WAY THAT LYIN' FINK TRIED TO DO!
IT'S ALL RIGHT, FLINT! THERE'S NO NEED FOR CONCERN!
I'M NOT IN ANY DANGER AT ALL!
NOW I'LL SEE IF THE KINGPIN IS AS GOOD AS HE CLAIMS HE IS!
WE'RE MERELY FACED WITH A LITTLE DISCIPLINARY PROBLEM--AN I'LL HANDLE IT IN MY OWN FOOL-PROOF WAY!
HOLD IT, YOU PUNKS! MAKE ANOTHER MOVE TOWARD THE KINGPIN, AND I'LL VENTILATE THE BOTH OF YA!
YOU GENTLEMEN ARE ABOUT TO LEARN A LESSON YOU'LL NEVER FORGET..!

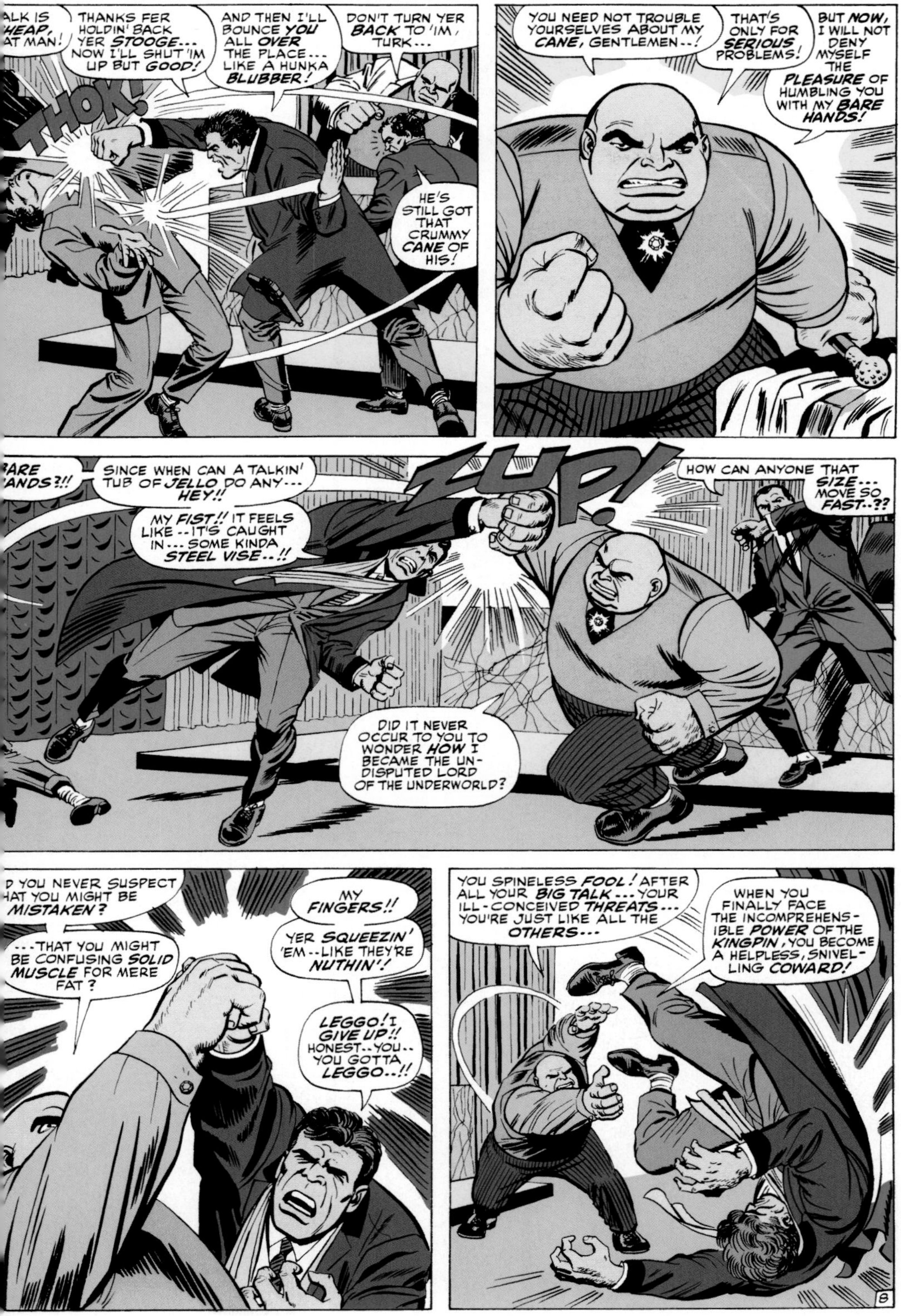

ALK IS HEAP, AT MAN!
THANKS FER HOLDIN' BACK YER STOOGE... NOW I'LL SHUT 'IM UP BUT GOOD!
THOK!
AND THEN I'LL BOUNCE YOU ALL OVER THE PLACE... LIKE A HUNKA BLUBBER!
DON'T TURN YER BACK TO 'IM, TURK...
HE'S STILL GOT THAT CRUMMY CANE OF HIS!
YOU NEED NOT TROUBLE YOURSELVES ABOUT MY CANE, GENTLEMEN--!
THAT'S ONLY FOR SERIOUS PROBLEMS!
BUT NOW, I WILL NOT DENY MYSELF THE PLEASURE OF HUMBLING YOU WITH MY BARE HANDS!
ARE ANDS?!!
SINCE WHEN CAN A TALKIN' TUB OF JELLO DO ANY--- HEY!!
MY FIST!! IT FEELS LIKE--IT'S CAUGHT IN... SOME KINDA STEEL VISE--!!
ZUP!
HOW CAN ANYONE THAT SIZE... MOVE SO FAST--??
DID IT NEVER OCCUR TO YOU TO WONDER HOW I BECAME THE UN-DISPUTED LORD OF THE UNDERWORLD?
D YOU NEVER SUSPECT HAT YOU MIGHT BE MISTAKEN?
...THAT YOU MIGHT BE CONFUSING SOLID MUSCLE FOR MERE FAT?
MY FINGERS!!
YER SQUEEZIN' 'EM--LIKE THEY'RE NUTHIN'!
LEGGO! I GIVE UP!! HONEST--YOU--YOU GOTTA LEGGO--!!
YOU SPINELESS FOOL! AFTER ALL YOUR BIG TALK... YOUR ILL-CONCEIVED THREATS... YOU'RE JUST LIKE ALL THE OTHERS...
WHEN YOU FINALLY FACE THE INCOMPREHENS-IBLE POWER OF THE KINGPIN, YOU BECOME A HELPLESS, SNIVEL-LING COWARD!
8

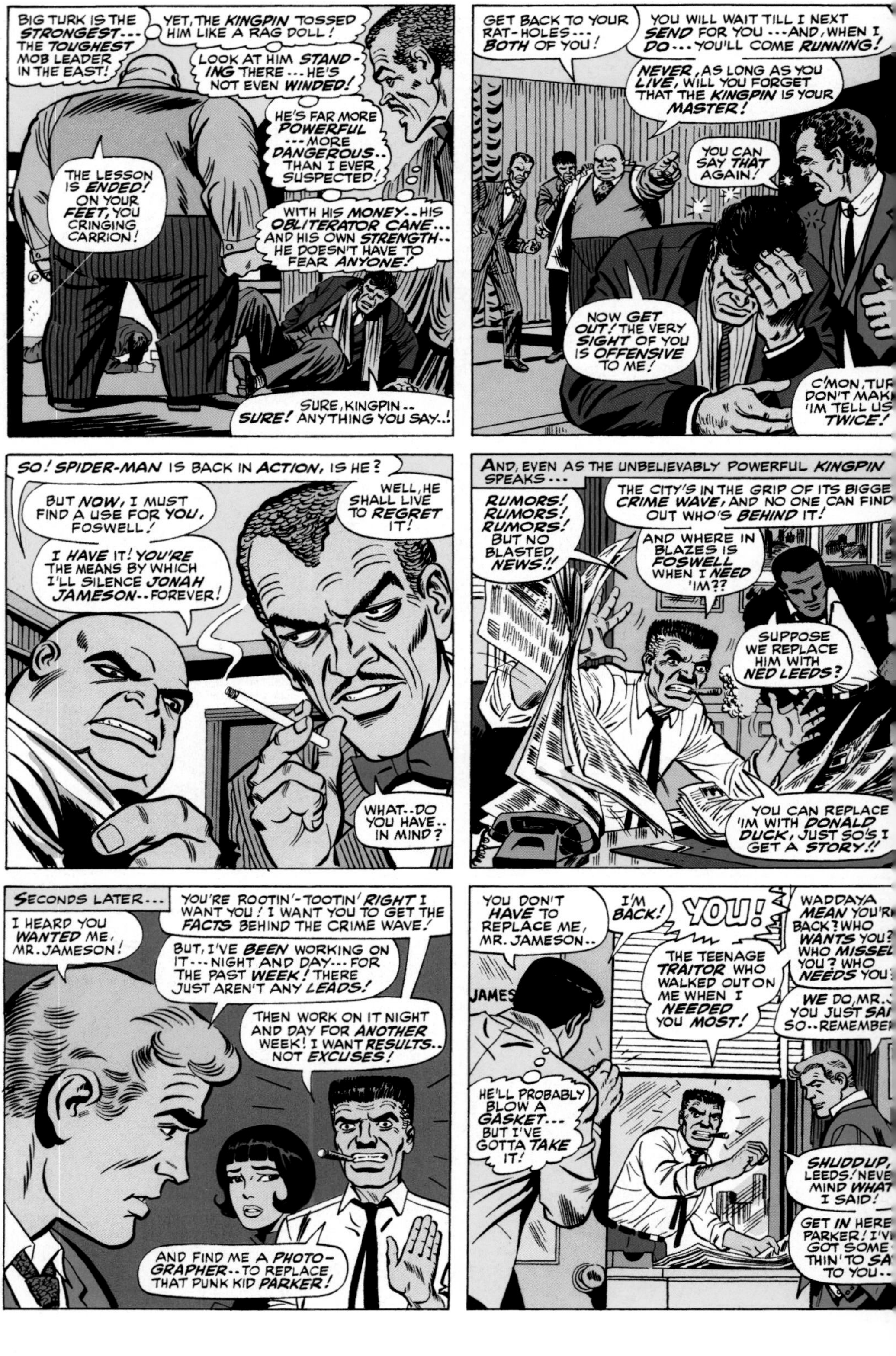
BIG TURK IS THE STRONGEST--- THE TOUGHEST MOB LEADER IN THE EAST!
YET, THE KINGPIN TOSSED HIM LIKE A RAG DOLL!
LOOK AT HIM STANDING THERE --- HE'S NOT EVEN WINDED!
HE'S FAR MORE POWERFUL --- MORE DANGEROUS.. THAN I EVER SUSPECTED!
THE LESSON IS ENDED! ON YOUR FEET, YOU CRINGING CARRION!
WITH HIS MONEY--HIS OBLITERATOR CANE... AND HIS OWN STRENGTH.. HE DOESN'T HAVE TO FEAR ANYONE!
SURE, KINGPIN -- SURE! ANYTHING YOU SAY..!
GET BACK TO YOUR RAT-HOLES --- BOTH OF YOU!
YOU WILL WAIT TILL I NEXT SEND FOR YOU ---AND, WHEN I DO--- YOU'LL COME RUNNING!
NEVER, AS LONG AS YOU LIVE, WILL YOU FORGET THAT THE KINGPIN IS YOUR MASTER!
YOU CAN SAY THAT AGAIN!
NOW GET OUT! THE VERY SIGHT OF YOU IS OFFENSIVE TO ME!
C'MON, TUR DON'T MAK 'IM TELL US TWICE!
SO! SPIDER-MAN IS BACK IN ACTION, IS HE?
BUT NOW, I MUST FIND A USE FOR YOU, FOSWELL!
WELL, HE SHALL LIVE TO REGRET IT!
I HAVE IT! YOU'RE THE MEANS BY WHICH I'LL SILENCE JONAH JAMESON--FOREVER!
WHAT--DO YOU HAVE.. IN MIND?
AND, EVEN AS THE UNBELIEVABLY POWERFUL KINGPIN SPEAKS...
RUMORS! RUMORS! RUMORS! BUT NO BLASTED NEWS!!
THE CITY'S IN THE GRIP OF ITS BIGGE CRIME WAVE, AND NO ONE CAN FIND OUT WHO'S BEHIND IT!
AND WHERE IN BLAZES IS FOSWELL WHEN I NEED 'IM??
SUPPOSE WE REPLACE HIM WITH NED LEEDS?
YOU CAN REPLACE 'IM WITH DONALD DUCK, JUST SO'S I GET A STORY!!
SECONDS LATER...
I HEARD YOU WANTED ME, MR. JAMESON!
YOU'RE ROOTIN'-TOOTIN' RIGHT I WANT YOU! I WANT YOU TO GET THE FACTS BEHIND THE CRIME WAVE!
BUT, I'VE BEEN WORKING ON IT --- NIGHT AND DAY --- FOR THE PAST WEEK! THERE JUST AREN'T ANY LEADS!
THEN WORK ON IT NIGHT AND DAY FOR ANOTHER WEEK! I WANT RESULTS.. NOT EXCUSES!
AND FIND ME A PHOTOGRAPHER--TO REPLACE THAT PUNK KID PARKER!
YOU DON'T HAVE TO REPLACE ME, MR. JAMESON..
I'M BACK!
YOU!
THE TEENAGE TRAITOR WHO WALKED OUT ON ME WHEN I NEEDED YOU MOST!
WADDAYA MEAN YOU'R BACK? WHO WANTS YOU? WHO MISSE YOU? WHO NEEDS YOU
WE DO, MR. J YOU JUST SAI SO--REMEMBE
JAMES
HE'LL PROBABLY BLOW A GASKET--- BUT I'VE GOTTA TAKE IT!
SHUDDUP, LEEDS! NEVE MIND WHAT I SAID!
GET IN HERE PARKER! I'V GOT SOME-THIN' TO SA TO YOU--

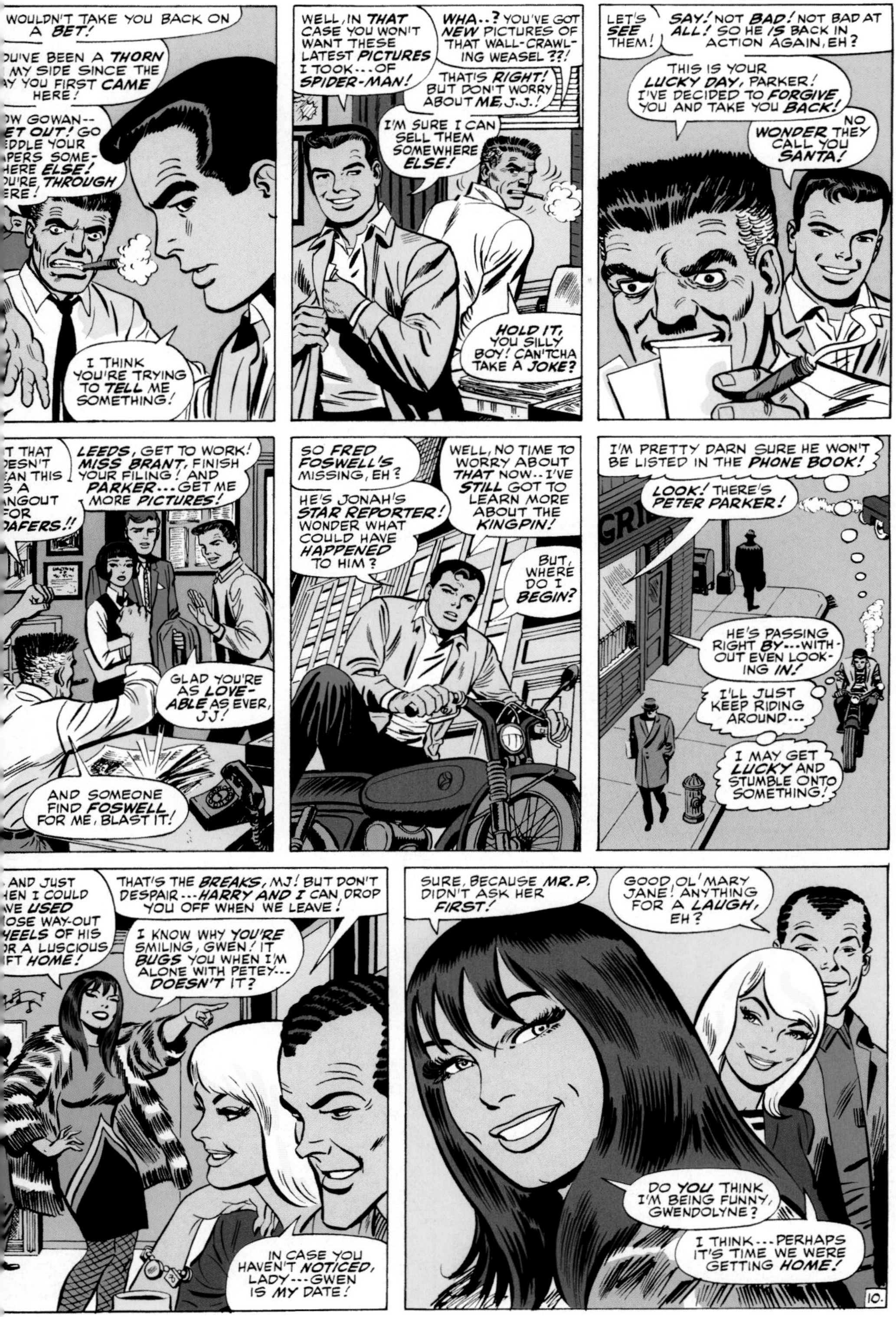
WOULDN'T TAKE YOU BACK ON A BET!
OU'VE BEEN A THORN MY SIDE SINCE THE AY YOU FIRST CAME HERE!
OW GOWAN-- ET OUT! GO EDDLE YOUR APERS SOME- HERE ELSE! OU'RE THROUGH ERE!
I THINK YOU'RE TRYING TO TELL ME SOMETHING!
WELL, IN THAT CASE YOU WON'T WANT THESE LATEST PICTURES I TOOK--- OF SPIDER-MAN!
WHA..? YOU'VE GOT NEW PICTURES OF THAT WALL-CRAWLING WEASEL ??!
THAT'S RIGHT! BUT DON'T WORRY ABOUT ME, J.J.!
I'M SURE I CAN SELL THEM SOMEWHERE ELSE!
HOLD IT, YOU SILLY BOY! CAN'TCHA TAKE A JOKE?
LET'S SEE THEM!
SAY! NOT BAD! NOT BAD AT ALL! SO HE IS BACK IN ACTION AGAIN, EH?
THIS IS YOUR LUCKY DAY, PARKER! I'VE DECIDED TO FORGIVE YOU AND TAKE YOU BACK!
NO WONDER THEY CALL YOU SANTA!
T THAT OESN'T EAN THIS S A ANGOUT FOR OAFERS!!
LEEDS, GET TO WORK! MISS BRANT, FINISH YOUR FILING! AND PARKER... GET ME MORE PICTURES!
GLAD YOU'RE AS LOVE-ABLE AS EVER, JJ!
AND SOMEONE FIND FOSWELL FOR ME, BLAST IT!
SO FRED FOSWELL'S MISSING, EH?
HE'S JONAH'S STAR REPORTER! WONDER WHAT COULD HAVE HAPPENED TO HIM?
WELL, NO TIME TO WORRY ABOUT THAT NOW.. I'VE STILL GOT TO LEARN MORE ABOUT THE KINGPIN!
BUT, WHERE DO I BEGIN?
I'M PRETTY DARN SURE HE WON'T BE LISTED IN THE PHONE BOOK!
LOOK! THERE'S PETER PARKER!
HE'S PASSING RIGHT BY--- WITH-OUT EVEN LOOKING IN!
I'LL JUST KEEP RIDING AROUND---
I MAY GET LUCKY AND STUMBLE ONTO SOMETHING!
AND JUST HEN I COULD AVE USED OSE WAY-OUT HEELS OF HIS OR A LUSCIOUS IFT HOME!
THAT'S THE BREAKS, MJ! BUT DON'T DESPAIR --- HARRY AND I CAN DROP YOU OFF WHEN WE LEAVE!
I KNOW WHY YOU'RE SMILING, GWEN! IT BUGS YOU WHEN I'M ALONE WITH PETEY--- DOESN'T IT?
IN CASE YOU HAVEN'T NOTICED, LADY --- GWEN IS MY DATE!
SURE, BECAUSE MR. P. DIDN'T ASK HER FIRST!
GOOD OL' MARY JANE! ANYTHING FOR A LAUGH, EH?
DO YOU THINK I'M BEING FUNNY, GWENDOLYNE?
I THINK --- PERHAPS IT'S TIME WE WERE GETTING HOME!

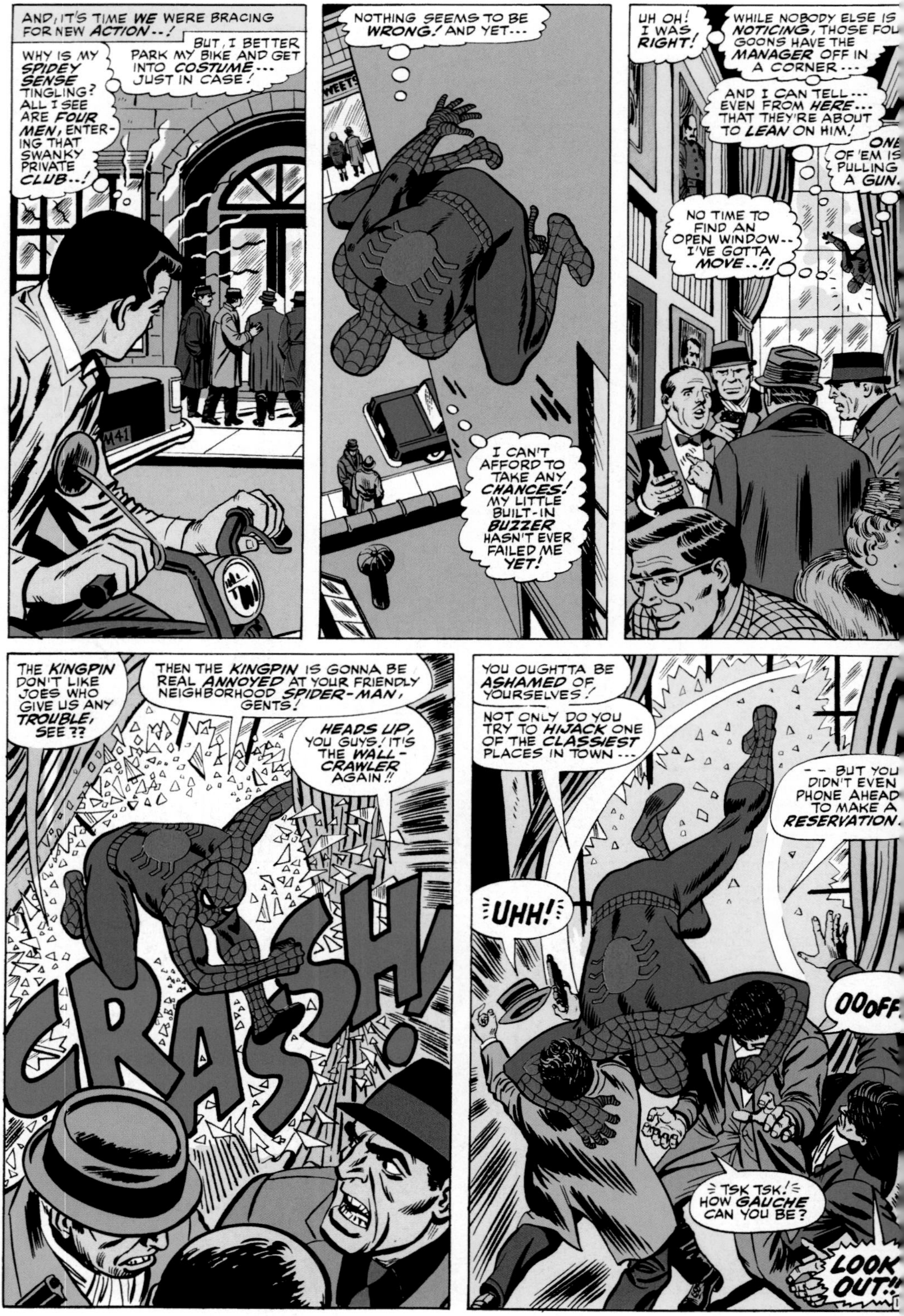
AND, IT'S TIME WE WERE BRACING FOR NEW ACTION--!
WHY IS MY SPIDEY SENSE TINGLING? ALL I SEE ARE FOUR MEN, ENTERING THAT SWANKY PRIVATE CLUB--!
BUT, I BETTER PARK MY BIKE AND GET INTO COSTUME--- JUST IN CASE!
NOTHING SEEMS TO BE WRONG! AND YET---
I CAN'T AFFORD TO TAKE ANY CHANCES! MY LITTLE BUILT-IN BUZZER HASN'T EVER FAILED ME YET!
UH OH! I WAS RIGHT!
WHILE NOBODY ELSE IS NOTICING, THOSE FOU GOONS HAVE THE MANAGER OFF IN A CORNER---
AND I CAN TELL--- EVEN FROM HERE--- THAT THEY'RE ABOUT TO LEAN ON HIM!
ONE OF 'EM IS PULLING A GUN.
NO TIME TO FIND AN OPEN WINDOW-- I'VE GOTTA MOVE--!!
THE KINGPIN DON'T LIKE JOES WHO GIVE US ANY TROUBLE, SEE??
THEN THE KINGPIN IS GONNA BE REAL ANNOYED AT YOUR FRIENDLY NEIGHBORHOOD SPIDER-MAN, GENTS!
HEADS UP, YOU GUYS! IT'S THE WALL-CRAWLER AGAIN!!
CRASH!
YOU OUGHTTA BE ASHAMED OF YOURSELVES!
NOT ONLY DO YOU TRY TO HIJACK ONE OF THE CLASSIEST PLACES IN TOWN---
--BUT YOU DIDN'T EVEN PHONE AHEAD TO MAKE A RESERVATION.
UHH!
OOOFF
TSK TSK! HOW GAUCHE CAN YOU BE?
LOOK OUT!!

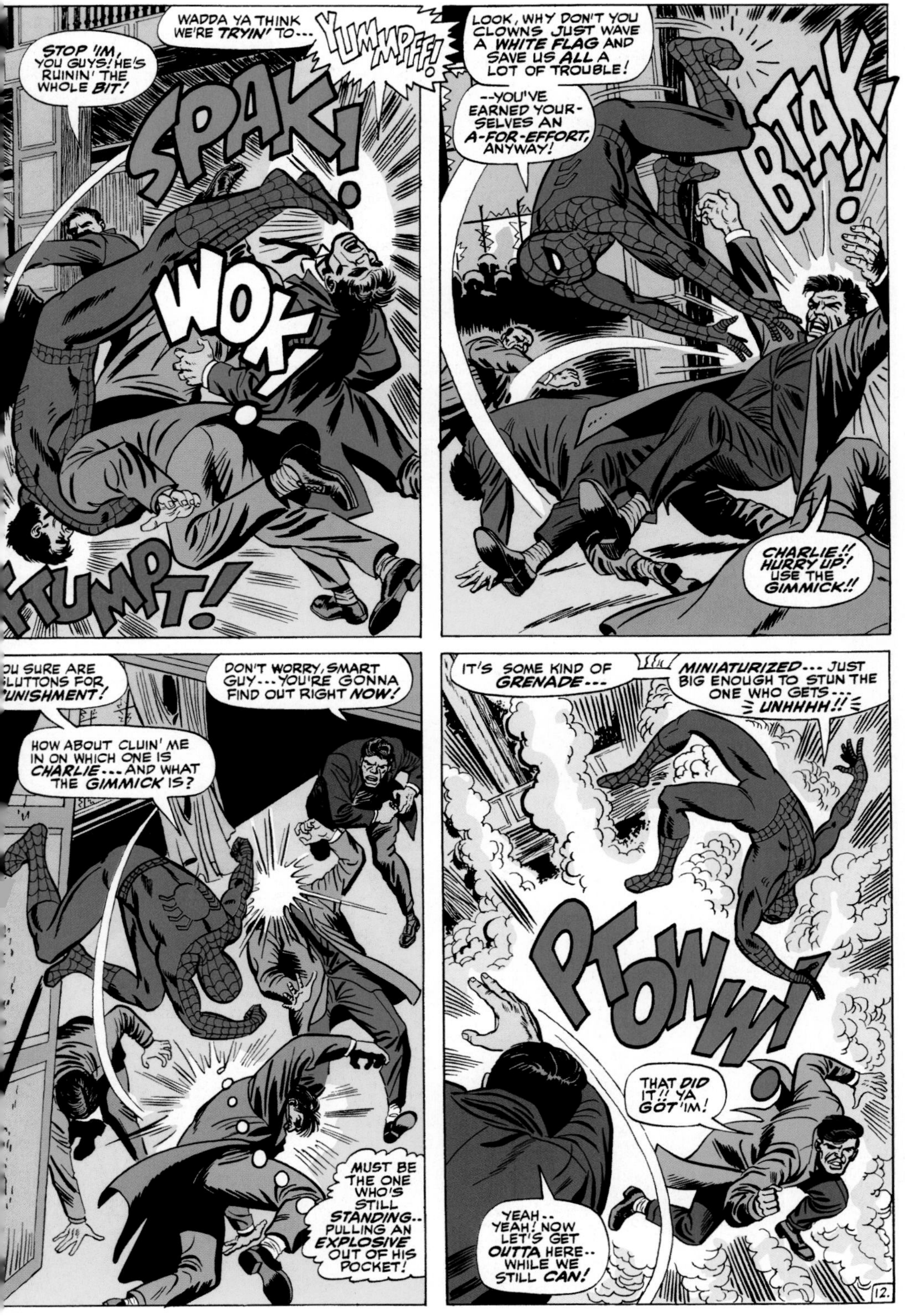
STOP 'IM, YOU GUYS! HE'S RUININ' THE WHOLE BIT!
WADDA YA THINK WE'RE TRYIN' TO---
YUMMPFF!
SPAK!
WOK!
THUMPT!
LOOK, WHY DON'T YOU CLOWNS JUST WAVE A WHITE FLAG AND SAVE US ALL A LOT OF TROUBLE!
--YOU'VE EARNED YOURSELVES AN A-FOR-EFFORT, ANYWAY!
BTAK!
CHARLIE!! HURRY UP! USE THE GIMMICK!!
OU SURE ARE GLUTTONS FOR PUNISHMENT!
DON'T WORRY, SMART GUY--- YOU'RE GONNA FIND OUT RIGHT NOW!
HOW ABOUT CLUIN' ME IN ON WHICH ONE IS CHARLIE--- AND WHAT THE GIMMICK IS?
MUST BE THE ONE WHO'S STILL STANDING.. PULLING AN EXPLOSIVE OUT OF HIS POCKET!
IT'S SOME KIND OF GRENADE---
MINIATURIZED--- JUST BIG ENOUGH TO STUN THE ONE WHO GETS--- UNHHHH!!
PTOWW!
THAT DID IT!! YA GOT 'IM!
YEAH-- YEAH! NOW LET'S GET OUTTA HERE-- WHILE WE STILL CAN!
12.

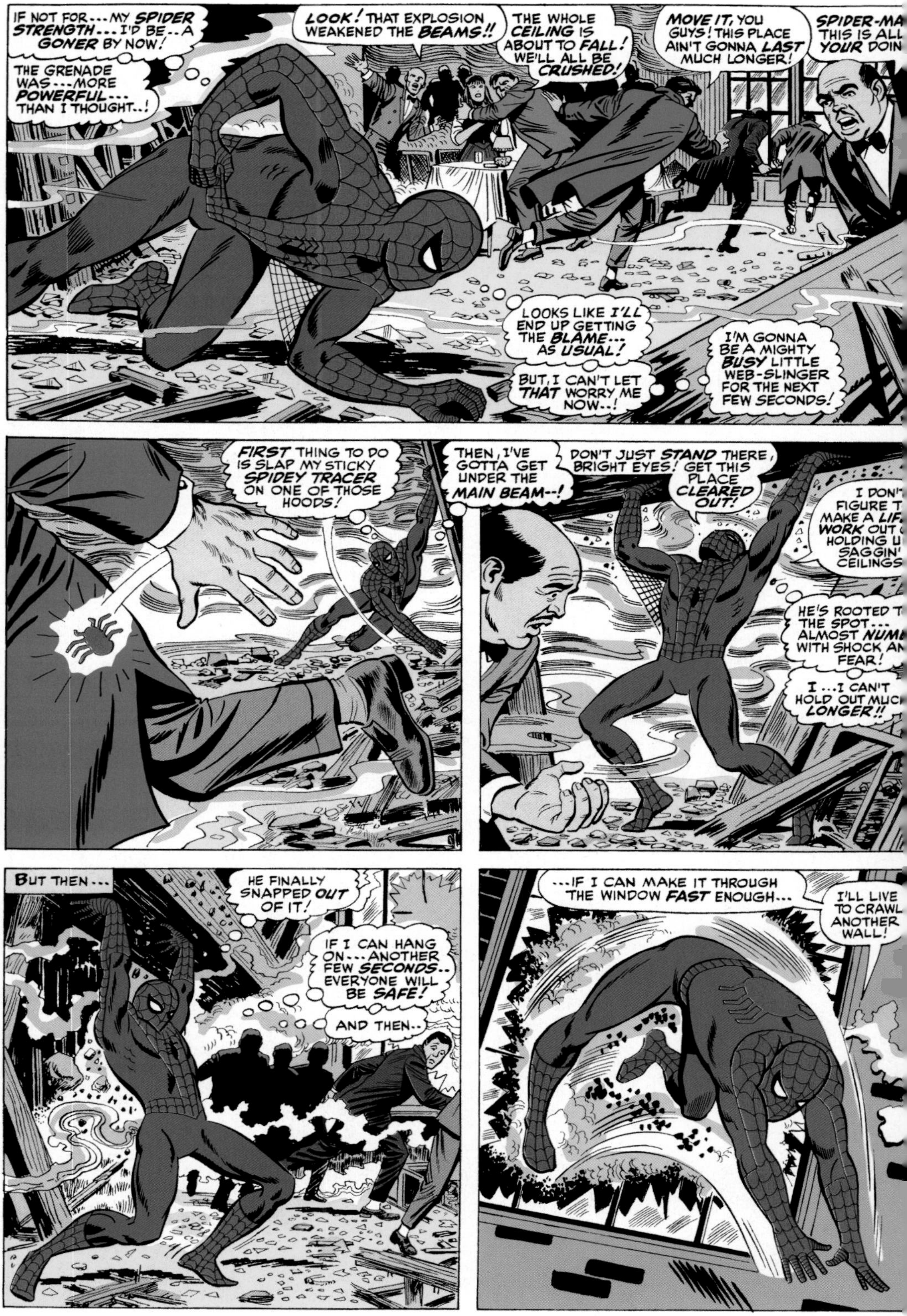
IF NOT FOR... MY SPIDER STRENGTH... I'D BE.. A GONER BY NOW!
THE GRENADE WAS... MORE POWERFUL... THAN I THOUGHT..!
LOOK! THAT EXPLOSION WEAKENED THE BEAMS!!
THE WHOLE CEILING IS ABOUT TO FALL! WE'LL ALL BE CRUSHED!
MOVE IT, YOU GUYS! THIS PLACE AIN'T GONNA LAST MUCH LONGER!
SPIDER-MA THIS IS ALL YOUR DOIN
LOOKS LIKE I'LL END UP GETTING THE BLAME... AS USUAL!
BUT, I CAN'T LET THAT WORRY ME NOW..!
I'M GONNA BE A MIGHTY BUSY LITTLE WEB-SLINGER FOR THE NEXT FEW SECONDS!
FIRST THING TO DO IS SLAP MY STICKY SPIDEY TRACER ON ONE OF THOSE HOODS!
THEN, I'VE GOTTA GET UNDER THE MAIN BEAM--!
DON'T JUST STAND THERE, BRIGHT EYES! GET THIS PLACE CLEARED OUT!
I DON' FIGURE T MAKE A LIF WORK OUT HOLDING U SAGGIN' CEILINGS
HE'S ROOTED T THE SPOT... ALMOST NUM WITH SHOCK AN FEAR!
I... I CAN'T HOLD OUT MUC LONGER!!
BUT THEN...
HE FINALLY SNAPPED OUT OF IT!
IF I CAN HANG ON... ANOTHER FEW SECONDS.. EVERYONE WILL BE SAFE!
AND THEN..
...IF I CAN MAKE IT THROUGH THE WINDOW FAST ENOUGH...
I'LL LIVE TO CRAWL ANOTHER WALL!

[panel 1] ...ERE SHE *GOES!* I GUESS THEY ...ST DON'T *BUILD* ...M LIKE THEY ...USED TO!

WELL, IT COULDA BEEN *WORSE!* AT LEAST NO ONE WAS *HURT!*

[panel 2] NOW, ALL I'VE GOT TO *DO* IS PICK UP MY LITTLE *TRACER'S* TRAIL!

AND, UNLESS I'M WAY *OFF BASE,* IT'LL LEAD ME RIGHT TO COUSIN *KINGPIN!*

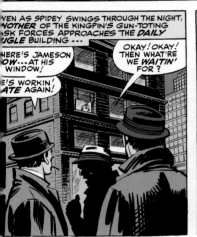

[panel 3] ...VEN AS SPIDEY SWINGS THROUGH THE NIGHT, ...NOTHER OF THE KINGPIN'S GUN-TOTING ...ASK FORCES APPROACHES THE *DAILY* ...UGLE BUILDING ...

...HERE'S JAMESON ...OW... AT HIS ...WINDOW!

...E'S WORKIN' ...ATE AGAIN!

OKAY! OKAY! THEN WHAT'RE WE *WAITIN'* FOR?

[panel 4] ON YOUR *FEET,* MISTER! YOU BEEN *WORKIN'* TOO HARD... SO WE'RE GIVIN' YOU A *VACATION!*

YEAH! WE'RE TAKIN' YA FOR A NICE LITTLE *RIDE*...TO VISIT THE *KINGPIN!*

THE *KINGPIN!* THEN...I WAS *RIGHT!* THERE *IS* SOMEONE BEHIND THE CRIME WAVE!

BUT... WHAT DOES HE WANT WITH *ME??*

[panel 5] ...RIEF MINUTES LATER ...

...RE YOU ...ICE AND ...OMFY, ...AMESON?

THIS IS *INSANE!* NOBODY GETS TAKEN FOR *RIDES* ANY MORE...

...EXCEPT ON *THE UNTOUCHABLES!*

WHEN THE *KINGPIN* SAYS RIDE, BROTHER.. YOU *RIDE!*

WHO IN BLAZES *IS* THE KINGPIN??

HE'S OUR *SCOUTMASTER!* NOW *SHUDDUP!*

[panel 6] FINALLY...

WELL, WELL! IF IT ISN'T *JONAH JAMESON!*

HOW *NICE* OF YOU TO DROP IN!

COME, COME, GENTLEMEN.. DON'T KEEP OUR *GUEST* STANDING OUT IN THE *HALL!*

YOU *HEARD* THE KINGPIN!

WALK!!

14.

I *KNOW* WHAT A BUSY MAN YOU ARE, SO I'LL COME RIGHT TO THE *POINT*..

I WANT YOU TO *STOP* STEAMING UP THE PUBLIC ABOUT THE SO-CALLED *CRIME WAVE* HERE IN THE CITY!

IN A *PIG'S EYE!* NOBODY TELLS *ME* WHAT TO WRITE IN MY PAPER!

EXCELLENT! SPOKEN LIKE THE TRUE *CRUSADER* THAT YOU ARE!

I APPLAUD YOUR OBVIOUS *COURAGE*...

BUT ALAS---YOU WILL LIVE TO *REGRET* IT!

WHAT--DO YOU... *MEAN?* WHAT ARE YOU..GONNA *DO?!*

ALL IN GOOD TIME, JAMESON!! BUT FIRST... WHAT IS *THIS?*

IT'S *CHARLIE* AND HIS BOYS, KINGPIN. THEY SAY THAT *SPIDER-MAN* KIBOSHED THE CAPER!

SPIDER-MAN.. *AGAIN?!!*

BUT THE WHOLE JOINT *CAVED* IN---AND HE WAS STILL *INSIDE!*

I *FIGGER* WE KISSED 'IM OFF AT *LAST!*

IN *THAT* CASE, YOUR MISSION *SUCCEEDED*.. BEYOND MY FONDEST HOPES!

BUT NOW, I STILL HAVE *ANOTHER* MINOR MATTER TO *DISPOSE* OF..!

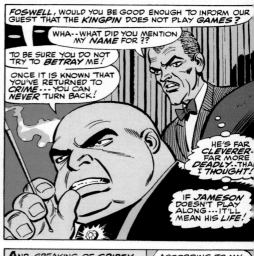

FOSWELL, WOULD YOU BE GOOD ENOUGH TO INFORM OUR GUEST THAT THE *KINGPIN* DOES NOT PLAY *GAMES?*

WHA--WHAT DID YOU MENTION MY *NAME* FOR ??

TO BE SURE YOU DO NOT TRY TO *BETRAY* ME!

ONCE IT IS KNOWN THAT YOU'VE RETURNED TO *CRIME*--- YOU CAN *NEVER* TURN BACK!

HE'S FAR *CLEVERER*.. FAR MORE *DEADLY*.-THAN I *THOUGHT!*

IF *JAMESON* DOESN'T PLAY ALONG---IT'LL MEAN HIS *LIFE!*

FOSWELL! ARE YOU REALLY *THERE?*

IS IT *TRUE* THAT YOU'VE JOINED FORCES WITH THE *KINGPIN??*

NEVER MIND ABOUT *ME*, JAMESON!

I'M *ADVISING* YOU-- DO WHAT THE KINGPIN *TELLS* YOU TO!

SO! I WAS *WRONG* TO EVER *TRUST* YOU!!

YOU'RE NO *BETTER* THAN---THAT SKUNK *SPIDER-MAN!*

AND, SPEAKING OF *SPIDEY*...

ACCORDING TO MY LITTLE *TRACER*, THE TRAIL ENDS IN THAT *PENTHOUSE* JUST AHEAD!

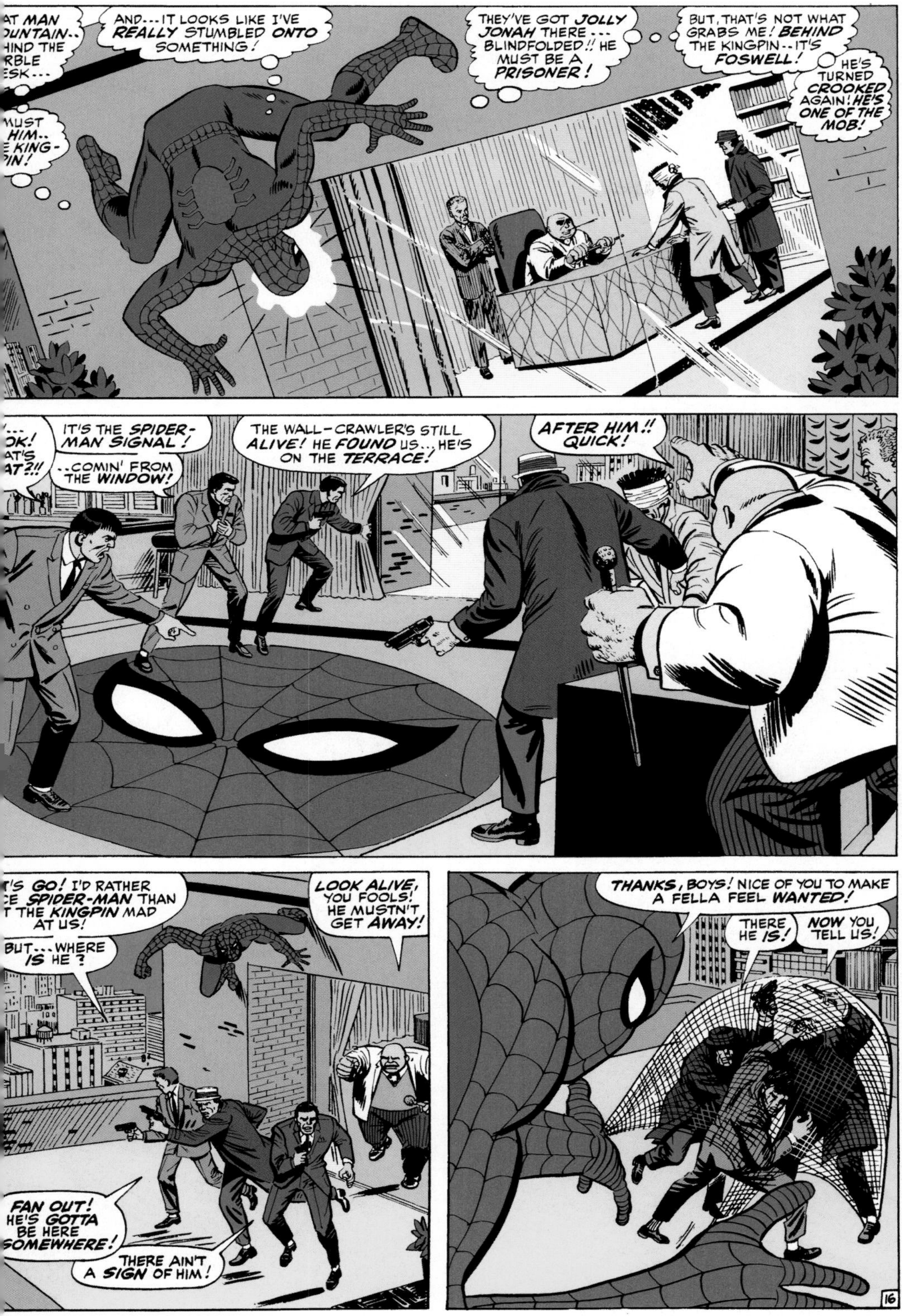AT MAN
OUNTAIN..
HIND THE
RBLE
ESK---
MUST
HIM..
E KING-
PIN!
AND---IT LOOKS LIKE I'VE REALLY STUMBLED ONTO SOMETHING!
THEY'VE GOT JOLLY JONAH THERE--- BLINDFOLDED!! HE MUST BE A PRISONER!
BUT, THAT'S NOT WHAT GRABS ME! BEHIND THE KINGPIN--IT'S FOSWELL!
HE'S TURNED CROOKED AGAIN! HE'S ONE OF THE MOB!
OK!
AT'S
AT?!!
IT'S THE SPIDER-MAN SIGNAL!
..COMIN' FROM THE WINDOW!
THE WALL-CRAWLER'S STILL ALIVE! HE FOUND US... HE'S ON THE TERRACE!
AFTER HIM!! QUICK!
T'S GO! I'D RATHER
CE SPIDER-MAN THAN
T THE KINGPIN MAD
AT US!
BUT... WHERE IS HE?
LOOK ALIVE, YOU FOOLS! HE MUSTN'T GET AWAY!
FAN OUT! HE'S GOTTA BE HERE SOMEWHERE!
THERE AIN'T A SIGN OF HIM!
THANKS, BOYS! NICE OF YOU TO MAKE A FELLA FEEL WANTED!
THERE HE IS!
NOW YOU TELL US!
16

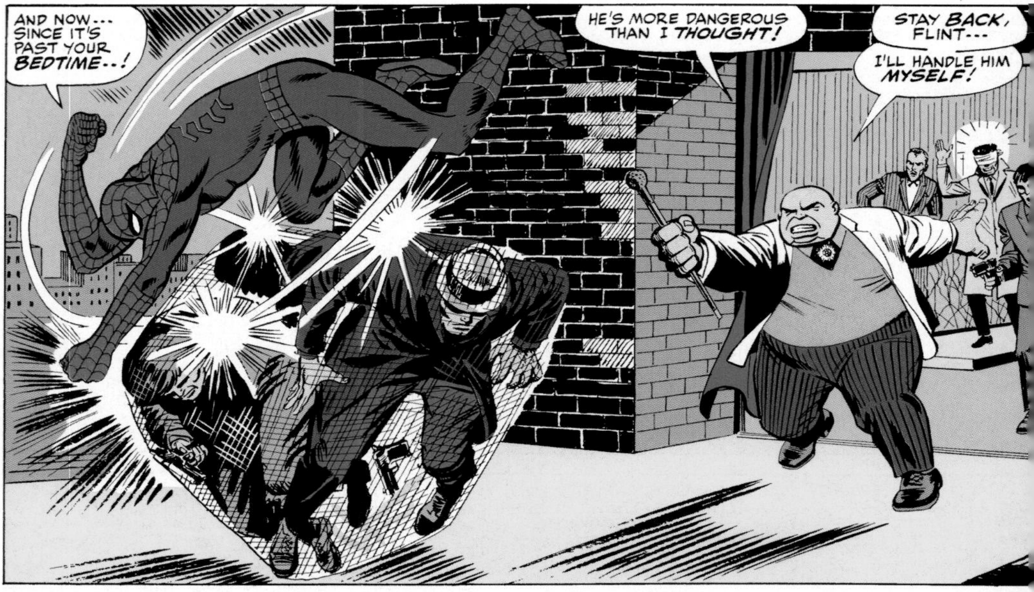
AND NOW... SINCE IT'S PAST YOUR BEDTIME..!
HE'S MORE DANGEROUS THAN I THOUGHT!
STAY BACK, FLINT---
I'LL HANDLE HIM MYSELF!

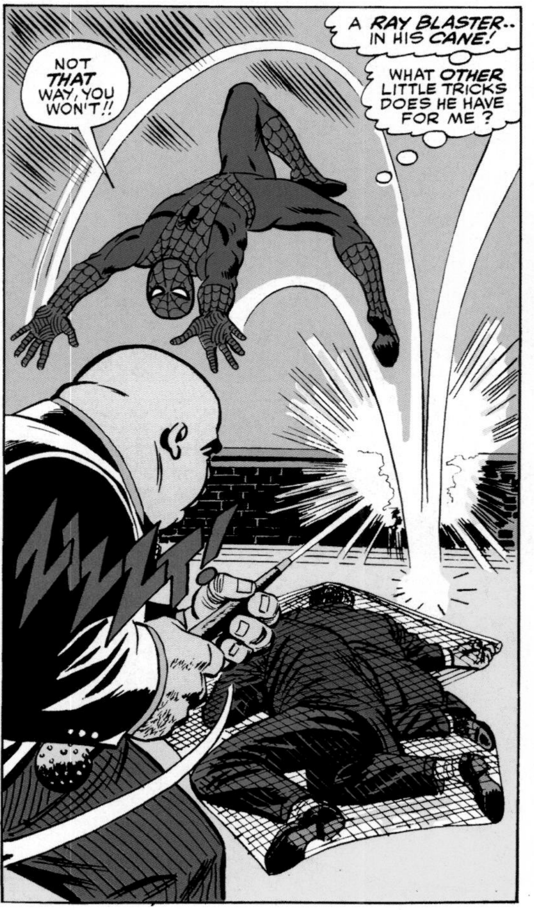
A RAY BLASTER.. IN HIS CANE!
NOT THAT WAY, YOU WON'T!!
WHAT OTHER LITTLE TRICKS DOES HE HAVE FOR ME?

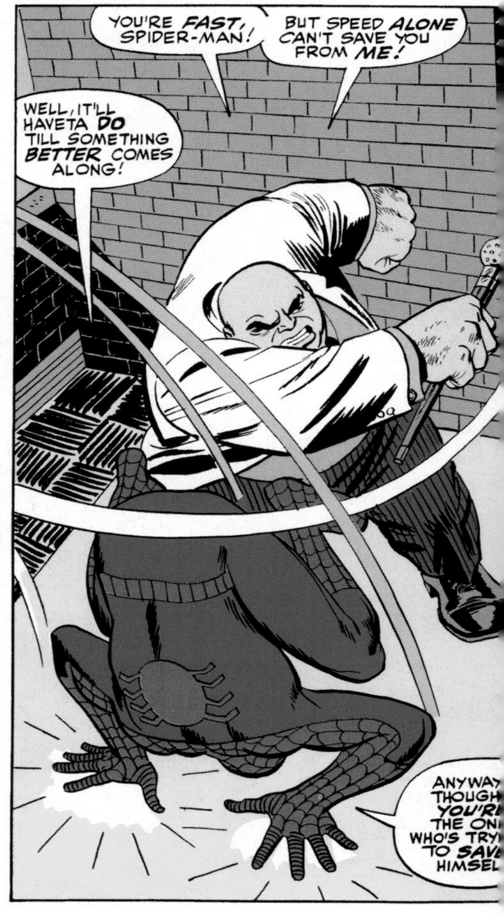
YOU'RE FAST, SPIDER-MAN!
BUT SPEED ALONE CAN'T SAVE YOU FROM ME!
WELL, IT'LL HAVETA DO TILL SOMETHING BETTER COMES ALONG!

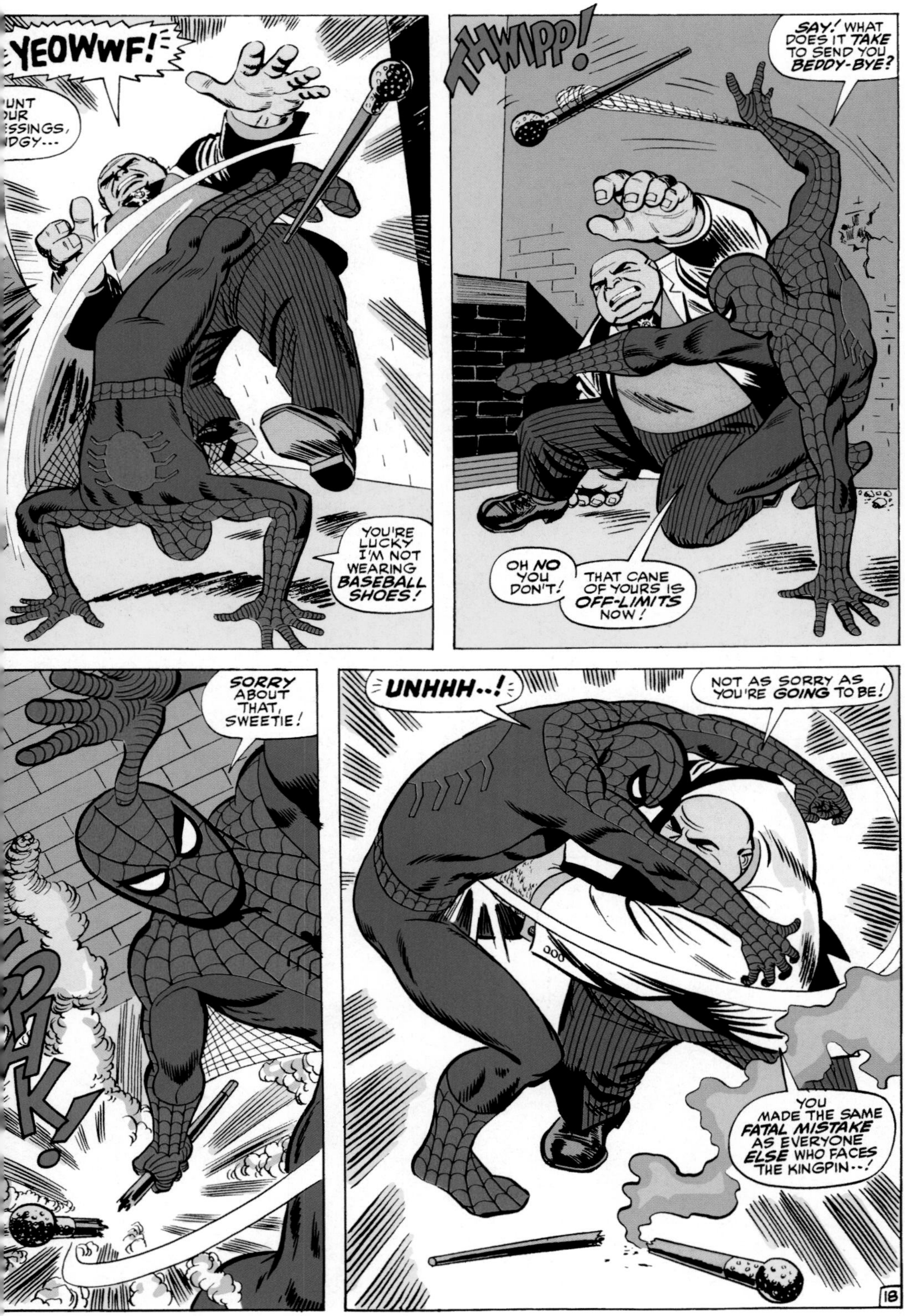
YEOWWF!
UNT OUR ESSINGS, DGY...
YOU'RE LUCKY I'M NOT WEARING BASEBALL SHOES!
THWIPP!
SAY! WHAT DOES IT TAKE TO SEND YOU BEDDY-BYE?
OH NO YOU DON'T!
THAT CANE OF YOURS IS OFF-LIMITS NOW!
SORRY ABOUT THAT, SWEETIE!
UNHHH..!
NOT AS SORRY AS YOU'RE GOING TO BE!
YOU MADE THE SAME FATAL MISTAKE AS EVERYONE ELSE WHO FACES THE KINGPIN..!

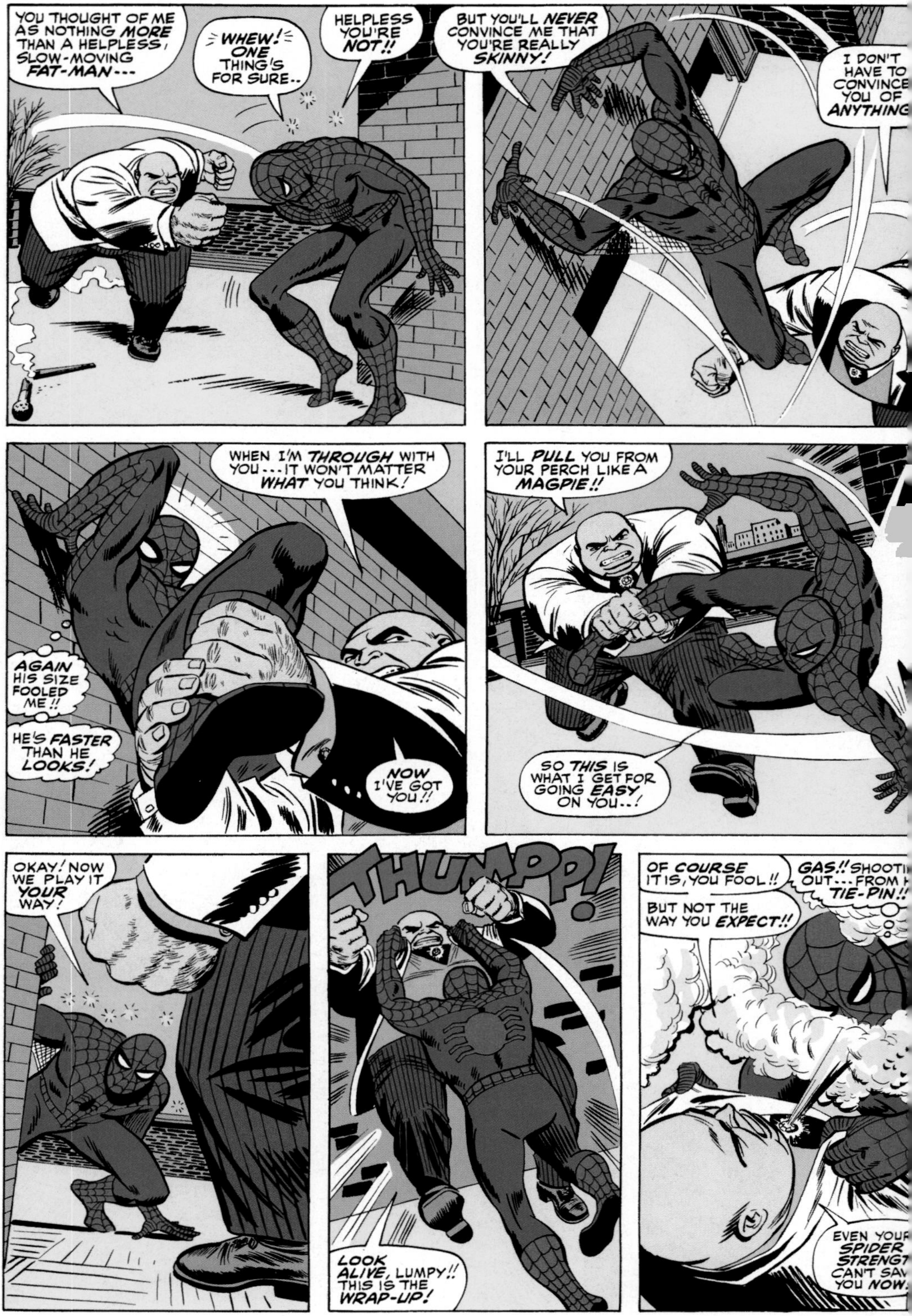
YOU THOUGHT OF ME AS NOTHING MORE THAN A HELPLESS, SLOW-MOVING FAT-MAN---
WHEW! ONE THING'S FOR SURE..
HELPLESS YOU'RE NOT!!
BUT YOU'LL NEVER CONVINCE ME THAT YOU'RE REALLY SKINNY!
I DON'T HAVE TO CONVINCE YOU OF ANYTHING
WHEN I'M THROUGH WITH YOU...IT WON'T MATTER WHAT YOU THINK!
AGAIN HIS SIZE FOOLED ME!!
HE'S FASTER THAN HE LOOKS!
NOW I'VE GOT YOU!!
I'LL PULL YOU FROM YOUR PERCH LIKE A MAGPIE!!
SO THIS IS WHAT I GET FOR GOING EASY ON YOU..!
OKAY! NOW WE PLAY IT YOUR WAY!
THUMPP!
LOOK ALIVE, LUMPY!! THIS IS THE WRAP-UP!
OF COURSE IT IS, YOU FOOL!!
BUT NOT THE WAY YOU EXPECT!!
GAS!! SHOOTI OUT---FROM H TIE-PIN!!
EVEN YOUR SPIDER STRENGT CAN'T SAV YOU NOW.

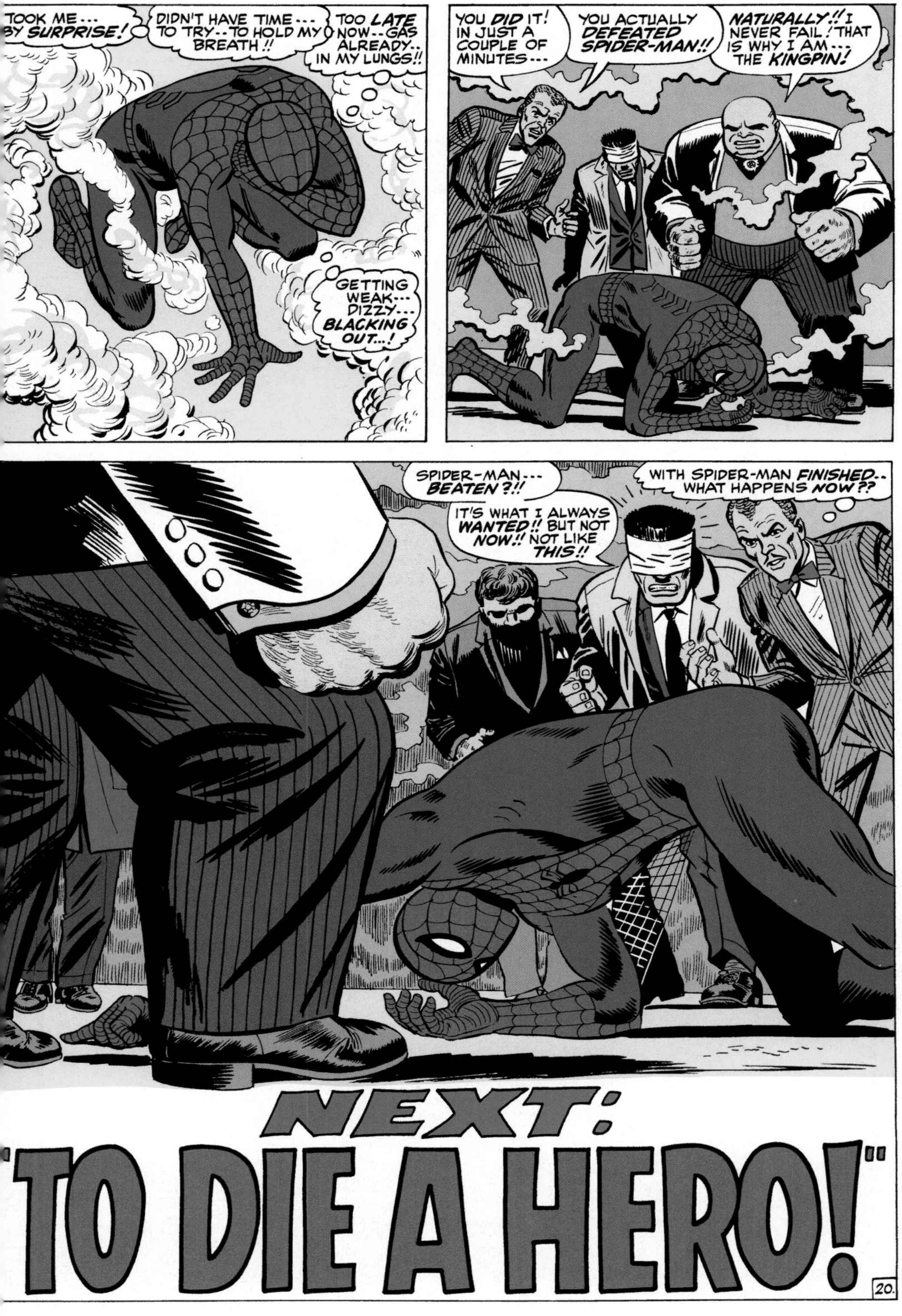
TOOK ME... BY SURPRISE!
DIDN'T HAVE TIME... TO TRY--TO HOLD MY BREATH!!
TOO LATE NOW--GAS ALREADY.. IN MY LUNGS!!
GETTING WEAK... DIZZY... BLACKING OUT...!
YOU DID IT! IN JUST A COUPLE OF MINUTES...
YOU ACTUALLY DEFEATED SPIDER-MAN!!
NATURALLY!! I NEVER FAIL! THAT IS WHY I AM... THE KINGPIN!
SPIDER-MAN... BEATEN?!!
IT'S WHAT I ALWAYS WANTED!! BUT NOT NOW!! NOT LIKE THIS!!
WITH SPIDER-MAN FINISHED.. WHAT HAPPENS NOW??
NEXT:
"TO DIE A HERO!"
20.

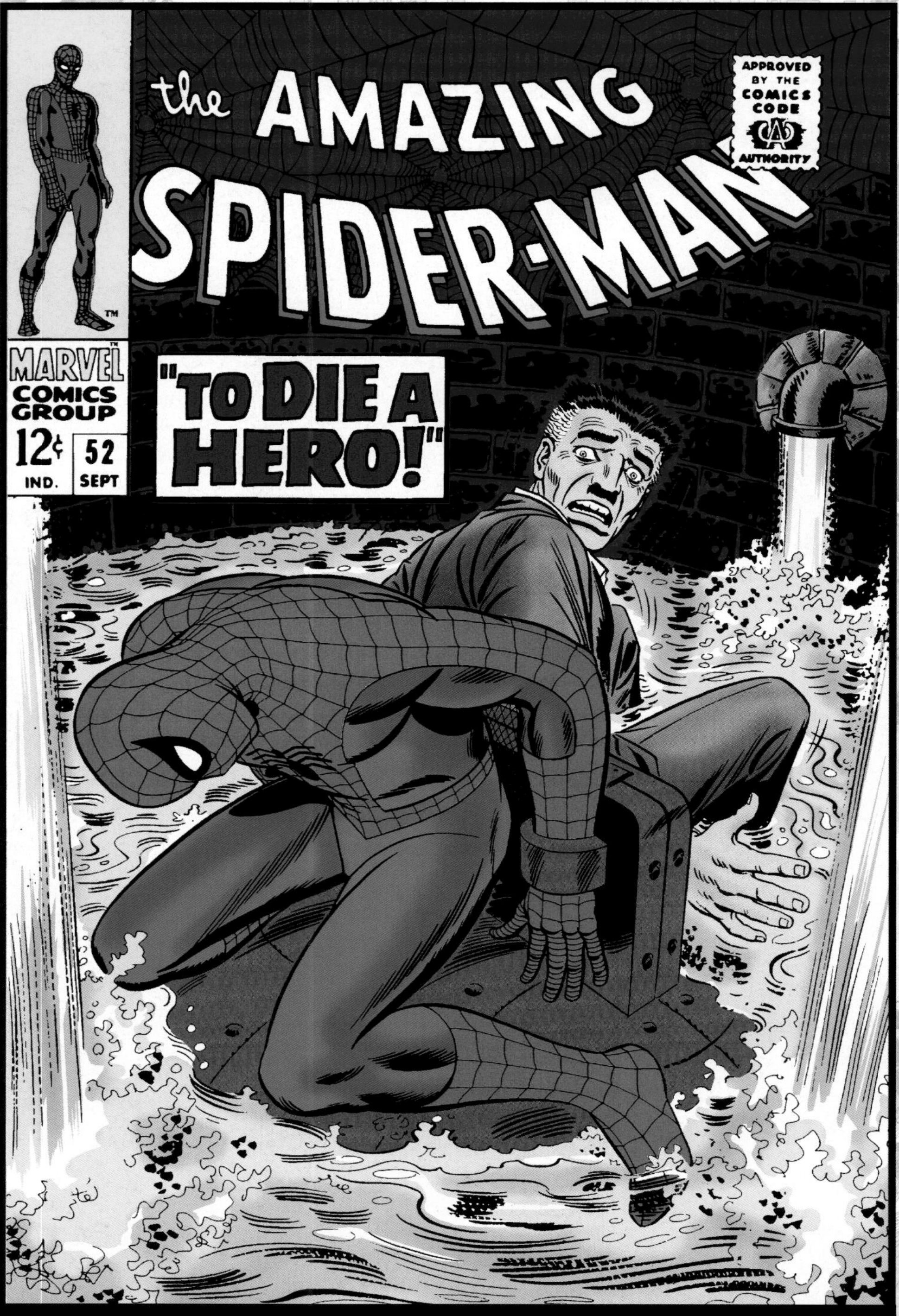
APPROVED BY THE COMICS CODE AUTHORITY
the AMAZING SPIDER-MAN
MARVEL COMICS GROUP
12¢ IND.
52 SEPT
"TO DIE A HERO!"

AMAZING SPIDER-MAN #52

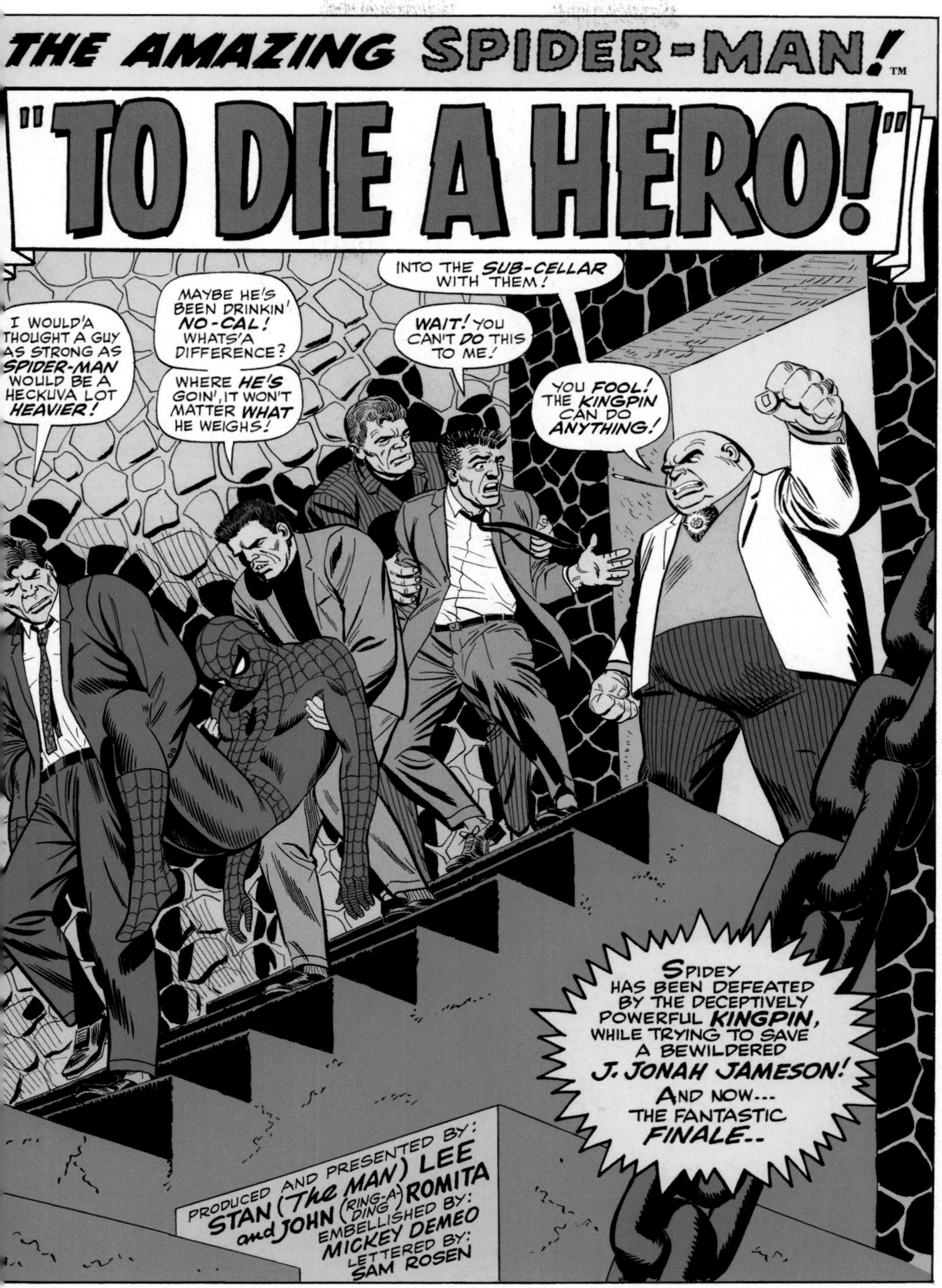
THE AMAZING SPIDER-MAN!
"TO DIE A HERO!"
I WOULD'A THOUGHT A GUY AS STRONG AS SPIDER-MAN WOULD BE A HECKUVA LOT HEAVIER!
MAYBE HE'S BEEN DRINKIN' NO-CAL! WHATS'A DIFFERENCE?
WHERE HE'S GOIN', IT WON'T MATTER WHAT HE WEIGHS!
INTO THE SUB-CELLAR WITH THEM!
WAIT! YOU CAN'T DO THIS TO ME!
YOU FOOL! THE KINGPIN CAN DO ANYTHING!
SPIDEY HAS BEEN DEFEATED BY THE DECEPTIVELY POWERFUL KINGPIN, WHILE TRYING TO SAVE A BEWILDERED J. JONAH JAMESON! AND NOW... THE FANTASTIC FINALE..
PRODUCED AND PRESENTED BY: STAN (The MAN) LEE and JOHN (RING-A-DING) ROMITA EMBELLISHED BY: MICKEY DEMEO LETTERED BY: SAM ROSEN

KEEP MOVIN', MISTER...WE AIN'T GETTIN' ANY YOUNGER!

WAIT! STOP! TELL ME...! I'VE A RIGHT TO KNOW...!

WHAT ARE YOU PLANNING.. TO DO TO ME...AND WHY??

YOU HAD YOUR CHANCE, JAMESON!

I WARNED YOU TO STOP PUBLISHING REPORTS ABOUT THE CRIME WAVE...TO STOP INCITING THE PUBLIC...BUT YOU REFUSED!

NOW YOU'LL LEARN THAT NOBODY CAN REFUSE THE KINGPIN!

NOW...YOU AND SPIDER-MAN WILL BE.. ELIMINATED!

HOLD IT! WHAT'S THE RUSH?? LET'S..TALK IT..OVER!

THIS'LL BE NICE, 'N CLEAN, N' QUIET!

YEAH! JUST THE WAY THE KINGPIN LIKES IT!

YOU'RE MAKING.. A BIG MISTAKE...!!

HOW'D YA LIKE HOW FAST HE POLISHED OFF THE WEB-SLINGER!

EVEN SPIDER-MAN COULDN'T SAVE HIMSELF FROM THE GAS THAT SPRAYED OUTTA THE BOSS'S TIEPIN!

YOU HEARD THE KINGPIN!

SO YA BETTER START PRAYIN'!!

YOU WALL-CRAWLING WEASEL... WAKE UP!!

WHERE'S YOUR BLASTED SPIDER-STRENGTH WHEN I NEED IT?

SPIDER-MAN..C'MON!! CAN'T YOU HEAR ME??

IT'S LIKE I ALWAYS SAID! ...YOU'RE NOTHING BUT A FRAUD!

KEEP TALKIN', JAMESON!

IT'S THE LAST CHANCE YA'LL EVER HAVE!

WATER...GUSHING OUT OF THAT PIPE!

WAIT!! YOU'VE GOTTA UNTIE US! WE'RE LIABLE TO DROWN!

KNOW SOME-THIN', MISTER? YOU CATCH ON REAL QUICK!

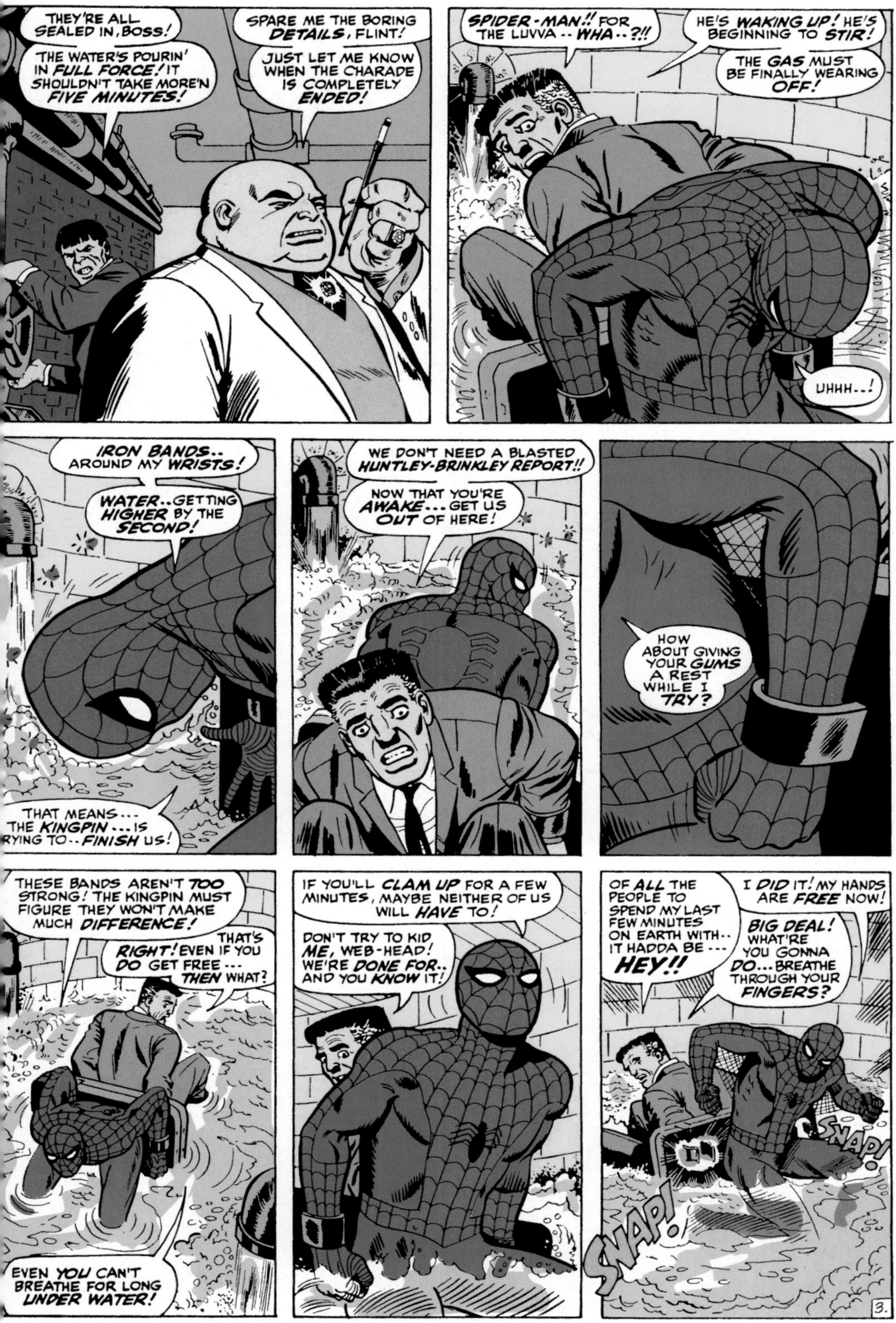
THEY'RE ALL SEALED IN, BOSS!
THE WATER'S POURIN' IN FULL FORCE! IT SHOULDN'T TAKE MORE'N FIVE MINUTES!
SPARE ME THE BORING DETAILS, FLINT!
JUST LET ME KNOW WHEN THE CHARADE IS COMPLETELY ENDED!
SPIDER-MAN!! FOR THE LUVVA -- WHA--?!!
HE'S WAKING UP! HE'S BEGINNING TO STIR!
THE GAS MUST BE FINALLY WEARING OFF!
UHHH--!
IRON BANDS.. AROUND MY WRISTS!
WATER..GETTING HIGHER BY THE SECOND!
THAT MEANS... THE KINGPIN...IS RYING TO--FINISH US!
WE DON'T NEED A BLASTED HUNTLEY-BRINKLEY REPORT!!
NOW THAT YOU'RE AWAKE...GET US OUT OF HERE!
HOW ABOUT GIVING YOUR GUMS A REST WHILE I TRY?
THESE BANDS AREN'T TOO STRONG! THE KINGPIN MUST FIGURE THEY WON'T MAKE MUCH DIFFERENCE!
THAT'S RIGHT! EVEN IF YOU DO GET FREE... THEN WHAT?
EVEN YOU CAN'T BREATHE FOR LONG UNDER WATER!
IF YOU'LL CLAM UP FOR A FEW MINUTES, MAYBE NEITHER OF US WILL HAVE TO!
DON'T TRY TO KID ME, WEB-HEAD! WE'RE DONE FOR.. AND YOU KNOW IT!
OF ALL THE PEOPLE TO SPEND MY LAST FEW MINUTES ON EARTH WITH.. IT HADDA BE --- HEY!!
I DID IT! MY HANDS ARE FREE NOW!
BIG DEAL! WHAT'RE YOU GONNA DO...BREATHE THROUGH YOUR FINGERS?
SNAP!
SNAP!
3.

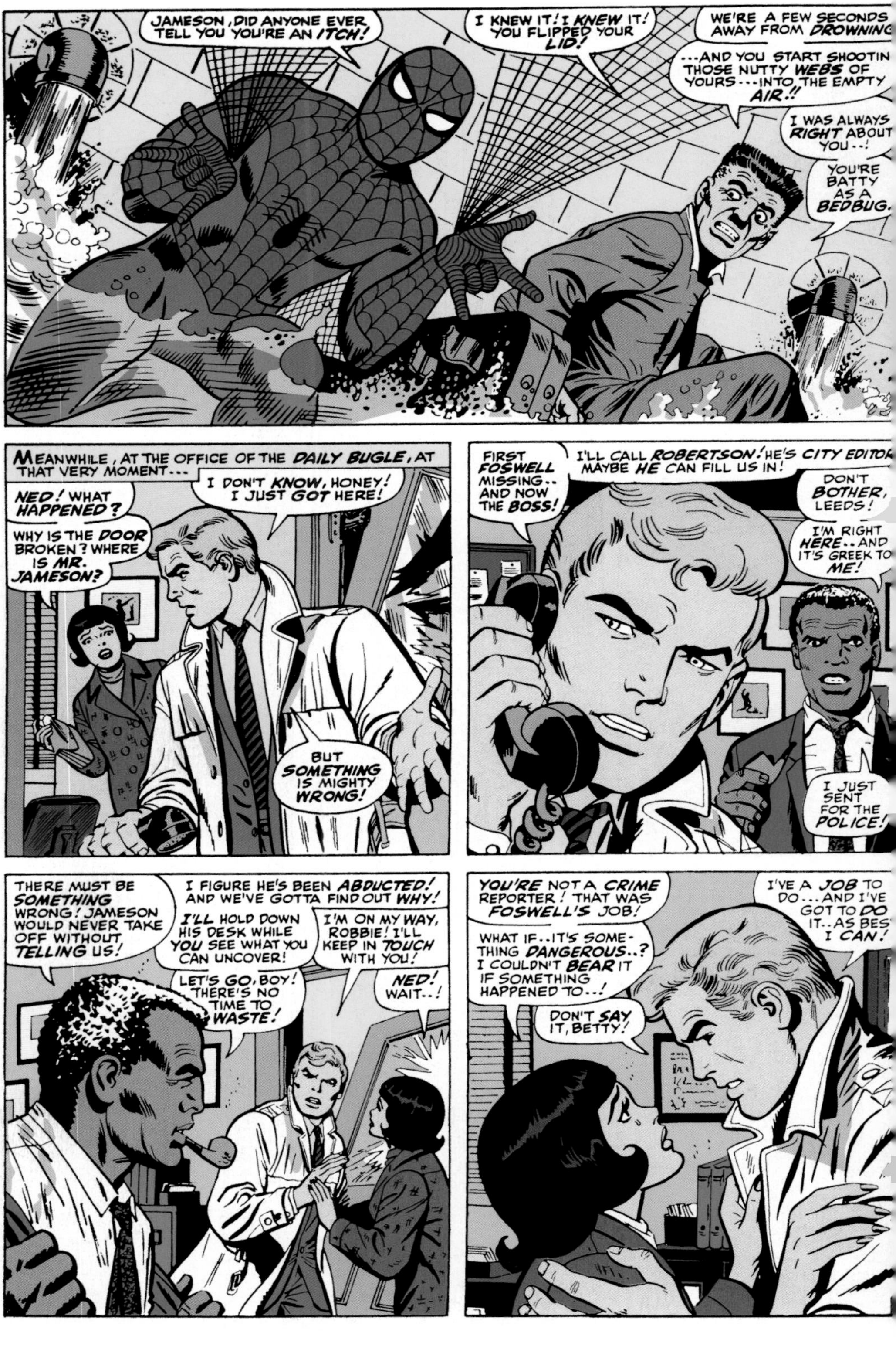

JAMESON, DID ANYONE EVER TELL YOU YOU'RE AN ITCH!
I KNEW IT! I KNEW IT! YOU FLIPPED YOUR LID!
WE'RE A FEW SECONDS AWAY FROM DROWNING
...AND YOU START SHOOTIN THOSE NUTTY WEBS OF YOURS---INTO THE EMPTY AIR!!
I WAS ALWAYS RIGHT ABOUT YOU--!
YOU'RE BATTY AS A BEDBUG.
MEANWHILE, AT THE OFFICE OF THE DAILY BUGLE, AT THAT VERY MOMENT...
NED! WHAT HAPPENED?
WHY IS THE DOOR BROKEN? WHERE IS MR. JAMESON?
I DON'T KNOW, HONEY! I JUST GOT HERE!
BUT SOMETHING IS MIGHTY WRONG!
FIRST FOSWELL MISSING.. AND NOW THE BOSS!
I'LL CALL ROBERTSON! HE'S CITY EDITOR MAYBE HE CAN FILL US IN!
DON'T BOTHER, LEEDS!
I'M RIGHT HERE..AND IT'S GREEK TO ME!
I JUST SENT FOR THE POLICE!
THERE MUST BE SOMETHING WRONG! JAMESON WOULD NEVER TAKE OFF WITHOUT TELLING US!
I FIGURE HE'S BEEN ABDUCTED! AND WE'VE GOTTA FIND OUT WHY!
I'LL HOLD DOWN HIS DESK WHILE YOU SEE WHAT YOU CAN UNCOVER!
I'M ON MY WAY, ROBBIE! I'LL KEEP IN TOUCH WITH YOU!
LET'S GO, BOY! THERE'S NO TIME TO WASTE!
NED! WAIT--!
YOU'RE NOT A CRIME REPORTER! THAT WAS FOSWELL'S JOB!
WHAT IF..IT'S SOMETHING DANGEROUS..? I COULDN'T BEAR IT IF SOMETHING HAPPENED TO--!
I'VE A JOB TO DO...AND I'VE GOT TO DO IT..AS BEST I CAN!
DON'T SAY IT, BETTY!

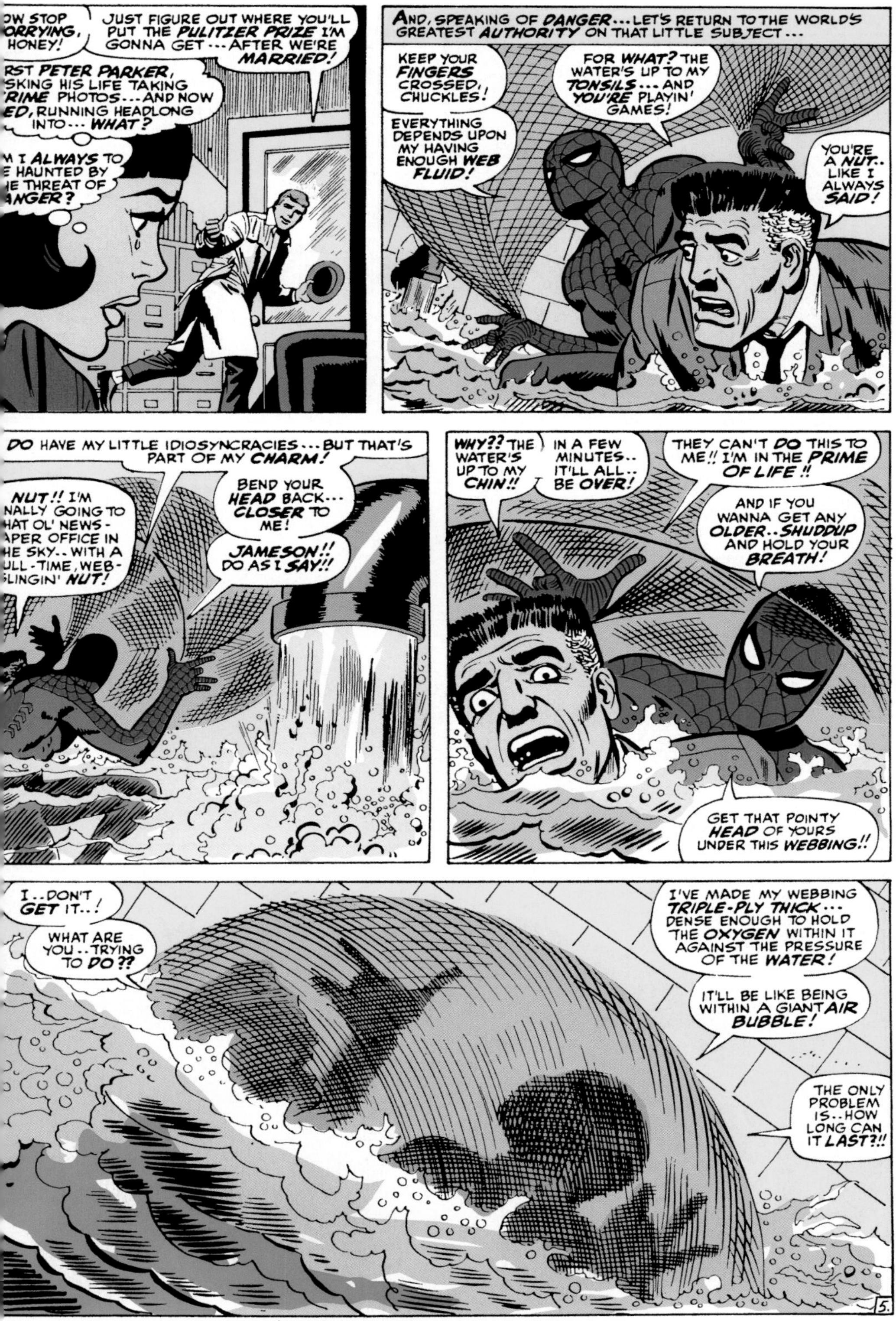
OW STOP
ORRYING, HONEY!
JUST FIGURE OUT WHERE YOU'LL PUT THE PULITZER PRIZE I'M GONNA GET... AFTER WE'RE MARRIED!
RST PETER PARKER, SKING HIS LIFE TAKING RIME PHOTOS... AND NOW ED, RUNNING HEADLONG INTO... WHAT?
M I ALWAYS TO E HAUNTED BY HE THREAT OF ANGER?
AND, SPEAKING OF DANGER... LET'S RETURN TO THE WORLD'S GREATEST AUTHORITY ON THAT LITTLE SUBJECT...
KEEP YOUR FINGERS CROSSED, CHUCKLES!
FOR WHAT? THE WATER'S UP TO MY TONSILS... AND YOU'RE PLAYIN' GAMES!
EVERYTHING DEPENDS UPON MY HAVING ENOUGH WEB FLUID!
YOU'RE A NUT.. LIKE I ALWAYS SAID!
DO HAVE MY LITTLE IDIOSYNCRACIES... BUT THAT'S PART OF MY CHARM!
NUT!! I'M NALLY GOING TO HAT OL' NEWS- APER OFFICE IN HE SKY.. WITH A ULL-TIME, WEB- LINGIN' NUT!
BEND YOUR HEAD BACK... CLOSER TO ME!
JAMESON!! DO AS I SAY!!
WHY?? THE WATER'S UP TO MY CHIN!!
IN A FEW MINUTES.. IT'LL ALL.. BE OVER!
THEY CAN'T DO THIS TO ME!! I'M IN THE PRIME OF LIFE!!
AND IF YOU WANNA GET ANY OLDER.. SHUDDUP AND HOLD YOUR BREATH!
GET THAT POINTY HEAD OF YOURS UNDER THIS WEBBING!!
I.. DON'T GET IT..!
WHAT ARE YOU.. TRYING TO DO??
I'VE MADE MY WEBBING TRIPLE-PLY THICK... DENSE ENOUGH TO HOLD THE OXYGEN WITHIN IT AGAINST THE PRESSURE OF THE WATER!
IT'LL BE LIKE BEING WITHIN A GIANT AIR BUBBLE!
THE ONLY PROBLEM IS.. HOW LONG CAN IT LAST?!!
5.

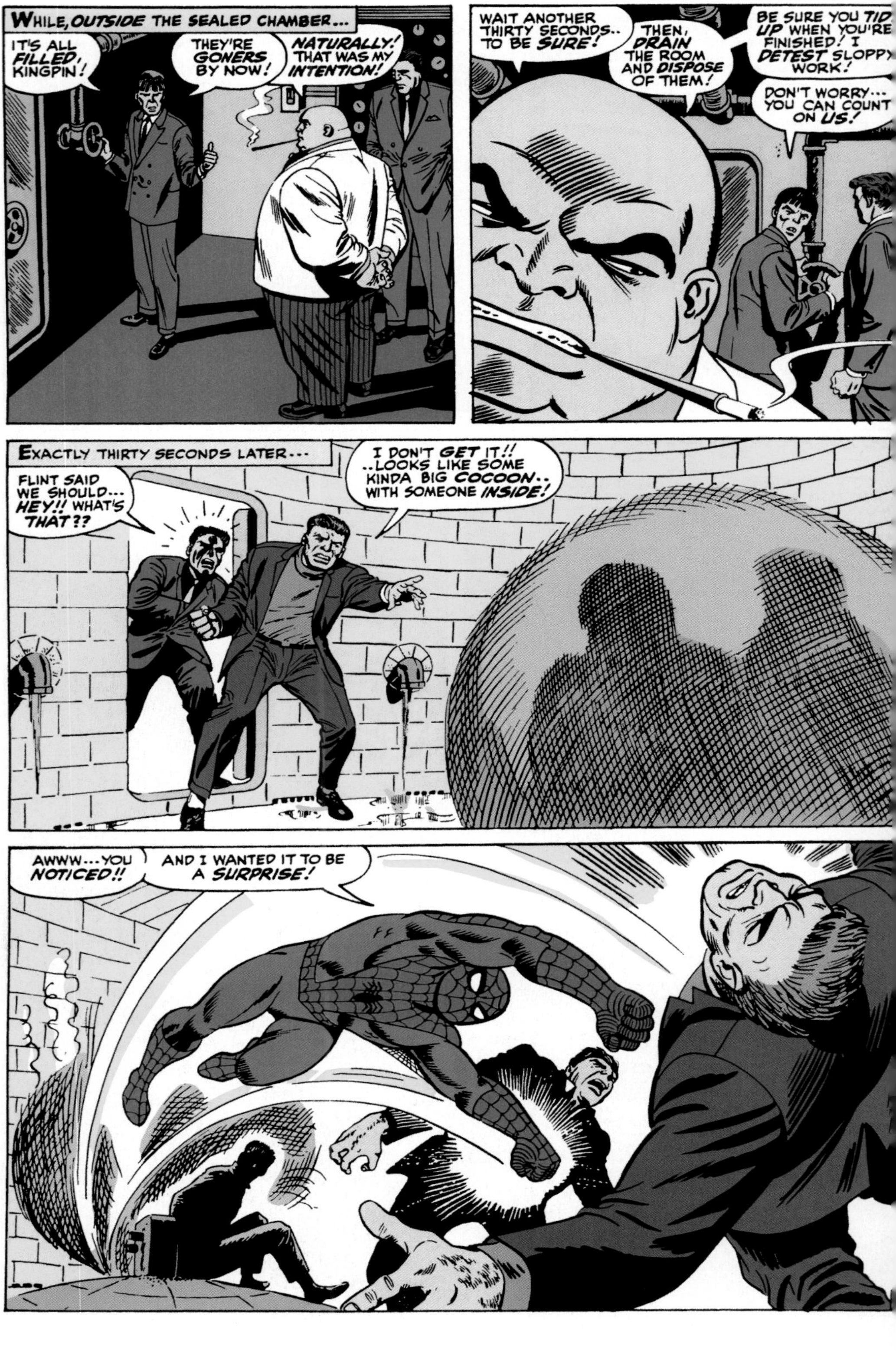
WHILE, OUTSIDE THE SEALED CHAMBER...
IT'S ALL FILLED, KINGPIN!
THEY'RE GONERS BY NOW!
NATURALLY! THAT WAS MY INTENTION!
WAIT ANOTHER THIRTY SECONDS.. TO BE SURE!
THEN, DRAIN THE ROOM AND DISPOSE OF THEM!
BE SURE YOU TIDY UP WHEN YOU'RE FINISHED! I DETEST SLOPPY WORK!
DON'T WORRY... YOU CAN COUNT ON US!
EXACTLY THIRTY SECONDS LATER...
FLINT SAID WE SHOULD... HEY!! WHAT'S THAT??
I DON'T GET IT!! ..LOOKS LIKE SOME KINDA BIG COCOON.. WITH SOMEONE INSIDE!
AWWW... YOU NOTICED!!
AND I WANTED IT TO BE A SURPRISE!

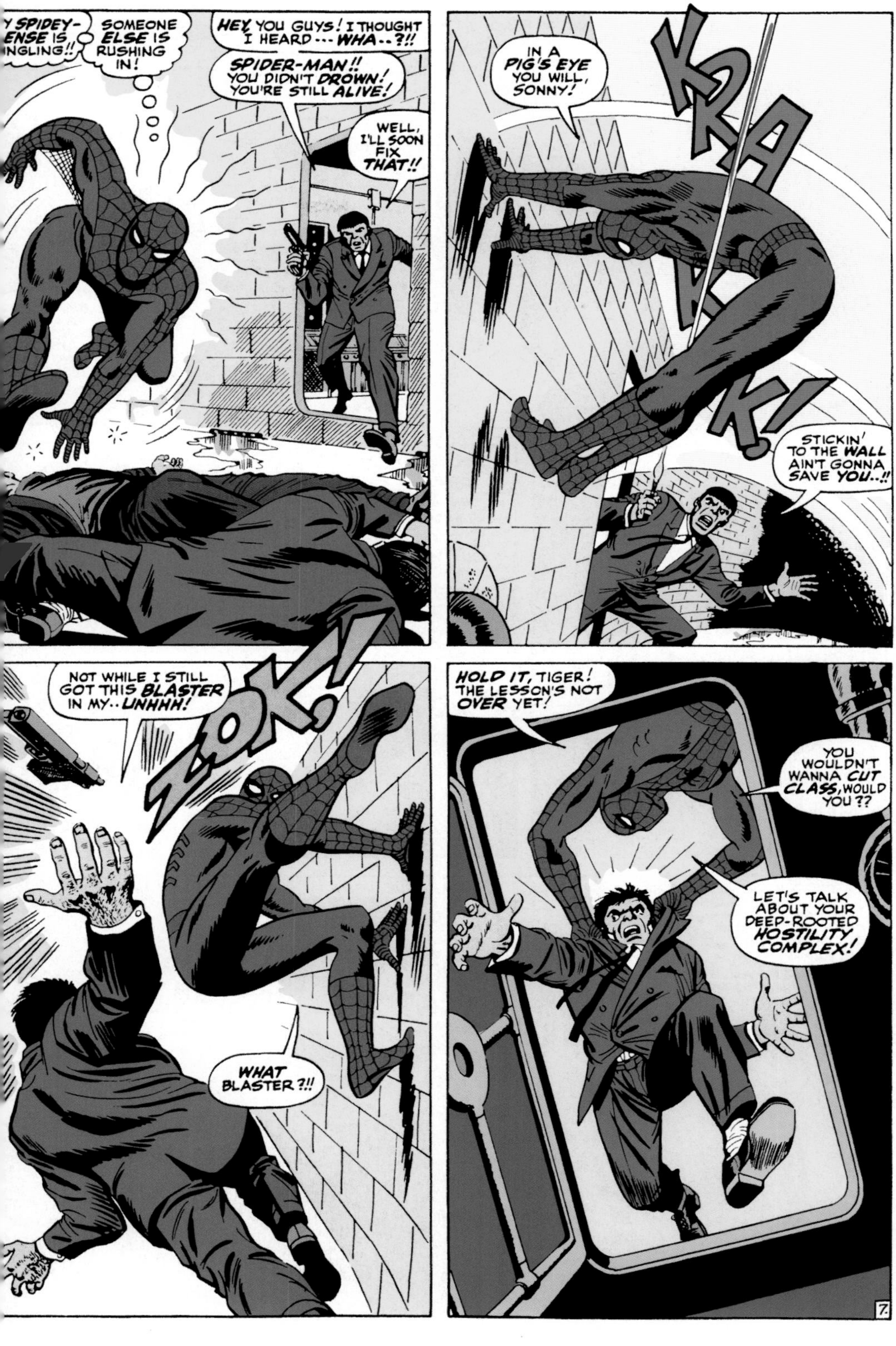

SOMEONE ELSE IS RUSHING IN!
HEY, YOU GUYS! I THOUGHT I HEARD --- WHA..?!!
SPIDER-MAN!! YOU DIDN'T DROWN! YOU'RE STILL ALIVE!
WELL, I'LL SOON FIX THAT!!
IN A PIG'S EYE YOU WILL, SONNY!
KRAKK!
STICKIN' TO THE WALL AIN'T GONNA SAVE YOU..!!
NOT WHILE I STILL GOT THIS BLASTER IN MY.. UNHHH!
ZOK!
WHAT BLASTER ?!!
HOLD IT, TIGER! THE LESSON'S NOT OVER YET!
YOU WOULDN'T WANNA CUT CLASS, WOULD YOU ??
LET'S TALK ABOUT YOUR DEEP-ROOTED HOSTILITY COMPLEX!
7

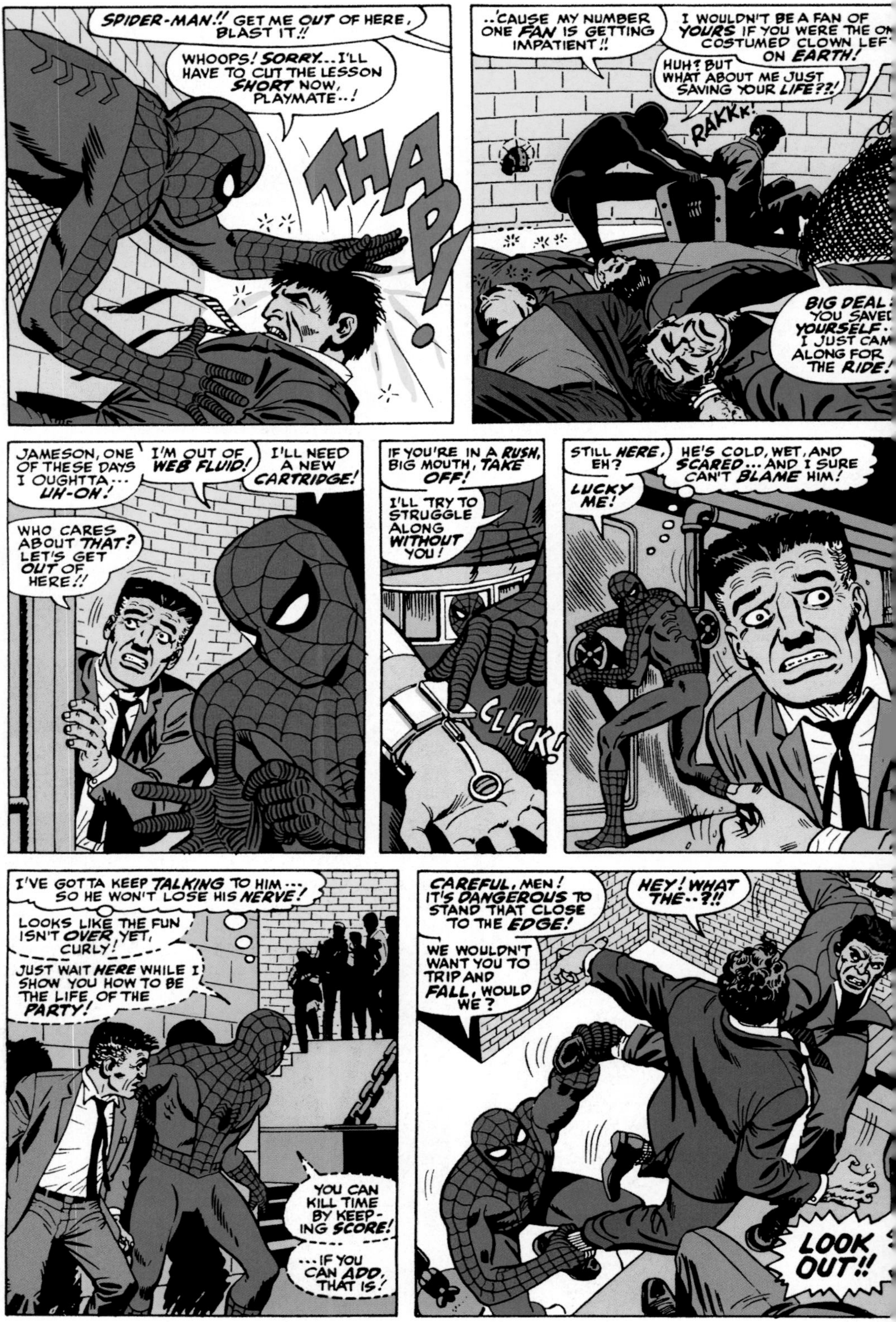
SPIDER-MAN!! GET ME OUT OF HERE, BLAST IT!!
WHOOPS! SORRY... I'LL HAVE TO CUT THE LESSON SHORT NOW, PLAYMATE..!
THAP!
..'CAUSE MY NUMBER ONE FAN IS GETTING IMPATIENT!!
I WOULDN'T BE A FAN OF YOURS IF YOU WERE THE ON COSTUMED CLOWN LEF ON EARTH!
HUH? BUT WHAT ABOUT ME JUST SAVING YOUR LIFE??!
RAKKK!
BIG DEAL: YOU SAVED YOURSELF.. I JUST CAM ALONG FOR THE RIDE!
JAMESON, ONE OF THESE DAYS I OUGHTTA... UH-OH!
I'M OUT OF WEB FLUID!
I'LL NEED A NEW CARTRIDGE!
WHO CARES ABOUT THAT? LET'S GET OUT OF HERE!!
IF YOU'RE IN A RUSH, BIG MOUTH, TAKE OFF!
I'LL TRY TO STRUGGLE ALONG WITHOUT YOU!
CLICK!
STILL HERE, EH?
LUCKY ME!
HE'S COLD, WET, AND SCARED... AND I SURE CAN'T BLAME HIM!
I'VE GOTTA KEEP TALKING TO HIM... SO HE WON'T LOSE HIS NERVE!
LOOKS LIKE THE FUN ISN'T OVER YET, CURLY!
JUST WAIT HERE WHILE I SHOW YOU HOW TO BE THE LIFE OF THE PARTY!
YOU CAN KILL TIME BY KEEP-ING SCORE!
...IF YOU CAN ADD, THAT IS!
CAREFUL, MEN! IT'S DANGEROUS TO STAND THAT CLOSE TO THE EDGE!
HEY! WHAT THE--?!!
WE WOULDN'T WANT YOU TO TRIP AND FALL, WOULD WE?
LOOK OUT!!

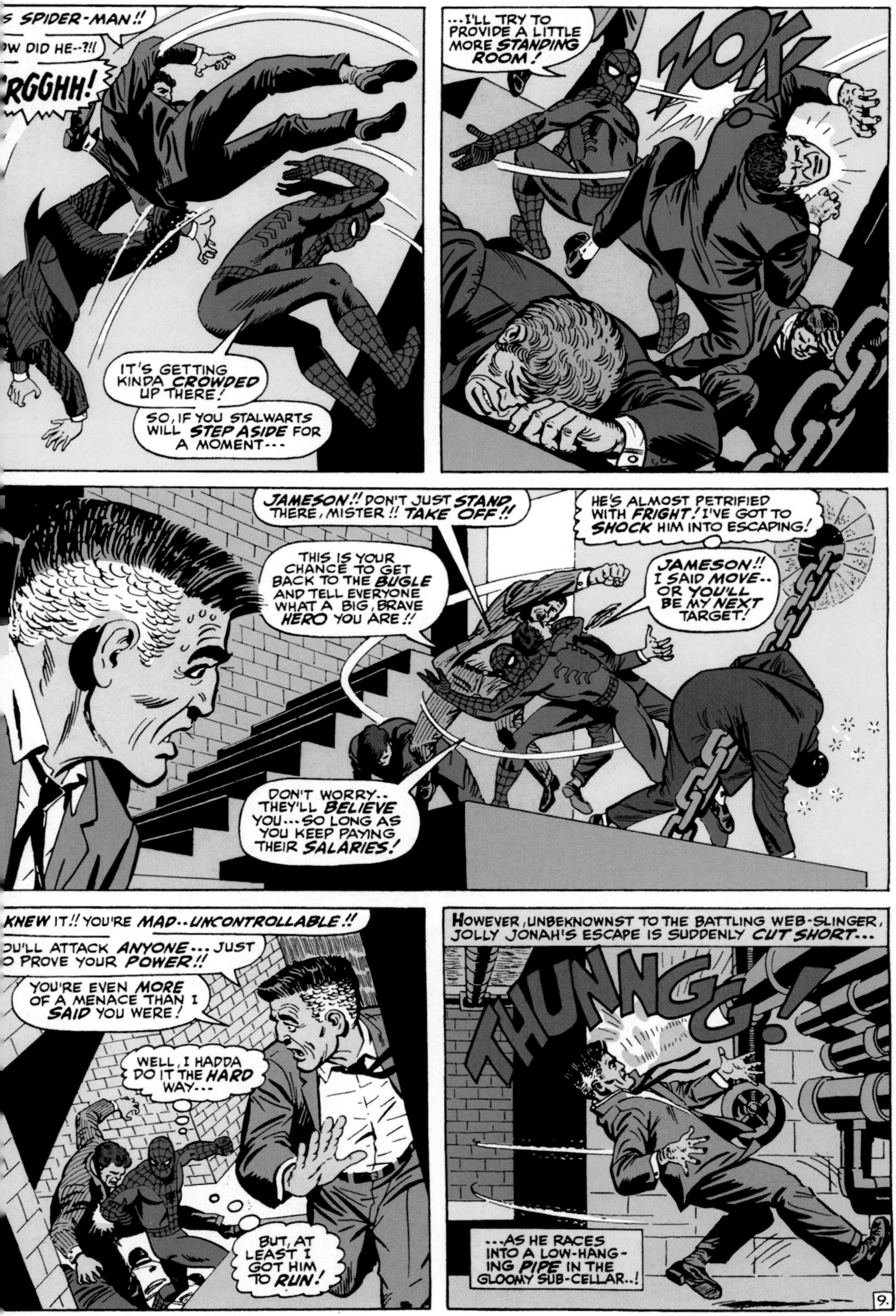

S SPIDER-MAN!!
W DID HE--?!!
RGGHH!
IT'S GETTING KINDA CROWDED UP THERE!
SO, IF YOU STALWARTS WILL STEP ASIDE FOR A MOMENT---
...I'LL TRY TO PROVIDE A LITTLE MORE STANDING ROOM!
JAMESON!! DON'T JUST STAND THERE, MISTER!! TAKE OFF!!
THIS IS YOUR CHANCE TO GET BACK TO THE BUGLE AND TELL EVERYONE WHAT A BIG, BRAVE HERO YOU ARE!!
DON'T WORRY.. THEY'LL BELIEVE YOU...SO LONG AS YOU KEEP PAYING THEIR SALARIES!
HE'S ALMOST PETRIFIED WITH FRIGHT! I'VE GOT TO SHOCK HIM INTO ESCAPING!
JAMESON!! I SAID MOVE.. OR YOU'LL BE MY NEXT TARGET!
KNEW IT!! YOU'RE MAD..UNCONTROLLABLE!!
OU'LL ATTACK ANYONE... JUST O PROVE YOUR POWER!!
YOU'RE EVEN MORE OF A MENACE THAN I SAID YOU WERE!
WELL, I HADDA DO IT THE HARD WAY...
BUT, AT LEAST I GOT HIM TO RUN!
HOWEVER, UNBEKNOWNST TO THE BATTLING WEB-SLINGER, JOLLY JONAH'S ESCAPE IS SUDDENLY CUT SHORT...
THUNNGG!
...AS HE RACES INTO A LOW-HANGING PIPE IN THE GLOOMY SUB-CELLAR..!
9.

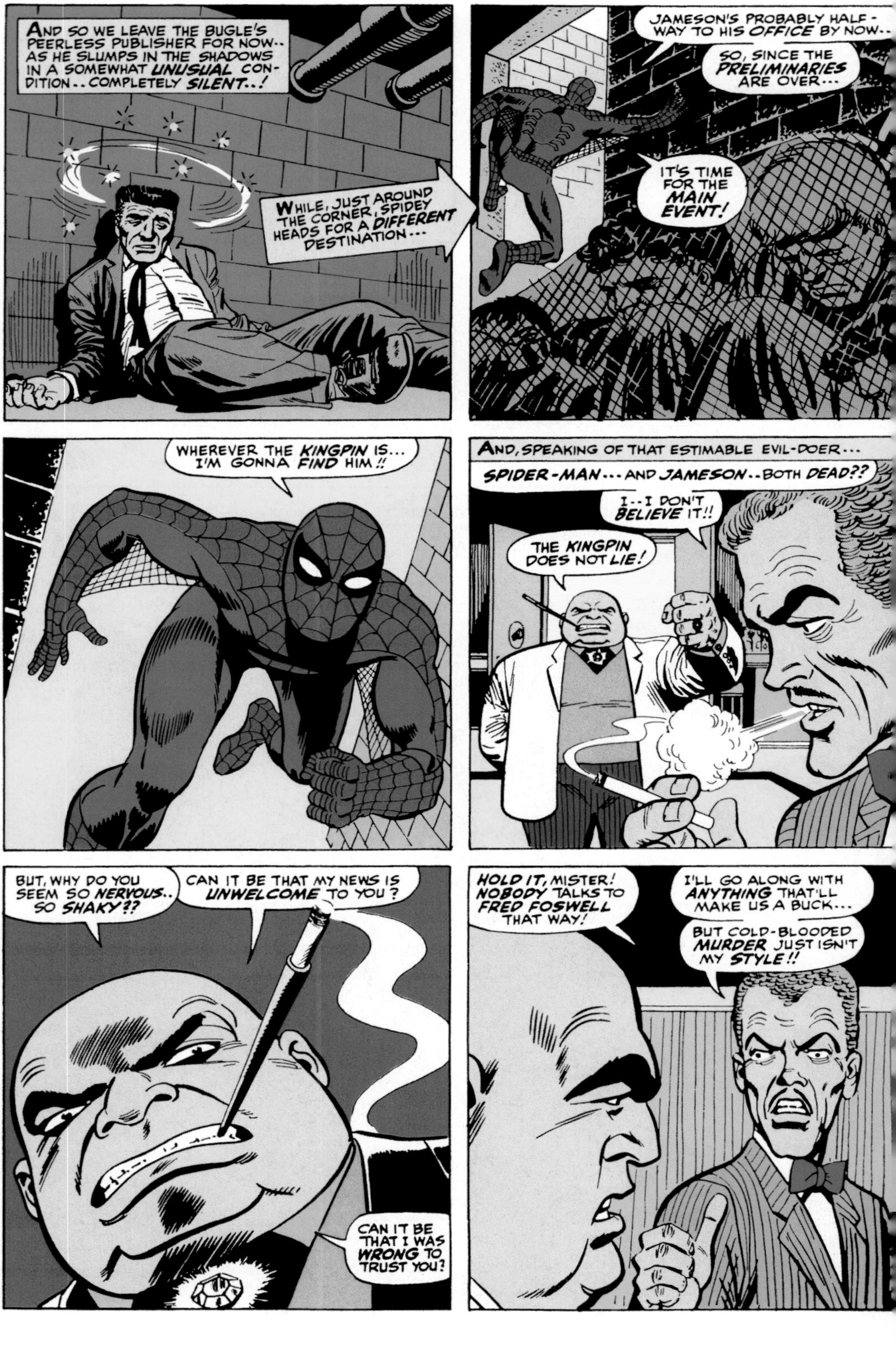
AND SO WE LEAVE THE BUGLE'S PEERLESS PUBLISHER FOR NOW.. AS HE SLUMPS IN THE SHADOWS IN A SOMEWHAT UNUSUAL CONDITION.. COMPLETELY SILENT..!
WHILE, JUST AROUND THE CORNER, SPIDEY HEADS FOR A DIFFERENT DESTINATION...
JAMESON'S PROBABLY HALF-WAY TO HIS OFFICE BY NOW--
SO, SINCE THE PRELIMINARIES ARE OVER...
IT'S TIME FOR THE MAIN EVENT!
WHEREVER THE KINGPIN IS... I'M GONNA FIND HIM!!
AND, SPEAKING OF THAT ESTIMABLE EVIL-DOER...
SPIDER-MAN... AND JAMESON.. BOTH DEAD??
I--I DON'T BELIEVE IT!!
THE KINGPIN DOES NOT LIE!
BUT, WHY DO YOU SEEM SO NERVOUS.. SO SHAKY??
CAN IT BE THAT MY NEWS IS UNWELCOME TO YOU?
CAN IT BE THAT I WAS WRONG TO TRUST YOU?
HOLD IT, MISTER! NOBODY TALKS TO FRED FOSWELL THAT WAY!
I'LL GO ALONG WITH ANYTHING THAT'LL MAKE US A BUCK...
BUT COLD-BLOODED MURDER JUST ISN'T MY STYLE!!

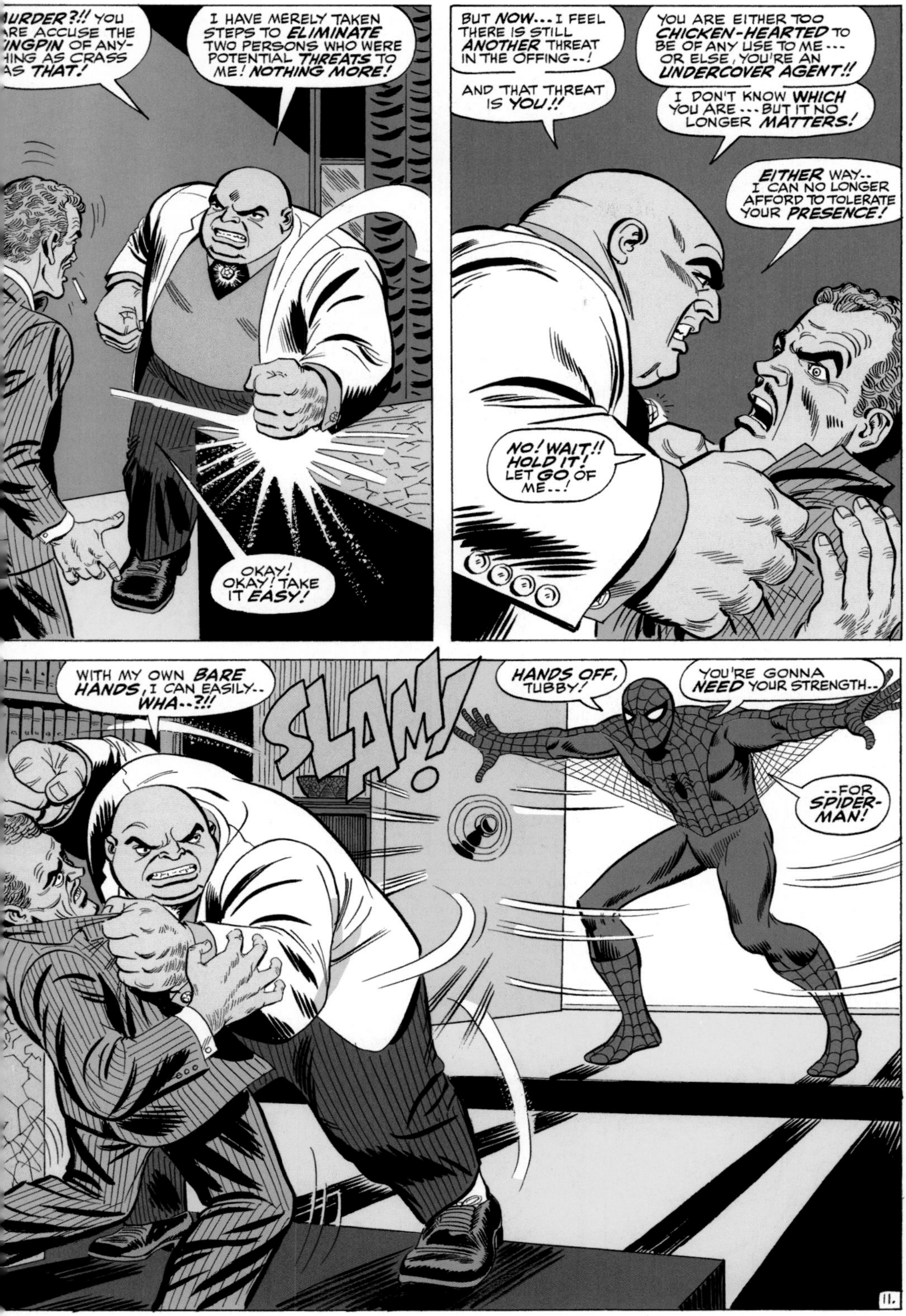
URDER?!! YOU RE ACCUSE THE INGPIN OF ANY- HING AS CRASS AS THAT!
I HAVE MERELY TAKEN STEPS TO ELIMINATE TWO PERSONS WHO WERE POTENTIAL THREATS TO ME! NOTHING MORE!
OKAY! OKAY! TAKE IT EASY!
BUT NOW... I FEEL THERE IS STILL ANOTHER THREAT IN THE OFFING--!
AND THAT THREAT IS YOU!!
YOU ARE EITHER TOO CHICKEN-HEARTED TO BE OF ANY USE TO ME--- OR ELSE, YOU'RE AN UNDERCOVER AGENT!!
I DON'T KNOW WHICH YOU ARE--- BUT IT NO LONGER MATTERS!
EITHER WAY.. I CAN NO LONGER AFFORD TO TOLERATE YOUR PRESENCE!
NO! WAIT!! HOLD IT! LET GO OF ME--!
WITH MY OWN BARE HANDS, I CAN EASILY.. WHA--?!!
SLAM!
HANDS OFF, TUBBY!
YOU'RE GONNA NEED YOUR STRENGTH..
--FOR SPIDER-MAN!

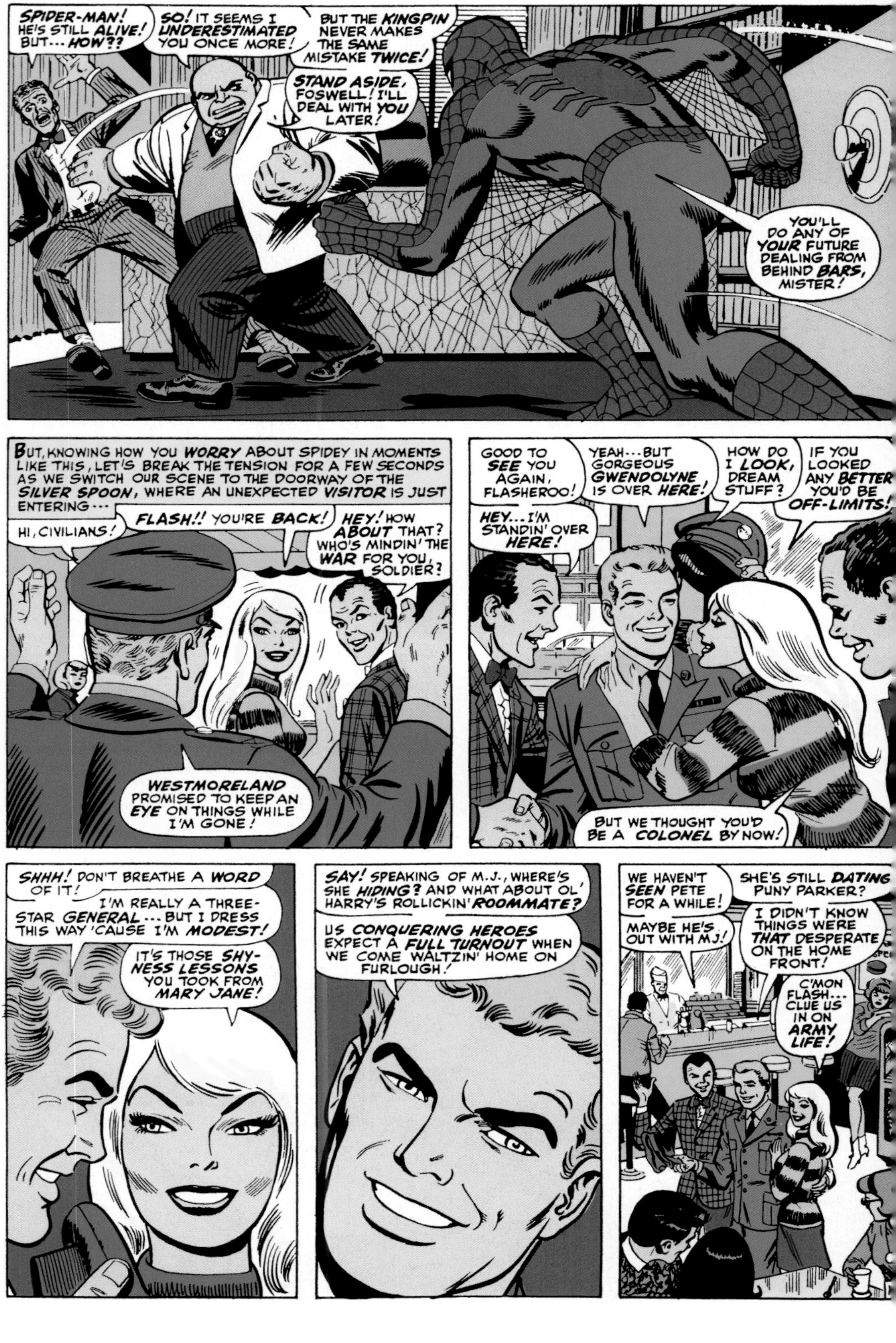
SPIDER-MAN! HE'S STILL ALIVE! BUT... HOW??
SO! IT SEEMS I UNDERESTIMATED YOU ONCE MORE!
BUT THE KINGPIN NEVER MAKES THE SAME MISTAKE TWICE!
STAND ASIDE, FOSWELL! I'LL DEAL WITH YOU LATER!
YOU'LL DO ANY OF YOUR FUTURE DEALING FROM BEHIND BARS, MISTER!
BUT, KNOWING HOW YOU WORRY ABOUT SPIDEY IN MOMENTS LIKE THIS, LET'S BREAK THE TENSION FOR A FEW SECONDS AS WE SWITCH OUR SCENE TO THE DOORWAY OF THE SILVER SPOON, WHERE AN UNEXPECTED VISITOR IS JUST ENTERING...
HI, CIVILIANS!
FLASH!! YOU'RE BACK!
HEY! HOW ABOUT THAT? WHO'S MINDIN' THE WAR FOR YOU, SOLDIER?
WESTMORELAND PROMISED TO KEEP AN EYE ON THINGS WHILE I'M GONE!
GOOD TO SEE YOU AGAIN, FLASHEROO!
YEAH... BUT GORGEOUS GWENDOLYNE IS OVER HERE!
HEY... I'M STANDIN' OVER HERE!
HOW DO I LOOK, DREAM STUFF?
IF YOU LOOKED ANY BETTER YOU'D BE OFF-LIMITS!
BUT WE THOUGHT YOU'D BE A COLONEL BY NOW!
SHHH! DON'T BREATHE A WORD OF IT!
I'M REALLY A THREE-STAR GENERAL... BUT I DRESS THIS WAY 'CAUSE I'M MODEST!
IT'S THOSE SHY-NESS LESSONS YOU TOOK FROM MARY JANE!
SAY! SPEAKING OF M.J., WHERE'S SHE HIDING? AND WHAT ABOUT OL' HARRY'S ROLLICKIN' ROOMMATE?
US CONQUERING HEROES EXPECT A FULL TURNOUT WHEN WE COME WALTZIN' HOME ON FURLOUGH!
WE HAVEN'T SEEN PETE FOR A WHILE!
MAYBE HE'S OUT WITH MJ!
SHE'S STILL DATING PUNY PARKER?
I DIDN'T KNOW THINGS WERE THAT DESPERATE ON THE HOME FRONT!
C'MON FLASH... CLUE US IN ON ARMY LIFE!

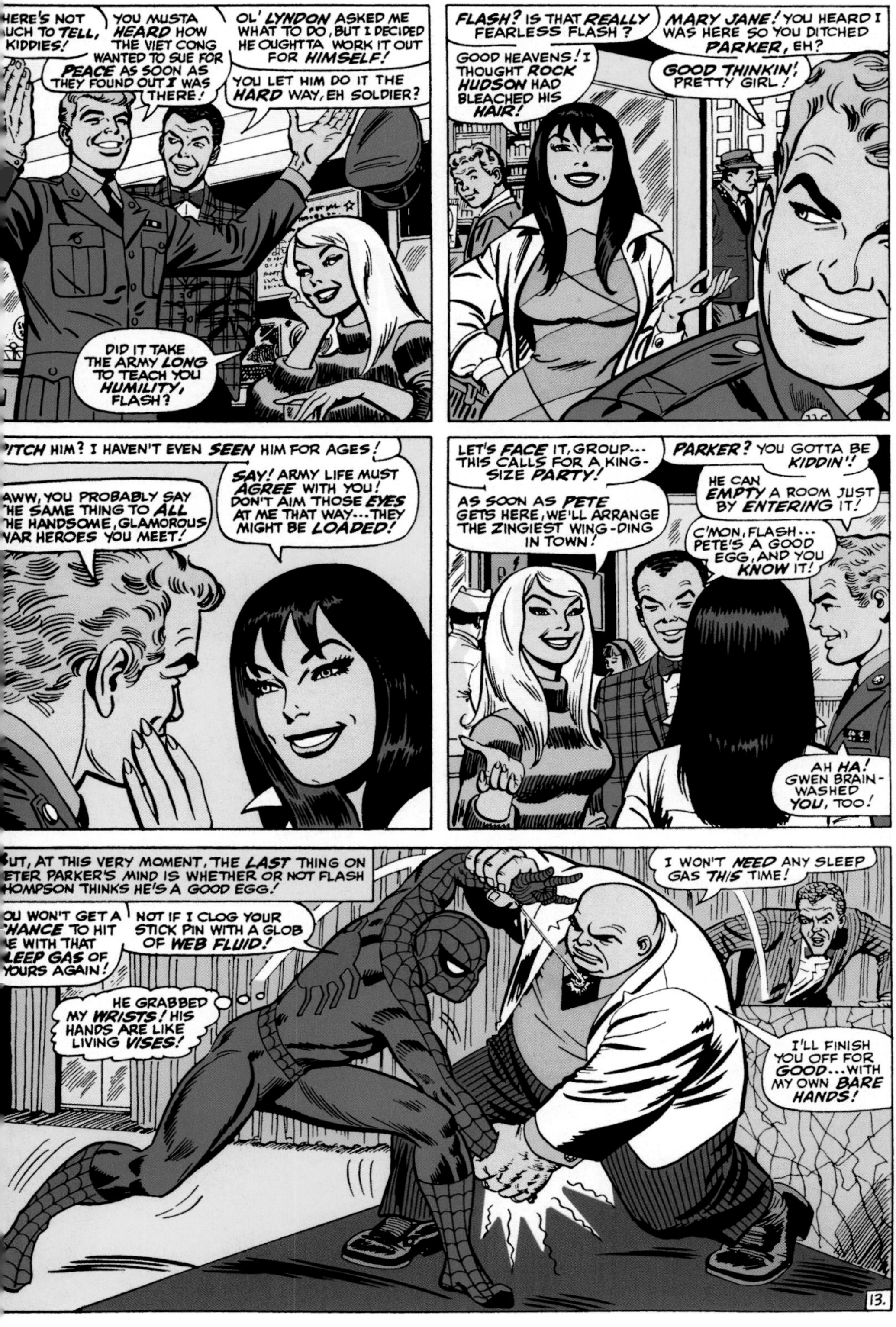
HERE'S NOT MUCH TO TELL, KIDDIES!
YOU MUSTA HEARD HOW THE VIET CONG WANTED TO SUE FOR PEACE AS SOON AS THEY FOUND OUT I WAS THERE!
OL' LYNDON ASKED ME WHAT TO DO, BUT I DECIDED HE OUGHTTA WORK IT OUT FOR HIMSELF!
YOU LET HIM DO IT THE HARD WAY, EH SOLDIER?
DID IT TAKE THE ARMY LONG TO TEACH YOU HUMILITY, FLASH?
FLASH? IS THAT REALLY FEARLESS FLASH?
GOOD HEAVENS! I THOUGHT ROCK HUDSON HAD BLEACHED HIS HAIR!
MARY JANE! YOU HEARD I WAS HERE SO YOU DITCHED PARKER, EH?
GOOD THINKIN', PRETTY GIRL!
DITCH HIM? I HAVEN'T EVEN SEEN HIM FOR AGES!
AWW, YOU PROBABLY SAY THE SAME THING TO ALL THE HANDSOME, GLAMOROUS WAR HEROES YOU MEET!
SAY! ARMY LIFE MUST AGREE WITH YOU! DON'T AIM THOSE EYES AT ME THAT WAY... THEY MIGHT BE LOADED!
LET'S FACE IT, GROUP... THIS CALLS FOR A KING-SIZE PARTY!
AS SOON AS PETE GETS HERE, WE'LL ARRANGE THE ZINGIEST WING-DING IN TOWN!
PARKER? YOU GOTTA BE KIDDIN'!
HE CAN EMPTY A ROOM JUST BY ENTERING IT!
C'MON, FLASH... PETE'S A GOOD EGG, AND YOU KNOW IT!
AH HA! GWEN BRAIN-WASHED YOU, TOO!
BUT, AT THIS VERY MOMENT, THE LAST THING ON PETER PARKER'S MIND IS WHETHER OR NOT FLASH THOMPSON THINKS HE'S A GOOD EGG!
YOU WON'T GET A CHANCE TO HIT ME WITH THAT SLEEP GAS OF YOURS AGAIN!
NOT IF I CLOG YOUR STICK PIN WITH A GLOB OF WEB FLUID!
HE GRABBED MY WRISTS! HIS HANDS ARE LIKE LIVING VISES!
I WON'T NEED ANY SLEEP GAS THIS TIME!
I'LL FINISH YOU OFF FOR GOOD... WITH MY OWN BARE HANDS!

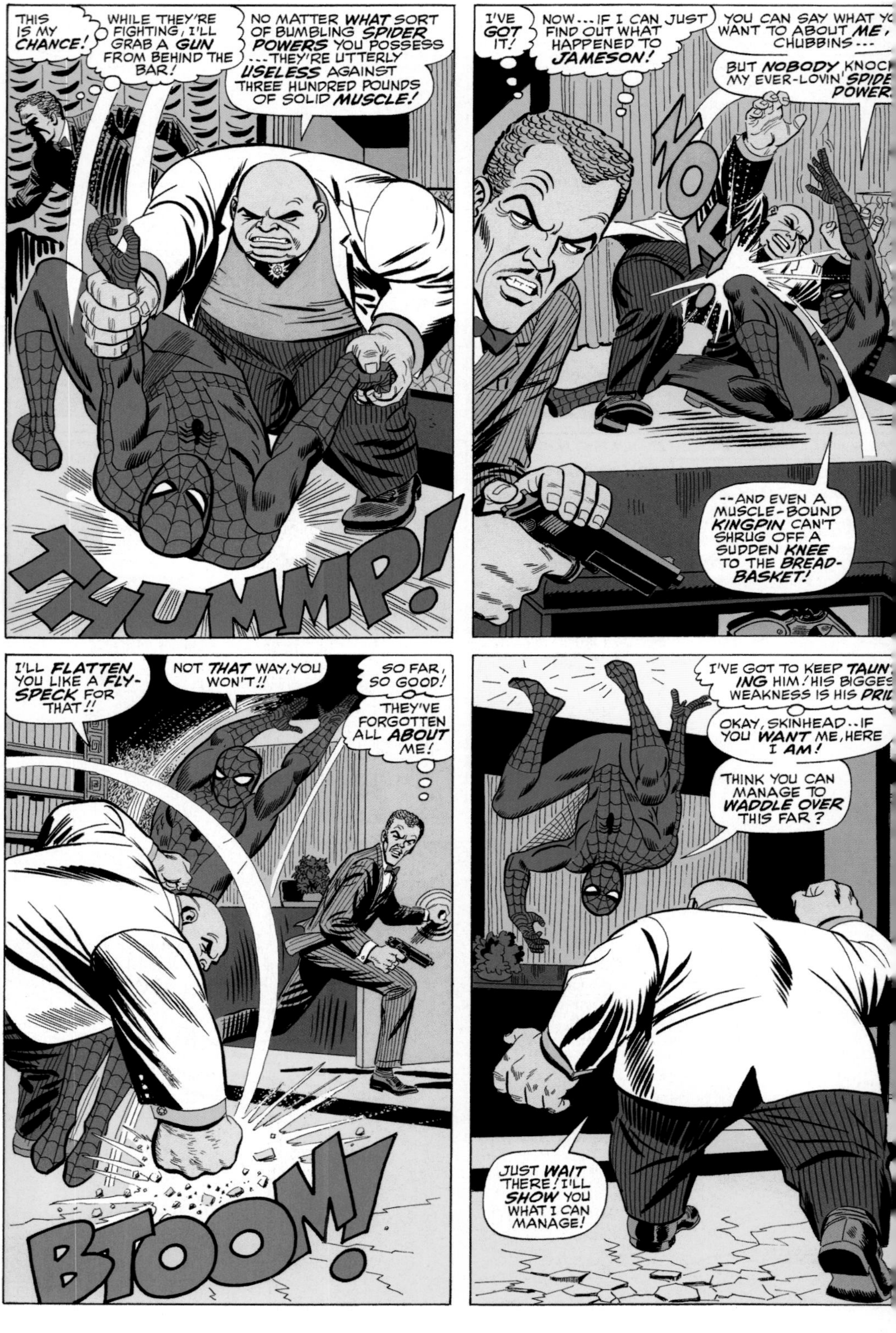
THIS IS MY CHANCE!
WHILE THEY'RE FIGHTING, I'LL GRAB A GUN FROM BEHIND THE BAR!
NO MATTER WHAT SORT OF BUMBLING SPIDER POWERS YOU POSSESS ...THEY'RE UTTERLY USELESS AGAINST THREE HUNDRED POUNDS OF SOLID MUSCLE!
THUMMP!
I'VE GOT IT!
NOW... IF I CAN JUST FIND OUT WHAT HAPPENED TO JAMESON!
YOU CAN SAY WHAT YO
WANT TO ABOUT ME, CHUBBINS---
BUT NOBODY KNOCK
MY EVER-LOVIN' SPIDE
POWER
WOK!
--AND EVEN A MUSCLE-BOUND KINGPIN CAN'T SHRUG OFF A SUDDEN KNEE TO THE BREAD-BASKET!
I'LL FLATTEN YOU LIKE A FLY-SPECK FOR THAT!!
NOT THAT WAY, YOU WON'T!!
SO FAR, SO GOOD!
THEY'VE FORGOTTEN ALL ABOUT ME!
BTOOM!
I'VE GOT TO KEEP TAUN
ING HIM! HIS BIGGES
WEAKNESS IS HIS PRID
OKAY, SKINHEAD..IF YOU WANT ME, HERE I AM!
THINK YOU CAN MANAGE TO WADDLE OVER THIS FAR?
JUST WAIT THERE! I'LL SHOW YOU WHAT I CAN MANAGE!

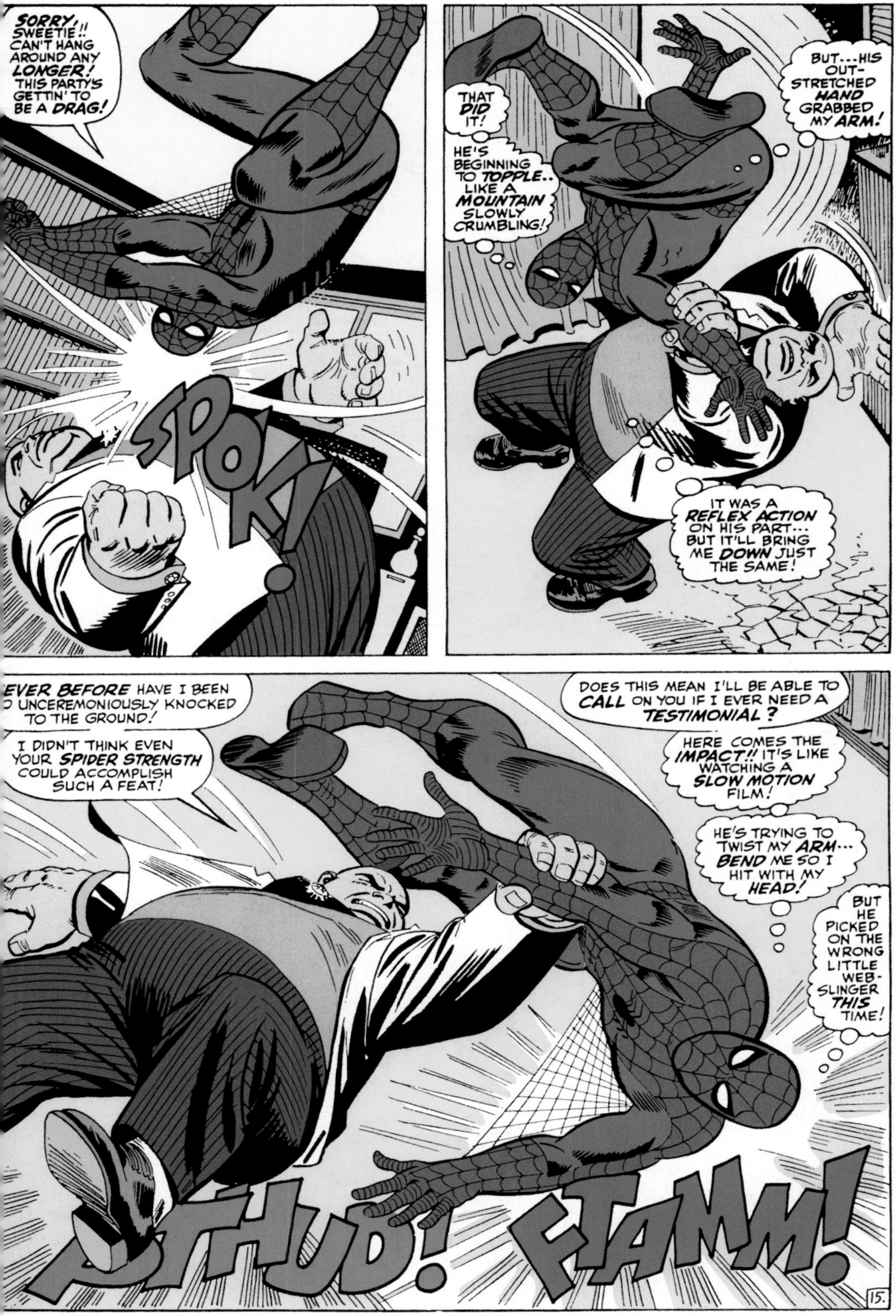
SORRY, SWEETIE!! CAN'T HANG AROUND ANY LONGER! THIS PARTY'S GETTIN' TO BE A DRAG!
SPOK!
THAT DID IT!
HE'S BEGINNING TO TOPPLE.. LIKE A MOUNTAIN SLOWLY CRUMBLING!
BUT---HIS OUT-STRETCHED HAND GRABBED MY ARM!
IT WAS A REFLEX ACTION ON HIS PART... BUT IT'LL BRING ME DOWN JUST THE SAME!
EVER BEFORE HAVE I BEEN O UNCEREMONIOUSLY KNOCKED TO THE GROUND!
I DIDN'T THINK EVEN YOUR SPIDER STRENGTH COULD ACCOMPLISH SUCH A FEAT!
DOES THIS MEAN I'LL BE ABLE TO CALL ON YOU IF I EVER NEED A TESTIMONIAL?
HERE COMES THE IMPACT!! IT'S LIKE WATCHING A SLOW MOTION FILM!
HE'S TRYING TO TWIST MY ARM... BEND ME SO I HIT WITH MY HEAD!
BUT HE PICKED ON THE WRONG LITTLE WEB-SLINGER THIS TIME!
THUD! FTAMM!

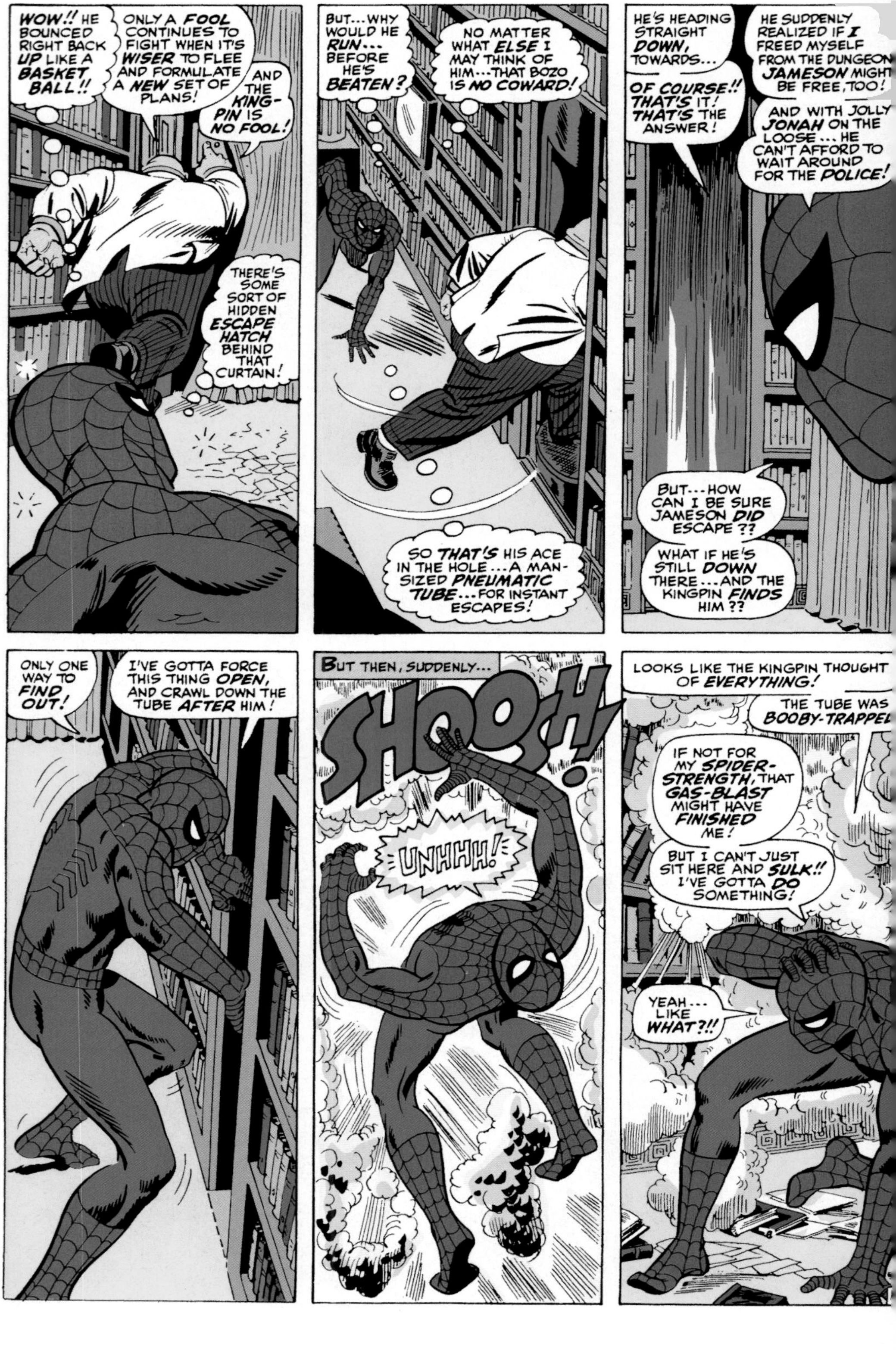
WOW!! HE BOUNCED RIGHT BACK UP LIKE A BASKET BALL!!
ONLY A FOOL CONTINUES TO FIGHT WHEN IT'S WISER TO FLEE AND FORMULATE A NEW SET OF PLANS!
AND THE KING-PIN IS NO FOOL!
THERE'S SOME SORT OF HIDDEN ESCAPE HATCH BEHIND THAT CURTAIN!
BUT...WHY WOULD HE RUN... BEFORE HE'S BEATEN?
NO MATTER WHAT ELSE I MAY THINK OF HIM...THAT BOZO IS NO COWARD!
SO THAT'S HIS ACE IN THE HOLE...A MAN-SIZED PNEUMATIC TUBE...FOR INSTANT ESCAPES!
HE'S HEADING STRAIGHT DOWN, TOWARDS...
OF COURSE!! THAT'S IT! THAT'S THE ANSWER!
HE SUDDENLY REALIZED IF I FREED MYSELF FROM THE DUNGEON JAMESON MIGHT BE FREE, TOO!
AND WITH JOLLY JONAH ON THE LOOSE...HE CAN'T AFFORD TO WAIT AROUND FOR THE POLICE!
BUT...HOW CAN I BE SURE JAMESON DID ESCAPE??
WHAT IF HE'S STILL DOWN THERE...AND THE KINGPIN FINDS HIM??
ONLY ONE WAY TO FIND OUT!
I'VE GOTTA FORCE THIS THING OPEN, AND CRAWL DOWN THE TUBE AFTER HIM!
BUT THEN, SUDDENLY...
SHOOSH!
UNHHH!
LOOKS LIKE THE KINGPIN THOUGHT OF EVERYTHING!
THE TUBE WAS BOOBY-TRAPPED
IF NOT FOR MY SPIDER-STRENGTH, THAT GAS-BLAST MIGHT HAVE FINISHED ME!
BUT I CAN'T JUST SIT HERE AND SULK!! I'VE GOTTA DO SOMETHING!
YEAH... LIKE WHAT?!!

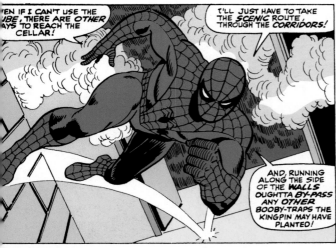

EN IF I CAN'T USE THE **UBE**, THERE ARE **OTHER** AYS TO REACH THE **CELLAR!**

I'LL JUST HAVE TO TAKE THE **SCENIC** ROUTE, THROUGH THE **CORRIDORS!**

AND, RUNNING ALONG THE SIDE OF THE **WALLS** OUGHTTA **BY-PASS** ANY **OTHER** BOOBY-TRAPS THE **KINGPIN** MAY HAVE PLANTED!

WHILE, MOVING SOMEWHAT **SLOWER**, A SHORT DISTANCE AHEAD---

I THOUGHT I HEARD A **GROAN**... FROM AROUND THAT CORNER!

IF IT'S **JAMESON**.. IT MEANS HE'S STILL **ALIVE!**

PLINK!

PLUNK!

PLINK...!

OHHHH... MY **HEAD**..!

WHERE AM I? ...WHAT **HAPPENED**!!

WHO'S POUNDING ON ME--- WITH A **SLEDGE HAMMER**--?

I **REMEMBER** NOW!! THE **KINGPIN**... HE TRIED TO **KILL** ME!!

AND THEN... **SPIDER-MAN** THREATENED ME!!

EVEN **FOSWELL** TURNED AGAINST.. **WAIT!!**

WHAT'S THIS..ON MY HEAD..?

IT'S **WET**!!

IT MUST BE **BLOOD!!**

I'M **WOUNDED!!** I'M **DYING!!**

HELP!! SOMEONE **HELLLP!**

OOK! IT'S AMESON!

WE'RE IN **LUCK!** LET'S GET 'IM---!

THE **KINGPIN'S** GUNMEN! **NOOOO!**

HE SOUNDS **SCARED!**

IT **FIGGERS!**

THEY'VE GOT GUNS!

WHERE CAN I **RUN** ?? WHAT CAN I.. **HUH** ?!!

ANOTHER ONE !!

IT'S **FOSWELL!**

JAMESON!! TURN THIS CORNER..**QUICK!!**

YOU'RE THE ONLY ONE WHO EVER **HELPED** ME.. OR GAVE ME A SECOND **CHANCE**--!

I DIDN'T WANT **YOU** TO BE HURT!

I'LL HOLD 'EM OFF FOR YOU---**SOMEHOW!**

HURRY, MAN... **HURRY!**

17.

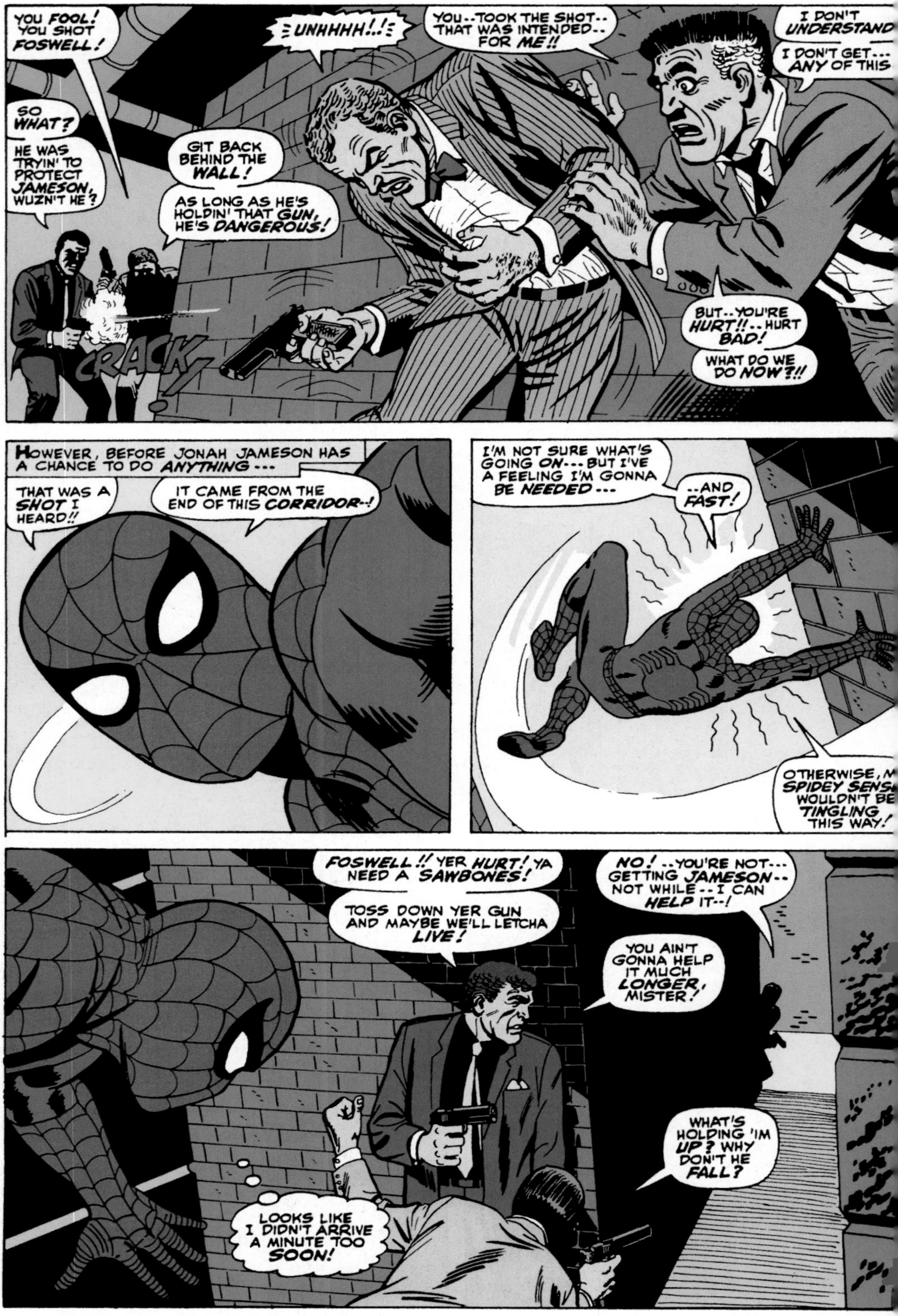
YOU FOOL! YOU SHOT FOSWELL!
UNHHHH!!!
YOU--TOOK THE SHOT-- THAT WAS INTENDED-- FOR ME!!
I DON'T UNDERSTAND
I DON'T GET--- ANY OF THIS
SO WHAT?
HE WAS TRYIN' TO PROTECT JAMESON, WUZN'T HE?
GIT BACK BEHIND THE WALL!
AS LONG AS HE'S HOLDIN' THAT GUN, HE'S DANGEROUS!
CRACK
BUT--YOU'RE HURT!!--HURT BAD!
WHAT DO WE DO NOW?!!
HOWEVER, BEFORE JONAH JAMESON HAS A CHANCE TO DO ANYTHING---
THAT WAS A SHOT I HEARD!!
IT CAME FROM THE END OF THIS CORRIDOR--!
I'M NOT SURE WHAT'S GOING ON--- BUT I'VE A FEELING I'M GONNA BE NEEDED---
--AND FAST!
OTHERWISE, M SPIDEY SENS WOULDN'T BE TINGLING THIS WAY!
FOSWELL!! YER HURT! YA NEED A SAWBONES!
TOSS DOWN YER GUN AND MAYBE WE'LL LETCHA LIVE!
NO! --YOU'RE NOT--- GETTING JAMESON-- NOT WHILE--I CAN HELP IT--!
YOU AIN'T GONNA HELP IT MUCH LONGER, MISTER!
WHAT'S HOLDING 'IM UP? WHY DON'T HE FALL?
LOOKS LIKE I DIDN'T ARRIVE A MINUTE TOO SOON!

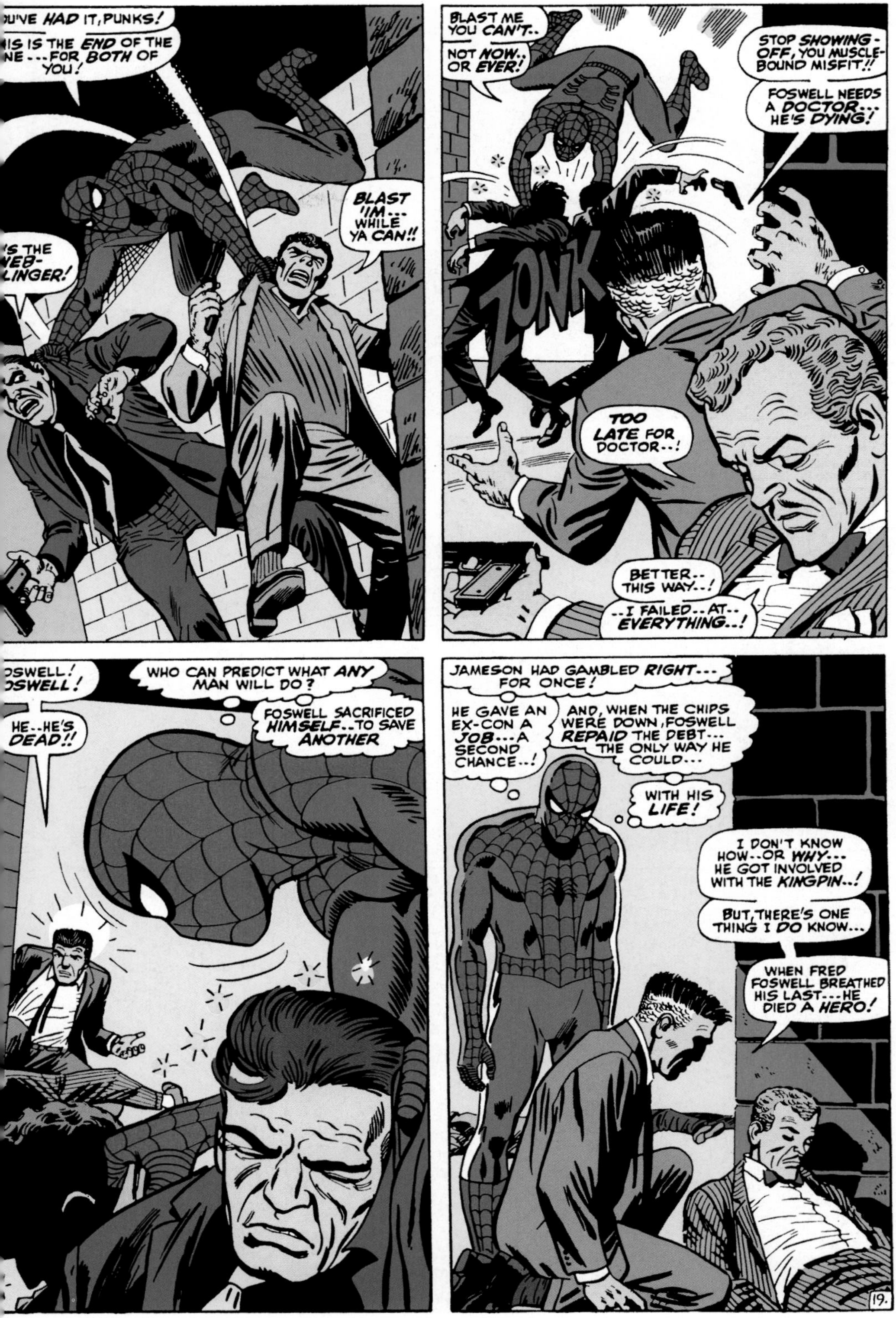

OU'VE HAD IT, PUNKS!
HIS IS THE END OF THE NE---FOR BOTH OF YOU!
'S THE WEB-LINGER!
BLAST 'IM... WHILE YA CAN!!
BLAST ME YOU CAN'T..
NOT NOW.. OR EVER!
STOP SHOWING-OFF, YOU MUSCLE-BOUND MISFIT!!
FOSWELL NEEDS A DOCTOR... HE'S DYING!
ZONK
TOO LATE FOR DOCTOR--!
BETTER.. THIS WAY--!
--I FAILED--AT-- EVERYTHING--!
OSWELL! OSWELL!
HE--HE'S DEAD!!
WHO CAN PREDICT WHAT ANY MAN WILL DO?
FOSWELL SACRIFICED HIMSELF..TO SAVE ANOTHER
JAMESON HAD GAMBLED RIGHT--- FOR ONCE!
HE GAVE AN EX-CON A JOB---A SECOND CHANCE--!
AND, WHEN THE CHIPS WERE DOWN, FOSWELL REPAID THE DEBT--- THE ONLY WAY HE COULD---
WITH HIS LIFE!
I DON'T KNOW HOW--OR WHY--- HE GOT INVOLVED WITH THE KINGPIN--!
BUT, THERE'S ONE THING I DO KNOW...
WHEN FRED FOSWELL BREATHED HIS LAST---HE DIED A HERO!
19.

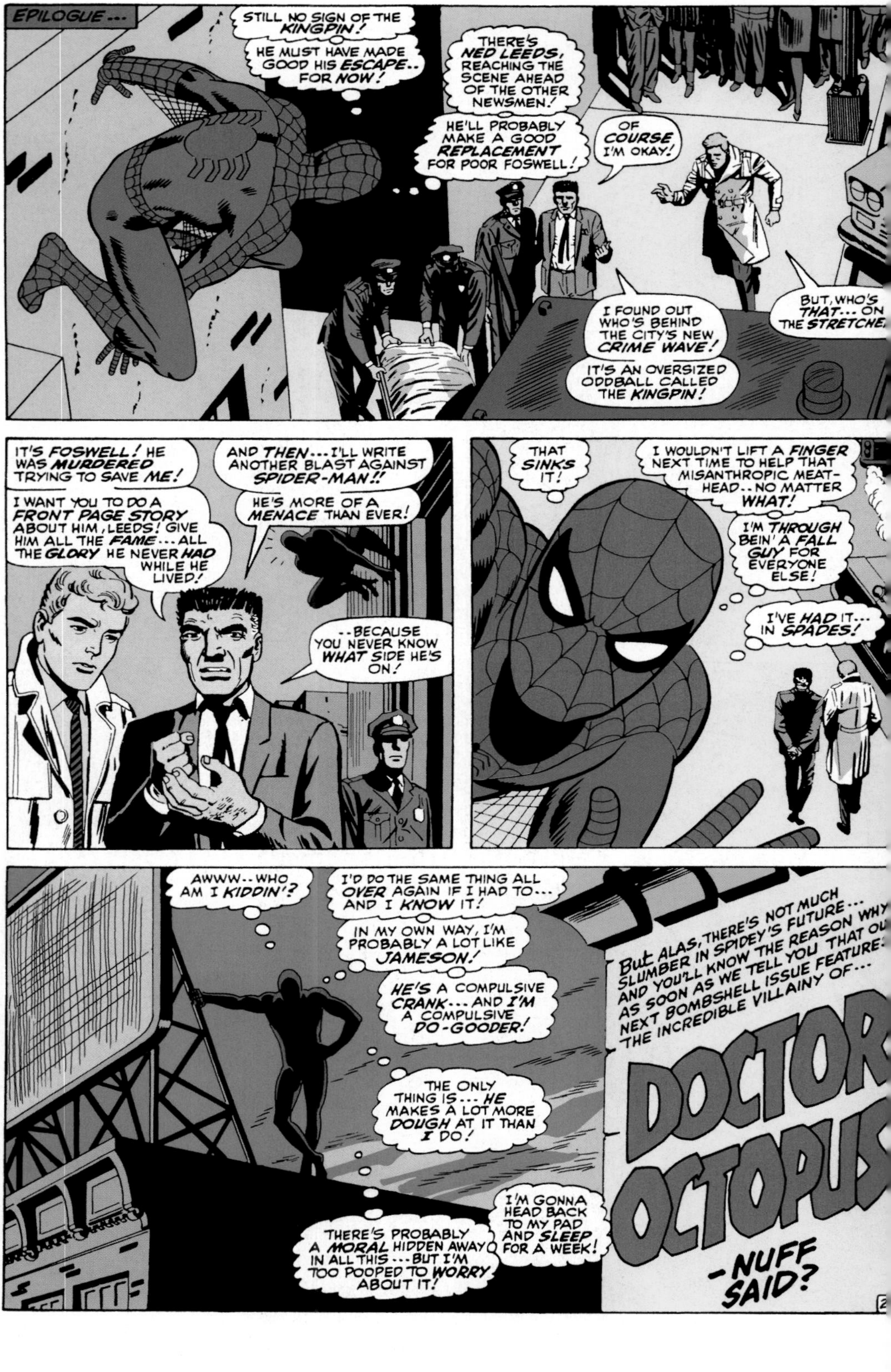
EPILOGUE ...
STILL NO SIGN OF THE KINGPIN!
HE MUST HAVE MADE GOOD HIS ESCAPE.. FOR NOW!
THERE'S NED LEEDS, REACHING THE SCENE AHEAD OF THE OTHER NEWSMEN!
HE'LL PROBABLY MAKE A GOOD REPLACEMENT FOR POOR FOSWELL!
OF COURSE I'M OKAY!
I FOUND OUT WHO'S BEHIND THE CITY'S NEW CRIME WAVE!
IT'S AN OVERSIZED ODDBALL CALLED THE KINGPIN!
BUT, WHO'S THAT... ON THE STRETCHE
IT'S FOSWELL! HE WAS MURDERED TRYING TO SAVE ME!
I WANT YOU TO DO A FRONT PAGE STORY ABOUT HIM, LEEDS! GIVE HIM ALL THE FAME... ALL THE GLORY HE NEVER HAD WHILE HE LIVED!
AND THEN... I'LL WRITE ANOTHER BLAST AGAINST SPIDER-MAN!!
HE'S MORE OF A MENACE THAN EVER!
--BECAUSE YOU NEVER KNOW WHAT SIDE HE'S ON!
THAT SINKS IT!
I WOULDN'T LIFT A FINGER NEXT TIME TO HELP THAT MISANTHROPIC MEAT-HEAD.. NO MATTER WHAT!
I'M THROUGH BEIN' A FALL GUY FOR EVERYONE ELSE!
I'VE HAD IT... IN SPADES!
AWWW.. WHO AM I KIDDIN'?
I'D DO THE SAME THING ALL OVER AGAIN IF I HAD TO... AND I KNOW IT!
IN MY OWN WAY, I'M PROBABLY A LOT LIKE JAMESON!
HE'S A COMPULSIVE CRANK... AND I'M A COMPULSIVE DO-GOODER!
THE ONLY THING IS... HE MAKES A LOT MORE DOUGH AT IT THAN I DO!
THERE'S PROBABLY A MORAL HIDDEN AWAY IN ALL THIS ... BUT I'M TOO POOPED TO WORRY ABOUT IT!
I'M GONNA HEAD BACK TO MY PAD AND SLEEP FOR A WEEK!
But ALAS, THERE'S NOT MUCH SLUMBER IN SPIDEY'S FUTURE... AND YOU'LL KNOW THE REASON WHY AS SOON AS WE TELL YOU THAT OU NEXT BOMBSHELL ISSUE FEATURE: THE INCREDIBLE VILLAINY OF...
DOCTOR OCTOPUS
-NUFF SAID?

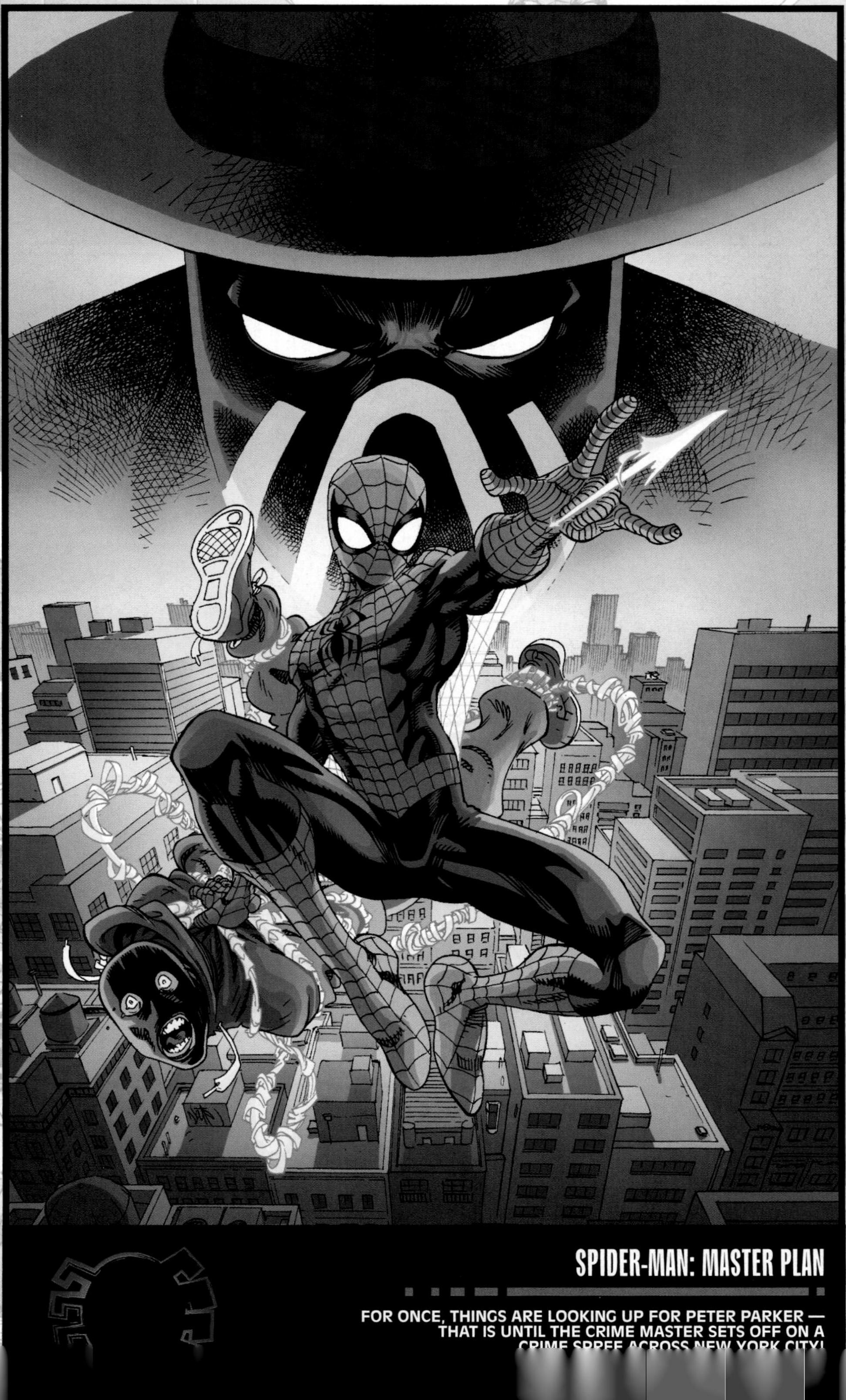
SPIDER-MAN: MASTER PLAN
FOR ONCE, THINGS ARE LOOKING UP FOR PETER PARKER — THAT IS UNTIL THE CRIME MASTER SETS OFF ON A CRIME SPREE ACROSS NEW YORK CITY!

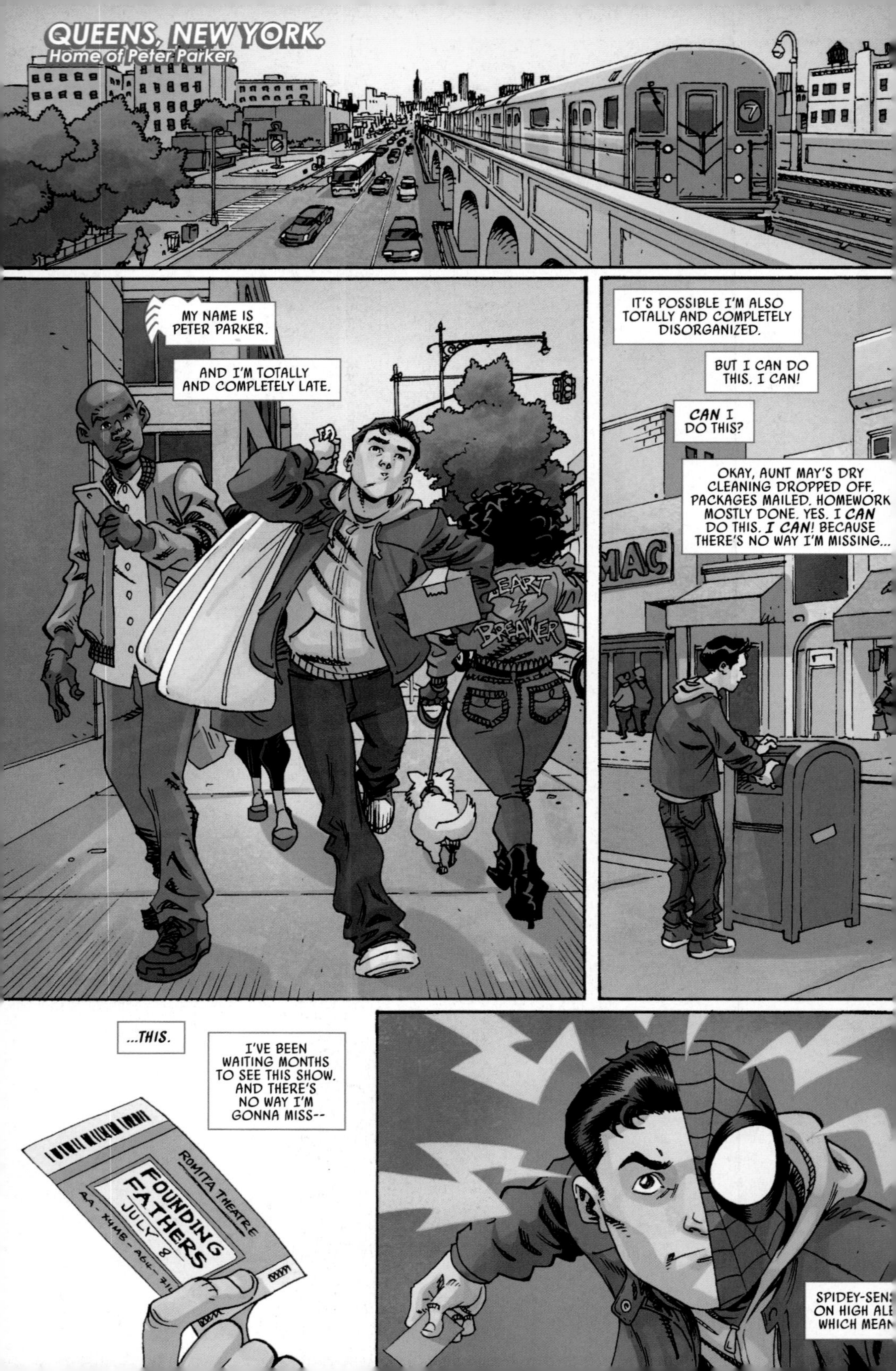
QUEENS, NEW YORK.
Home of Peter Parker.
MY NAME IS PETER PARKER.
AND I'M TOTALLY AND COMPLETELY LATE.
HEART BREAKER
IT'S POSSIBLE I'M ALSO TOTALLY AND COMPLETELY DISORGANIZED.
BUT I CAN DO THIS. I CAN!
CAN I DO THIS?
OKAY, AUNT MAY'S DRY CLEANING DROPPED OFF. PACKAGES MAILED. HOMEWORK MOSTLY DONE. YES. I CAN DO THIS. I CAN! BECAUSE THERE'S NO WAY I'M MISSING...
...THIS.
I'VE BEEN WAITING MONTHS TO SEE THIS SHOW. AND THERE'S NO WAY I'M GONNA MISS--
ROMITA THEATRE
FOUNDING FATHERS
JULY 8
SPIDEY-SENS
ON HIGH ALE
WHICH MEAN

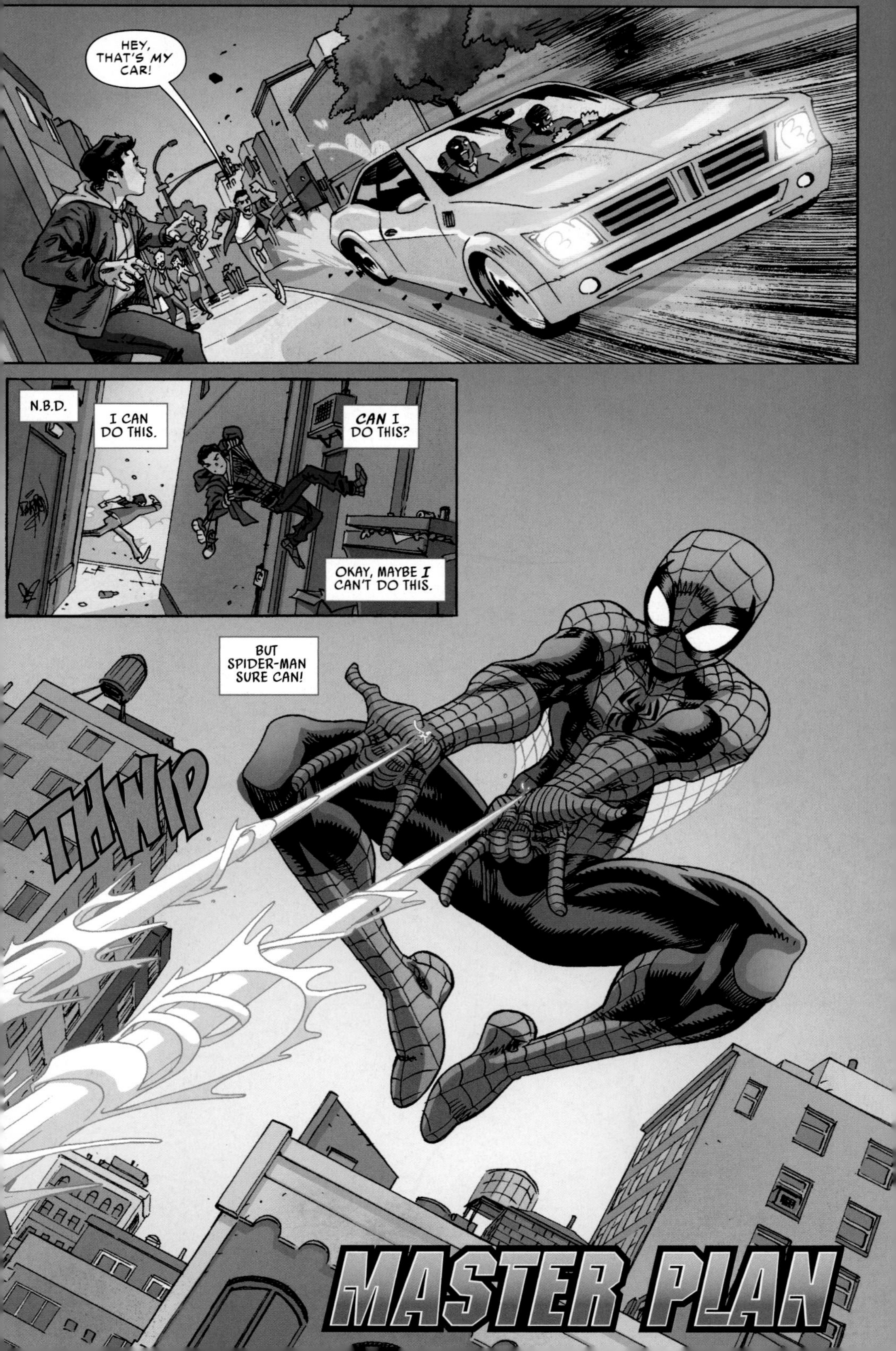

HEY, THAT'S MY CAR!
N.B.D.
I CAN DO THIS.
CAN I DO THIS?
OKAY, MAYBE I CAN'T DO THIS.
BUT SPIDER-MAN SURE CAN!
THWIP
MASTER PLAN

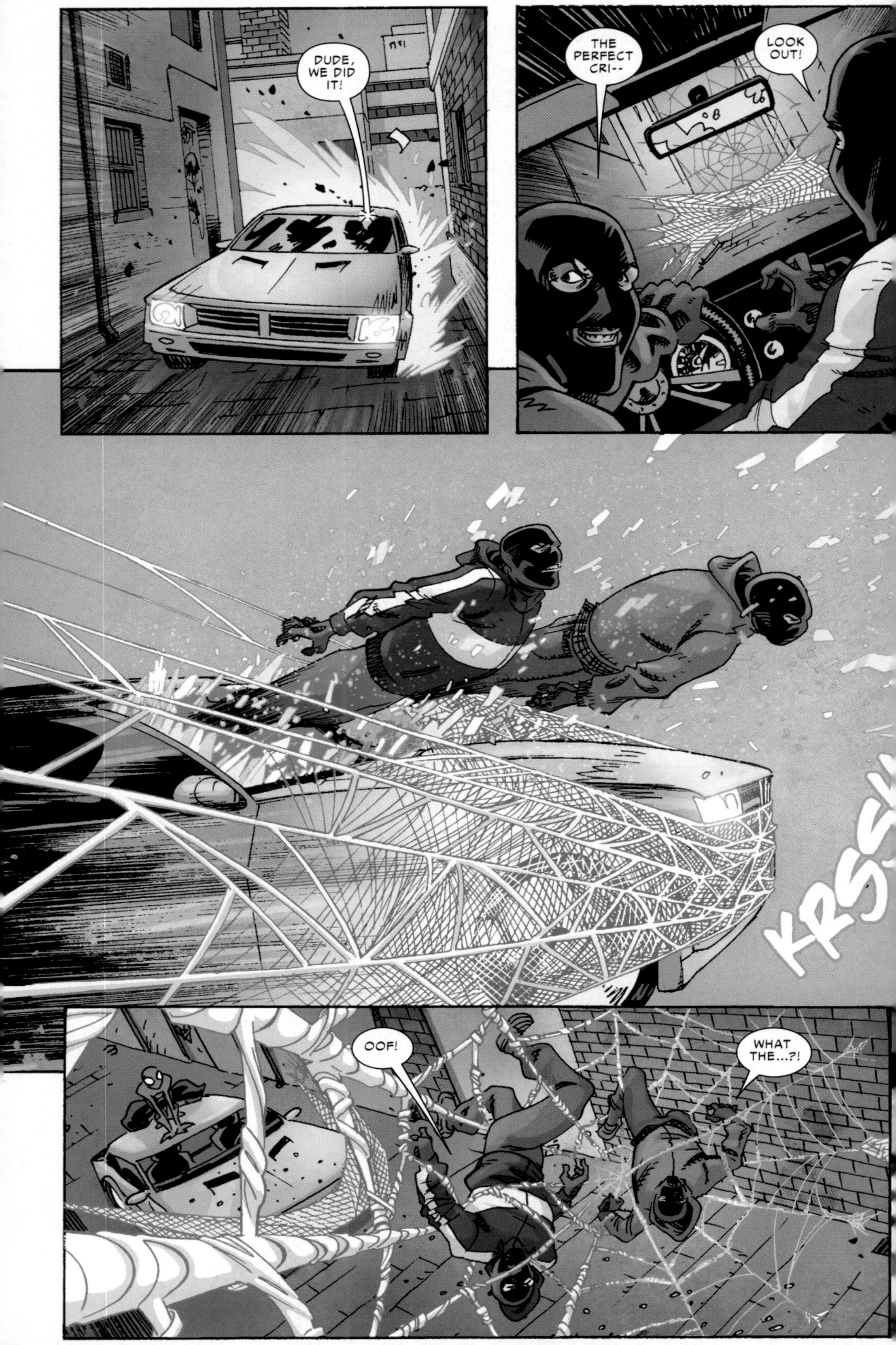
DUDE, WE DID IT!
THE PERFECT CRI--
LOOK OUT!
KRSSH
OOF!
WHAT THE...?!

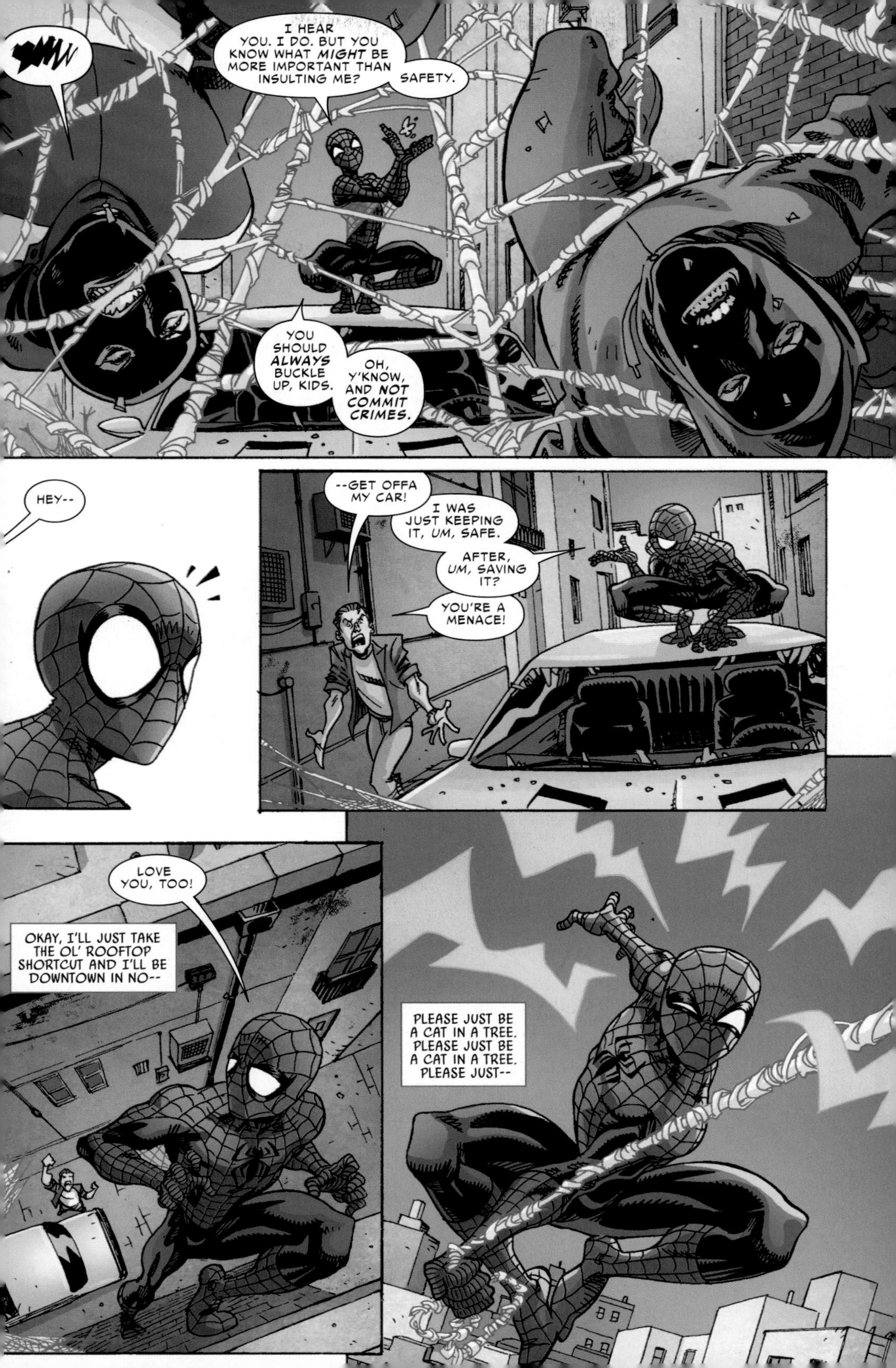

I HEAR YOU. I DO. BUT YOU KNOW WHAT MIGHT BE MORE IMPORTANT THAN INSULTING ME?
SAFETY.
YOU SHOULD ALWAYS BUCKLE UP, KIDS.
OH, Y'KNOW, AND NOT COMMIT CRIMES.
HEY--
--GET OFFA MY CAR!
I WAS JUST KEEPING IT, UM, SAFE.
AFTER, UM, SAVING IT?
YOU'RE A MENACE!
LOVE YOU, TOO!
OKAY, I'LL JUST TAKE THE OL' ROOFTOP SHORTCUT AND I'LL BE DOWNTOWN IN NO--
PLEASE JUST BE A CAT IN A TREE. PLEASE JUST BE A CAT IN A TREE. PLEASE JUST--

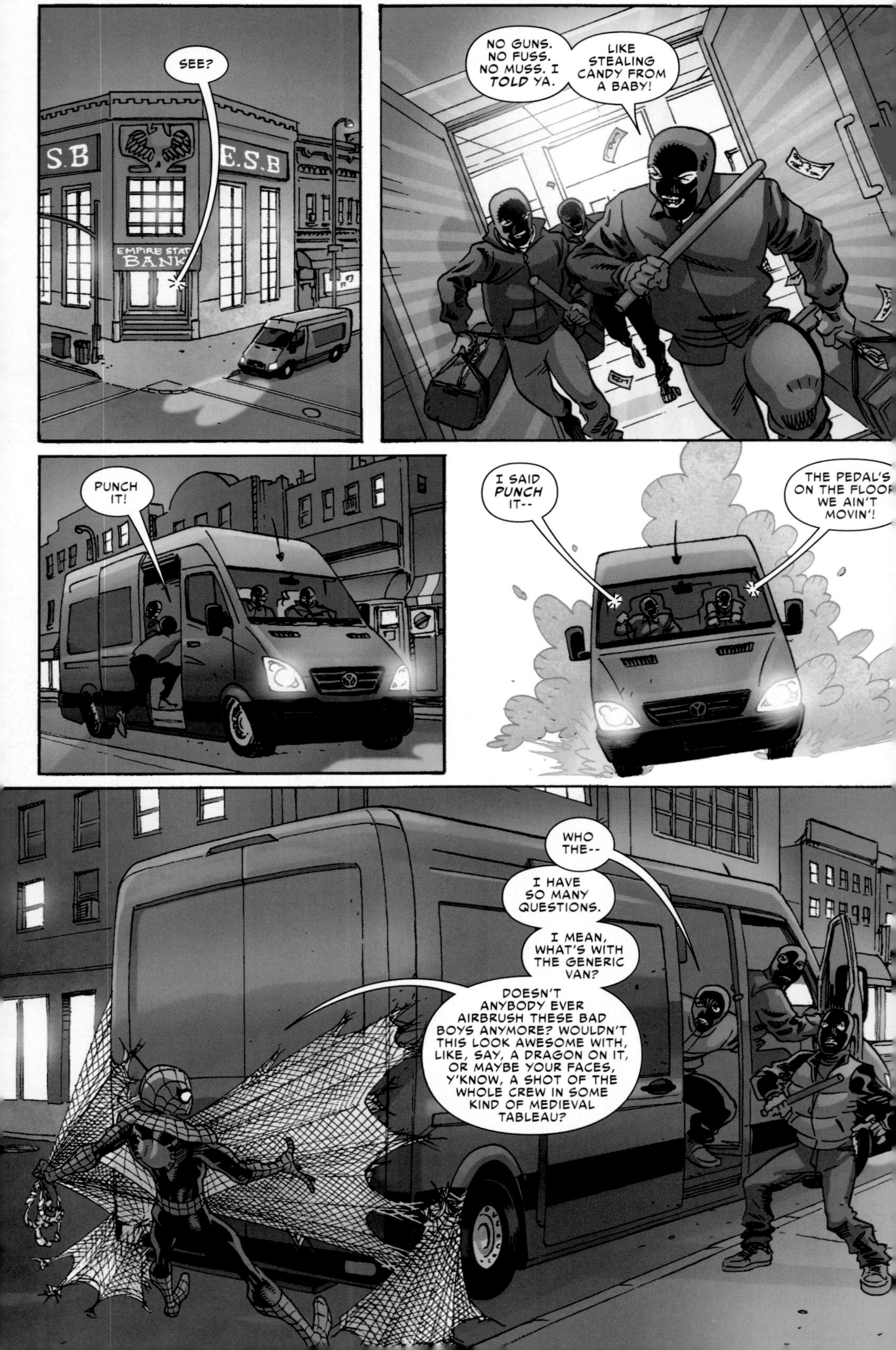
S.B
E.S.B
EMPIRE STAT
BANK
SEE?
NO GUNS. NO FUSS. NO MUSS. I *TOLD* YA.
LIKE STEALING CANDY FROM A BABY!
PUNCH IT!
I SAID *PUNCH* IT--
THE PEDAL'S ON THE FLOOR WE AIN'T MOVIN'!
WHO THE--
I HAVE SO MANY QUESTIONS.
I MEAN, WHAT'S WITH THE GENERIC VAN?
DOESN'T ANYBODY EVER AIRBRUSH THESE BAD BOYS ANYMORE? WOULDN'T THIS LOOK AWESOME WITH, LIKE, SAY, A DRAGON ON IT, OR MAYBE YOUR FACES, Y'KNOW, A SHOT OF THE WHOLE CREW IN SOME KIND OF MEDIEVAL TABLEAU?

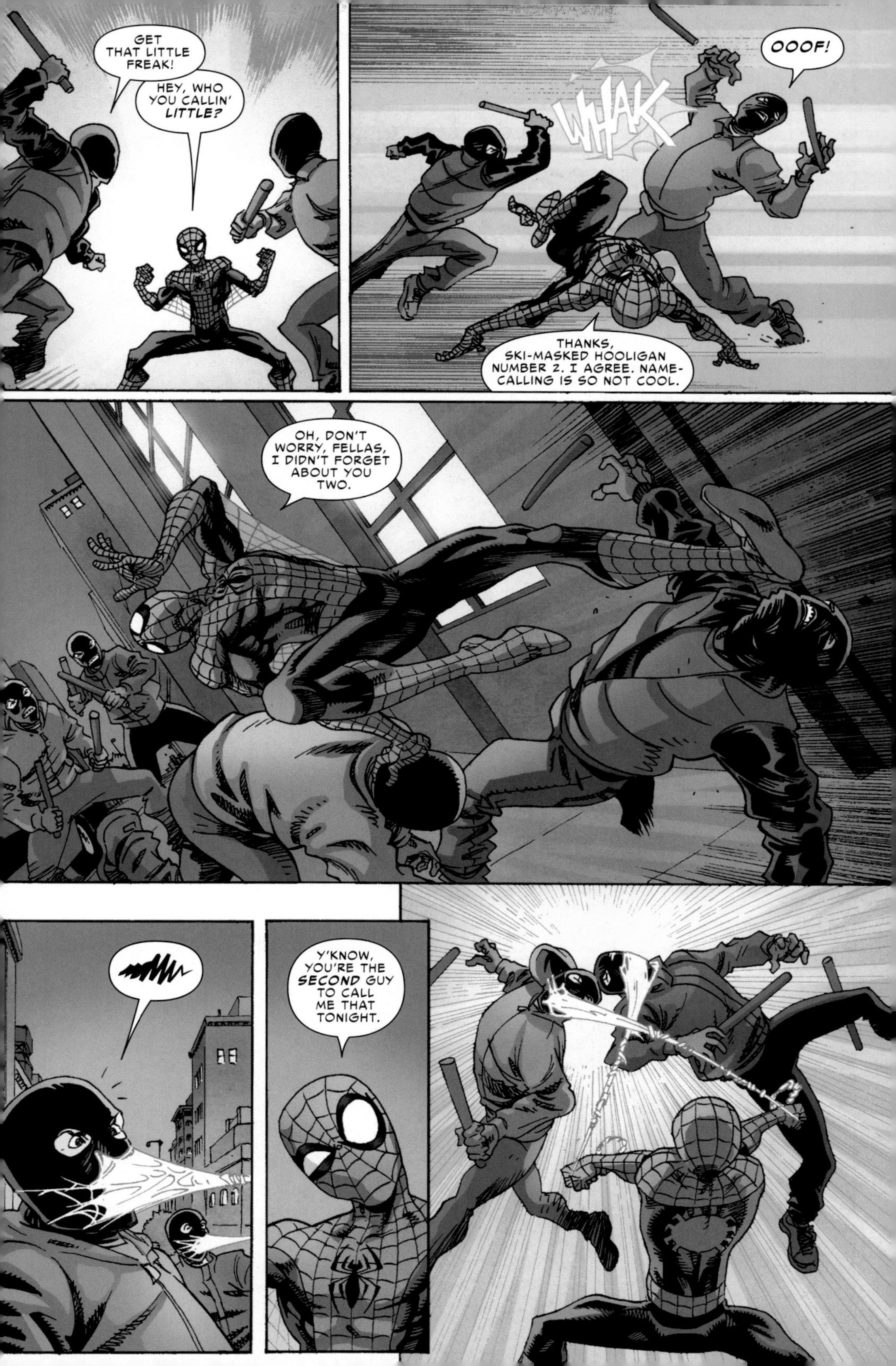
GET THAT LITTLE FREAK!
HEY, WHO YOU CALLIN' *LITTLE?*
WHAK
OOOF!
THANKS, SKI-MASKED HOOLIGAN NUMBER 2. I AGREE. NAME-CALLING IS SO NOT COOL.
OH, DON'T WORRY, FELLAS, I DIDN'T FORGET ABOUT YOU TWO.
Y'KNOW, YOU'RE THE ***SECOND*** GUY TO CALL ME THAT TONIGHT.

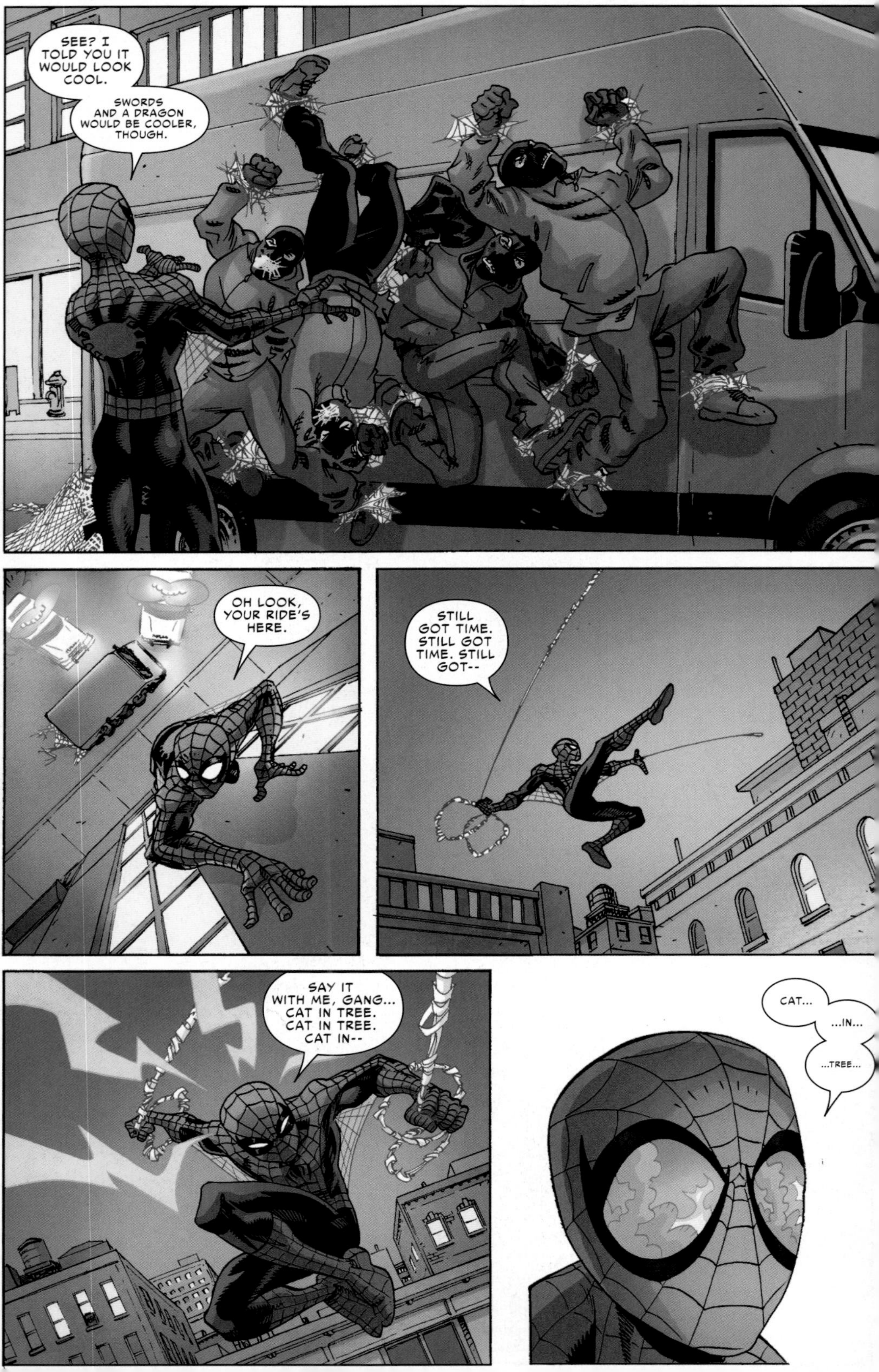
SEE? I TOLD YOU IT WOULD LOOK COOL.
SWORDS AND A DRAGON WOULD BE COOLER, THOUGH.
OH LOOK, YOUR RIDE'S HERE.
STILL GOT TIME. STILL GOT TIME. STILL GOT--
SAY IT WITH ME, GANG... CAT IN TREE. CAT IN TREE. CAT IN--
CAT...
...IN...
...TREE...

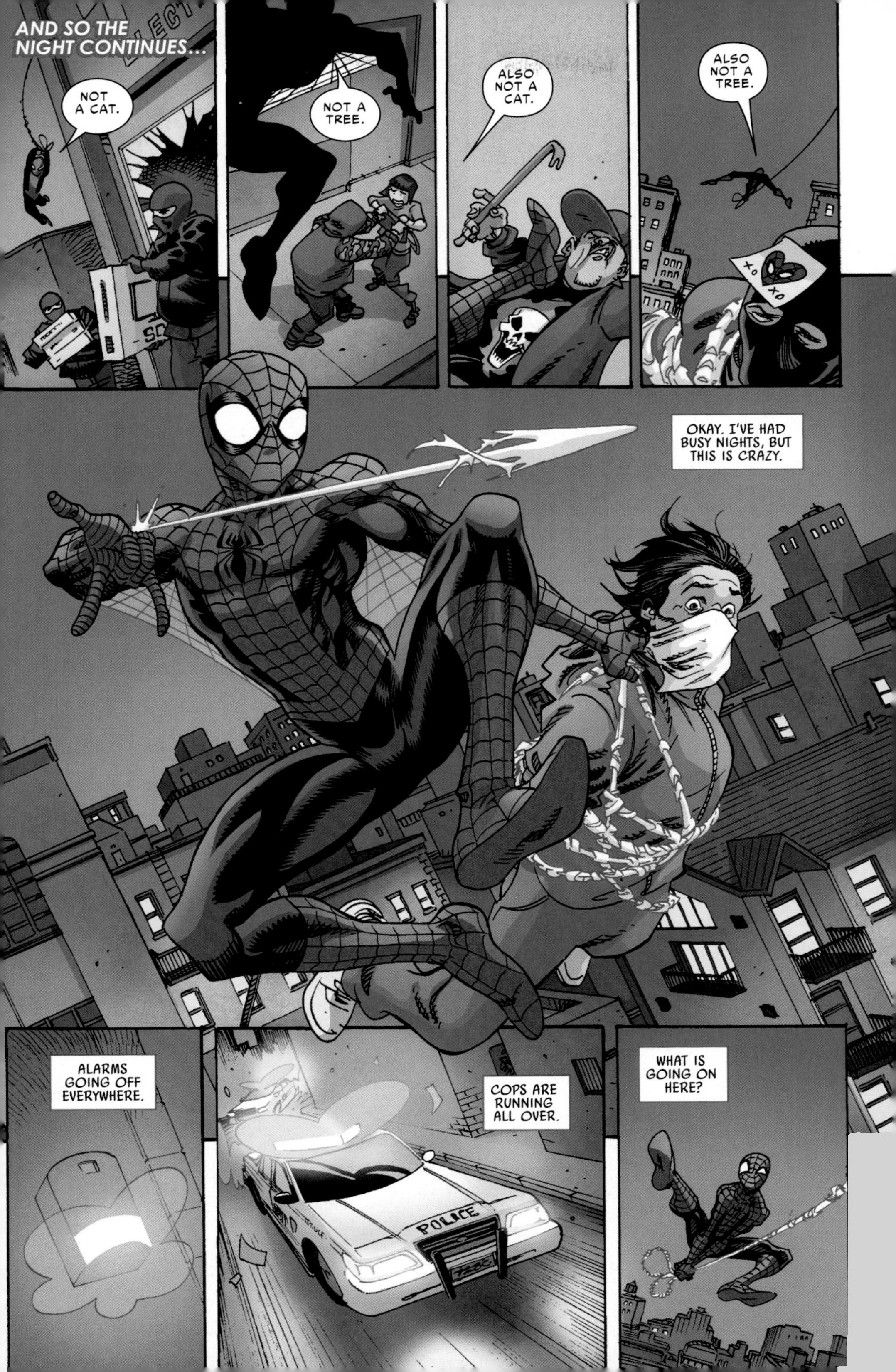
AND SO THE NIGHT CONTINUES...
NOT A CAT.
NOT A TREE.
ALSO NOT A CAT.
ALSO NOT A TREE.
OKAY. I'VE HAD BUSY NIGHTS, BUT THIS IS CRAZY.
ALARMS GOING OFF EVERYWHERE.
COPS ARE RUNNING ALL OVER.
POLICE
WHAT IS GOING ON HERE?

AS I WAS JUST SAYING: WHAT IS GOING ON HERE?

IS THERE A CRIME CONVENTION IN TOWN?

WAS THERE A SALE ON SKI MASKS?

WAIT. IS CRIMECON A THING?

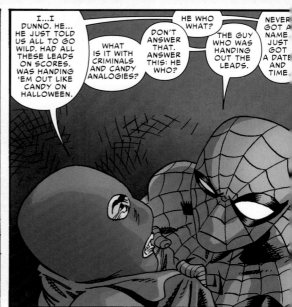

I...I DUNNO. HE... HE JUST TOLD US ALL TO GO WILD. HAD ALL THESE LEADS ON SCORES. WAS HANDING 'EM OUT LIKE CANDY ON HALLOWEEN.

WHAT IS IT WITH CRIMINALS AND CANDY ANALOGIES?

DON'T ANSWER THAT. ANSWER THIS: HE WHO?

HE WHO WHAT?

THE GUY WHO WAS HANDING OUT THE LEADS.

NEVER GOT A NAME. JUST GOT A DATE AND TIME.

LEMME GUESS: TODAY. NOW.

YOU GOT IT, YOU FILTHY

THWIP

COORDINATED ATTACKS. BUT THE ATTACKS ARE RANDOM. WHY IS THIS HAPPENING? AND WHO IS BEHIND IT?

OKAY, THIS VIEW ISN'T REALLY NARROWING IT DOWN FOR ME. SO, LET'S GET A CLOSER LOOK-SEE...

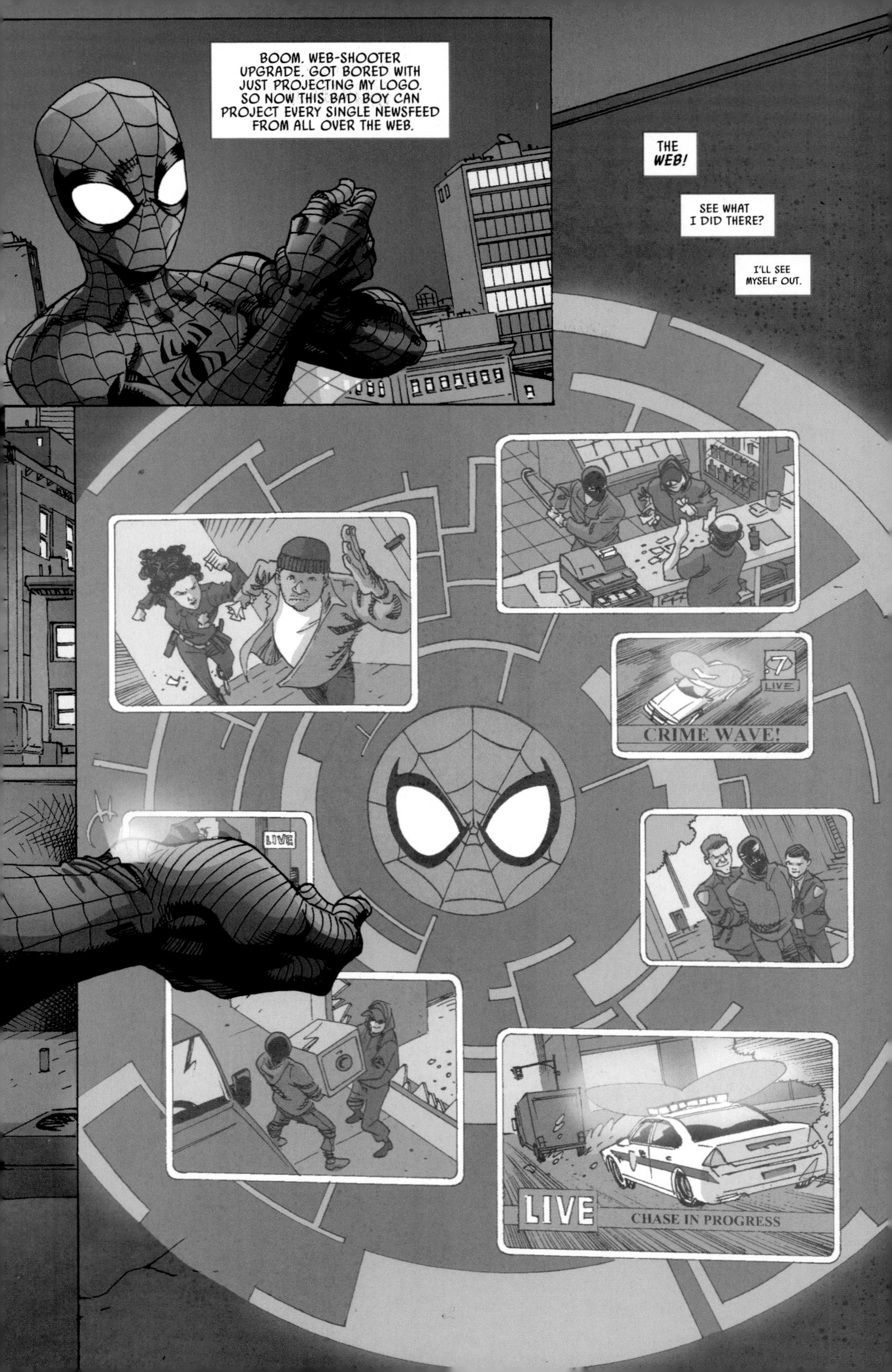
BOOM. WEB-SHOOTER UPGRADE. GOT BORED WITH JUST PROJECTING MY LOGO. SO NOW THIS BAD BOY CAN PROJECT EVERY SINGLE NEWSFEED FROM ALL OVER THE WEB.
THE *WEB!*
SEE WHAT I DID THERE?
I'LL SEE MYSELF OUT.
7
LIVE
CRIME WAVE!
LIVE
LIVE
CHASE IN PROGRESS

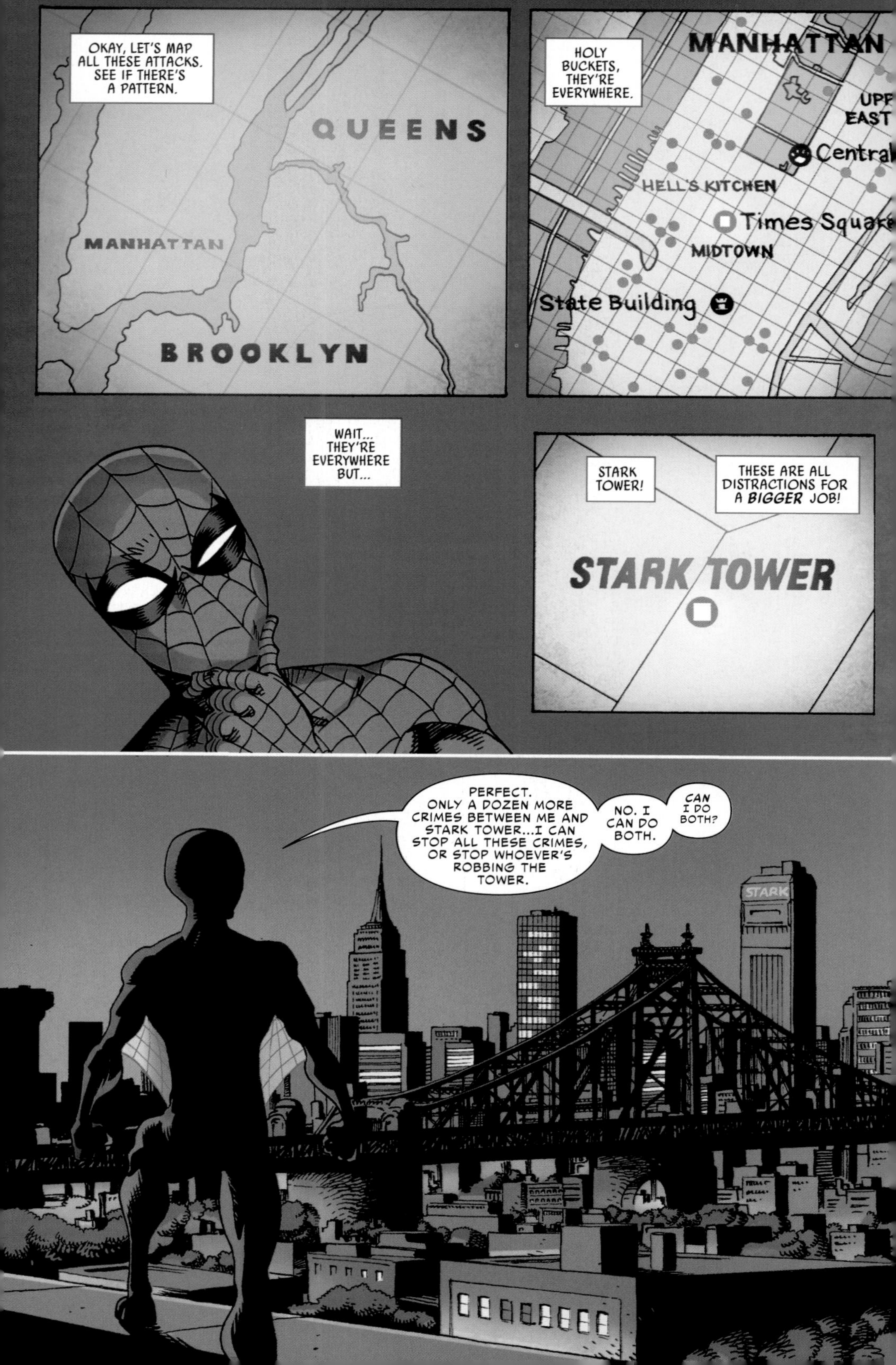
OKAY, LET'S MAP ALL THESE ATTACKS. SEE IF THERE'S A PATTERN.
QUEENS
MANHATTAN
BROOKLYN
HOLY BUCKETS, THEY'RE EVERYWHERE.
MANHATTAN
HELL'S KITCHEN
Times Square
MIDTOWN
State Building
WAIT... THEY'RE EVERYWHERE BUT...
STARK TOWER!
THESE ARE ALL DISTRACTIONS FOR A BIGGER JOB!
STARK TOWER
PERFECT. ONLY A DOZEN MORE CRIMES BETWEEN ME AND STARK TOWER...I CAN STOP ALL THESE CRIMES, OR STOP WHOEVER'S ROBBING THE TOWER.
NO. I CAN DO BOTH.
CAN I DO BOTH?
STARK

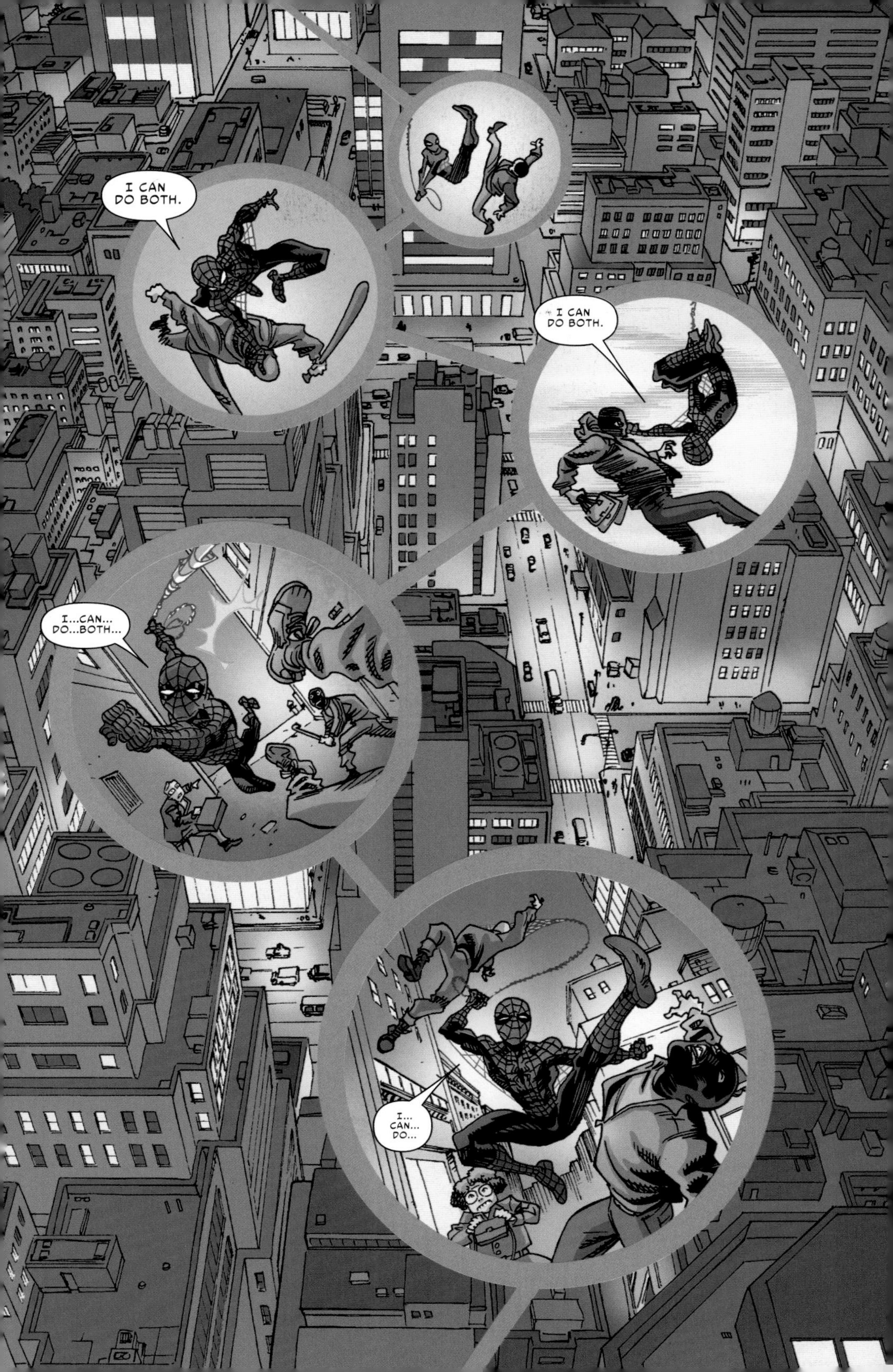
I CAN DO BOTH.
I CAN DO BOTH.
I...CAN... DO...BOTH...
I... CAN... DO...

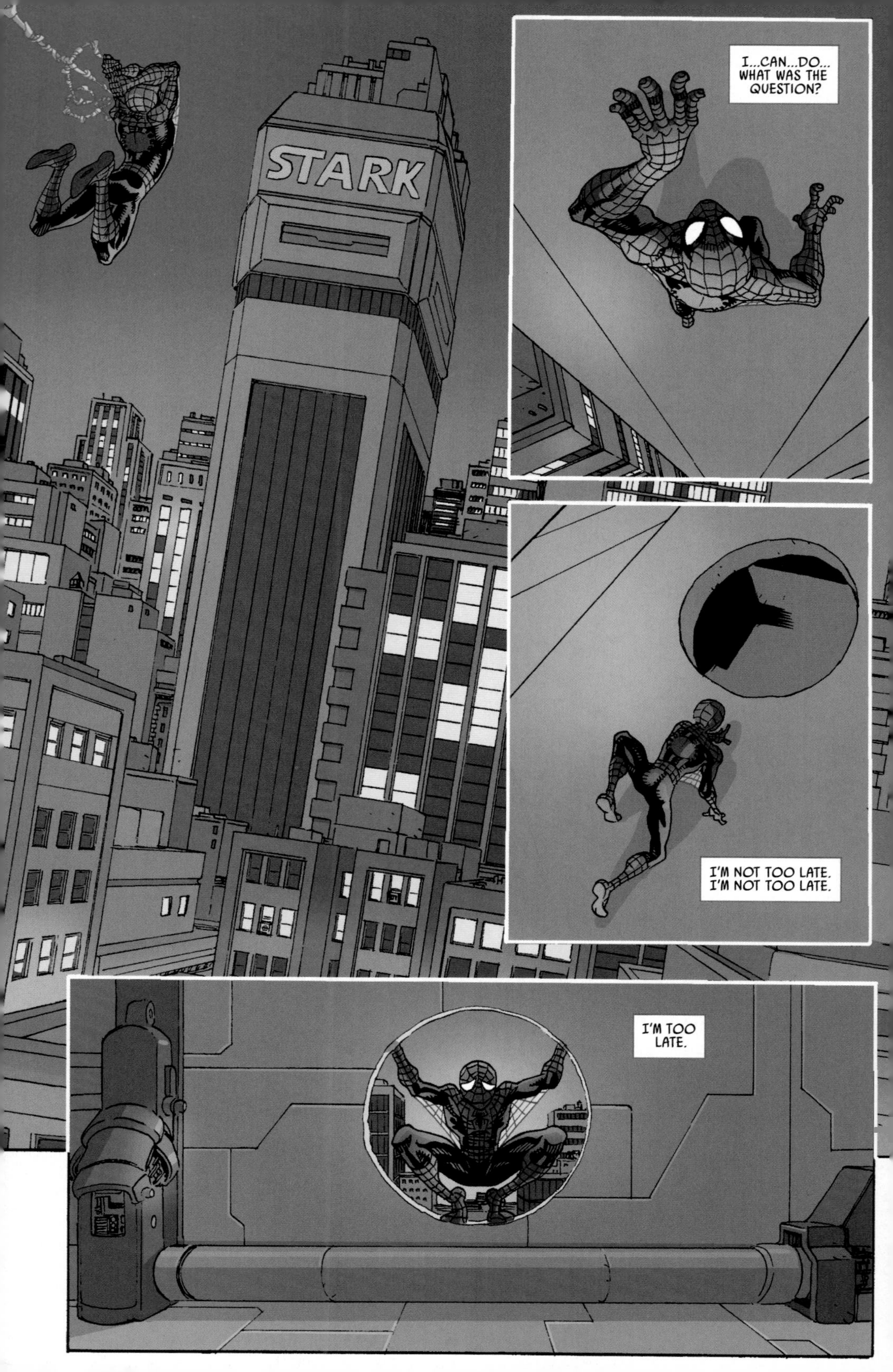
STARK
I...CAN...DO... WHAT WAS THE QUESTION?
I'M NOT TOO LATE. I'M NOT TOO LATE.
I'M TOO LATE.

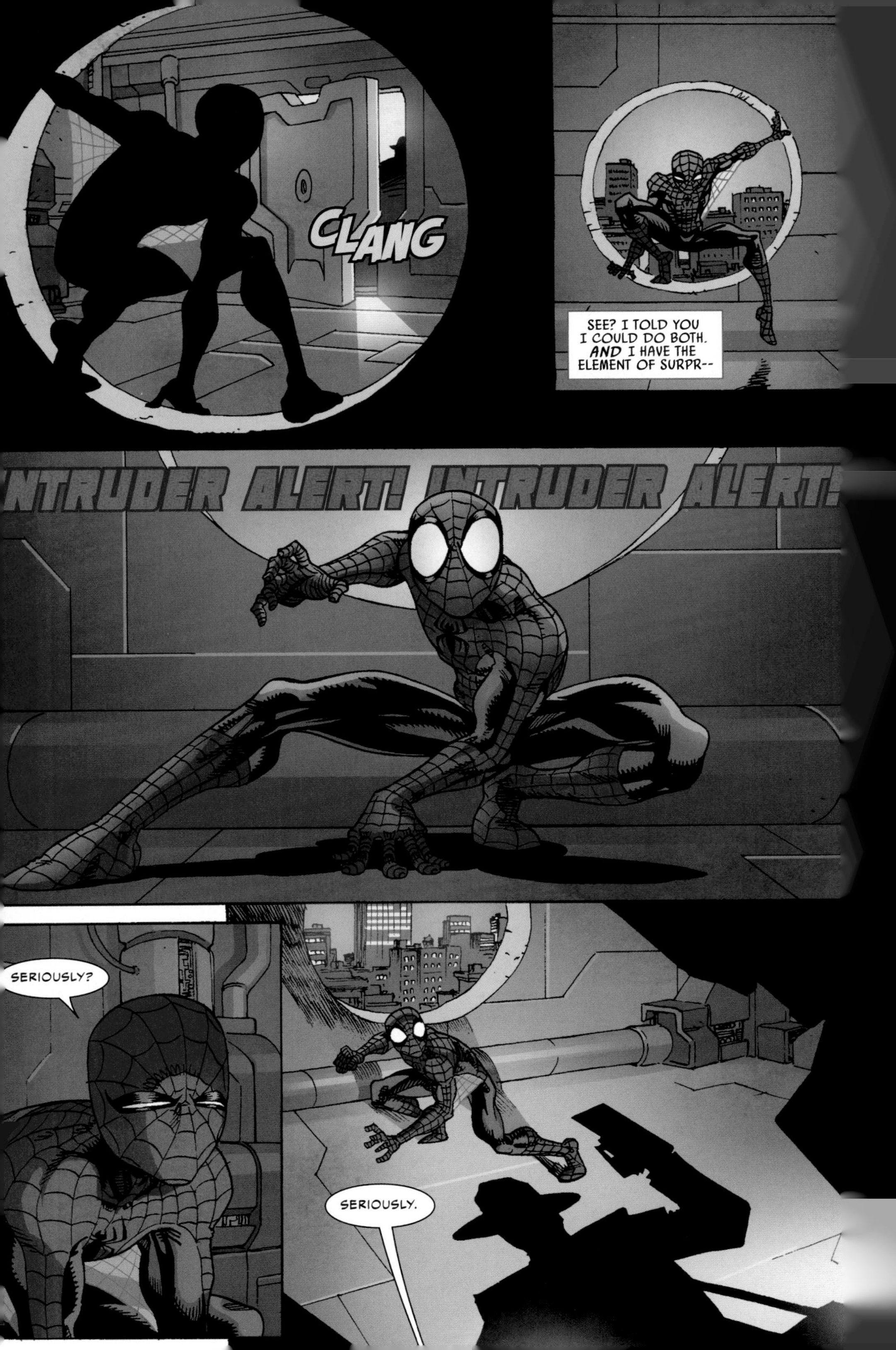
CLANG
SEE? I TOLD YOU I COULD DO BOTH. AND I HAVE THE ELEMENT OF SURPR--
NTRUDER ALERT! INTRUDER ALERT!
SERIOUSLY?
SERIOUSLY.

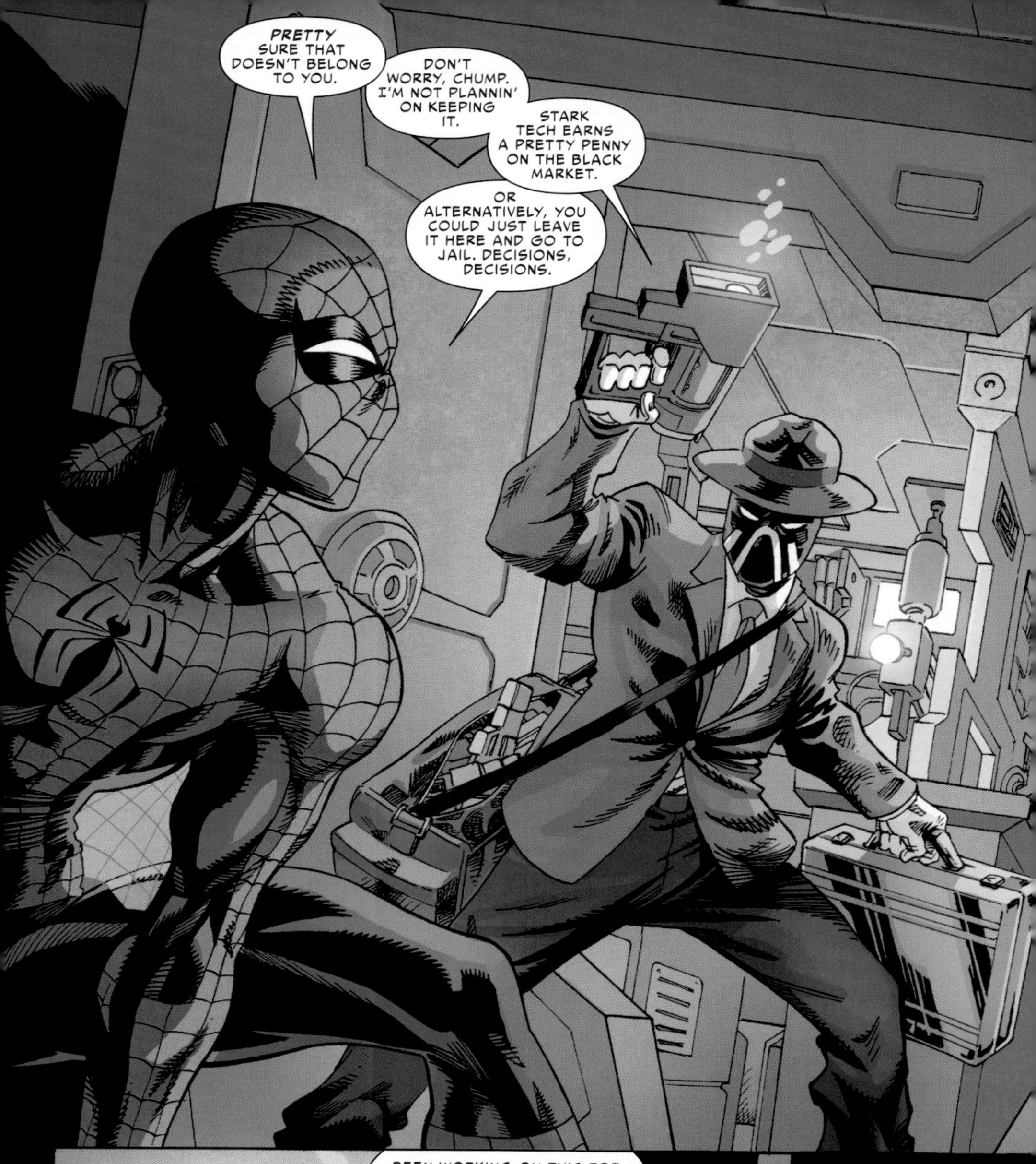
PRETTY SURE THAT DOESN'T BELONG TO YOU.
DON'T WORRY, CHUMP. I'M NOT PLANNIN' ON KEEPING IT.
STARK TECH EARNS A PRETTY PENNY ON THE BLACK MARKET.
OR ALTERNATIVELY, YOU COULD JUST LEAVE IT HERE AND GO TO JAIL. DECISIONS, DECISIONS.

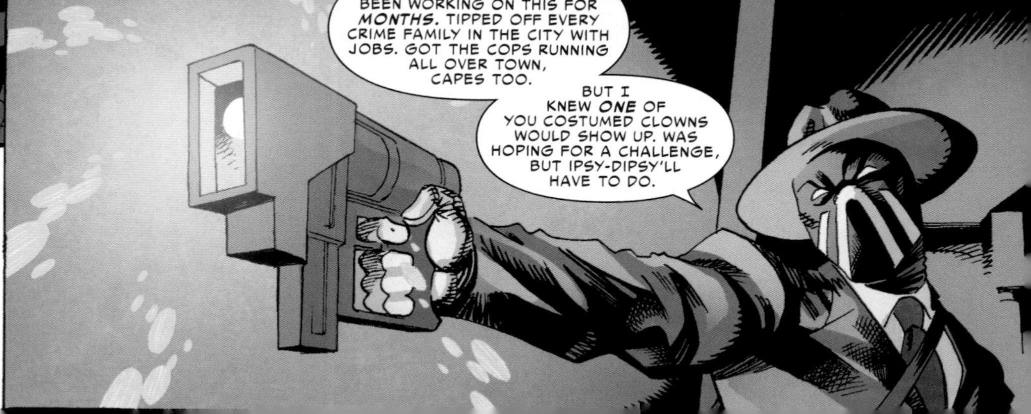
BEEN WORKING ON THIS FOR MONTHS. TIPPED OFF EVERY CRIME FAMILY IN THE CITY WITH JOBS. GOT THE COPS RUNNING ALL OVER TOWN, CAPES TOO.
BUT I KNEW ONE OF YOU COSTUMED CLOWNS WOULD SHOW UP. WAS HOPING FOR A CHALLENGE, BUT IPSY-DIPSY'LL HAVE TO DO.

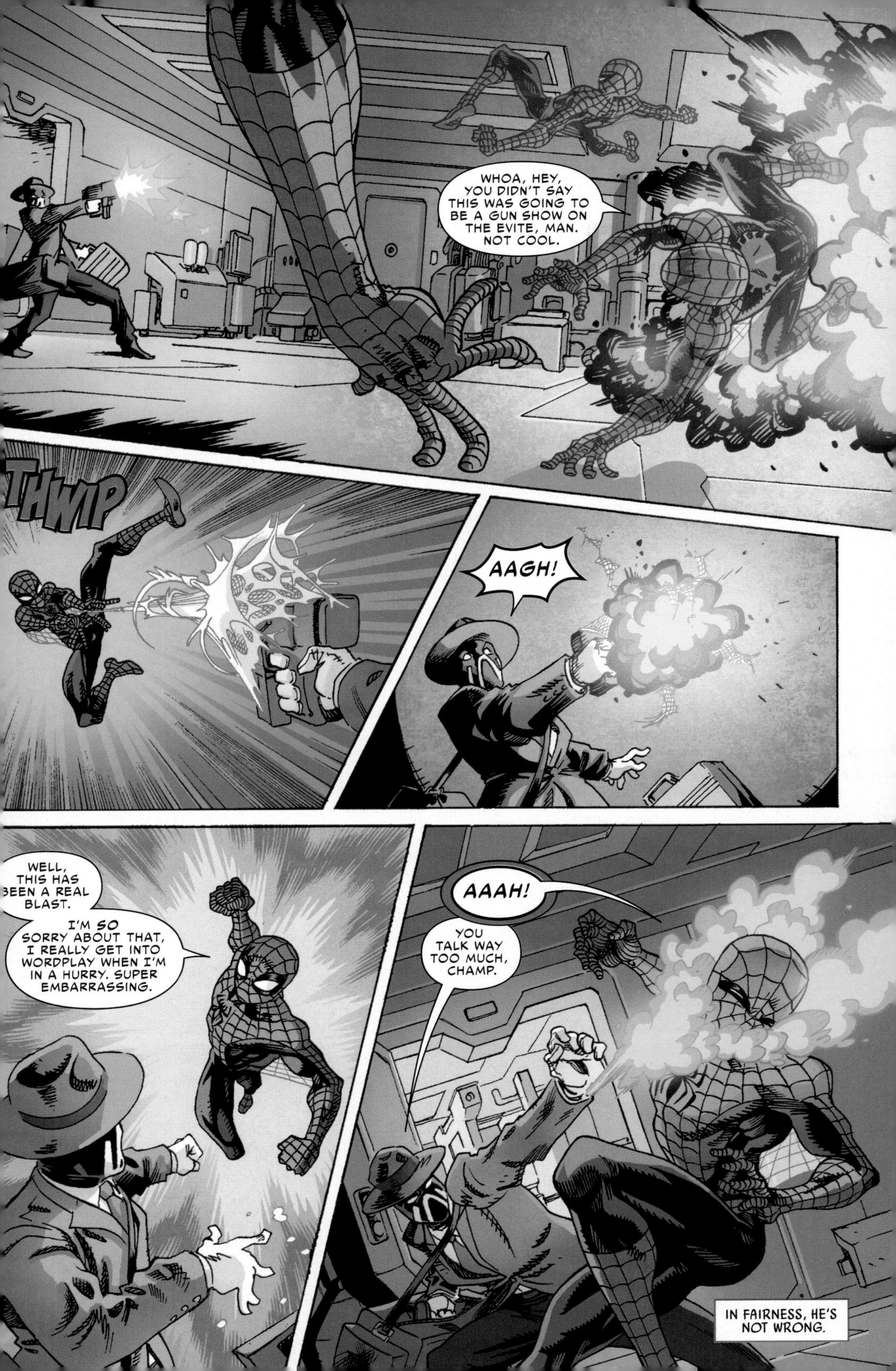
WHOA, HEY, YOU DIDN'T SAY THIS WAS GOING TO BE A GUN SHOW ON THE EVITE, MAN. NOT COOL.
THWIP
AAGH!
WELL, THIS HAS BEEN A REAL BLAST.
I'M SO SORRY ABOUT THAT, I REALLY GET INTO WORDPLAY WHEN I'M IN A HURRY. SUPER EMBARRASSING.
AAAH!
YOU TALK WAY TOO MUCH, CHAMP.
IN FAIRNESS, HE'S NOT WRONG.

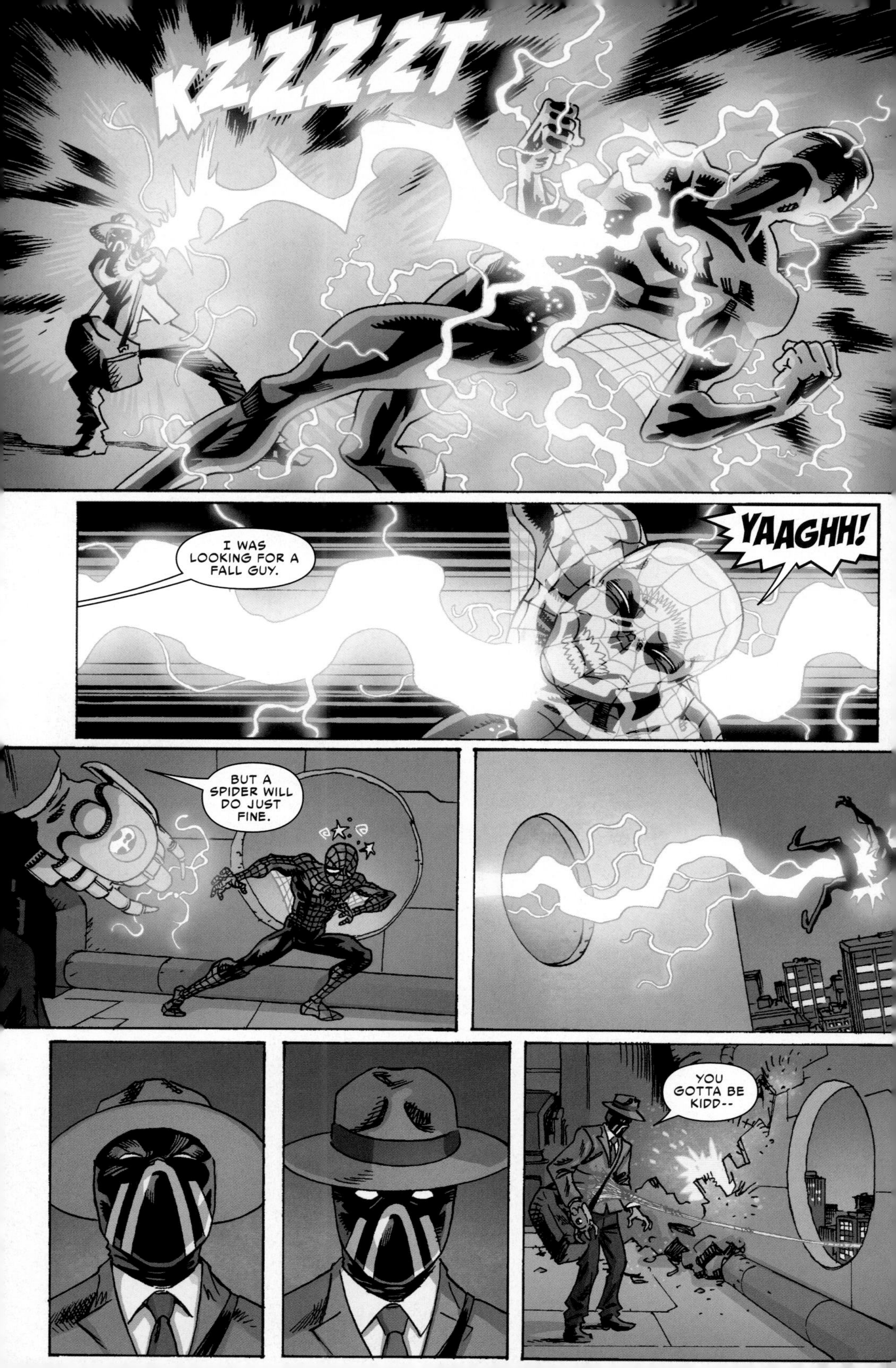
KZZZZZT
I WAS LOOKING FOR A FALL GUY.
YAAGHH!
BUT A SPIDER WILL DO JUST FINE.
YOU GOTTA BE KIDD--

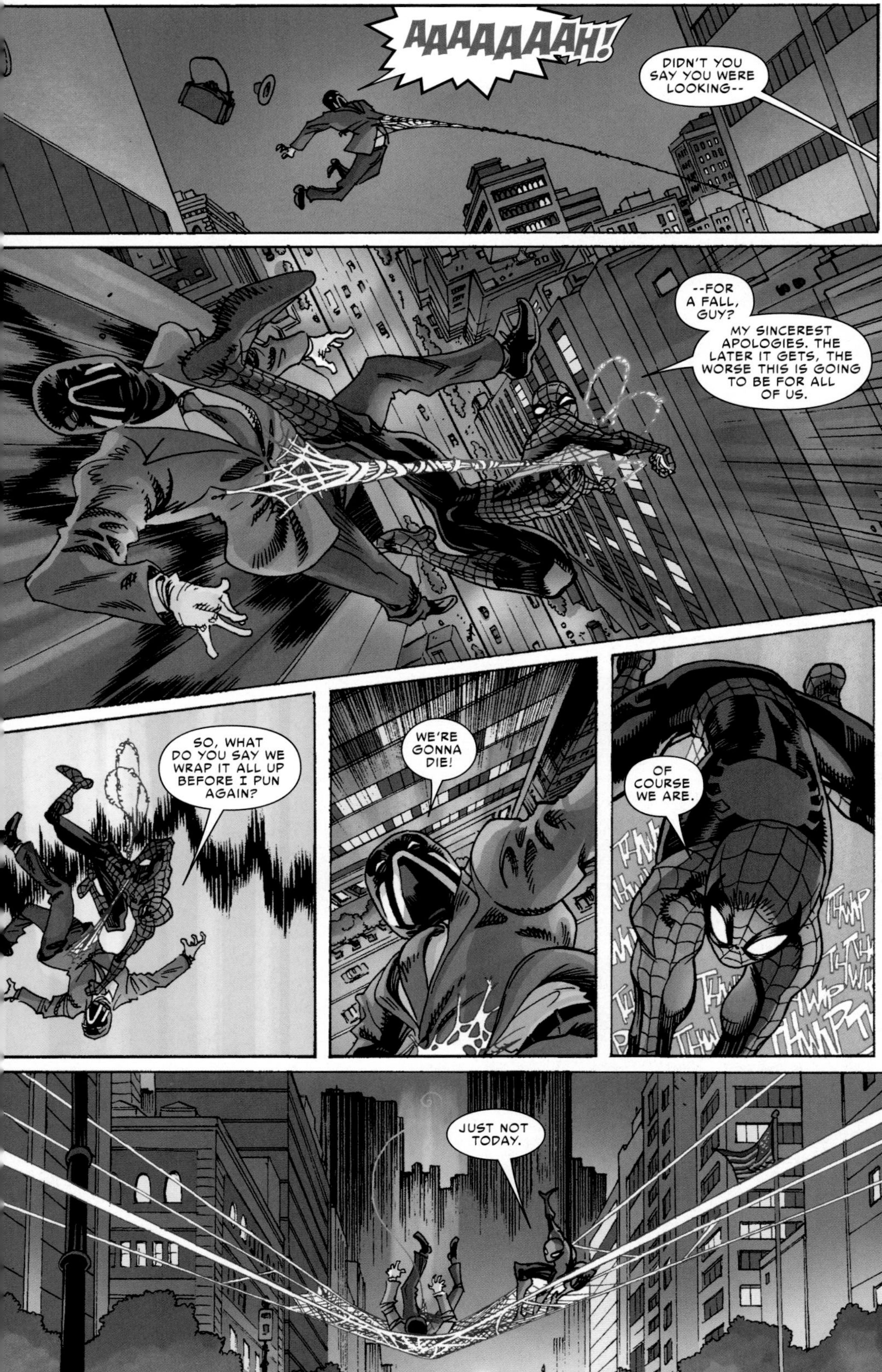
AAAAAAAH!
DIDN'T YOU SAY YOU WERE LOOKING--
--FOR A FALL, GUY?
MY SINCEREST APOLOGIES. THE LATER IT GETS, THE WORSE THIS IS GOING TO BE FOR ALL OF US.
SO, WHAT DO YOU SAY WE WRAP IT ALL UP BEFORE I PUN AGAIN?
WE'RE GONNA DIE!
OF COURSE WE ARE.
JUST NOT TODAY.

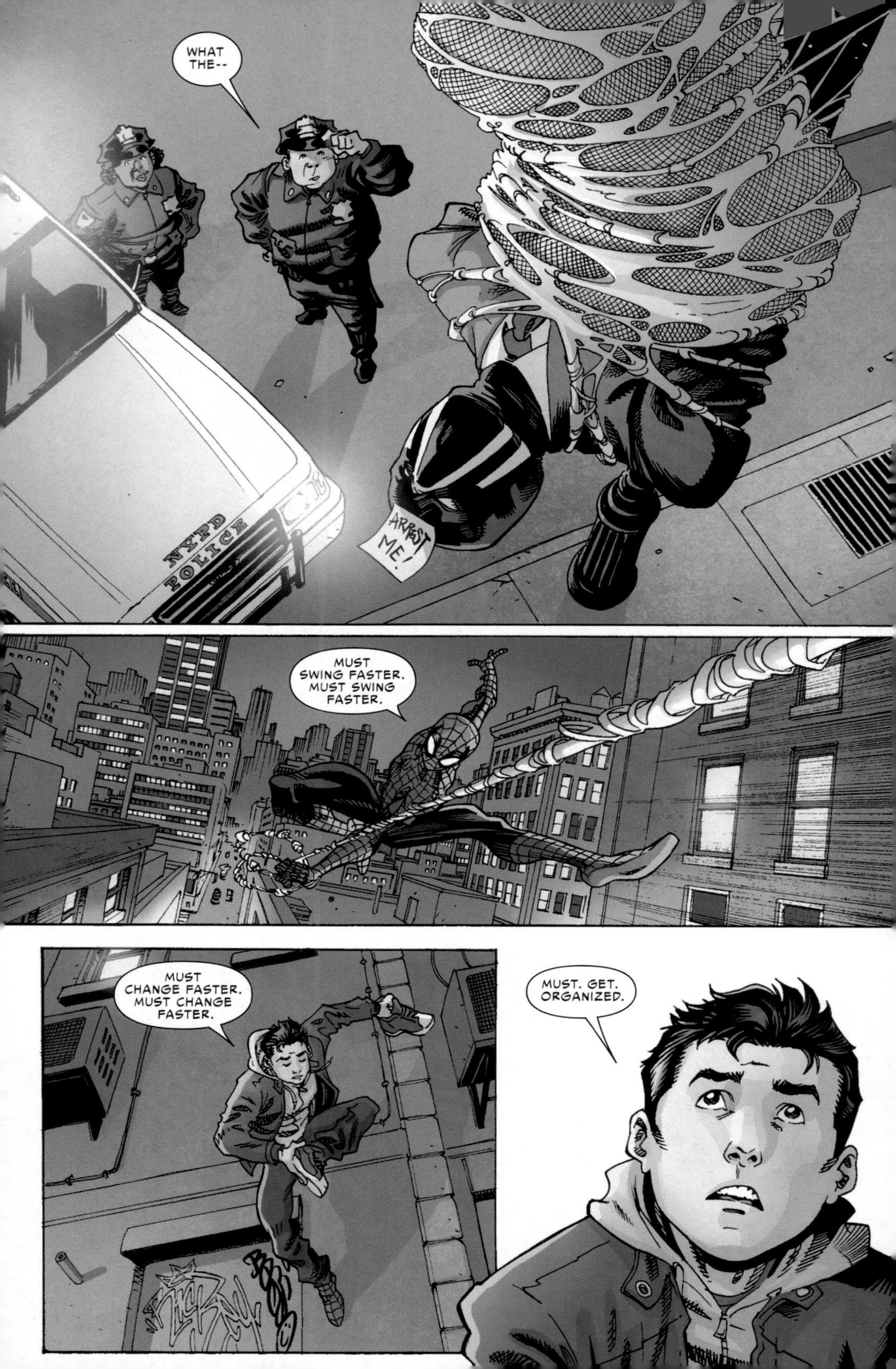
WHAT THE--
NYPD POLICE
ARREST ME!
MUST SWING FASTER. MUST SWING FASTER.
MUST CHANGE FASTER. MUST CHANGE FASTER.
MUST. GET. ORGANIZED.

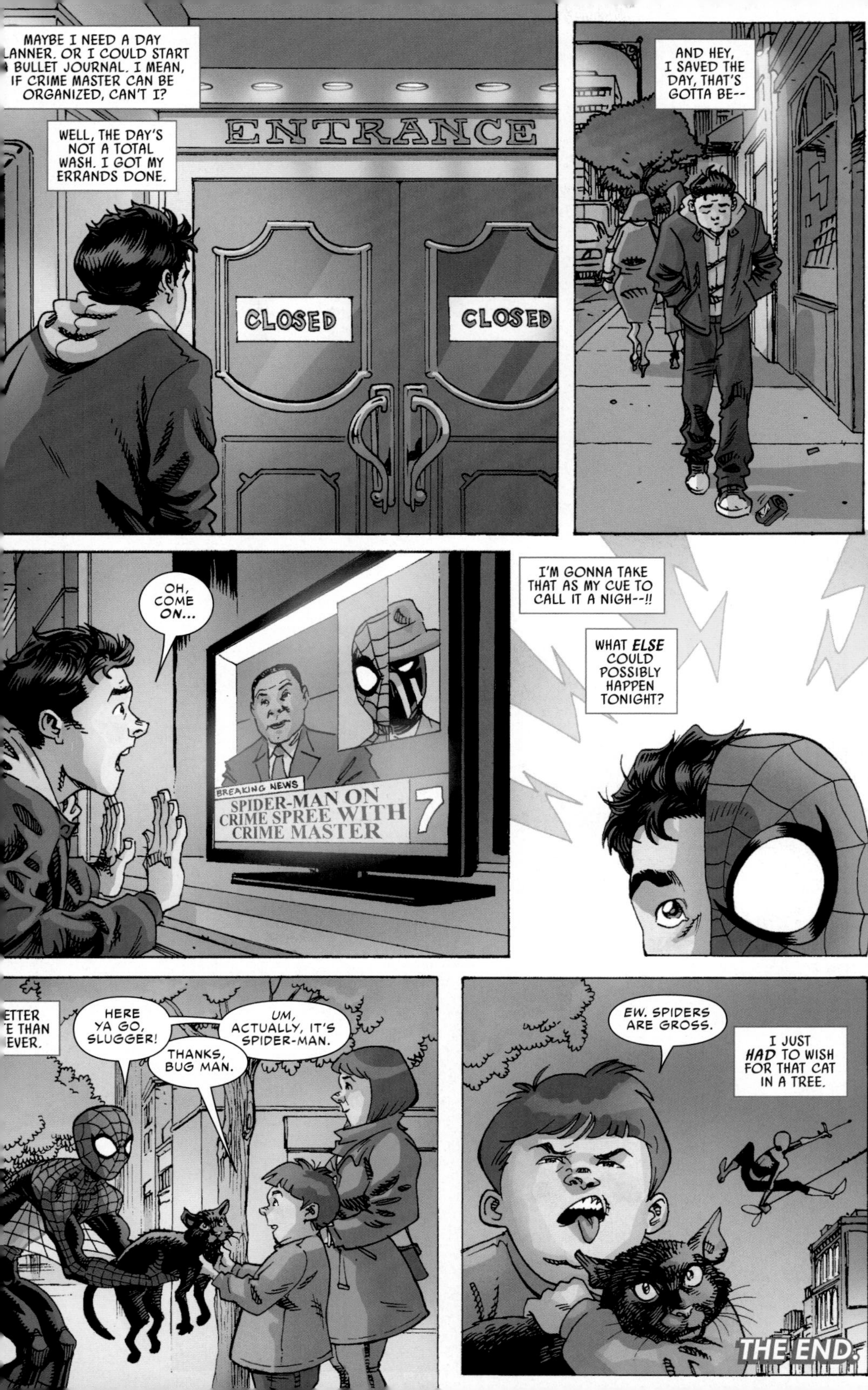

MAYBE I NEED A DAY
LANNER. OR I COULD START
A BULLET JOURNAL. I MEAN, IF CRIME MASTER CAN BE ORGANIZED, CAN'T I?
ENTRANCE
WELL, THE DAY'S NOT A TOTAL WASH. I GOT MY ERRANDS DONE.
CLOSED
CLOSED
AND HEY, I SAVED THE DAY, THAT'S GOTTA BE--
OH, COME ON...
BREAKING NEWS
SPIDER-MAN ON CRIME SPREE WITH CRIME MASTER
7
I'M GONNA TAKE THAT AS MY CUE TO CALL IT A NIGH--!!
WHAT ELSE COULD POSSIBLY HAPPEN TONIGHT?
ETTER
E THAN
EVER.
HERE YA GO, SLUGGER!
UM, ACTUALLY, IT'S SPIDER-MAN.
THANKS, BUG MAN.
EW. SPIDERS ARE GROSS.
I JUST HAD TO WISH FOR THAT CAT IN A TREE.
THE END.

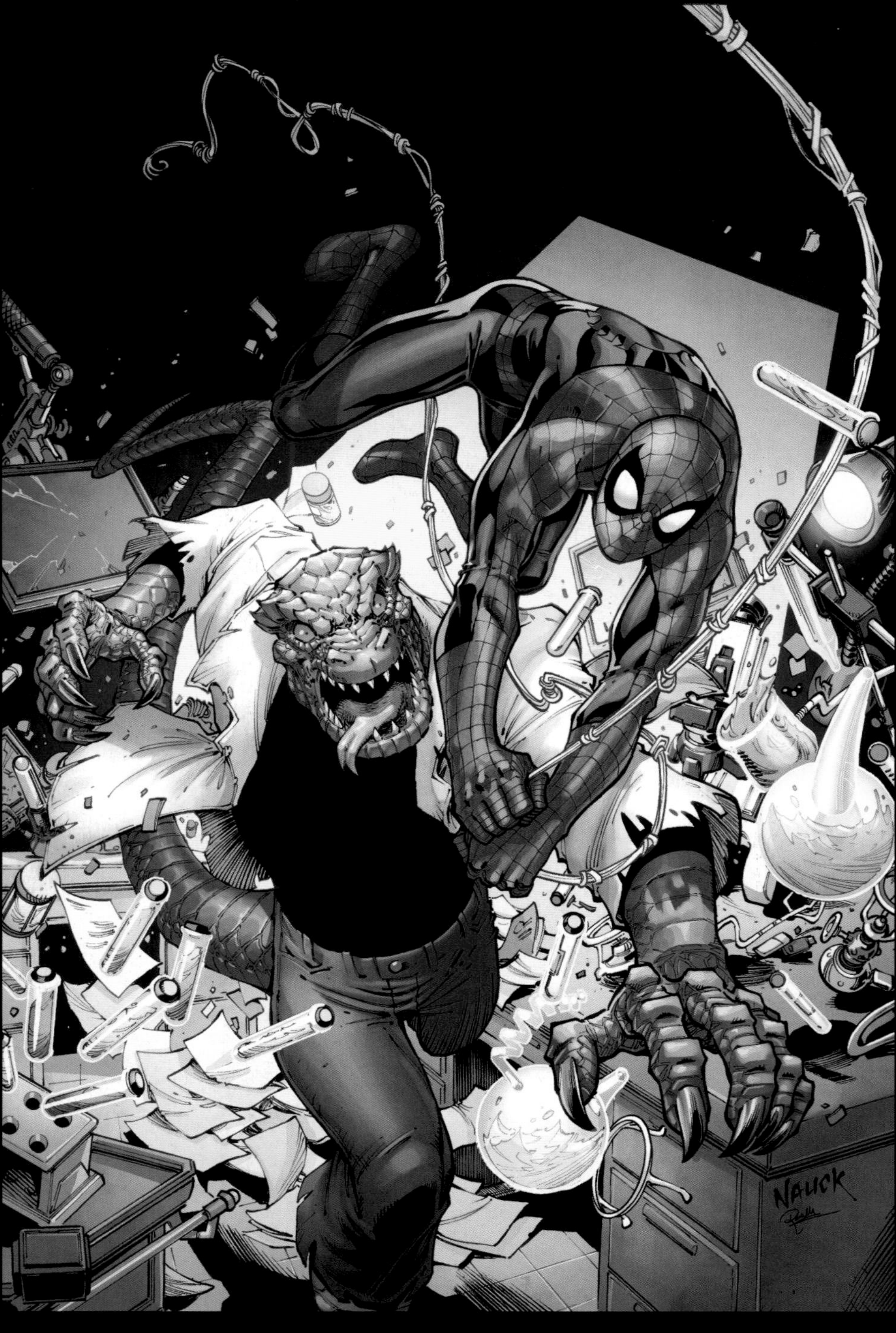
NAUCK

SPIDER-MAN: REPTILIAN RAGE

HIGH SCHOOL STUDENT PETER PARKER HAS A REAL SHOT AT ENTERING A PRESTIGIOUS ACADEMIC PROGRAM. THE ONLY PROBLEM IS, THE LIZARD

Empire State University. One of the premier institutions of higher learning in New York City.

WE HAVE SO MUCH TO OFFER HERE TO QUALIFIED APPLICANTS. MANY ESU GRADUATES HAVE GONE ON TO MAKE *MAJOR* BREAKTHROUGHS IN ALL AREAS OF SCIENTIFIC ENDEAVOR.

WE EVEN HAD THE WORLD'S FOREMOST BIOCHEMIST, DOCTOR *HENRY PYM*, AS A GUEST PROFESSOR LAST SEMESTER.

I WANT TO STRESS THE *IMPORTANCE* OF THE SUMMER INTERNSHIP PROGRAM. IT COULD BE A CRITICAL ELEMENT IN PAVING THE WAY FOR *YOUR* LATER ENTRY INTO THIS UNIVERSITY.

ESU BLDG - ISCA INTEGRATED SCIENCES

DIRECTORY

THE ...MPETITION ...OR IT IS ...RCE, AND ...OU KNOW ...ARE ONLY ...FERING IT ...A *SINGLE* ...H SCHOOL ...DENT FROM ...HE NEW ...ORK CITY ...AREA.

YOUR INTERVIEW WITH ME WILL BE *CRUCIAL*.

OH, THAT OFFICE OVER THERE BELONGS TO OUR RECENT ADDITION, DOCTOR *CURT CONNORS*, WHO INVENTED A SERUM FOR REGENERATING LIMBS AFTER HE LOST HIS RIGHT ARM WHILE SERVING AS A SURGEON IN THE MILITARY.

ARE YOU PAYING ATTENTION, MISTER PARKER?

UHH, YES MA'AM, MRS. MURRAY.

DR. CONNORS? HERE?

LAB 4

WHEN HE USED THE SERUM HE'D EXTRACTED FROM A REPTILE ON HIMSELF, IT TURNED HIM INTO A HUMANOID *LIZARD*!*

...AND HERE AT ESU, WE FOSTER THE BRILLIANCE OF YOUNG MINDS FOR THE NEXT...

ALTHOUGH I BATTLED HIM AS *SPIDER-MAN*, IT WAS MY *SCIENCE SKILLS* THAT ALLOWED ME TO CREATE AN *ANTIDOTE* THAT TURNED HIM HUMAN AGAIN.

*WAAAY BACK IN *AMAZING SPIDER-MAN #6.* --BACK-ISSUE BASSO

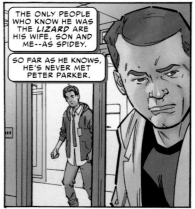

THE ONLY PEOPLE WHO KNOW HE WAS THE *LIZARD* ARE HIS WIFE, SON AND ME--AS SPIDEY.

SO FAR AS HE KNOWS, HE'S NEVER MET PETER PARKER.

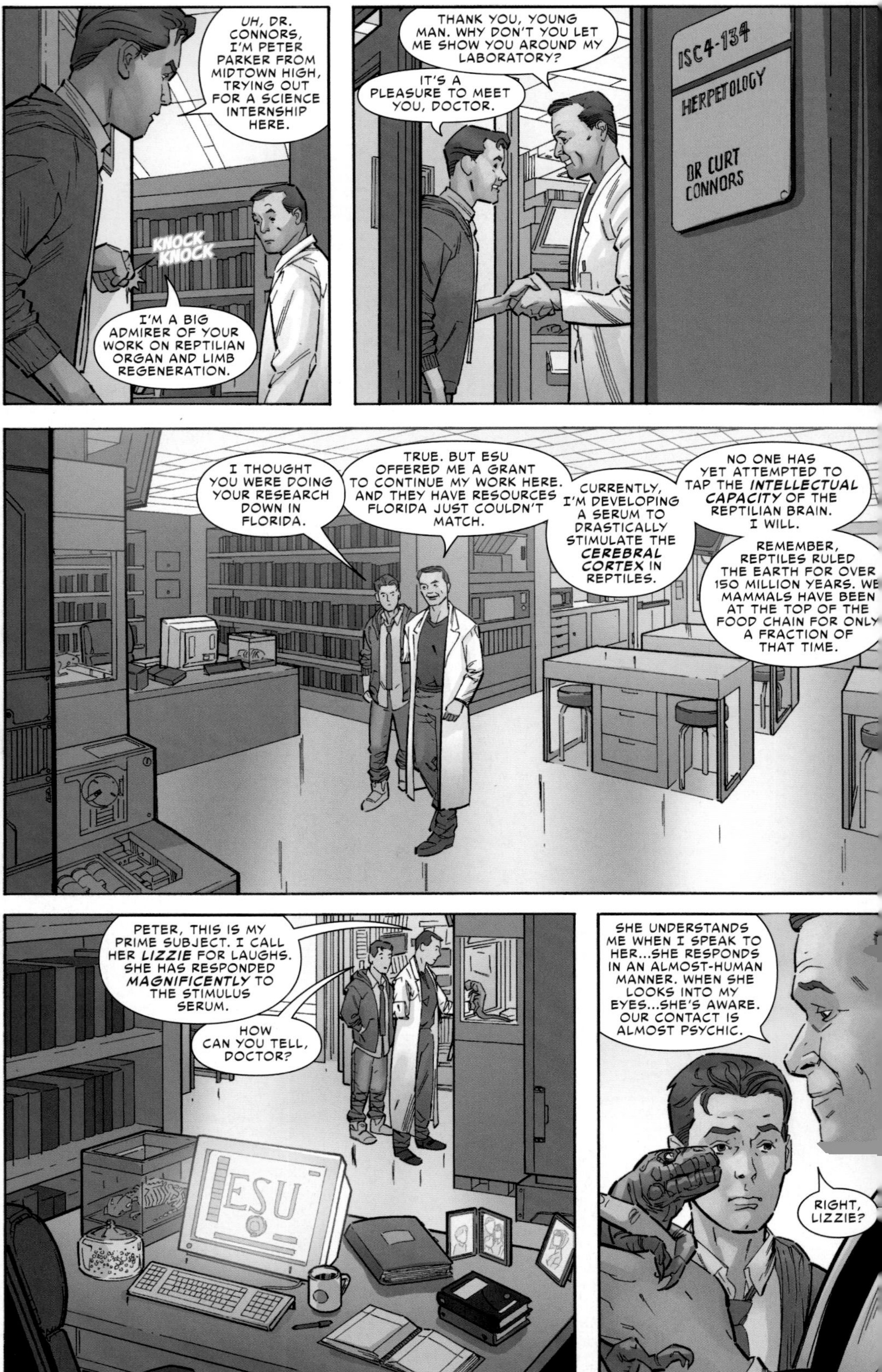
UH, DR. CONNORS, I'M PETER PARKER FROM MIDTOWN HIGH, TRYING OUT FOR A SCIENCE INTERNSHIP HERE.
KNOCK KNOCK
I'M A BIG ADMIRER OF YOUR WORK ON REPTILIAN ORGAN AND LIMB REGENERATION.
THANK YOU, YOUNG MAN. WHY DON'T YOU LET ME SHOW YOU AROUND MY LABORATORY?
IT'S A PLEASURE TO MEET YOU, DOCTOR.
ISC4-134
HERPETOLOGY
DR CURT CONNORS
I THOUGHT YOU WERE DOING YOUR RESEARCH DOWN IN FLORIDA.
TRUE. BUT ESU OFFERED ME A GRANT TO CONTINUE MY WORK HERE. AND THEY HAVE RESOURCES FLORIDA JUST COULDN'T MATCH.
CURRENTLY, I'M DEVELOPING A SERUM TO DRASTICALLY STIMULATE THE CEREBRAL CORTEX IN REPTILES.
NO ONE HAS YET ATTEMPTED TO TAP THE INTELLECTUAL CAPACITY OF THE REPTILIAN BRAIN. I WILL.
REMEMBER, REPTILES RULED THE EARTH FOR OVER 150 MILLION YEARS. WE MAMMALS HAVE BEEN AT THE TOP OF THE FOOD CHAIN FOR ONLY A FRACTION OF THAT TIME.
PETER, THIS IS MY PRIME SUBJECT. I CALL HER LIZZIE FOR LAUGHS. SHE HAS RESPONDED MAGNIFICENTLY TO THE STIMULUS SERUM.
HOW CAN YOU TELL, DOCTOR?
ESU
SHE UNDERSTANDS ME WHEN I SPEAK TO HER...SHE RESPONDS IN AN ALMOST-HUMAN MANNER. WHEN SHE LOOKS INTO MY EYES...SHE'S AWARE. OUR CONTACT IS ALMOST PSYCHIC.
RIGHT, LIZZIE?

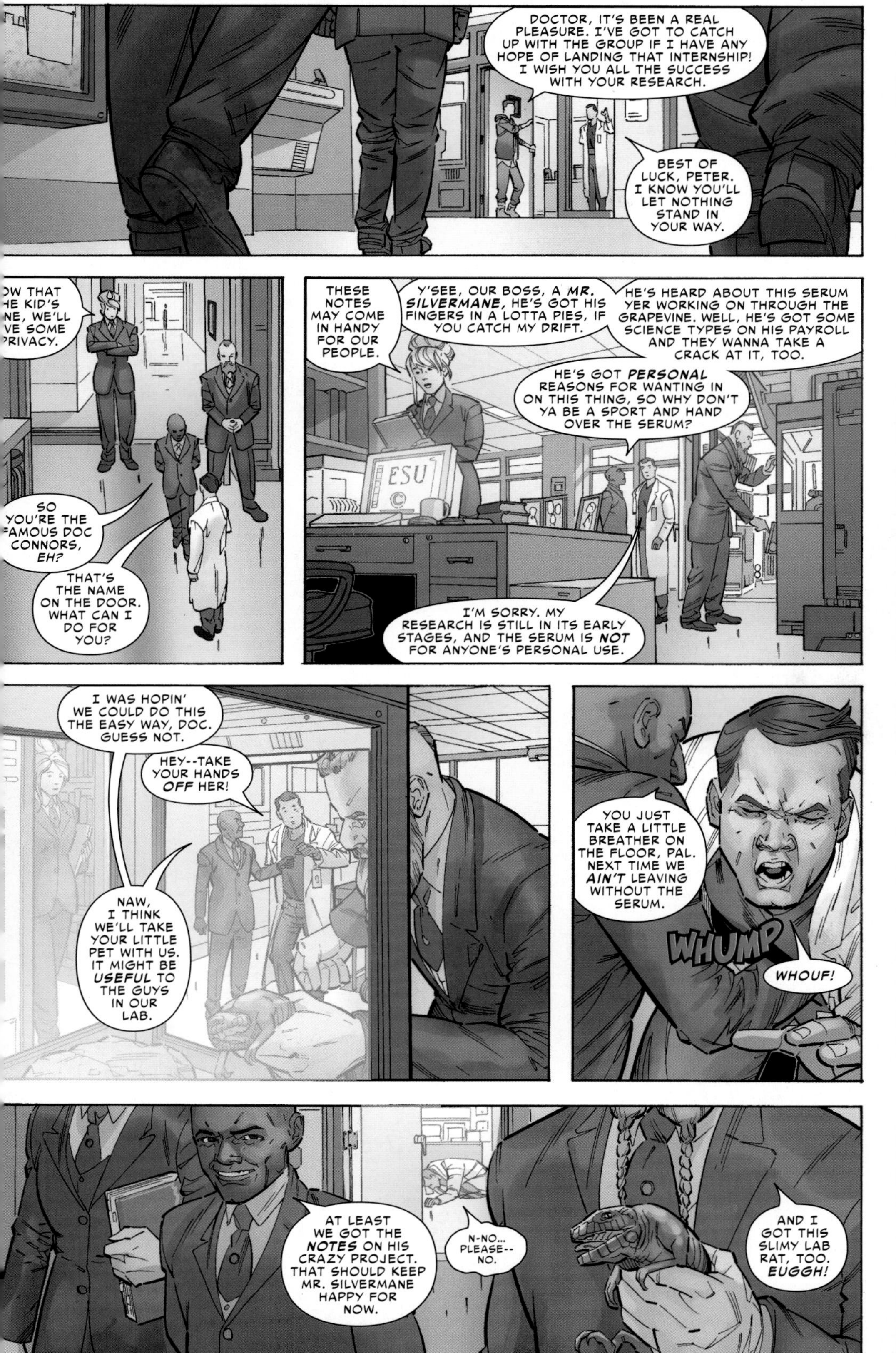
DOCTOR, IT'S BEEN A REAL PLEASURE. I'VE GOT TO CATCH UP WITH THE GROUP IF I HAVE ANY HOPE OF LANDING THAT INTERNSHIP! I WISH YOU ALL THE SUCCESS WITH YOUR RESEARCH.
BEST OF LUCK, PETER. I KNOW YOU'LL LET NOTHING STAND IN YOUR WAY.
OW THAT HE KID'S NE, WE'LL VE SOME PRIVACY.
SO YOU'RE THE AMOUS DOC CONNORS, *EH?*
THAT'S THE NAME ON THE DOOR. WHAT CAN I DO FOR YOU?
THESE NOTES MAY COME IN HANDY FOR OUR PEOPLE.
Y'SEE, OUR BOSS, A ***MR. SILVERMANE,*** HE'S GOT HIS FINGERS IN A LOTTA PIES, IF YOU CATCH MY DRIFT.
HE'S HEARD ABOUT THIS SERUM YER WORKING ON THROUGH THE GRAPEVINE. WELL, HE'S GOT SOME SCIENCE TYPES ON HIS PAYROLL AND THEY WANNA TAKE A CRACK AT IT, TOO.
HE'S GOT ***PERSONAL*** REASONS FOR WANTING IN ON THIS THING, SO WHY DON'T YA BE A SPORT AND HAND OVER THE SERUM?
I'M SORRY. MY RESEARCH IS STILL IN ITS EARLY STAGES, AND THE SERUM IS ***NOT*** FOR ANYONE'S PERSONAL USE.
I WAS HOPIN' WE COULD DO THIS THE EASY WAY, DOC. GUESS NOT.
HEY--TAKE YOUR HANDS ***OFF*** HER!
NAW, I THINK WE'LL TAKE YOUR LITTLE PET WITH US. IT MIGHT BE ***USEFUL*** TO THE GUYS IN OUR LAB.
YOU JUST TAKE A LITTLE BREATHER ON THE FLOOR, PAL. NEXT TIME WE ***AIN'T*** LEAVING WITHOUT THE SERUM.
WHUMP
WHOUF!
AT LEAST WE GOT THE ***NOTES*** ON HIS CRAZY PROJECT. THAT SHOULD KEEP MR. SILVERMANE HAPPY FOR NOW.
N-NO... PLEASE-- NO.
AND I GOT THIS SLIMY LAB RAT, TOO. ***EUGGH!***

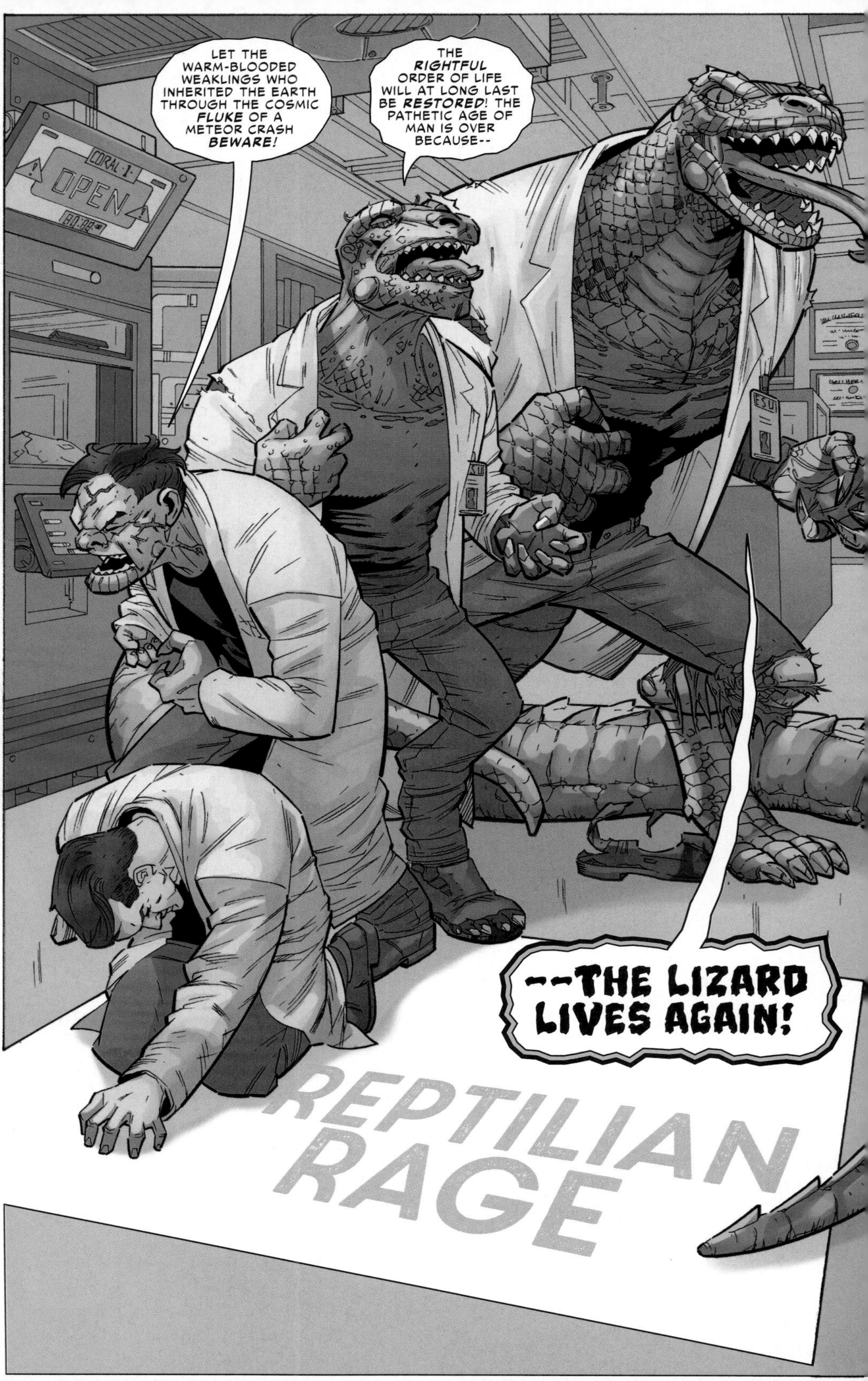
CORAL-1
OPEN
LET THE WARM-BLOODED WEAKLINGS WHO INHERITED THE EARTH THROUGH THE COSMIC FLUKE OF A METEOR CRASH BEWARE!
THE RIGHTFUL ORDER OF LIFE WILL AT LONG LAST BE RESTORED! THE PATHETIC AGE OF MAN IS OVER BECAUSE--
ESU
--THE LIZARD LIVES AGAIN!
REPTILIAN RAGE

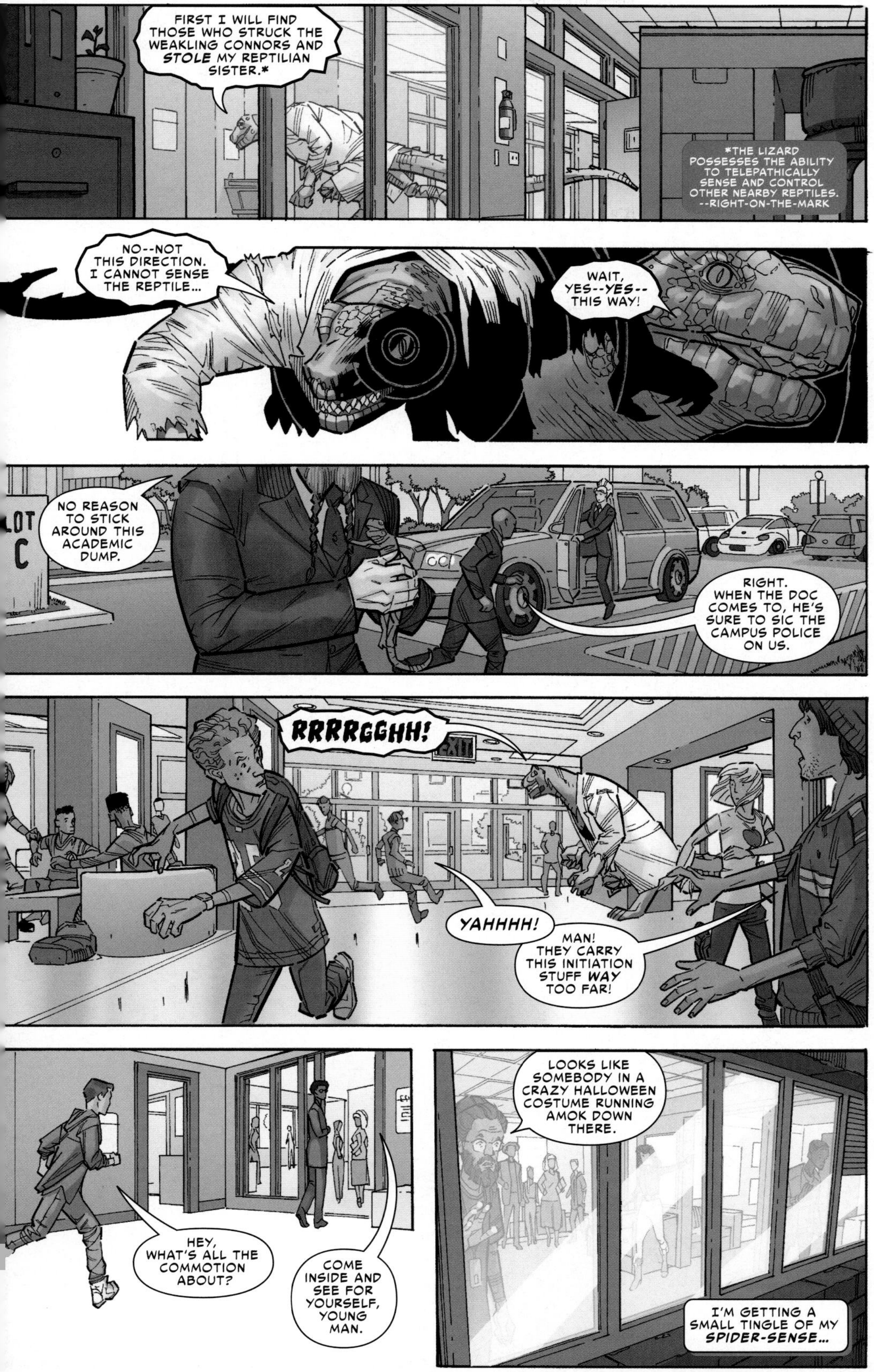
FIRST I WILL FIND THOSE WHO STRUCK THE WEAKLING CONNORS AND *STOLE* MY REPTILIAN SISTER.*
*THE LIZARD POSSESSES THE ABILITY TO TELEPATHICALLY SENSE AND CONTROL OTHER NEARBY REPTILES. --RIGHT-ON-THE-MARK
NO--NOT THIS DIRECTION. I CANNOT SENSE THE REPTILE...
WAIT, YES--*YES*-- THIS WAY!
LOT C
NO REASON TO STICK AROUND THIS ACADEMIC DUMP.
RIGHT. WHEN THE DOC COMES TO, HE'S SURE TO SIC THE CAMPUS POLICE ON US.
RRRRGGHH!
EXIT
YAHHHH!
MAN! THEY CARRY THIS INITIATION STUFF *WAY* TOO FAR!
HEY, WHAT'S ALL THE COMMOTION ABOUT?
COME INSIDE AND SEE FOR YOURSELF, YOUNG MAN.
LOOKS LIKE SOMEBODY IN A CRAZY HALLOWEEN COSTUME RUNNING AMOK DOWN THERE.
I'M GETTING A SMALL TINGLE OF MY *SPIDER-SENSE*...

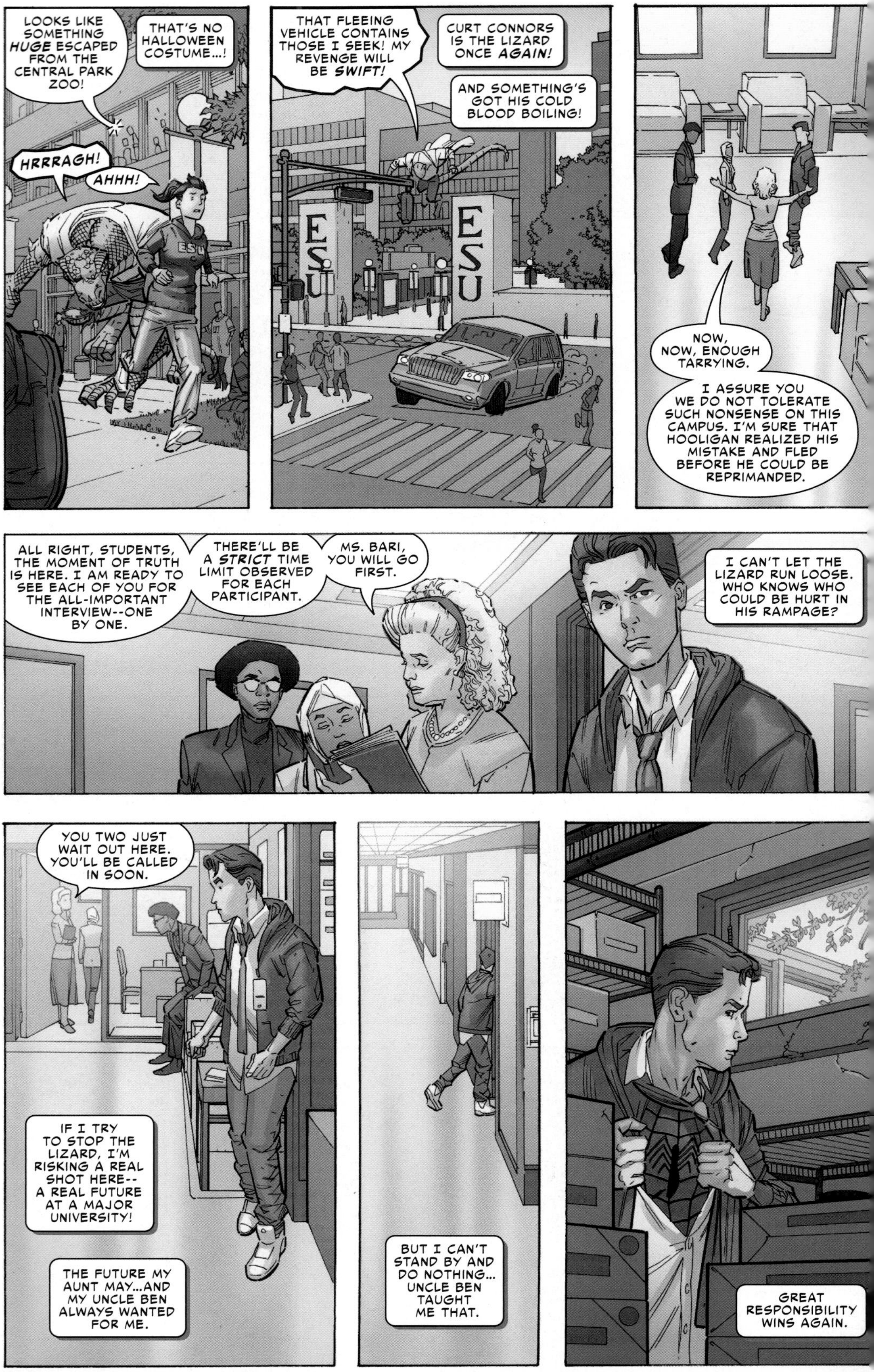
LOOKS LIKE SOMETHING HUGE ESCAPED FROM THE CENTRAL PARK ZOO!
THAT'S NO HALLOWEEN COSTUME...!
HRRRAGH!
AHHH!
THAT FLEEING VEHICLE CONTAINS THOSE I SEEK! MY REVENGE WILL BE SWIFT!
CURT CONNORS IS THE LIZARD ONCE AGAIN!
AND SOMETHING'S GOT HIS COLD BLOOD BOILING!
ESU
ESU
NOW, NOW, ENOUGH TARRYING.
I ASSURE YOU WE DO NOT TOLERATE SUCH NONSENSE ON THIS CAMPUS. I'M SURE THAT HOOLIGAN REALIZED HIS MISTAKE AND FLED BEFORE HE COULD BE REPRIMANDED.
ALL RIGHT, STUDENTS, THE MOMENT OF TRUTH IS HERE. I AM READY TO SEE EACH OF YOU FOR THE ALL-IMPORTANT INTERVIEW--ONE BY ONE.
THERE'LL BE A STRICT TIME LIMIT OBSERVED FOR EACH PARTICIPANT.
MS. BARI, YOU WILL GO FIRST.
I CAN'T LET THE LIZARD RUN LOOSE. WHO KNOWS WHO COULD BE HURT IN HIS RAMPAGE?
YOU TWO JUST WAIT OUT HERE. YOU'LL BE CALLED IN SOON.
IF I TRY TO STOP THE LIZARD, I'M RISKING A REAL SHOT HERE-- A REAL FUTURE AT A MAJOR UNIVERSITY!
THE FUTURE MY AUNT MAY...AND MY UNCLE BEN ALWAYS WANTED FOR ME.
BUT I CAN'T STAND BY AND DO NOTHING... UNCLE BEN TAUGHT ME THAT.
GREAT RESPONSIBILITY WINS AGAIN.

I THOUGHT I'D SEEN *EVERYTHING* IN THIS NUTTY CITY--BUT SOME CLOWN IN A *REPTILE OUTFIT* AND *LAB COAT* LEAPING AROUND EIGHTH AVENUE-- NO FREAKIN' WAY!

LOOKS LIKE WE'LL BE BACK AT THE BOSS' PLACE BEFORE LONG.

UHH... GANG?

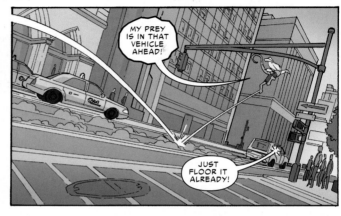

MY PREY IS IN THAT VEHICLE AHEAD!

JUST FLOOR IT ALREADY!

HSSS! THE SIGHTS AND SMELLS OF THIS CITY ASSAULT MY [S]ENSES--*DISGUST* ME! [I]S *BREEDING GROUND* FOR THE UPRIGHT [M]AMMALS WHO CLAIM OWNERSHIP OF THE EARTH!

THEY *POISON* THE [P]LANET--*DRAIN* THE LIFE- [G]IVING SWAMPS AND PASS [JU]DGMENT ON WHAT SPECIES WILL *LIVE* AND *DIE!*

NO *LONGER!* NOW *THEY* WILL BECOME THE *HUNTED*--THE *VICTIMS*--THE *FOOD* THAT WILL FILL REPTILIAN BELLIES!

AND IT BEGINS WITH THE *UNSUSPECTING* MAMMALS BELOW WHOSE LIVES ARE ABOUT TO BE SNUFFED OUT!

WH- WHAT'S THAT THING DOING?!

OH MY GOD!

SKRAKT

LOOK AT THE ROAD OR WE'LL *CRASH!*

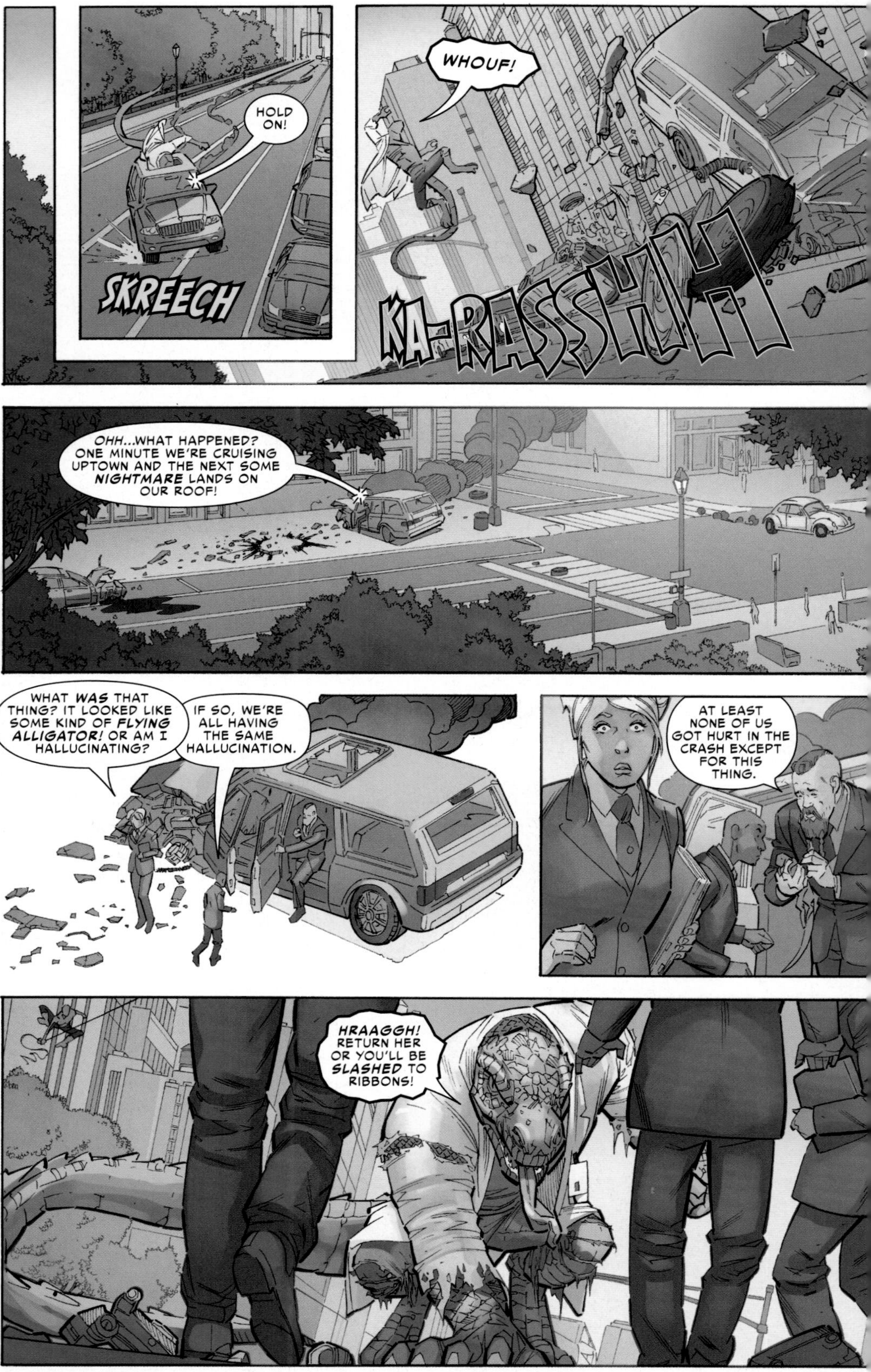
HOLD ON!
SKREECH
WHOUF!
KA-RASSHHH
OHH...WHAT HAPPENED? ONE MINUTE WE'RE CRUISING UPTOWN AND THE NEXT SOME NIGHTMARE LANDS ON OUR ROOF!
WHAT WAS THAT THING? IT LOOKED LIKE SOME KIND OF FLYING ALLIGATOR! OR AM I HALLUCINATING?
IF SO, WE'RE ALL HAVING THE SAME HALLUCINATION.
AT LEAST NONE OF US GOT HURT IN THE CRASH EXCEPT FOR THIS THING.
HRAAGGH! RETURN HER OR YOU'LL BE SLASHED TO RIBBONS!

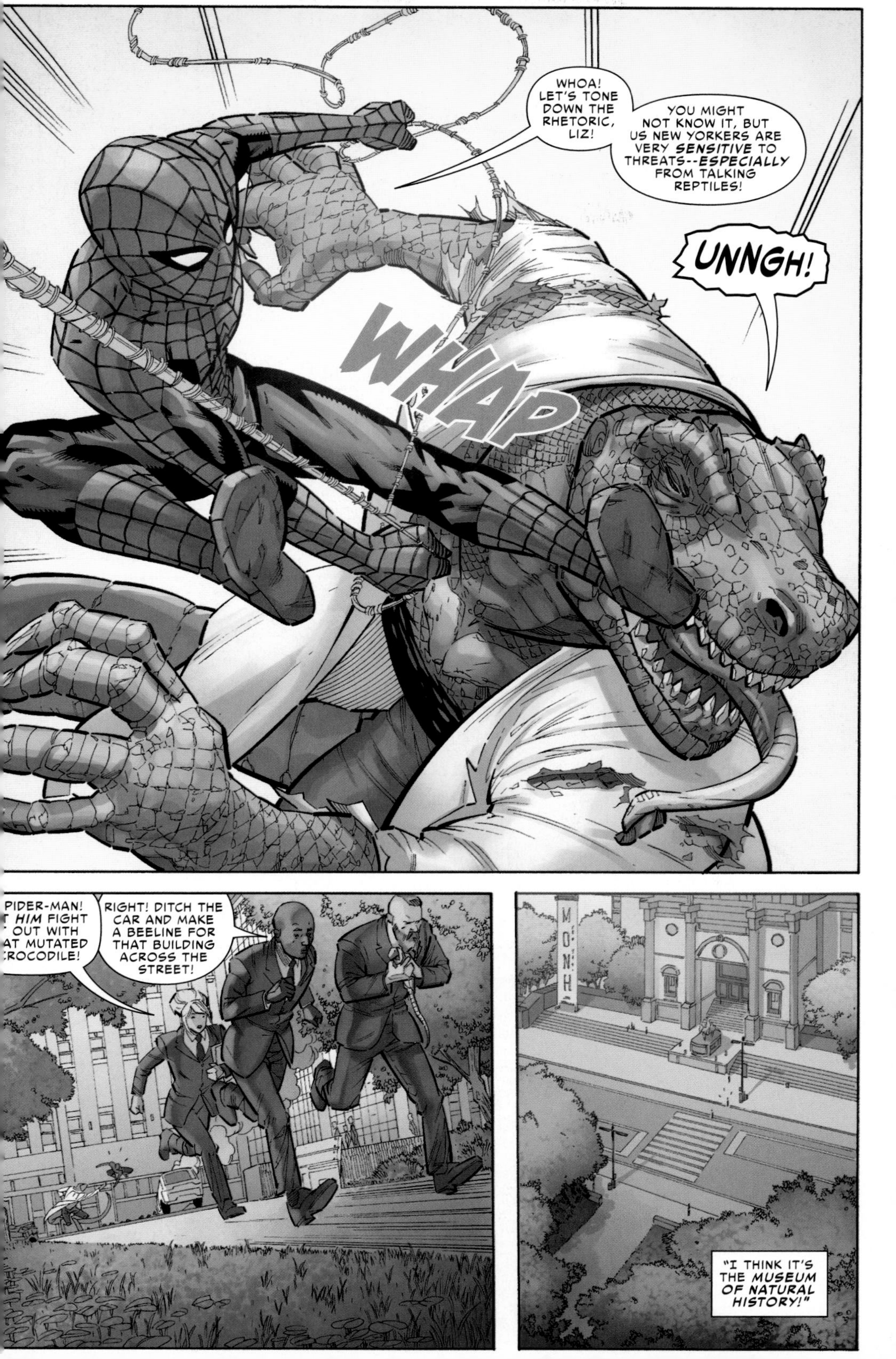
WHOA! LET'S TONE DOWN THE RHETORIC, LIZ!
YOU MIGHT NOT KNOW IT, BUT US NEW YORKERS ARE VERY SENSITIVE TO THREATS--ESPECIALLY FROM TALKING REPTILES!
UNNGH!
WHAP
PIDER-MAN! T HIM FIGHT OUT WITH AT MUTATED ROCODILE!
RIGHT! DITCH THE CAR AND MAKE A BEELINE FOR THAT BUILDING ACROSS THE STREET!
"I THINK IT'S THE MUSEUM OF NATURAL HISTORY!"

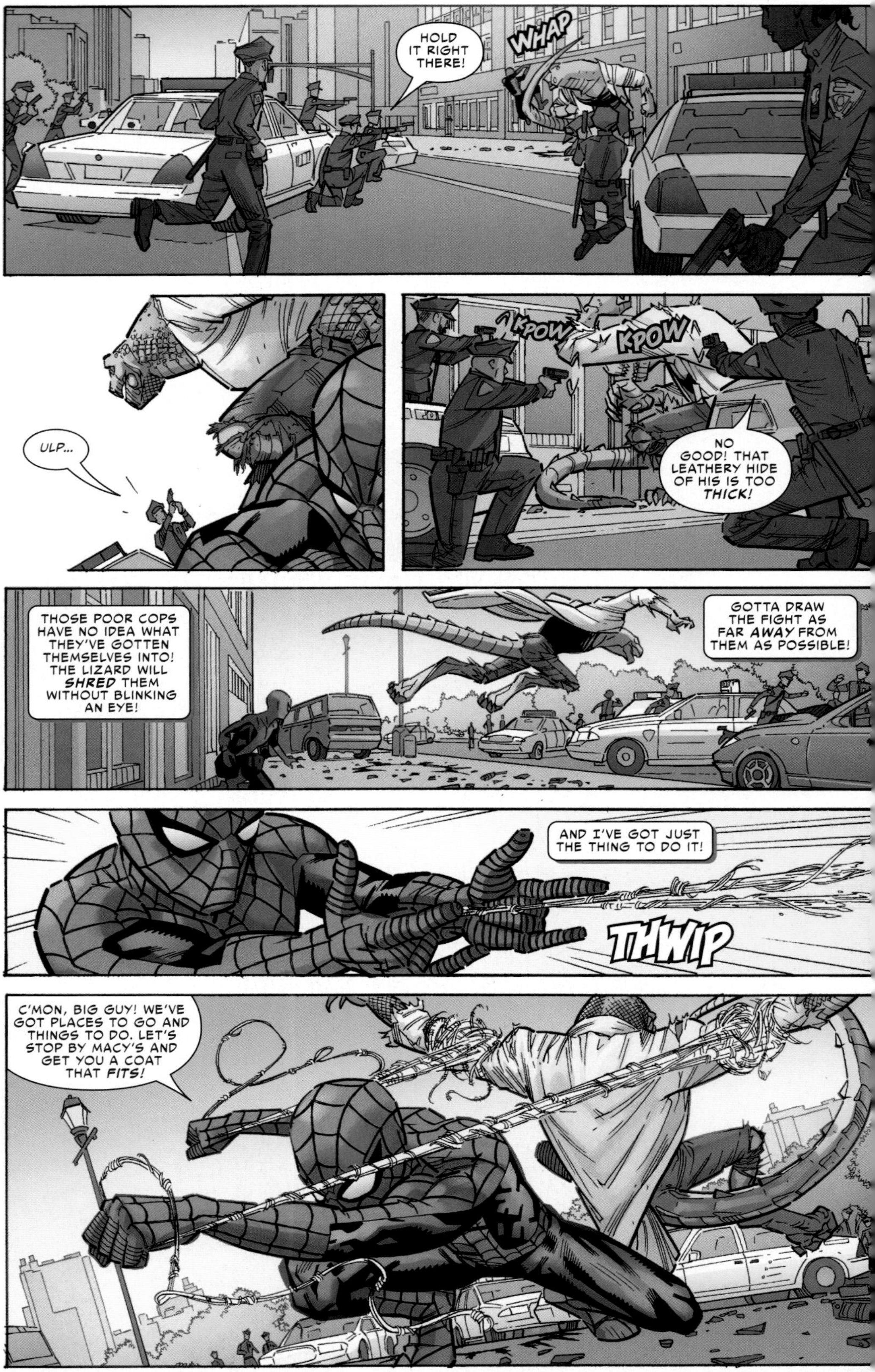
HOLD IT RIGHT THERE!
WHAP
ULP...
KPOW
KPOW
NO GOOD! THAT LEATHERY HIDE OF HIS IS TOO THICK!
THOSE POOR COPS HAVE NO IDEA WHAT THEY'VE GOTTEN THEMSELVES INTO! THE LIZARD WILL SHRED THEM WITHOUT BLINKING AN EYE!
GOTTA DRAW THE FIGHT AS FAR AWAY FROM THEM AS POSSIBLE!
AND I'VE GOT JUST THE THING TO DO IT!
THWIP
C'MON, BIG GUY! WE'VE GOT PLACES TO GO AND THINGS TO DO. LET'S STOP BY MACY'S AND GET YOU A COAT THAT FITS!

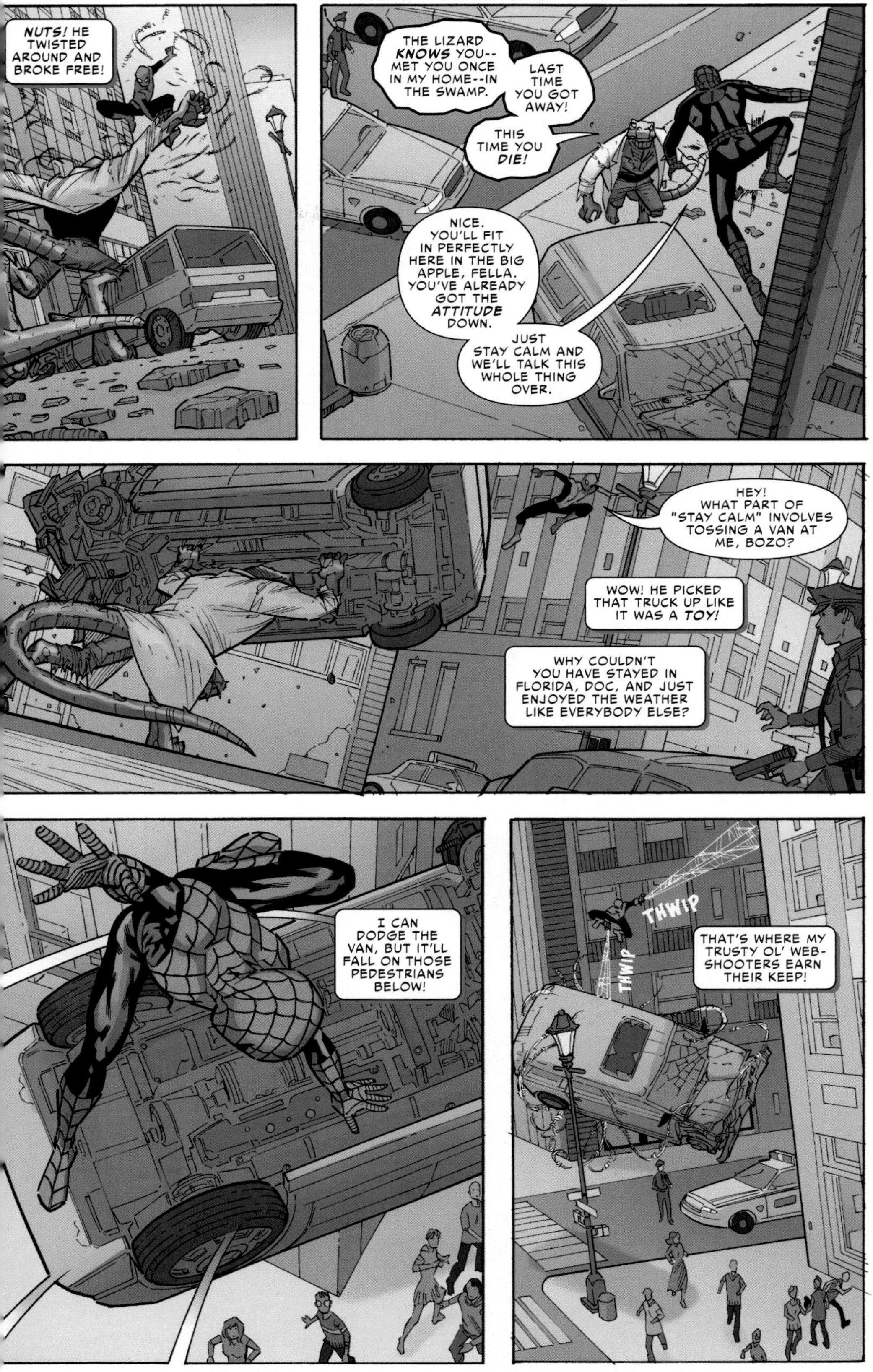
NUTS! HE TWISTED AROUND AND BROKE FREE!
THE LIZARD KNOWS YOU-- MET YOU ONCE IN MY HOME--IN THE SWAMP.
LAST TIME YOU GOT AWAY!
THIS TIME YOU DIE!
NICE. YOU'LL FIT IN PERFECTLY HERE IN THE BIG APPLE, FELLA. YOU'VE ALREADY GOT THE ATTITUDE DOWN.
JUST STAY CALM AND WE'LL TALK THIS WHOLE THING OVER.
HEY! WHAT PART OF "STAY CALM" INVOLVES TOSSING A VAN AT ME, BOZO?
WOW! HE PICKED THAT TRUCK UP LIKE IT WAS A TOY!
WHY COULDN'T YOU HAVE STAYED IN FLORIDA, DOC, AND JUST ENJOYED THE WEATHER LIKE EVERYBODY ELSE?
I CAN DODGE THE VAN, BUT IT'LL FALL ON THOSE PEDESTRIANS BELOW!
THWIP
THWIP
THAT'S WHERE MY TRUSTY OL' WEB-SHOOTERS EARN THEIR KEEP!

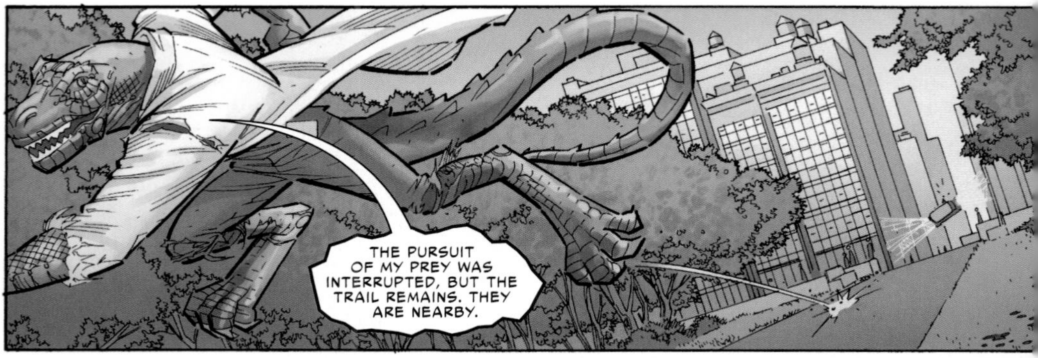
THE PURSUIT OF MY PREY WAS INTERRUPTED, BUT THE TRAIL REMAINS. THEY ARE NEARBY.

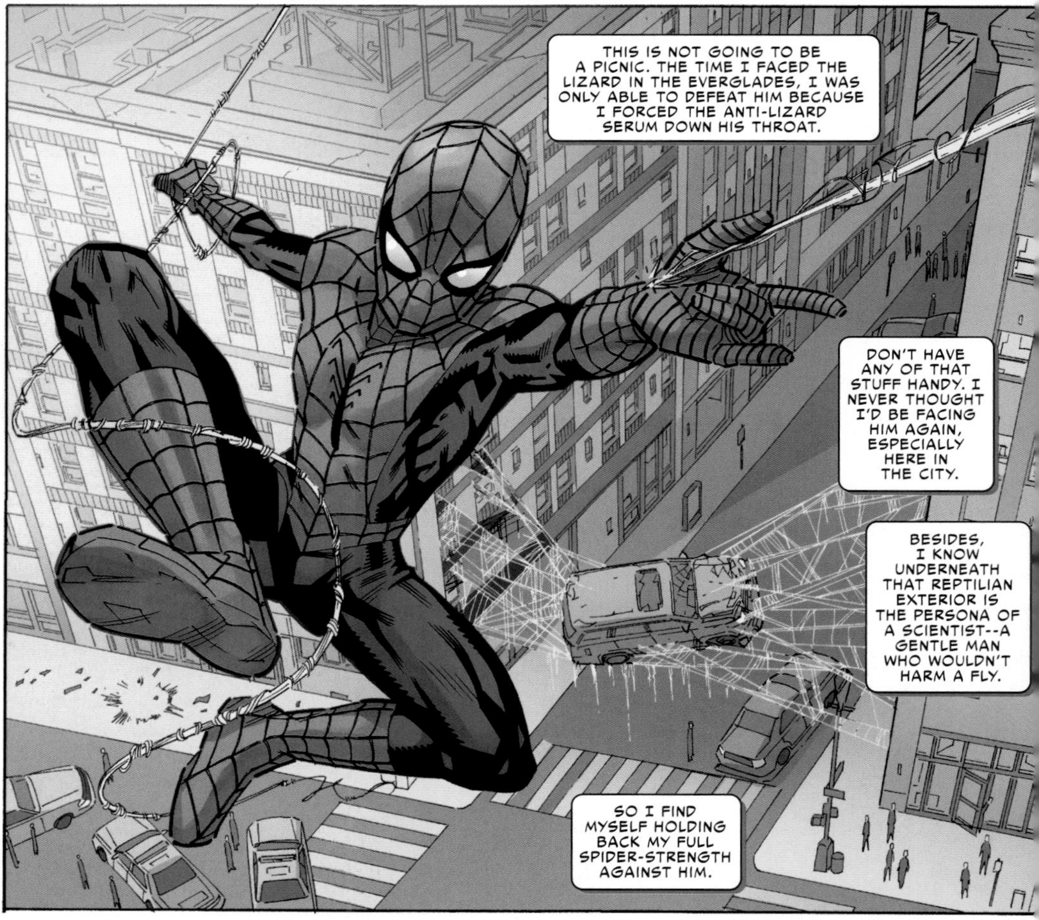
THIS IS NOT GOING TO BE A PICNIC. THE TIME I FACED THE LIZARD IN THE EVERGLADES, I WAS ONLY ABLE TO DEFEAT HIM BECAUSE I FORCED THE ANTI-LIZARD SERUM DOWN HIS THROAT.
DON'T HAVE ANY OF THAT STUFF HANDY. I NEVER THOUGHT I'D BE FACING HIM AGAIN, ESPECIALLY HERE IN THE CITY.
BESIDES, I KNOW UNDERNEATH THAT REPTILIAN EXTERIOR IS THE PERSONA OF A SCIENTIST--A GENTLE MAN WHO WOULDN'T HARM A FLY.
SO I FIND MYSELF HOLDING BACK MY FULL SPIDER-STRENGTH AGAINST HIM.

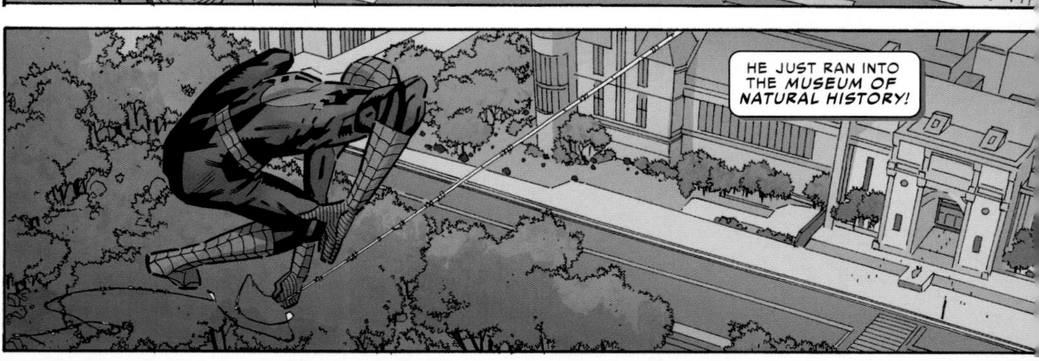
HE JUST RAN INTO THE *MUSEUM OF NATURAL HISTORY!*

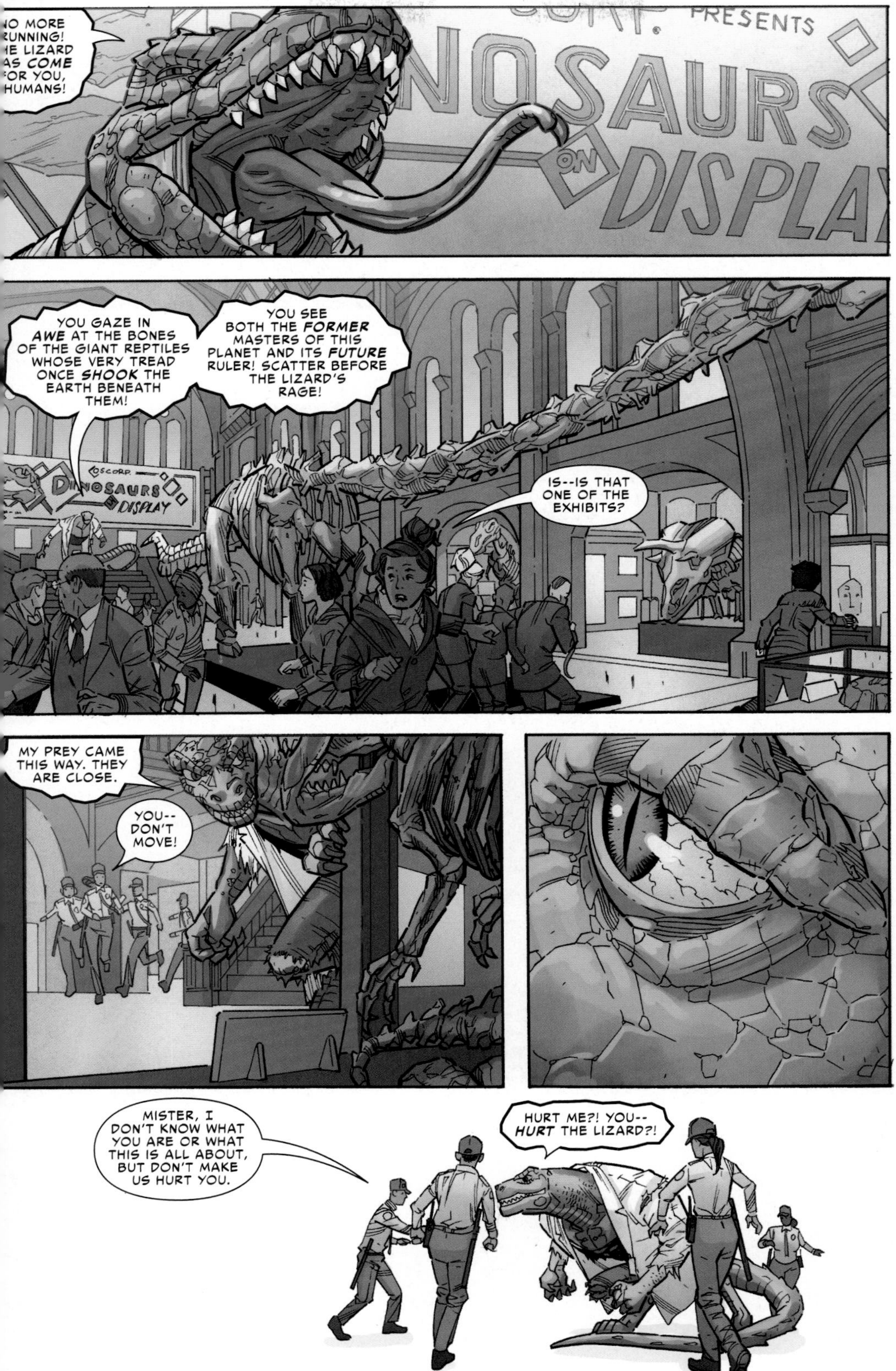

NO MORE RUNNING! THE LIZARD HAS COME FOR YOU, HUMANS!
PRESENTS
NOSAURS ON DISPLAY
YOU GAZE IN AWE AT THE BONES OF THE GIANT REPTILES WHOSE VERY TREAD ONCE SHOOK THE EARTH BENEATH THEM!
YOU SEE BOTH THE FORMER MASTERS OF THIS PLANET AND ITS FUTURE RULER! SCATTER BEFORE THE LIZARD'S RAGE!
OSCORP
DINOSAURS DISPLAY
IS--IS THAT ONE OF THE EXHIBITS?
MY PREY CAME THIS WAY. THEY ARE CLOSE.
YOU-- DON'T MOVE!
MISTER, I DON'T KNOW WHAT YOU ARE OR WHAT THIS IS ALL ABOUT, BUT DON'T MAKE US HURT YOU.
HURT ME?! YOU-- HURT THE LIZARD?!

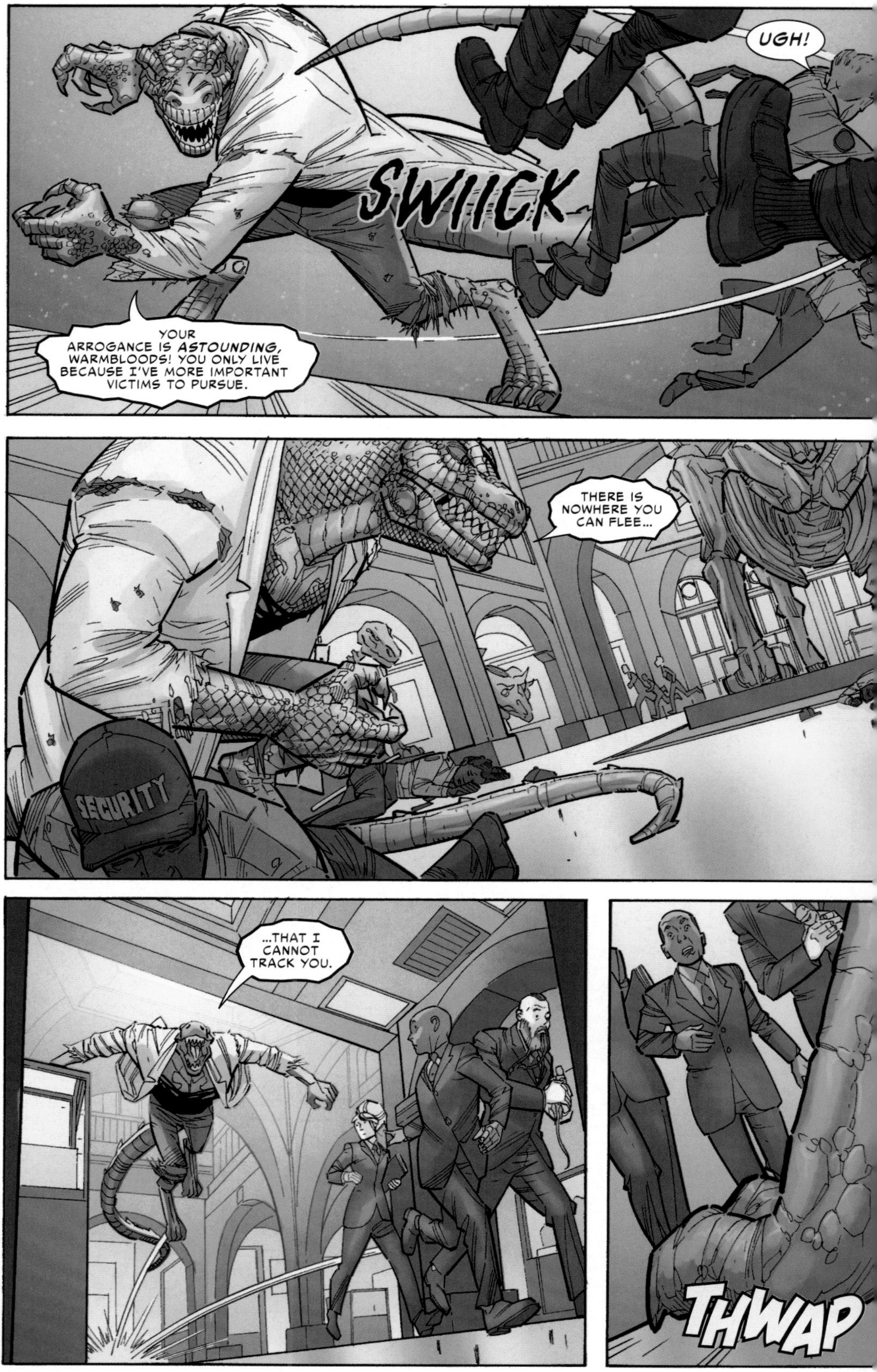
UGH!
SWIICK
YOUR ARROGANCE IS ASTOUNDING, WARMBLOODS! YOU ONLY LIVE BECAUSE I'VE MORE IMPORTANT VICTIMS TO PURSUE.
THERE IS NOWHERE YOU CAN FLEE...
SECURITY
...THAT I CANNOT TRACK YOU.
THWAP

LOOKS LIKE I GOT HERE IN THE NICK OF TIME. NO ONE'S BEEN SERIOUSLY INJURED.

THIS DISPLAY BROUGHT TO YOU BY OSCORP.

ALTHOUGH THE LIZARD SEEMS INTENT ON STALKING THAT PARTICULAR TRIO FOR SOME REASON.

WAIT A MINUTE! THIS IS STARTING TO MAKE A LITTLE SENSE. I SAW THOSE THREE ENTER DOCTOR CONNORS' OFFICE JUST AFTER I LEFT.

[A]ND IT APPEARS THEY'VE GOT [T]HAT SMALL REPTILE HE WAS [E]XPERIMENTING ON WITH THEM.

THEY MUST'VE TAKEN IT...AND LIZARD WANTS HIS FRIEND BACK!

STILL YOU PURSUE ME, INSECT! MOVE ASIDE-- I WILL DEAL WITH YOU SOON.

NO CAN DO, MR. LIZARD. THE SUPER HERO MANUAL EXPRESSLY FORBIDS LEAVING CIVILIANS IN HARM'S WAY. PAGE SIXTEEN, PARAGRAPH TWO.

YOU CANNOT ESCAPE ME! ONE [LE]AP AND I'LL BE ON [Y]OUR BACK SINKING MY CLAWS INTO YOUR SOFT FLESH!

WHAT'S THE MATTER, ALLIGATOR MAN? YOU AFRAID TO MIX IT UP WITH SOMEONE WHO CAN FIGHT BACK? YOU KEEP RUNNING FROM ME.

WORRIED I'LL EMBARRASS YOU HERE WITH YOUR BONY ANCESTORS LOOKING ON? YOU GOT THE LAB COAT ON TO HIDE A YELLOW STREAK DOWN YOUR BACK?

NOW YOU DID IT, SPIDEY. YOU JUST GOADED ABOUT 800 POUNDS OF REPTILIAN FEROCITY INTO ATTACKING YOU!

ALL RIGHT--LET'S RUMBLE!

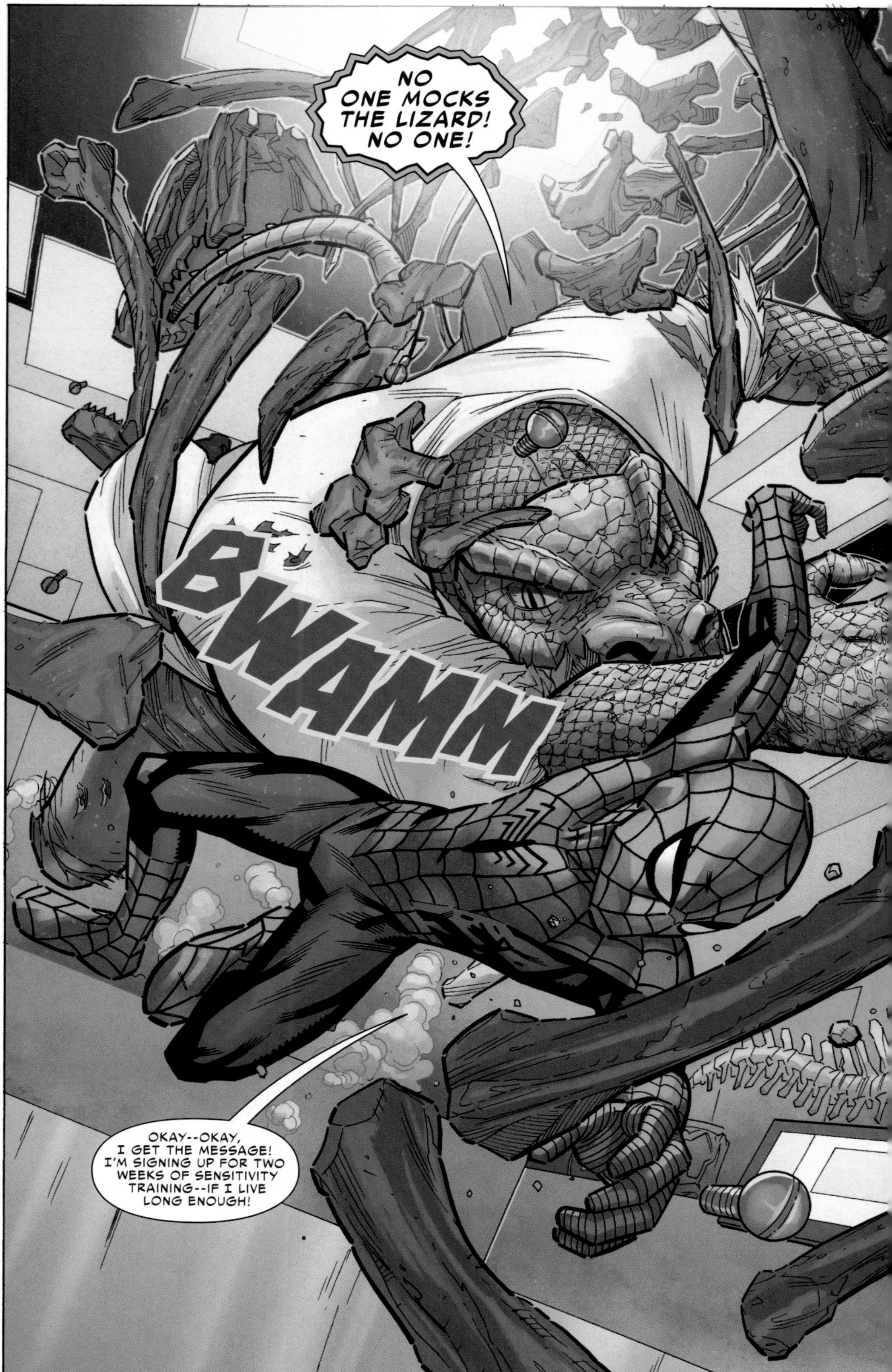
NO ONE MOCKS THE LIZARD! NO ONE!
BWAMM
OKAY--OKAY, I GET THE MESSAGE! I'M SIGNING UP FOR TWO WEEKS OF SENSITIVITY TRAINING--IF I LIVE LONG ENOUGH!

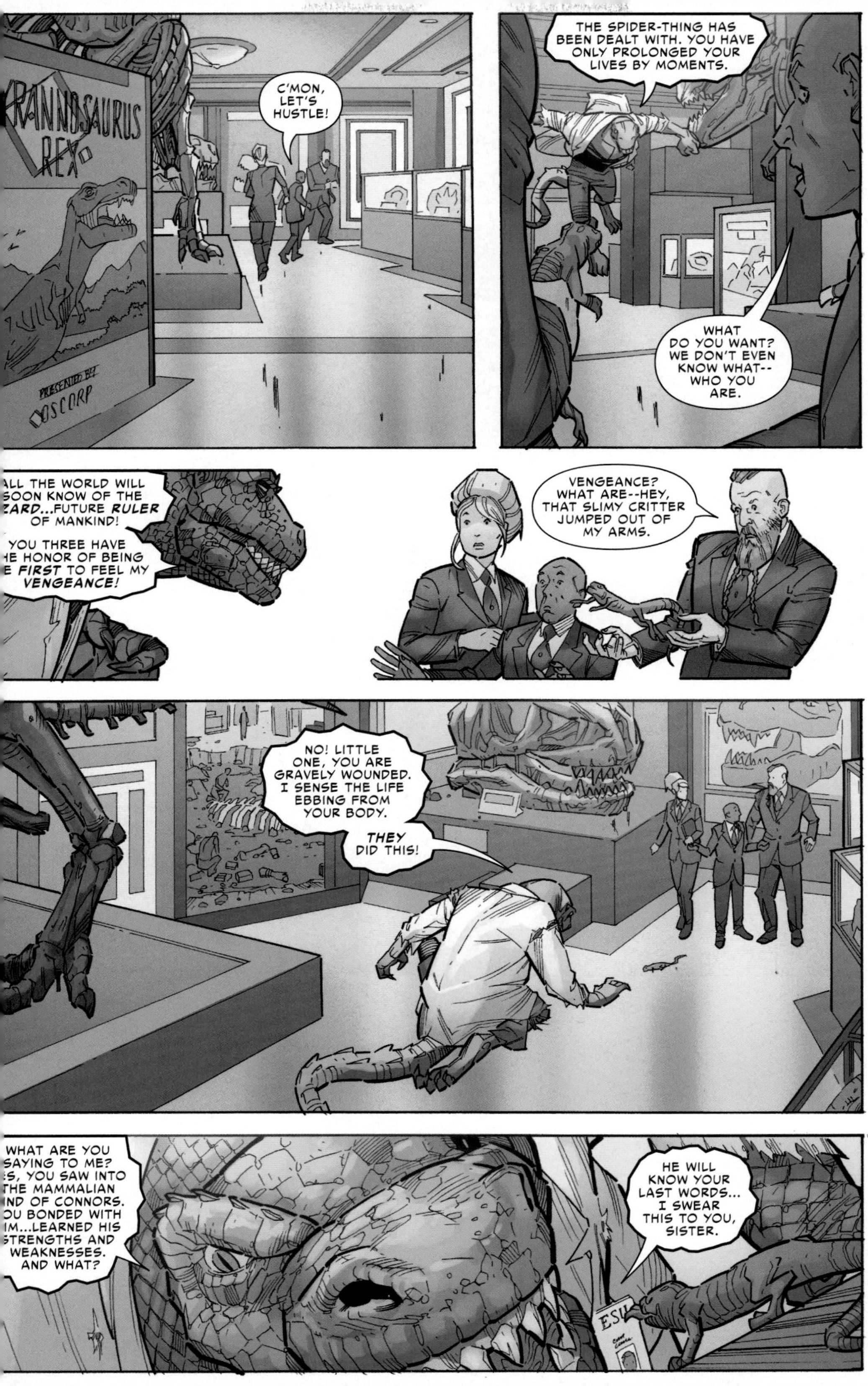

RANNOSAURUS REX
PRESENTED BY OSCORP
C'MON, LET'S HUSTLE!
THE SPIDER-THING HAS BEEN DEALT WITH. YOU HAVE ONLY PROLONGED YOUR LIVES BY MOMENTS.
WHAT DO YOU WANT? WE DON'T EVEN KNOW WHAT-- WHO YOU ARE.
ALL THE WORLD WILL SOON KNOW OF THE ZARD...FUTURE RULER OF MANKIND!
YOU THREE HAVE HE HONOR OF BEING E FIRST TO FEEL MY VENGEANCE!
VENGEANCE? WHAT ARE--HEY, THAT SLIMY CRITTER JUMPED OUT OF MY ARMS.
NO! LITTLE ONE, YOU ARE GRAVELY WOUNDED. I SENSE THE LIFE EBBING FROM YOUR BODY.
THEY DID THIS!
WHAT ARE YOU SAYING TO ME? ES, YOU SAW INTO THE MAMMALIAN IND OF CONNORS. OU BONDED WITH IM...LEARNED HIS STRENGTHS AND WEAKNESSES. AND WHAT?
HE WILL KNOW YOUR LAST WORDS... I SWEAR THIS TO YOU, SISTER.
ESU

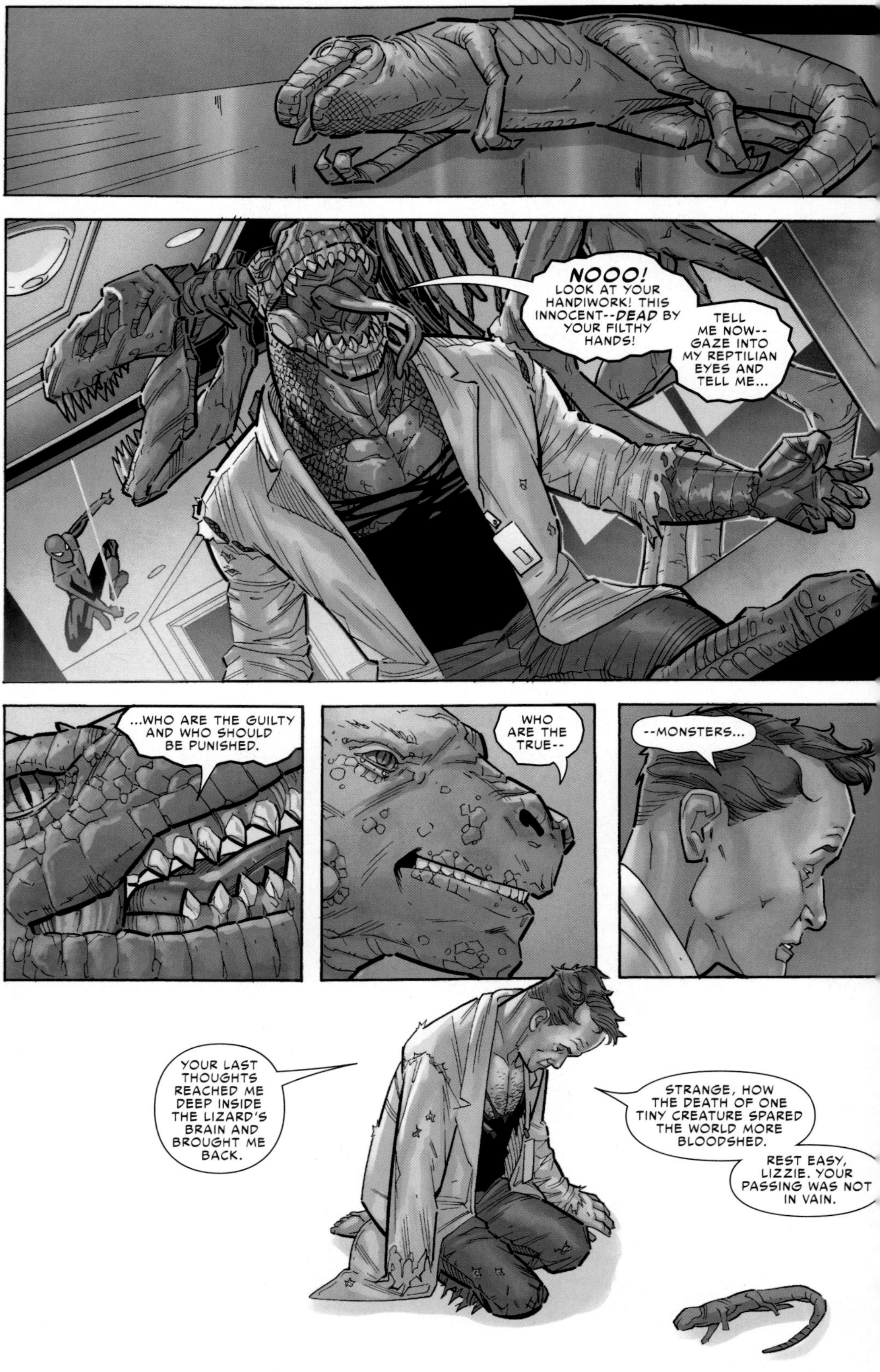
NOOO! LOOK AT YOUR HANDIWORK! THIS INNOCENT--DEAD BY YOUR FILTHY HANDS!
TELL ME NOW--GAZE INTO MY REPTILIAN EYES AND TELL ME...
...WHO ARE THE GUILTY AND WHO SHOULD BE PUNISHED.
WHO ARE THE TRUE--
--MONSTERS...
YOUR LAST THOUGHTS REACHED ME DEEP INSIDE THE LIZARD'S BRAIN AND BROUGHT ME BACK.
STRANGE, HOW THE DEATH OF ONE TINY CREATURE SPARED THE WORLD MORE BLOODSHED.
REST EASY, LIZZIE. YOUR PASSING WAS NOT IN VAIN.

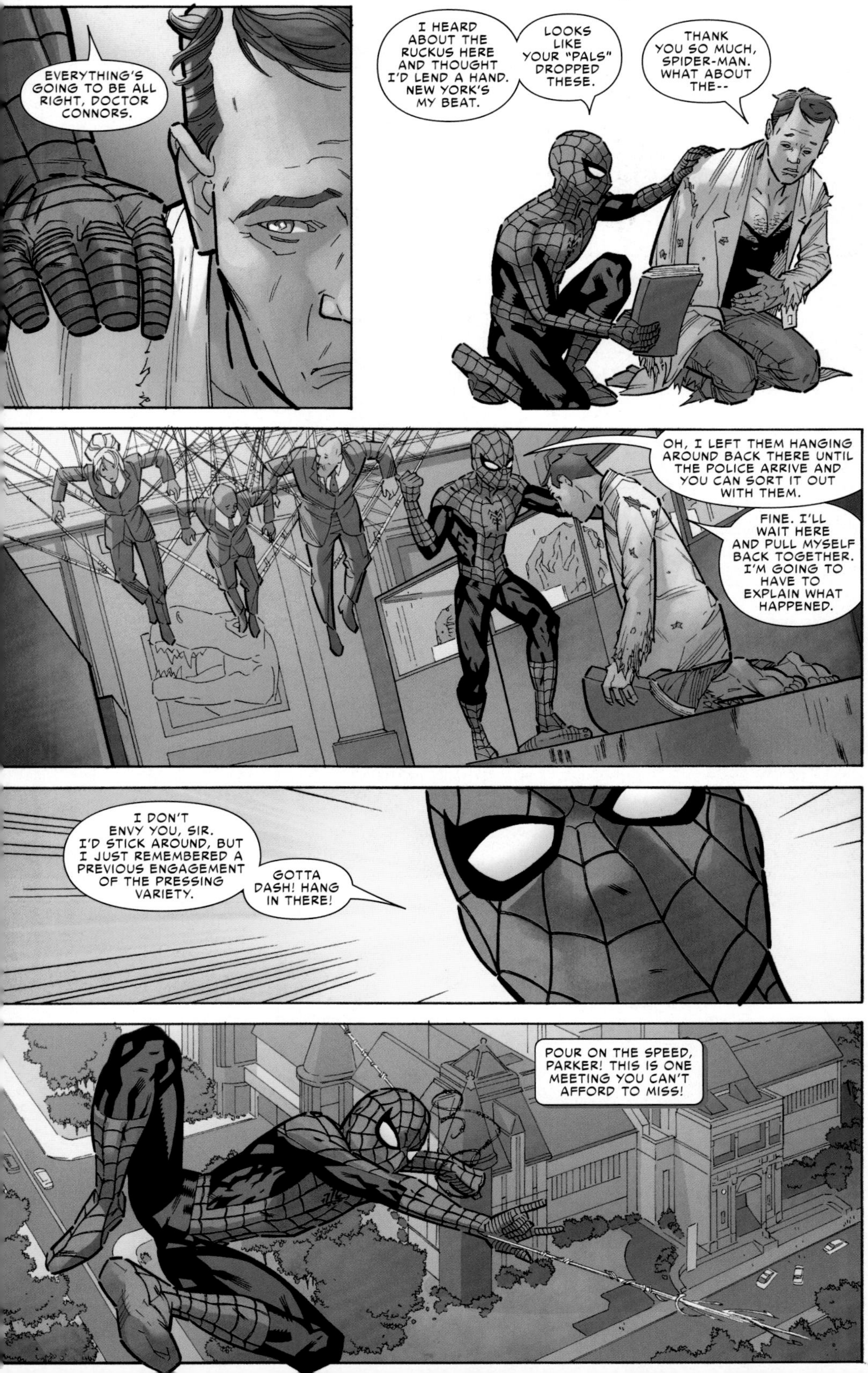
EVERYTHING'S GOING TO BE ALL RIGHT, DOCTOR CONNORS.
I HEARD ABOUT THE RUCKUS HERE AND THOUGHT I'D LEND A HAND. NEW YORK'S MY BEAT.
LOOKS LIKE YOUR "PALS" DROPPED THESE.
THANK YOU SO MUCH, SPIDER-MAN. WHAT ABOUT THE--
OH, I LEFT THEM HANGING AROUND BACK THERE UNTIL THE POLICE ARRIVE AND YOU CAN SORT IT OUT WITH THEM.
FINE. I'LL WAIT HERE AND PULL MYSELF BACK TOGETHER. I'M GOING TO HAVE TO EXPLAIN WHAT HAPPENED.
I DON'T ENVY YOU, SIR. I'D STICK AROUND, BUT I JUST REMEMBERED A PREVIOUS ENGAGEMENT OF THE PRESSING VARIETY.
GOTTA DASH! HANG IN THERE!
POUR ON THE SPEED, PARKER! THIS IS ONE MEETING YOU CAN'T AFFORD TO MISS!

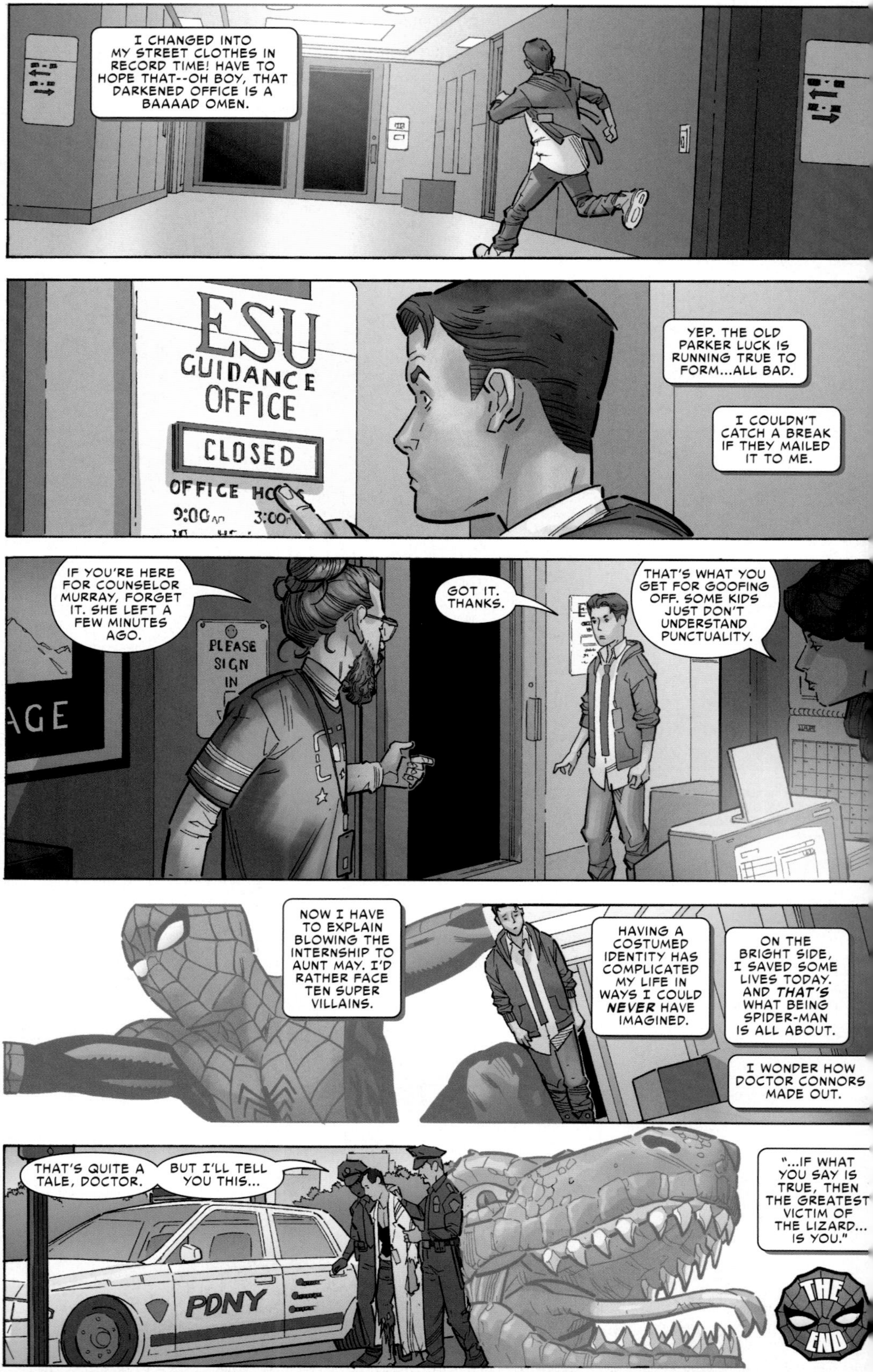
I CHANGED INTO MY STREET CLOTHES IN RECORD TIME! HAVE TO HOPE THAT--OH BOY, THAT DARKENED OFFICE IS A BAAAAD OMEN.
ESU GUIDANCE OFFICE
CLOSED
OFFICE HO
9:00
3:00
YEP. THE OLD PARKER LUCK IS RUNNING TRUE TO FORM...ALL BAD.
I COULDN'T CATCH A BREAK IF THEY MAILED IT TO ME.
IF YOU'RE HERE FOR COUNSELOR MURRAY, FORGET IT. SHE LEFT A FEW MINUTES AGO.
PLEASE SIGN IN
AGE
GOT IT. THANKS.
THAT'S WHAT YOU GET FOR GOOFING OFF. SOME KIDS JUST DON'T UNDERSTAND PUNCTUALITY.
NOW I HAVE TO EXPLAIN BLOWING THE INTERNSHIP TO AUNT MAY. I'D RATHER FACE TEN SUPER VILLAINS.
HAVING A COSTUMED IDENTITY HAS COMPLICATED MY LIFE IN WAYS I COULD NEVER HAVE IMAGINED.
ON THE BRIGHT SIDE, I SAVED SOME LIVES TODAY. AND THAT'S WHAT BEING SPIDER-MAN IS ALL ABOUT.
I WONDER HOW DOCTOR CONNORS MADE OUT.
THAT'S QUITE A TALE, DOCTOR.
BUT I'LL TELL YOU THIS...
PDNY
"...IF WHAT YOU SAY IS TRUE, THEN THE GREATEST VICTIM OF THE LIZARD... IS YOU."
THE END

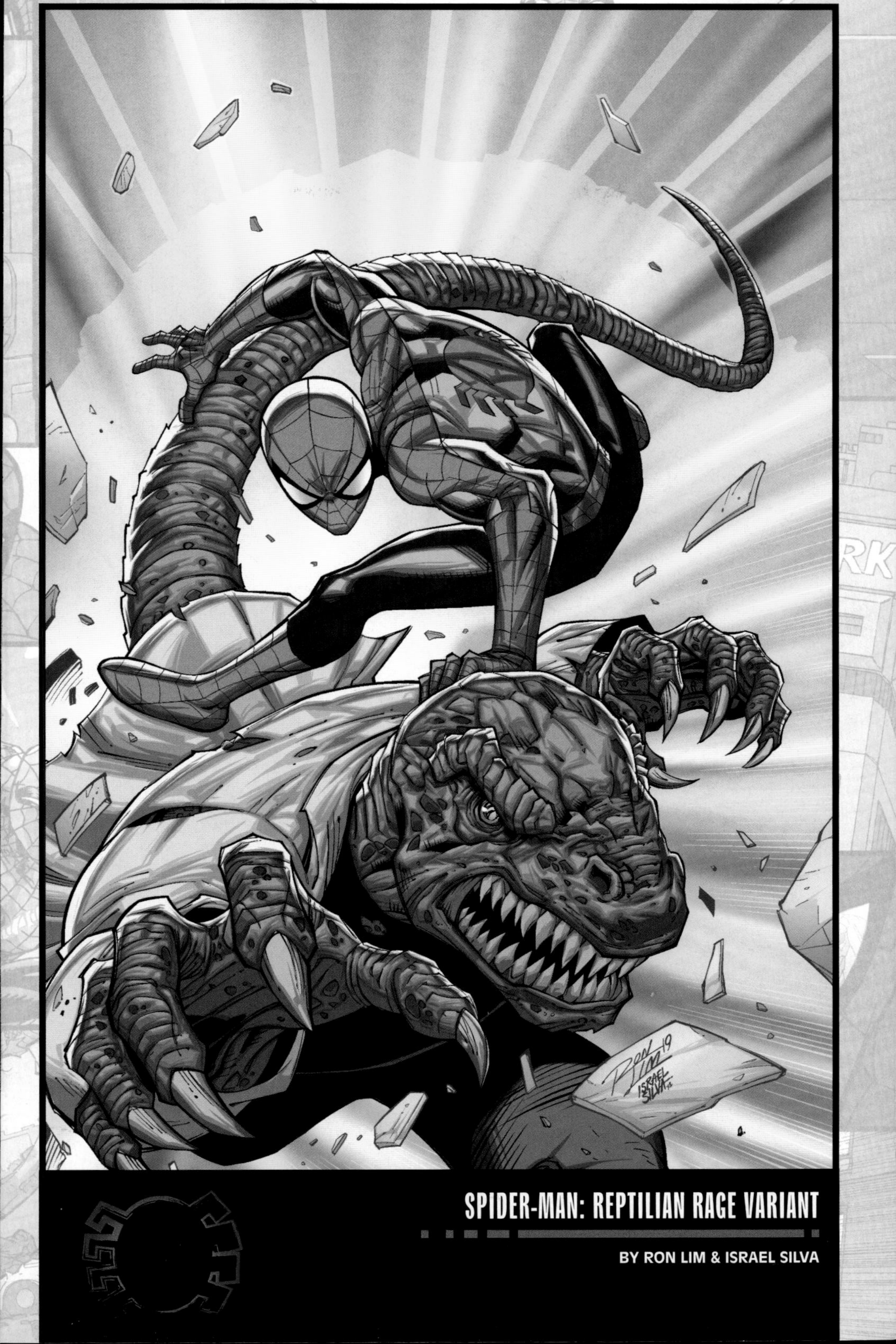

SPIDER-MAN: REPTILIAN RAGE VARIANT

BY RON LIM & ISRAEL SILVA

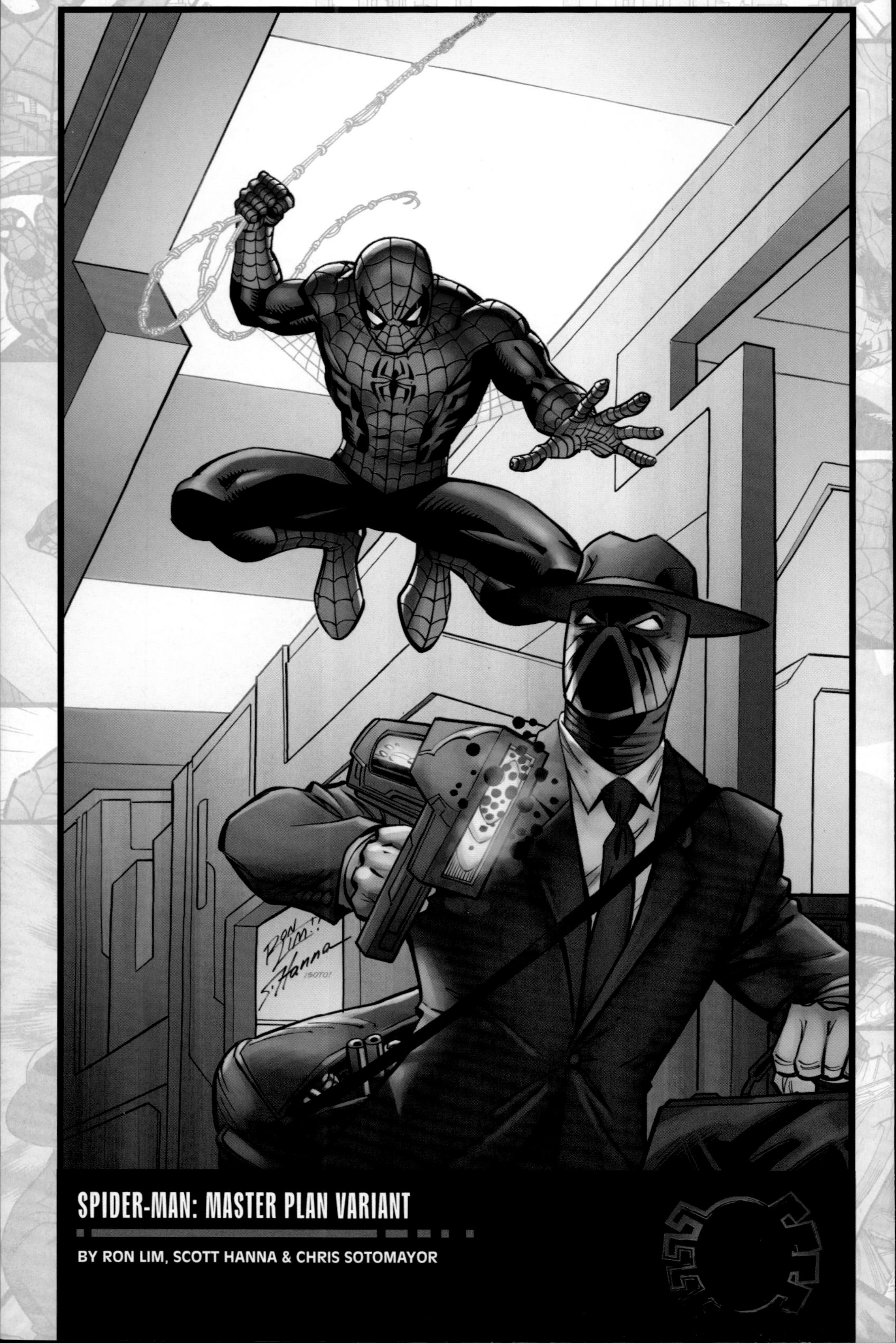

SPIDER-MAN: MASTER PLAN VARIANT

BY RON LIM, SCOTT HANNA & CHRIS SOTOMAYOR

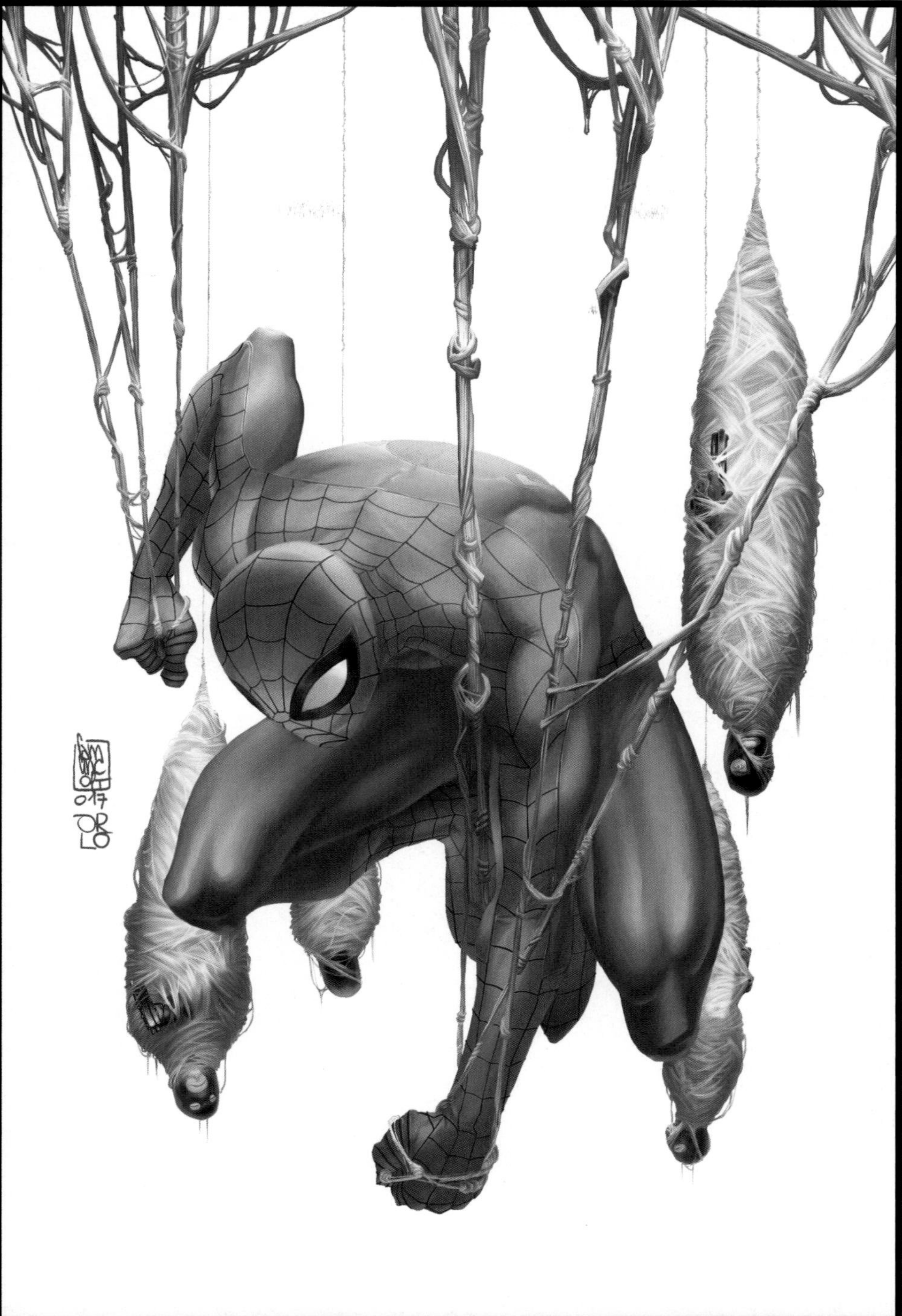

SPIDER-MAN: MASTER PLAN VARIANT

BY GIUSEPPE CAMUNCOLI & DANIELE ORLANDINI

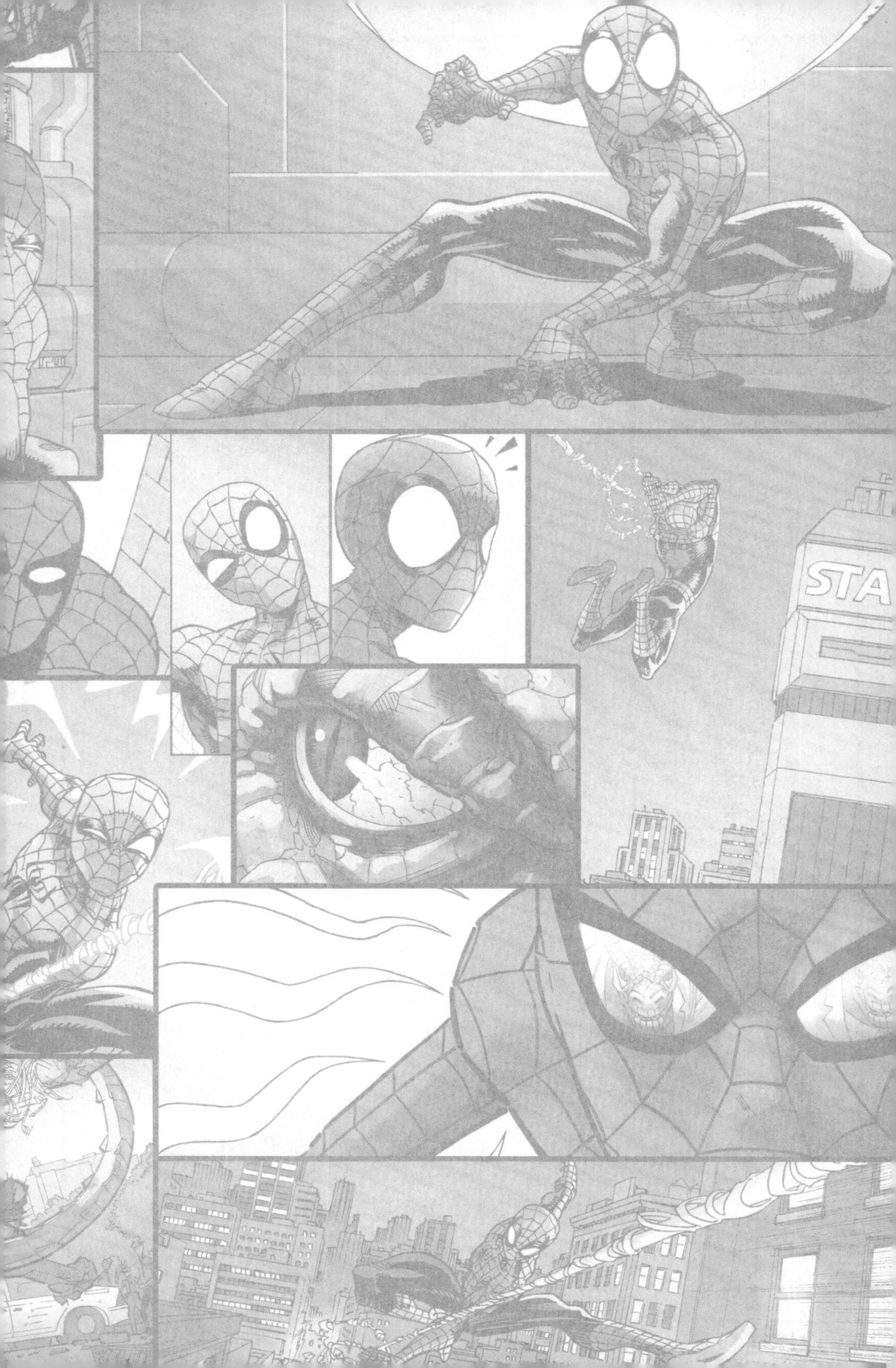
STA